LANDFALL

ALSO BY SCOTT JAMES MAGNER

THE FOREWORLD SAGA

Hearts of Iron

Blood and Ashes

THE TRANSGENIC WARS

Homefront

The Homefront trilogy:

Invasion

Landfall

Beachhead

The Reclamation's End trilogy:

Starfarer's Legacy

Red Genesis

Black Destiny

THE HUNTERS CHRONICLE

Seasons of Truth

Empire of Night

Crusade of Shadows

LANDFALL

A NOVEL OF THE TRANSGENIC WARS

SCOTT JAMES MAGNER

www.arusentertainment.com

FOR ABSENT FRIENDS, AND THOSE WHO FELL BEHIND.

HUMAN EVOLUTIONARY RESPONSE TO THE PRESENCE OF EXTRA-SOLAR TRANSGENIC PLASMIDS

Dr. Micah Harrison. Biological Sciences Division, University of Chicago

ABSTRACT. ANALYSIS OF CRYSTALLINE STRUCTURES FOUND IN THE Copernicus system reveals them to be organic in nature, and compatible with human biology. Transgenic plasmids derived from these structures were unintentionally released on Earth during the period of 20 October to 11 November, 2168. In this study, through systematic analysis of the resulting biological transformations, we propose a probabilistic strategy to contain and direct these unexplained genetic expressions, with the goal of preserving the history, culture, and genetic future of the human race.

KEYWORDS: Transgenic, Evolution, Transformation, Containment, Diversity.

1. Introduction

IN 2168, our examination of anomalous crystalline structures found on the planet Brahe in the Copernicus system by CEV *Prometheus* in 2167 concluded that not only are the samples organic, but that they are also compatible with human biology.

Initial quarantine of the *Prometheus* crew members at the Star City, facility ended before analysis of the supposedly inert structures was complete. As such, during the period of 20 October to 11 November, undiscovered, extra-solar transgenic plasmids present in their bodies were distributed throughout the world, and at the time of this writing only those humans who exist in extreme isolation or in hermetically sealed environments have avoided exposure. Given the interconnected nature of our world, it is only a matter of time until those communities are also effected.

Individuals exposed to these plasmids experience episomal integration within minutes, and within twenty-four to ninety-six hours may express profound metamorphic changes including (but not limited to): additional sensory organs, growth of additional limbs, enhanced metabolic rate, and rapid cellular repair (including the spontaneous remission of cancerous growths).

Since these changes appear to bypass the normal process of evolutionary mutation, it is our contention that they must be engineered for this precise purpose. Given the aggressive, and absolute nature of the transformations, the Biological Sciences Division has come to the inescapable conclusion that individuals with active expressions are no longer classifiable as *homo sapiens sapiens*.

There is no known method of reversing an active expression, and for the most part these mutations are benign, adapting their hosts near-perfectly to living conditions both on Earth and in near-Earth orbit. Our study documents, and it is our contention, that without careful, guided study of this phenomenon the human race as we know it will be extinct within three generations.

If we are to survive as a species, the human race must jump-start our physical and societal evolution to match that of our changed children. We as a race must make every effort to understand this transgenesis, and learn how to guide it to its ultimate end...

17 JULY, 2640 OER

MIRA

THIS IS ABSOLUTELY NOT how I thought I'd die.

With at least three different alarms adding to her already monster headache, Lieutenant Commander Mira Harlan clawed her way across the blood-slicked floor of the flight deck to the co-pilot's chair.

The shuttle was spinning on multiple axes, fast enough to overcome its internal grav generators and press her solidly to the floor. Only the boosted strength of her armored hardsuit allowed her to make any progress at all, and when another explosion rocked the shuttle, she had to trigger her boot jets to avoid getting splattered across the back wall of the compartment.

Fucking idiots. I told them we'd get shot down.

It had been less than two hours since her life had come completely apart, and given their current trajectory, today showed absolutely no signs of getting better. First, an unknown object came out of nowhere, and smashed its way through her battlegroup until it lodged amidships in *SDF Valiant*. Then she'd been forced to fire on her own crew during an attempted mutiny, while at the same time dodging fire from a small force of gennie invaders from the outer colonies who had ultimately taken control of their escape shuttle, and the cargo she'd loaded into it right before everything really went to shit.

Captain Aloysius Martin, now unconscious and secured to a bulkhead behind Mira, hadn't exactly made things easier when he told her what the cargo was—a centuries-old sleeper unit containing an Alpha, a special kind of gennie who was apparently supposed to save the human race.

All of us, including the ones who got me into this mess in the first place, and are probably going to get us killed anyway.

Head pounding, face still hurting from where the gennie commander Jantine had punched her in the nose, Mira grabbed the base of the chair and hauled herself up, activating both the emergency restraints and her magnetic boots to hold her in place. She wasn't half the pilot her wife was, but she knew a hell of a lot more about SDF shuttles than the maniac gennie in the other seat.

Despite the chaos of their situation, the gangly teenager in the black skinsuit the other gennies called Janbi seemed completely unconcerned with the fact that they were in an uncontrolled, tumbling descent through Earth's atmosphere.

So much so, in fact, that once she was squared away, he calmly turned his head to address her while still moving his hands through more control holos than Mira could count.

"We haven't been formally introduced. My name is—"

"We don't have time for that! Strap in, Janbi. Your harness is activated by a button on the side of your chair."

Mira didn't look to see if the strange boy with the lopsided smile complied, she had enough problems of her own. Her head was still pounding from whatever psychic whammie the big orange gennie put on her, and—

The pain in Mira's skull tripled as the dozens of new voices in her brain admonished her for not showing the Omegas proper respect. A cascade of other people's memories rushed to the fore, and she experienced again the thrill—and dread—of meeting the three-meter-plus tall aliens with orange skin and way too many eyes for the first time.

Every one of the voices held "the Builders" in incredible reverence, and all but one felt she should be punished for her insolence.

All of you can fuck the hell right off. I didn't ask for you to be shoved into my head, and the sooner you get off my metaphorical back, the faster I can do something keep your precious Omegas alive.

Mira had no idea what it was the Omega had done to her, other than that it hurt, and showed no signs of getting better. The Omega was still crouched in the corridor, hanging on to the sides of the out hatch with enough grip strength to dent the supposedly indestructible frame.

Another explosion rocked the shuttle, and Janbi started screaming something in a language Mira had never heard before. A second or two later, the new voices in her head supplied a translation, though she really wished they hadn't bothered.

"Everybody hold on. We just lost primary engine control, and we may be in for a rough landing."

Oh, hell no.

"Are you fucking serious? Pull up! We can't land without—"

Mira slammed against her restraints hard enough to black out for a few seconds. When she came to, air was rushing past her face and the shuttle's tumbling had worsened. If she hadn't already thrown up when the Omega breathed his strange mist into her lungs and gave her multiple lifetimes of gennie memories, she was sure she'd pop now from the spinning.

Mira opened her mouth to equalize pressure, and it was only after she instinctively took a deep breath that she realized the pain in her broken nose was gone. In fact, she felt better than ever, if you didn't count all the screaming inside her head, and the intense fear she felt radiating from Janbi.

"I may need some help to get the propulsion systems back online."

Janbi's measured words were impossibly calm, considering what Mira could sense of his emotions, another "gift" from the Omega. But her own fear spiked a moment later when she saw their rapidly plummeting altitude, and just how little time was left to stabilize their descent.

Without waiting for permission, Mira pulled up a holo interface and transferred shuttle control to her station. Janbi was right, the ship was spinning dead, unable to generate any effective thrust while they were tumbling. But more to the point, the reactors were running at full power, just not doing anything with it. It was almost like...

Almost like what happened to Valiant *when that rock hit us.*

"Janbi, I have two very important questions and I need real answers to both of them. First, where are these missiles coming from? And second..."

Mira's next words were canceled by a white-hot knife of pain pushing deep into her brain. It only lasted a moment, and was followed by a deep wave of sadness that had the same "flavor" as when the Omegas wanted to tell her something.

But Mira didn't need an update, she already knew what it was. There were fewer people alive on the shuttle than there were before, and unless she could do something to arrest their fall, that number was going to drop to zero sooner, rather than later.

She wasn't sure which of the strange, emotional messes from another star had just died, but they'd been terrified at the time, and their leader Jantine had gone unconscious soon after.

"—ny missiles. The debris field around us is reacting poorly to Earth's radiation belts, and is known to be...energetic."

What?

"What?"

"I said, no-one is firing missiles at us. I programmed our insertion to come in over Earth's north magnetic pole, away from all the satellite clutter and orbiting stations you've got surrounding your planet. Even those few devices that noted our arrival think we're a transient meteor strike, and active sensors aren't registering any ground installations along our path. Everything was going well until the—"

≈*ohshitoshitoshit*≈

Now it was Janbi's turn to clutch his head, and Mira frantically tried to shut down whatever search routine Janbi was running while at the same time trying to reroute power to the shuttle's engines.

Part of her brain that was no longer hers registered that her uncontrolled panic was causing the gennie pain, but the part that was still recognizably Mira was more worried about what might happen if their indiscriminate sensor scans were picked up as they burned a path across the dead center of the North American Reclamation.

Not only by who, but by what.

"Janbi! Stop pinging the ground! For the love of all that's holy, we have to appear as a natural phenomenon for as long as...humanly possible."

"But we need to find the—"

"Just do it! I don't have time to explain."

Mira felt, rather than heard, his assent, and refocused her attention on maneuvering thrusters. Calming waves of something from the Omega behind her steadied her nerves enough to fire thrusters in short bursts to stop their spin, then use a longer burn to flip the shuttle over so that the heavier shielding on its underside took the brunt of the damage caused by their insane deorbit strategy.

All I have to do is get us down in as few pieces as possible. It's not like this thing ever has to fly again...

Mira programmed an aerocapture maneuver, hoping to dump as much velocity as possible before one of the wings came off. They were already far too deep in the atmosphere for it to work, but it was the only thing she could think of at the moment, and the Omega seemed to agree it was a good idea. A Shrike could have handled their current trajectory, but a transfer shuttle this old wasn't designed to handle this kind of stress, and unless she could get the gravitic drive back online, it couldn't really land either.

One problem at a time.

It was hard to hear exactly what Janbi was saying over the atmospheric roar just a few meters away outside the hull, but something about her strange new brain kept filling in the gaps a second or two after he started talking. The words were in Elac—or at least, she thought they were, and he seemed to have recovered from her earlier whatever-it-was assault on his mind.

"—lled all sensor sweeps, and increased thruster efficiency by 20%. If you adjust our angle by—"

Another explosion rocked the shuttle, enough so that it lifted Mira out of her chair, and only her boots and harness kept her from slamming into the compartment's ceiling. Spent microslugs from the gennies' initial assault on the flight deck stopped bouncing off the walls and rained down around them, pinging off every flat surface. Including the drive status indicator, which stopped flashing red and started glowing a solid, healthy green.

"Oh, nevermind. The last of the slug debris just disintegrated, and all power has been restored to main propulsion. May I now resume the search parameters please?"

Mira couldn't stop herself from staring at Janbi, her eyes wide and mouth hanging open. It wasn't just the words, but the complete innocence with which he spoke them. Janbi had yet to activate his restraints, and for all she knew had been sitting perfectly still in place the entire time.

And to make the moment even more surreal, blood trapped in her sinuses from her earlier broken nose chose that exact moment to break loose, finally picking a single direction to flow and bubble down the back of her throat.

It took her several swallows and a hacking cough to find her words, during which the drives kicked in and stopped their descent somewhere over the center of the continent. The shuttle was standing almost on its end, and out the display glass window behind Janbi's head Mira had a perfect view of the bluest sky she'd ever seen, tinged with the cherry red glow of the superheated hull outside.

"No, I think we're good for now." Mira killed the drives, and the shuttle dropped like a stone, with maneuvering thrusters keeping them upright as they fell. Even with their relative plane of reference aligned to the shuttle's "floor", she was pressed against her emergency harness and barely touching the chair, while Janbi remained half-turned and relaxed in the pilot's seat.

"Who the hell are you people, and what the hell you going to do with us once we're on the ground?" Mira's question hung in the air between them, and she kept one eye on the altimeter while she waited for his response, counting down the seconds until her next braking maneuver. This whole morning so far seemed like a dream, from the first minutes she was on shift until her explosive exit from *Valiant*'s transfer bay, and she couldn't help but think she'd forgotten something in all the chaos.

And with everything else going on in my head right now, I'm not even sure I want to remember.

"We're the good guys. And with your help, I think we can save the human race from itself. If that's what you want too, I think now would be a good time to land, ma'am."

Ma'am? What the fuck are you...oh, right.

Mira activated the grav drive at five kilometers above impact, gradually slowing them down until the shuttle came to rest in a corn field with little more than a puff of dust marking their impact.

What the hell. Let's save the human race. But first, I need a good strong drink, a clean shirt, and...oh, shit.

Marcus.

CALLAWAY

COMMANDER MARCUS CALLAWAY awoke to the sound of an air exchanger whirring to life, and several other noises he couldn't identify. He sat up, or at least tried to, until the netting holding down the covers on his borrowed bunk pulled tight across his chest.

"Mira?"

Idiot, she's long gone, remember? Harlan's got an actual job on this ship, instead of just hanging around while Captain Martin makes up his mind about what to do with the gennie.

There had been gravity and light in the compartment when Mira put on her hardsuit and left for first shift, and Marcus had enjoyed every second of watching her pull on his uniform blouse by mistake through half-lidded eyes. The efficiency with which the woman moved extended to everything she did, which he'd experienced first-hand as they consummated their relationship the night before.

Shit, I still need to tell Aloysius about us. Provided I can unhook myself and get out of here without being seen, that is.

It wasn't that he dreaded telling the captain that he'd started sleeping with one of his most promising officers, or even that he'd finally cleared her for membership in their conspiracy. It was the thought of admitting to Mira afterward that their initial conversations had been more about vetting her than getting to know her that made him truly nervous.

She'll break me in half. And given how close she came last night, I should probably be as far away as possible when I tell her. In another solar system, perhaps.

On the other hand...

Marcus allowed himself a smile before returning to the problem at hand. The air in Mira's quarters didn't taste off, so the exchanger hadn't been malfunctioning for long. He'd either caught the last bit of charge in its batteries, or there was something else happening that he should probably get up to speed on sooner rather than later.

Releasing himself from the netting, Marcus floated free with one hand still on the bunk, a sign that there was definitely a problem aboard *Valiant*.

We're tumbling. What the hell happened while I was sleeping, and for that matter, how did I not wake up when it did?

Marcus drew the room in his head, placing the door, sanitary sink, and the hamper where he remembered them relative to Mira's bunk. She'd kept the room almost completely unfurnished, a rare style among officers her age and a habit he kept himself.

No use settling in, if you might have to bug out at any time.

A quick push moved him to the wall, and he grabbed for the hamper he assumed was still attached to the bulkhead. Finding it, he opened the lid and rooted around inside for his pants. Mira may have left with half his uniform, but nothing else in her quarters would come close to fitting him.

More importantly, my command key is right where I left it.

Marcus performed a quick, one-handed spin and slid into the pants, then drew himself to the floor to look for his boots and control belt. He'd been in space long enough to know that without at least some frame of reference, he'd be ineffectual in the pitch black room.

His hand found a smooth, solid surface beneath the bunk, fifteen or so centimeters tall and secured to the deck by some method his fingers couldn't identify. Following its top edge, Marcus sketched in his mind a case of some kind, approximately 1.5 meters long and half as deep. He also found his boots magnetically locked at the edge of her rack, which occupied him for a few seconds while he thought about the situation.

Whatever Mira's got in there is either private, or for emergencies, and I'm not sure the current situation qualifies me to check it out.

Not yet, anyway. Let's see about getting out of here first.

Marcus gave his boots a quick once over, and then snapped their control unit into place over his normal belt. He was just about to activate them when the lights, air exchanger, and the alarm he remembered reaching over Mira to set (mainly to make her snuggle in closer) all came to life. He took an involuntary step back, raising his left arm from his waist to cover his eyes. The combined motions sent him spinning up over the bed, and as the lights went out again his head slammed into the compartment's ceiling.

"FuckfuckFUCK!"

Marcus felt warmth spreading across his face, but didn't compound his earlier mistakes by trying to examine his brand new scar. The pain was enough of a reminder of how stupid he'd just been, and the last thing he wanted to do was cancel out his inertia while in the middle of the room, floating helplessly until one of Mira's damage control teams—or worse yet, Mira herself—came to rescue him. Instead, he let himself go loose, spreading his fingers to maximize his chance of grabbing some solid object.

As he spun, Marcus used the last glow of the clock panel to fix the floating end of the netting in his mind, timing his spin to grab it the next time it came close. It brushed by the fingers of his outstretched right hand in the darkness, and he decided to risk grabbing for it with his left.

The resulting spin was enough to give him a serious moment of vertigo, but with the netting in hand he was able to both kill his rotation and activate the boots. His hand was slippery on the controls, and Marcus felt several drops of something burst against his chest.

Great, an uncontrolled bleed in null-g is the last thing I need right now. And is that smoke?

Marcus couldn't place the source, but there was definitely something burning in the compartment. The harsh smell stung his nose, and a quick survey of the darkness revealed no sparks or flames.

So it's either in the walls, or in my head. Either way, I need to get out of here as fast as possible.

While regs suggested walking across the ceiling to, and then down, one of the compartment's walls, if there was an electrical fire in the room Marcus wanted to minimize his contact with it as much as possible. So instead, he bent his legs up to his chest and used both hands to pull on the netting until he returned to the bunk and could swing himself to the deck.

Once he was secured to the compartment's nominal floor, he raised a hand to his head and encountered a small cloud of blood bubbles. Based on the pain alone, it felt like there was a massive tear in the skin, but probing with his fingers he found a contusion no more than a centimeter in length.

Small enough to worry about later. For now, I need to get out of here and find a working comm.

Keeping pressure on the wound with one hand, Marcus crouch-walked forward, listening to the echoes as his boots pulled free from the floor. It had been a while since he'd had to practice this particular maneuver, but Fleet emergency escape procedures were in place for a reason, and he quickly found the outlines of the hatch and triggered the emergency release.

Marcus cranked it open a few centimeters, and waited. Even while crouched, air was definitely flowing past him into the corridor, and with it the burning smell. There was an emergency beacon out there somewhere, and the amount of smoke revealed by the blue light told him Mira's wasn't the only compartment producing smoke on this level.

Okay. Time to go. But first...

Marcus made his way back to Mira's bunk, and used the beacon's light to examine the case. It took him a few seconds to find and release the pressure locks holding it to the deck, and once he wrestled it free there was just enough illumination for him to read the words stenciled on its cover.

Mirabelle Agnes McCallister-Andreison-Harlan

Right. Her wives. In all the excitement, I'd almost forgotten.

Mira had been very open about her marriage, and equally assuring that neither of her wives would mind her taking a lover. At first, it was just one more thing for Marcus to investigate, but in the course of her —and their—background checks, he not only came to understand their arrangement, but also the reasons behind it and why it worked.

And now, I'm about to betray that trust, on the off-chance that things out there really are as dire as they seem and in the hope that Mira might have prepared for an even worse situation.

With the pressure locks released, it took him only a few seconds to figure out not only how to open it, but what it probably contained.

You're just full of surprises, aren't you Mira?

Inside the case were two top-of-the-line induction pistols with custom grips, perfectly fitted into an indestructible inner compartment along with thirty canisters of micro-slugs, a brace of spare barrels, and an engraved metal box with the initials ERH.

Okay. Decidedly non-regulation, but probably more accurate and powerful than anything in Valiant's stores. From what I understand, her wife Debra's weapon designs have put a lot of Fleet engineers out of a job.

And as for her other wife, the less said, the better...

Marcus closed the case, not wanting to handle pistols clearly designed for Mira's hands and no other. After another second of thought, he returned it to where he'd found it, sealed the pressure locks, then smoothed the covers under the netting to shield it from casual discovery.

A conversation for another time, Lieutenant McCallister-Andreison-Harlan.

Back at the hatch, Marcus cranked it open until he had just enough space to slide out into the corridor. There was no way to seal it after him without a portable generator and a welding torch, but from what he'd observed in the last six weeks, Mira's belongings were as safe now as they'd ever been.

Now let's see about me.

Marcus used the corridor's catch rings to propel himself down to the beacon. Secured to the grating around it were emergency supplies, and someone had scrawled instructions above the beacon.

<CH-2>FT-1>COMMAND>

If Fire Team One wants me to go to the command deck, who am I to argue? But first things first.

Marcus opened one of the medkits and sealed his head wound with an aerosol bandage before claiming one of the portable comms, a holo map, and a hand beacon from the supply cache. Almost as an afterthought, he undid his belt and resecured it over an emergency blanket as a sort of makeshift poncho.

Once he was in a state more befitting a senior command pilot, Marcus turned on the comm, thumbing it over to channel two for emergency instructions as per protocol. But instead of a recorded message, the unit produced only a soft hiss. The map also refused to load *Valiant*'s layout, which made Marcus stop and think.

Must have something to do with the intermittent power spikes, but the main core should be on an independent circuit. If both are down...

Guess I'll have to get my answers the old-fashioned way.

Fixing the comm to his belt, Marcus set off toward the command deck, swinging his way between catch rings.

Unless we're in a lot more trouble than I think we are, both Captain Martin and Mira should be there, having the time of their lives fixing every last thing wrong with this ship.

And won't that be a fun conversation to drop into looking like a space hobo?

DEMARCO

EVEN WHEN THEY'D served together as fresh-faced lieutenants, Sam DeMarco had never liked the sound of Horace Kołodziejski's voice. And now that his fellow fleet captain had a full head of steam going on his favorite rant in the worlds, he liked it even less.

Projecting into the council chamber from an unspecified location, Horace had been shouting at the most powerful people in the home system for almost an hour about the evils of the outer colonies, and what he considered the latest salvo in a centuries-long war.

"The gennies have crossed the only line we had left, and this time the result is the destruction of an entire battlegroup. The evidence is clear; you've seen the footage and our preliminary analysis. What more justification do you people need?"

The man never gets tired of hearing himself talk. But I supposed that's to be expected from Vice-Admiral Worthy's fair-haired boy.

Sitting in front of Sam at the main table, Commodore Ykaterina Maranova wasn't bothering to hide her dislike of Kołodziejski, but so far had said nothing to rebut the claims he'd brought before the Reclamation Council. The diminutive flag officer was studying a file on her display, face scrunched up like she'd just swallowed something sour.

Kołodziejski's holo flickered, then shifted from his projected face and torso to a static image of a Redstone dreadnaught with the legend SDF *Indomitable*. The assembled councilors used the time to review their own screens and deal with whatever problems had cropped up in their districts since their last check-in. Only Dr. Mordecai Harrison, representing the North American Reclamation, was still looking at the holo, and the lighted nameplate in front of him indicated it was his turn to speak.

Of the people in the room, Harrison was the oldest, and the only one who really looked it. Still healing from a recent Separatist attack, he slumped forward in his chair, the worst of his scars hidden by his formal councilor's robes.

The other councilors all had variations on the bland, blended face of someone who'd never left Earth's orbit. Transgenesis had done its best to homogenize the human race on its homeworld, and the elected representatives around the table reflected that.

To avoid any possible conflicts of interest, fleet officers like DeMarco, Maranova, and even Horace Kołodziejski were required to submit to regular genetic testing intended to detect any transgenic activity. Only humans with no, or completely benign, expressions were allowed to serve on active duty. In fact, the virus was so successful at adapting humans to live on what was left of Planet Earth, after a few generations Fleet personnel were almost a distinct species of their own, set apart visually and physically from both the councilors and the rest of the human race.

Mordecai Harrison, however, was one of a kind, and his particular unaltered genome was both a blessing and a curse. The Harrisons had remained on Earth during the troubles, studying, treating, and expanding humanity's knowledge of the T-virus. It was a minor miracle that none of them had expressed any changes beyond those of the initial global exposure centuries ago, but that miracle had the unfortunate drawback of making him unresponsive to advanced regenerative techniques.

The white patch over his right eye stood out in stark contrast to skin almost as dark as Sam's own, as did his wild, towering hair. But there was nothing he could do to hide the still healing burns on his face and hands, and the ceroplastic cane leaning against the table spoke to his other injuries.

But what really set him apart from the assembled leaders of humanity was the calm, steady way he had of dealing with Kołodziejski's demands.

I really have to hand it to him. After what he's been through, dealing with Horace's bullshit would drive me mad.

The wait for a stable connection gave Sam a bit more time to think about what he'd just seen. The footage recovered from *Valiant* was hard to refute, and Sam had an even harder time trying to figure out why he wasn't willing to agree with Kołodziejski just yet.

Maybe it's because even millions of kilometers away, something about that man makes me want to take a shower every time I see him.

Commodore Maranova—and by extension, the council, had little choice but to accept Kołodziejski as Worthy's surrogate when the Admiral shipped out for the corridor colonies. But other than the preternaturally calm Harrison, none of them seemed willing to engage him directly.

Sam shifted in his chair, trying not to appear completely uncomfortable with furniture meant for much smaller humans. It was the same everywhere in the fleet, and was one of many reasons he'd followed Captain Martin's lead and reconfigured EFS *Clarke's* command center so he could walk around a sensor pit on shift, rather than sit in a central command chair and receive information from every angle.

Even though I know Aloysius isn't a collaborator, even though he and Valiant are all apparently dead from a supposed gennie attack, I can't shake the feeling that whatever he's been up to with Marcus Callaway for the last month or so is why we're here today.

And until the commodore reads me in further on Aloysius's mission, my function here is to observe, and to be seen observing.

The Kołodziejski holo returned to life, and now Sam couldn't shake the feeling that Horace had changed his shirt in the time he'd been away.

"Well? What are you going to do about this? Whether you like it or not, we're at war. Make the declaration already!"

Councilor Harrison waited another second to be sure Kołodziejski was finished, then spoke in a deep, rolling voice only a lifetime of public speaking could produce.

"Captain Kołodziejski, you claim Captain Martin's battlegroup, a collection of the most advanced warships the System Defense Force has to offer, was on a fact-gathering mission when they were attacked and subsequently destroyed by an unknown Colonial force." Harrison winced, and paused for a drink of water. The man looked tired, much more so than the other councilors in the chamber. Artificial gravity sometimes had that effect on people, especially those as old as Harrison. Sam had spent most of his life in space, and on the rare occasions when he was down a gravity well he felt like the ground was trying to drag him under.

What has it been, five years now? Six?

Harrison's hypnotic voice continued.

"And while you have certainly shown us footage of a conflict, I have a hard time making the leap from blurry images of black-clad figures to a full-scale invasion. Further, we have yet to hear from any other sources who can substantiate your report, either from your own battlegroup, or the surviving members of Captain Martin's. The Magellan Accords require full Council confirmation, and I for one will not commit us to a war without it. The stakes for this planet are far too high. You have the floor, sir."

After the delay, Horace's image sat up a bit taller in his chair, and opened his mouth to speak. But before he could do so, the light in front of the holographic representation of Martian President Victor Darbin came on, and he, too, reached for a glass of water.

Like Sam and Commodore Maranova, Darbin was more of an advisor than an active participant in the Council. While the Reclamation government technically included the Mars Confederation, the assembled councilors were all from Earth, the only planet to have truly fought a transgenic war. Still, the look of pure hatred on the man's face was matched only by the one still smoldering on Kołodziejski's.

"Councilor Harrison, Captain Kołodziejski has served us all, with distinction, for many years. I'm inclined to believe his testimony, and call for an immediate vote."

Harrison's light snapped on, and in a surprising breach of FTL communications protocol the councilor did not wait the requisite second for acknowledgment before speaking.

"Mr. President, I do not question Captain Kołodziejski's integrity, but rather his motives. I cannot, and will not move for a vote until the conditions of the Accords are satisfied. And if I may be so bold, sir, despite the generous contributions your planet makes to the System Defense Force, control of it lies with this body, and no other."

"Ha! He's got you there, Victor!" Maranova's cackling interjection caught every eye in the room, and a second later drew angry stares from both Kołodziejski and Darbin. And while the Martian president was content to fume silently, Kołodziejski had no problem continuing his tirade.

"You may vote, or not, Mr. Harrison. You may debate, and dither, and hide in your hole while the universe burns, but when the time comes for action, it will be Martian ships, crewed by Martians, who will protect the human race from the evils of the cosmos. All I'm asking for is the chance to do my job, while there's still something for me to protect!"

"It's Doctor Harrison, Captain, or more precisely, while I'm in this chamber and wearing these robes, Councilor. And while it's true many of our ships are built on Mars, they're all paid for by Earth, just like the domes you live in and the orbital elevators that make your planet's manufacturing base possible. And what, exactly, is it you think you are protecting? Or rather, whom?"

Kołodziejski's holo cut out again, and Sam leaned over to whisper into Maranova's ear, mindful of the attention it drew from nearby councilors.

"Are council meetings always like this?"

Maranova smiled, her lined face and shock of white hair magnifying her expression. As the de-facto commanding officer of the Home Fleet, she'd attended most of the council sessions since Vice-Admiral Worthy left the system, and she appeared to be enjoying this one quite a bit.

"Hell no. Usually we have to wait a couple hours for the good stuff. Although Horace is definitely running right up to the line with this diatribe. He always wants more money and ships, but now he thinks he's got something, or rather, someone to use them on."

DeMarco considered the footage he'd seen so far. The tactics of the black-clad commandos attacking *Valiant*'s crew were all speed and force, but something wasn't quite right with the footage. Kołodziejski said he'd sent a pod with all the collected data, but it had yet to arrive at a capture point, leaving a few blurry holos as the only evidence for his claims of colonial infiltrators.

No one wants another war, especially with the Reclamation finally yielding results. So what's his real agenda, and what will it cost me to find out? I'm already down my best pilot and second-in-command.

Horace's holographic face appeared again, and this time it really was just a face. He looked different, more angular than normal. And Sam just couldn't shake the feeling that this time, he wasn't wearing a shirt at all.

"You can hide down in your institute's hole for another hundred years, Councilor, just like your family has been hiding since this mess began. It still won't change what we have to do. The gennie menace is real—the pod data backs me up on that. Whether you want to declare one or not, we are now at war with the outer colonies, and you're going to have to decide how and when to fight them."

The image froze, but the green light beneath it signaled the channel was still open, and receiving. Mordecai Harrison saw it too, and somehow kept his cool despite the personal attack.

I'm pretty sure I'd be making strangling motions towards Horace's floating face right now if it was me in the hot seat, Sam thought. *There's a reason Harrison is one of the most powerful people on Earth, and I fly back and forth between meetings.*

"We haven't been hiding down here, Captain, but I am glad you mentioned my family. When Mars closed its borders to Earth's refugees, my family helped move them to safe zones around the Home System. When plagues ravaged the Earth, the Harrison Institute found cures while your planet lived safe and segregated inside your domes. And when war broke out amongst your people, it was my grandfather, Commodore Andrew Harrison, who commanded the fleet that ended it.

"I'm not ashamed of my history, Captain Kołodziejski. I celebrate it. And I'm not prepared to subject the people of Earth, or Mars, or any other human settlement to a needless war without hard evidence. The Reclamation Council will review the data you've supplied, and make its recommendations accordingly. Now, if there is no other new business, I recommend we adjourn for the day."

One of the other councilors brought up food redistribution, and Horace's holo winked out for the last time as he left the meeting. Sam considered doing the same, but something Harrison had said raised a question in his own mind. In a whisper that seemed like a shout among the quiet murmurs of the councilors, he asked it of Commodore Maranova.

"How many people live on Mars right now?"

Maranova's answer was immediate, and Sam wondered if she'd been thinking the same thing.

"Three million, eight hundred thousand, with another thousand or so on ships around the system and in the fleet. They'd lose any serious engagement in about two hours, even without high energy weapons. And if someone's committed to throwing rocks at us from an unknown vector, we're all dead no matter how many ships we have."

If Ykaterina was as terrified as he was, she gave no sign. An enemy willing to use mass drivers against civilian targets was completely unpredictable, especially when those civilians were the only thing keeping the rest of humanity alive.

And without any real embassy for the gennies, we have no idea what they're thinking right now.

Horace Kołodziejski wasn't afraid to wear his heart on his sleeve, but he also had a lot of sleeve to work with. If he'd done the same math, come to the same conclusions, Horace wasn't just arguing for his own agenda, but for the survival of his entire planet.

Sam sat for a while and listened to the collected leadership of the human race talk about hydroponics and asteroid mining. The threat of a gennie invasion had to be on their minds as well, but the only thing they could do was keep moving forward with the Reclamation as planned.

We came so close to putting war behind us. But the fleet was built for a reason, and when the time comes, they're counting on us to be ready.

Sam's wrist comm chirped, and he quickly covered it with his hand. Maranova arched an eyebrow, but didn't turn away from the fascinating conversation she was having regarding rotating supplies from the Home Fleet to some of the smaller orbital habitats over the next two months.

The message on the comm was equal parts short and cryptic.

>>*Problem in O-Club. Only You.*

Sam's aide-de-camp knew not to bother him with casual issues, and knew even more how important it was to a fleet captain's career to be seen at council meetings like this one. So for him to forward on a problem now, it really must have been a big one.

He tapped out an acknowledgment, then sent a quick message to the commodore's wrist.

>>*Must leave. Sorry.*

Maranova had wisely turned off the her own comm's audio, but she'd already rolled her wrist up while speaking in anticipation of his message. She nodded her permission, and as quietly as he could Sam unfolded himself from his chair and left the council chamber.

This had better be good. And if I'm lucky, it'll take at least a couple hours to sort out.

ANDREISON

MARYA RAISED HER GLASS, admiring the cascade of bubbles as her beer settled. Lagrange 6 wasn't exactly the end of the line, but after her unceremonious exit from *City of Lights*, it might as well be.

It was a good dream while it lasted, but it's time to face facts. Even if they let me live, I'm finished in the fleet, and nothing I can do will change that.

Her drink tasted just as good as the three before it, but even after thirty hours in a jumpseat and with a few beers in her, Marya still had no idea of her next move.

She set the glass back on the counter next to her mess tunic. Unlike the rumpled mess of her flight suit, it was nearly pristine, a silent reminder of all the things she had yet to accomplish. After seven years of active duty, its main distinctions were the combat pilot's wings she'd never officially got to use, and the Distinguished Service Medal she'd earned the day she lost her eyes.

And if I could reverse that trade, I'd do it in a hot minute. The only reason it's there at all is because I'm required to wear it as part of any display.

In theory, the medal entitled her to a salute from other officers and a bump in pay. In practice, Marya was the only serving officer to have earned one since the Reclamation—*hell, in the last 200 years*—and in any event her reputation made the award mostly moot. She didn't regret her actions, either that day or since. But since her records always took a few bureaucratic detours when she moved between postings, the other commendations she'd earned never seemed to find her.

My real crime was getting caught. And, of course, refusing to quit after the trial.

Marya could have chosen a civvie bar to think in, but her feet took her on autopilot straight to the wardroom and she hadn't felt like moving since. Her only companion was the steward, a pleasant-enough NCO with old-Earth features and a slight limp. The man had noticed the medal as soon as she'd come in, and kept shooting it an occasional glance to make sure he'd read it right.

Besides, bartenders ask questions. This fella knows enough to keep the drinks coming, and how to disappear when necessary.

She took another sip of her beer, half closing her eyes to savor it without distractions. When she put it back down, she narrowed her eyes further to zoom in on the liquid itself.

Drinking out of a glass was a luxury in space, one only possible under constant acceleration or artificial gravity. Lagrange 6 had both, and the interplay between them made the bubbles take a slanting path up to meet the head. The bubbles themselves were interesting, undulating pockets of gas rather than the perfectly round ones people enjoyed down the gravity well.

There's probably some metaphor here for my situation, but I'm so thoroughly screwed I can't think of anything clever.

She finished her drink and signaled for another, and the steward hesitated before taking her glass away. He didn't flinch away from her stare, but also didn't start pouring.

"What?" The word was loaded with all the frustration of the last two shipdays, along with more than a little of the last few years.

"Most officers who choose this mess for lunch order food, ma'am. Are you sure you don't want anything else?

I want another fucking beer, damnit. I want the fucking universe to make some fucking sense. And I want some goddamned respect for once.

"I'm fine, thanks. Just beer for now."

Nodding, the steward pulled her another glass, and swapped it for the empty one before retreating to the prep room.

She turned her attention back to the tunic, and let her fingers brush over the flight wings. They were among the first things she'd seen after the implants healed, right after Mira's face and a bunch of investigators with questions about the accident. Mira had done a good job of shielding her from the inquest, but there was only so much a fresh sub-lieutenant could do in the face of a superior officer's demands, and Mira had a lot more to lose by bucking the system than Marya ever would.

At least she got the truth out. One of a million reasons I'm thankful she's still in my life.

Thoughts of Mira always led to thoughts of Deb, and that more than anything made up her mind to resign. She still had no idea what to do about the out-system transmission she'd decoded that ultimately led to her stowing away on a shuttle, or the fact that her superior officers had probably tried to have her killed on *City of Lights* to keep it quiet. But at least this was a problem she could solve.

Maybe Deb will design me a sweet little sub-orbital to ferry bigwigs around in. Because the odds of me getting back to space in any meaningful way just dropped from slim to none.

Maybe I won't blow my brains out from boredom inside a month.

Resigning her commission would be as easy as registering the decision and having it witnessed, especially since no-one really wanted her in the Fleet anyway. But Marya was tired of dealing with uniforms and bureaucracies, and she certainly didn't want to wait around in some office with a head full of drunk.

"Steward, can you bring me a handheld, please? I need core access."

There was a brief delay before the man appeared, and the look of fear on his face nearly killed Marya's buzz entirely.

"I'm sorry, ma'am. I can't do that."

Give me the damn handheld, you pissant sonuva...

"And why is that, exactly?

"Because I told him not to, Sub-Lieutenant. And around here people obey my orders."

It was a man's voice—deep, resonant, and accustomed to command. Part of her wanted to jump to attention and spin around with a hasty salute, but unlike the steward she was through with people telling her what to do.

Instead, Marya picked up her beer and took a long pull at it, setting it back down with a smile.

"It's probably a good thing I won't be around here much longer, then. Listen, whoever you are, this day's been the latest of a long string of bad ones, and I'd really like to get it over with. If you can help me with that, I'm happy to talk. Otherwise, I've got things to do."

"I was told you were smart, Andreison. Too smart to be pulling stunts like this, and definitely too smart to mouth off to a senior fleet captain. But by all means, please, finish your drink. I'm sure the rest of my day can wait until you realize how much trouble you're in."

Marya swallowed hard, and eased out of her chair. Determined not to back down, she turned and put a face to the voice, and once again regretted letting her mouth run.

She'd only seen the man standing before her once, during her graduation exercises. But Fleet Captain Samuel DeMarco wasn't someone you could easily forget.

DeMarco's body was matched well to his voice. He was the kind of man that had to have everything he wore tailored, since normal clothes would look ridiculous on so large a frame. Marya was no slouch herself, but pulling herself up to her full height only brought her eyes to DeMarco's third blouse button, and the bottom of his impressive set of ribbons. And unlike the peacockery of Ethan Phillips, none of DeMarco's ribbons were participation prizes.

Well, shit. This day just keeps getting better and better.

"I was in the process of resigning my commission, sir, so if you can see fit to expediting my request, I'll be off your station and out of your hair as soon as I can."

"Two more mistakes. First, your request is denied, so get back in uniform right now or we'll complete our conversation in the brig."

Marya reclaimed her tunic from the bar and sealed it over her jumpsuit as fast as she could, careful to smooth it down according to regs. DeMarco's slight nod of approval gave her some hope that she could salvage the situation, but his frown did not budge as he spoke.

"Second, this isn't my station, but I was understandably curious when half the ship's complement of *City of Lights* showed up out of nowhere, with one-way transfer orders and nowhere to go but 'away.' Even more so to get a call from Rivers here about a shavetail who walked straight off the transport into the wardroom and started tossing back beers on a stolen credit chip. An officer, I might add, who was not only missing from the shuttle's manifest, but also not listed as part of *City of Lights*' crew.

"Care to explain? Or should I call for station security and let them sort you out after all?"

Marya pressed her lips together, wondering which of her new problems to be angry about first.

"The chip's not stolen, it's mine. I just haven't had to use it in some time, and must have forgotten to update it."

Because my pig of a father did the worlds a favor and died a few years back, leaving me enough credit to build one of these stations for myself. I just didn't need any of it until today.

"But as for the rest, sir, yes, I can explain."

"Good. Come with me, Andreison. I get the feeling that whatever you have to say isn't meant for public consumption."

Marya nodded, and turned back to settle up with the steward. Her beer had been replaced on the counter with a glass of water and a couple sobriety pills, as well as her inherited credit chip. She looked up at the steward, who surprised her by offering one of the crispest salutes she'd seen in years.

Although Captain DeMarco was waiting, and she was under no obligation to do so, Marya returned the salute, holding it a few seconds longer than necessary as a thank you for the wordless respect before turning to follow the captain.

JANTINE

HEAD POUNDING, JANTINE SNUGGLED DEEPER INTO HER PILLOWS, WISHING whoever it was that kept saying her name would just go away. She'd already had this dream once today, and wanted it to be over as fast as possible.

"Jantine. Jantine!"

JonB's voice seemed far away. Darkness was closing around her as she fought for air, and she felt rumbling of some kind through the deck. The rumbling became a pounding, and then the weight on her back was gone.

A pair of tree trunk legs was standing in front of her, and Jantine rolled over to take in a painful, gasping breath. One of the Omegas was holding a crate high over her head, then spun around rapidly before releasing it. It sailed away like a rocket, and she felt rather than heard its impact. She raised her head, and saw a jumble of arms and legs struggling feebly beneath the crate as it came to rest in the corridor outside.

A warm feeling gathered at the base of her neck, nudging her to wakefulness. She hated this dream, hated what it was doing to her friends. Most of all, she hated what it was doing to her, and resolved to have better ones from now on.

Her pillow shifted, and Jantine felt herself sliding down a mountain.

"Jantine!"

"You should make the call, boss."

Malik's face glowed in the light of his computer screen, laughing with his eyes at some joke she didn't understand. He was always so good at...

Was...

Malik.

Jantine opened her eyes, and the rich yellow light pouring in from the hole in the cargo compartment made her headache even worse. She couldn't quite see who was talking to her, nor could she make out any of their words save for her name.

The sound of tiny bells echoed inside her head, dropping in intensity with each pass. The wall behind her shifted, and an orange something moved across her field of vision, slowly resolving into an eight-fingered hand larger than her head.

She clutched the Omega's arm tighter, pressing herself against its warmth while at the same time willing the emptiness inside her to end. She tried closing her eyes again, but JonB wasn't going to leave her alone, and no amount of wishing would bring back her dead team members.

Harren. Malik. Doria.

Jarl.

Crassus.

It started as a whisper, a single syllable mouthed as she exhaled, but steadily growing in volume with each breath.

"no."

Jarl's last step sent him crashing into one of the piston assemblies used to retract the ramp, and Jantine saw his eyes were wide and fixed. His encounter suit was covered in puckered scars, each one giving her another reason to get her team off the Valiant *as soon as possible.*

"Boss, shu...shuttle secured."

"No."

The shuttle lurched, and Jantine pitched forward into the sleeper unit. She hit her head on something, then fell to the deck as if pushed there. Then the shuttle stood on its nose, sending her sliding back up the blood-slick ramp.

Discarded micro-slugs scratched her face as the sounds of JonB's screaming came closer. Another change of direction slammed her into the wall, and then she was tumbling head over heels back down into the bay.

"COMMANDER!"

She tried to turn her head toward Crassus, but her neck was made of rubber. All she could manage was a pathetic gasp, and then the sound of tearing metal filled the room.

Her last sight before everything went black was of a tiny, six-limbed figure sailing away from a ragged hole in the hull, waving its arms madly as it fell.

"NO!"

Jantine fought her way free of the Omega's encircling arms, and unsteadily to her feat. Whichever one it was pulled back completely from her mind, and it took every bit of her composure not to drop to her knees in front of JonB and weep for her fallen soldiers. Everything in her eyeline was blurry save for JonB's face, and he had that frustrating look like he was about to tell her something else she didn't want to hear.

"Jantine, I we need to move. Now. The shuttle's down, we're all okay, but Mira says..."

Mira? Mira who?

Jantine took a wobbly step forward, then another. Her knees were shaking, her head pounding, and she still didn't know either where she was, or where to find the rest of her team. To make matters worse, JonB was in her way, again, and spouting an even more annoying brand of nonsense than usual.

"I give the orders here, JonB. I'll decide when we leave, and I...I..."

Jantine's vision clouded, and the room spun around her. The last thing she saw clearly was JonB's face going white as she pitched forward into his arms. She tried to push him away, but her body didn't obey her commands anymore than the civvie, and she raged silently as she leaned against him for unwanted support.

Have to get out of here. Have to find Katra!

JonB knelt over the Gamma, holding her arms while Carlton inserted a small tube into the left side of her chest. There was blood everywhere, and Jantine saw at least a dozen ugly holes on her bare skin.

Jarl staggered down the ramp, waving away fresh energizers in favor of a double handful of grenades, hoping to buy them enough time to...

Doria coughed, not bothering to wipe away the blood from her lips. Her left arm cradled Malik's buttered face to her chest, her right tucked in tight at her side against the pain. Jantine watched her as long as she could, before the Omegas knelt before the pair of dying mods, each one stretching out a hand to an unresisting face...

"make it stop. please, make it stop..."

Her whispered words didn't travel any farther than the fabric of JonB's jumpsuit, but the other Beta's hearing was every bit as acute as her own. Even in distress, Jantine noted that at some point he had taken off his encounter suit and changed his garments, while she was still wearing hers, minus her cowl, helmet, and given the lack of pressure across her breasts, her hand pulser.

JonB leaned forward, and wrapped his arms around her. Jantine tensed, ready to discipline him for the unwanted contact, but all she could do was rest there, listening to her pulse pounding inside her head.

Jantine's cheeks burned with shame, her breath caught in her throat, and her nose filled with an unfamiliar tingling sensation.

Please...

Then a third hand joined JonB's on her back, one large enough to apply gentle pressure to her entire spine at once. The warm feeling returned, but this time it didn't want to drag her back to sleep, but to push her gently into the world.

JonB broke the embrace, but kept supporting Janine with his hands on her upper arms. She didn't want to meet his eyes, didn't want to show any more weakness than she already had. But whatever this moment was could not last—JonB was right, they had to get moving, had to leave the Earth shuttle behind as fast as possible.

But there's some questions I want answered first, and this time I'm not taking a head shake for an answer.

Jantine steeled herself for another uncomfortable encounter with the Omegas, and as if sensing her mood, the hand at her back disappeared, along with whatever pain-relieving mental exercise the Omega had employed.

The Beta set her feet and pushed away from JonB, not opening her eyes until she was turned completely around and facing the other direction. When she did open them, the first thing she saw was the ancient sleeper unit they'd stolen along with the shuttle, and the delicate, ghostly face of the mod inside.

Anger brought a fresh blush to Jantine's cheeks, and she didn't bother to hide it. In response, the Omega moved between her and the unit, its tattered coveralls reminding her of how powerful—and terrifying—the Omegas could be if they put their minds to something.

The Omegas were moving across the bay now, transforming with each step they took from peaceful architects into orange-skinned engines of death. Powerful arms swatted enemies aside like flies. One armored trooper had enough time and presence of mind to fire a weapon, but the hypersonic volley of slugs bounced harmlessly off an Omega's chest as it advanced...

Jantine didn't have a slugthrower—at this point, she didn't even know if she still had her hand pulser. All she had was her anger, and a mind trained for years to take command—and keep it.

Reaching up to grab the fabric of the Omega's jumpsuit, she took a double handful and pulled. At first, nothing happened, but then the unyielding wall of orange flesh bent to her will, and slowly bowed to meet her eyes.

"What. Is. That?" Jantine kept a tight grip in the coverall with her right hand, gesturing with her left at the sleeper unit. The Omega's only response was to blink its eyes in sequence, one pair at a time. Something tickled the back of her head, but she was too angry to let the Omega in, and too inexperienced with mind-to-mind communication to understand it in any event.

"Just nod for yes. Is it an Alpha?" Nod. "Did you know it was an Alpha when you went off-mission?" Nod. "Did you know the humans had it captive before we launched?"

The Omega did not nod this time, nor did it attempt any further communication. After a few seconds, it stood up and squared its shoulders, forcing Jantine to relinquish her grip or be pulled off her feet. It turned and took three huge steps over to the sleeper unit before sitting down with its back to her, head gently swaying.

Jantine's rage reached a boiling point, and she slapped her chest, only to confirm that she'd either lost her hand pulser during their tumbling descent from orbit, or it had been removed sometime after. She looked around the shuttle's cargo area for something, anything, that would make an impression on the Omega if swung hard enough, but only saw sealed crates, the jagged breach in the hull, and a stunned civilian scientific advisor.

"JonB, fetch me the human female." Not looking back for his reaction, she circled left to get a better look at the sleeper unit. The Omega shifted and held out a many-fingered hand to block her view, which made her even angrier.

"I have questions for the Omegas, and we all need to know the answers. Drag her here if you have to, and the other Omega too, if you can figure out how."

"I can't," said JonB. His first words were a fearful whisper, but his next ones drove Jantine's temper way past boiling into a plasma state. "She won't leave the other human alone. He's—"

"Did I ask about that, JonB? Did I?" Jantine was on the Beta in an instant, one hand holding the fabric of his jumpsuit and the other at his throat, pushing him back over the edge of the hull breach until his arms flailed for balance.

"I gave you an *order*, JonB. Either follow it, or find me someone who can! As you said, we don't have time to waste, and like it or not, whatever they"—Jantine waved a hand angrily in the Omega's general direction—"did to her means she can talk to them. So go get her, bring her down here, and get. Them. Talking!"

Her last words weren't exactly shouted, but JonB's wide eyes and pale face took them as such. Disgusted by both his weakness and her loss of control, Jantine pulled him back inside and threw him to the deck.

"When one of you has something to tell me that I want to hear, I'll be out there." Jantine took an exploratory step to see if it was the shuttle's gravity holding her down, or Earth's, and decided it was the latter. She jumped from the shuttle, relaxing her legs and rolling to a stop on the uneven ground.

She heard motion to her right, and spun around to face it, grabbing at her chest once again for a weapon that wasn't there. Artemus was standing behind a stack of crates, cleaning a hand pulser with his bottom hands while assembling survival packs with his uppers. While she couldn't tell from her position whose weapon it was, she could do the math on the packs well enough.

Five of us left to wear them. Three Betas—myself, JonB, and Carlton; one Gamma, and Artemus. The Omegas don't use weapons and rarely even wear clothes, and right now I don't really care what they want to take with them when we leave.

Jantine stalked over to Artemus, who held out the now-reassembled weapon to her butt first, while selecting another from the row in front of him for maintenance. She took it gratefully, checking the energizer more out of habit than necessity—Artemus knew his craft well, and he'd given her a fresh one.

Her hand was halfway to sheathing it in her encounter suit when she changed her mind, and handed it back to him. Artemus cocked an eyebrow, and she answered the Delta's unspoken question by grabbing the pack he'd inscribed with her sigil.

Opening it, she pulled out her jumpsuit, still smelling of the cargo container the mods had spent almost three standard weeks in before their journey to Earth ended a million kilometers early. Setting it aside, she took two ration bars from an outside pocket, unwrapping one and taking a bite before placing both on top of the jumpsuit.

Jantine took a deep, full breath of Earth air, savoring its strange smell and the quick rush of oxygen coursing through her lungs. Letting it out, she saw the beginnings of a smile on Artemus's face, and felt one teasing the corner of her own mouth.

I can't lose control like that again. I need to stay in command for as long as I can, no matter how annoying JonB gets. We need each other, now more than ever.

And I don't know how this ends.

"Artemus?"

"Yes, Commander Jantine?"

"Make up three extra packs, one with as many energizers as you're comfortable storing in one place."

"Yes, Commander Jantine. Will there be anything else?"

Jantine took her time in answering as she removed her encounter suit, carefully unhooking and clearing the sanitary systems before handing it and her back to Artemus for proper maintenance. She set her boots aside, flexing her toes in the rich, dark soil of humanity's homeworld as a light breeze cooled her bare skin.

"JonB will be looking for me soon, possibly with the Earth woman in tow. I don't want to talk to him, but send her to me there," she said, pointing to a low rise to the west. "I need to think."

"Of course, Commander. I set aside some of our spare garments, if you would like first pick among the stores." Artemus pointed with a top hand to another stack of crates along the side of the shuttle, with articles of clothing sorted in front by size and fit. Jantine noted that there were no Delta-sized garments, and felt another pang of regret at the senseless loss of their team's other combat specialist.

I grieve for Crassus too, Artemus. But that's not what you need to hear right now, is it?

Jantine gave Artemus a quick nod, releasing him to his own tasks while she collected her pack. Doria's clothes were too small for her, and Harren's would be a better fit for his twin Carlton. But Malik's gear was a perfect fit—by design, rather than circumstance.

Just like the Alphas planned. Everything down to the last detail, except for what actually happened to us.

Jantine decided instead on a white cooling harness from her own pack, a seamless-one piece garment that would also monitor her bodily functions once she reactivated her handheld. She steadied herself against the crates with one hand as she stepped into it, careful not to get any dirt on the inside surfaces. Once it was snug between her legs and across her shoulders, she pulled on her jumpsuit, and walked toward the setting sun.

We made it to Earth. Most of us, anyway.

Now all I have to do is figure out how to survive with everyone in the worlds against us, with ninety percent of my colony missing and presumed dead, three combat effectives, two civvies, and a couple of humans I'd rather shoot than look at.

After all, it's what I'm here to do.

CALLAWAY

MARCUS WAS HALFWAY to the command deck when he found the first set of bodies. A mix of hardsuited troopers and vacsuited repair techs were stuffed behind piles of equipment, with too many holes in them and not enough heads.

Whoever had done the hiding—and the holing—was fairly good at their job. If Marcus hadn't stopped to scavenge some more supplies, he'd have missed the tiny, undulating blobs of blood rising up as *Valiant* tumbled around random axes as it died.

Before this very second I was desperate to get somebody on comms. Now I'd rather crawl back into Mira's bunk and wait for the universe to make sense again.

Marcus nearly retched as he uncovered the first body. Even though there were no insects or vermin to deal with, death had a smell all its own, one he knew far too well from a childhood spent patrolling his family's nature preserve in Kenya.

Never in a million years would I have expected to find this in space. And since now I know there's a killer—or killers—aboard my ship, my priorities have definitely shifted.

I need a weapon, and fast.

Marcus flashed back to the ones safely hidden under Mira's bunk, and was about to go back for them when he spotted the handle of an induction pistol amongst a jumble of shattered faceplates and punctured breastplates.

Working it free, he ran through the checklist Mira had drilled into him during their training sessions, checking first to see if it was loaded, then to determine whether or not it would fire.

Judging it functional, he set aside and looked for another one, careful not to move the bodies any more than he had to. The burn patterns on the hard suits were like nothing he'd ever seen; the closest analogy he could form was that of a glass probe melted from being shoved into moving lava. Some of the techs' bodies were burned completely through, adding even more texture to the already pungent aroma surrounding him.

After a few minutes of digging, Marcus pocketed several micro-slug canisters, an oxygen concentrator, and some ration bars sealed in heavy foil.

Hope it's enough to keep out the worst of this stink. I'm going to need a couple cycles in the sonic shower to feel even remotely clean again.

What he didn't find were the heavy slugthrowers the troopers should have been carrying, which meant their killers had either upgraded their arsenal here, or had enough carrying capacity not to worry about a couple dozen kilos of slugthrowers.

Whoever did this was not screwing around, and though they were armed enough to tear through these poor souls, they certainly didn't want to leave armed enemies at their back. Plus, whatever weapons they used here are probably literally light years ahead of this old thing.

Guess I'll need to up my game a bit. Luckily, I've still got a few tricks to take.

Marcus tidied up the area as best he could. He thought about taking along the cache's portable generator, but since someone on *Valiant* was clearly spoiling for a fight, he didn't want to carry any extra mass around if he didn't have to.

Doesn't matter if it's weightless, I still need to get it moving, and stop it on the other end. There's no telling what—or who—else I'll encounter on my way up to Command, and I've only got two hands to work with.

A few drops of blood brushed his unshaven cheek, losing their surface tension and mingling with a dried smear from his earlier injury.

Cursing under his breath, he tried to wipe it away with the hem of his makeshift poncho, but transfer from the bodies had irreparably soiled that garment. Instead, he exchanged it for an even bloodier vacsuit, after carefully removing the soiled inner liner. Unfortunately, the one he selected for its many pockets had no helmet, but another few seconds of scavenging produced a loosely fitting thermal cowl.

It took him about a minute to pull the jumpsuit on over his duty pants, most of which was spent getting into and out of his boots while they were anchored to the deck. Throughout the process, he kept one hand ready to snatch the induction pistol from where he'd left it hovering above a crate. He redistributed his scavenged kit across the vacsuit's outer pockets before sealing it up around his collar and bucking his control belt over the whole ensemble. It wasn't an ideal fit, and the jumpsuit chafed against the bare skin of his chest, but it would offer him a couple more seconds of life in an emergency, and more importantly, someplace to stow the pistol out of sight.

First impressions are very important, after all.

Before he left the cache behind, he opened an emergency medical kit and took out another concentrator. He crouched down behind one of the crates, taking slow, deep breaths of oxygen through its close-fitting mask while considering his next steps.

These bodies are cold, so all this happened while I was sleeping. And since no one but me's come looking for them, there have to be enough trouble spots around the ship that this team's missed check-ins rank lower than everybody else's problems.

Or, he thought morbidly, *there's nobody else to come looking.*

Marcus patted the pocket holding his scavenged comm, then pulled it out and thumbed through the frequencies he remembered from evacuation drills when he first came aboard. All he got was static, and try as he might, he couldn't remember Mira saying anything about any private channels during their conversations.

Should have paid more attention to what she was actually saying, I guess, instead of peeling apart her responses for any political commentary. Or staring at the intensity in her eyes, or admiring the way her freckles scrunch up when she smiles.

Or the combination of both when she's shooting those monster hand-cannons of hers.

The ease with which Mira could shift from warm conversationalist to cool, efficient professional was one of the most jarring things about the woman. Captain Martin had told him she was good at her job, but he had no idea how good an instructor Mira really was until she ran him through his pistol requalification out on the hull.

I always thought I was a good shot, but as a pilot, I never had much need to carry a personal weapon. But the way she could spot—and destroy— holotargets as soon as they spawned was almost superhuman, and in only a couple of sessions she got me almost a quarter as fast as she was, more than enough to earn another medal for my collection.

That's me now. Commander Callaway of the Spaceways. And it's a good thing, too, since from the looks of things I'm probably going to have to shoot someone on this trip sooner, rather than later.

Shit. I really need to find Mira, so she can rescue my dumb ass.

Marcus took one last, long drag on the concentrator, imagining his blood filling up with extra energy for a fight he hoped wasn't going to happen. He took the rest of the medical supplies and packed them into any pocket with enough room to hold them, then placed the empty kit under his abandoned blanket, swatting down a couple more drops of blood as he did.

He unlocked his boots and took a cautious first step from conceal-ment, only to grab a catch ring and duck back behind the crate as he heard an answering echo from the corridor ahead.

Make that echoes, he thought, counting off footfalls while he searched the darkened space in front of him for the people making them.

Three, no four...fuck. They're in step now, I've got no idea how many of them there are. I'm just going to have to get closer, and hope they're friendlies.

He unzipped the pocket holding the pistol, then slowly swung his way forward. Every ring brought him a few meters closer to the sounds of armored boots clomping their way to the middle of the ship, until he could finally see emergency suit lights about thirty meters ahead.

Six, seven, shit, that's a full squad of troopers, not a five-man fire team. And they're carrying enough firepower to hold this corridor against pretty much anybody.

Well, almost anybody. Those slugthrowers didn't kill these poor souls behind me, which means somebody else did, and they probably went in the same direction I'm heading right now.

Unlike Marcus, in addition to full weapons loadouts the troopers had either brought a couple generators with them, or were less discriminating than he in their scavenging. Even weighed down with extra gear, they were moving forward in a textbook, two-by-two formation he hadn't seen since the Academy, each pair making a full corridor survey before waving the next pair forward.

Marcus pressed himself as tightly to the corridor wall as he could, thankful that he'd grabbed the vacsuit when he did. Even with a mismatched cowl, its insulation almost completely masked his body heat, and his exposed face could easily be covered up by his gloved hands to avoid detection by a hardsuit's thermal sensors.

I can't hear them talking, so they must be using a private network. And although I could really use some backup right now, I still don't know friends from foes.

Marcus let them move farther ahead, then made a few more swings, crossing the corridor when it curved enough to obscure his view of the troopers ahead. He had crept up undetected to within twenty meters of the group when they stopped to slap a light pack against the overhead grating, illuminating another carefully staged supply cache, and much to his dismay, Marcus himself.

The rearmost troopers turned in unison, slugthrowers at the

ready. Marcus took the hint and floated down to the deck from his position against the wall, setting his boots to walking strength and raising his arms—and more importantly, empty hands—above his head.

Well, nothing for it now. Time to either make some new friends, or new enemies.

"Idle down, troopers. I'm Commander Callaway. What can you tell me about what's happening here?"

While Marcus wasn't officially part of *Valiant*'s crew, enough people had seen him with Captain Martin for word to get around about who he was, and who he knew.

And a few of the fire crews have seen me in Mira's company, which might stand me a little better with this lot.

Marcus allowed himself to hope this might actually *be* Mira and her squad, for exactly as long as it took for him to recognize the unit insignia blazed onto their chest plates and helmets as he stepped further into the light: the crossed swords and moons of *SDF Indomitable*.

Oops.

"That's far enough, Commander. Get down on your knees, and surrender to my authority."

The voice was female, lightly accented, and all business. Marcus wasn't even sure which trooper it was at first, until the wall of weapons facing him parted to let someone with the twin circles of a lieutenant on their collar.

"I'm afraid I can't do that, Lieutenant. Though I'm happy to accept yours, and those of your troopers." Marcus took another step forward, trying not to flinch as the troopers facing him tracked his every move with the barrels of their slugthrowers.

"And why should I do that, Commander Callaway? We have you outnumbered. You are unarmed. And, most importantly, you are also on our list of suspected traitors to arrest."

Well, that escalated quickly. Can't say she's wrong, though. I just hope I've read enough of the situation right for this to work...

"And you're alone, Lieutenant, with exactly as much authority as is granted by the troopers at your back. You wouldn't be scavenging supplies if you could call back for more of your own.

"Now me, I know this ship. I know the people on it, and how to get the best out of them. I also know you can feel the ship tumbling as well as I can, and this air isn't going to get any fresher any time soon. Don't you want someone on your side who can fix all that?"

Marcus took a breath, hoping the final part of his bluff would seal the deal.

"And I don't know if you've noticed, but somewhere on this ship, there's someone with a lot bigger weapons than yours. So either we all kill each other now, or we work together and see what happens. Because I'm thinking, if you can't get supplies from *Indomitable*—or whatever ship brought you here—you also can't get off *Valiant*, and you need me a lot more than you think."

Pretty sure I can kill a couple before they gun me down. At least one, probably.

Maybe. I just need a little—

Marcus felt a vibration through his boots, and instinctively looked down to see what it was. He didn't spot anything happening under the grating, but a second later, the vibration became a corridor-shaking rumble, followed by a low growl that quickly escalated into the scream of tearing metal. He dropped a hand to his belt controls just in time to lock down his boots and avoid being blown off his feet by a wall of air strong enough to bend him over backwards.

Fuck. A hull breach, and there's no hatch in sight. As if this day couldn't get any worse.

This far inside the ship, a breach had to be absolutely huge to vent this much atmosphere. And with the power down in this section, Marcus and the Martians had few options for escape.

Of course, all of them have nice, sealed helmets to provide them a steady supply of oxygen. Looks like Commander Callaway's thrilling space adventures are about to come to a close.

One of the troopers hadn't secured their boots in time and went sailing past him, surrounded by a cloud of supply crates and assorted weaponry. Marcus acted on instinct ingrained by fifteen years living and working in space and reached for them as they passed, grabbing just enough of a flailing gauntlet to swing the trooper towards a catch ring. Once he heard the Martian's boots catch, he let go, not wanting to take the trooper with him if one of the supply crates he was dodging knocked him loose as well.

The torrent of air continued, telling Marcus not only that the breach was closer—and larger— than his original estimate, but also that there were open hatches ahead of them on this deck. If left unchecked, they could vent the whole section, if not the rest of the ship.

Bracing himself against the unnatural wind, he made his way to the closest catch ring with painstakingly slow steps, face and eyes burning despite having one of his hands out in front of him.

We have got to get out of here, but how?

Something snapped the palm of his hand, and Marcus batted it away hard enough that he almost lost his grip on the ring. After blinking away stinging tears, he saw a carabiner dancing just out of his reach at the end of a long wire tether, the other end of which was in the hands of the *Indomitable* trooper he'd just been trading words with.

The tether was drifting further away from him, and the venting atmosphere was making it bob up and down as well. But instead of stretching out for it, Marcus doubled his grip on the catch ring and pulled, yanking his boots from the deck. Muscles straining, he brought his knees up to his chest, holding himself there for a moment before planting his feet on the bulkhead, one on either side of the ring, and waiting for the magnets to reattach.

Once he was secure, he unfolded himself out from the ring, laying out horizontally and praying not only that the tether was still within reach and approximately where he'd last seen it, but that there weren't enough crates left to knock him out into space. Something hit his left hand, and skipped away before he could grab it. Marcus craned his neck to see, and spotted the carabiner just before it slammed into his head, reopening and expanding the cut on his temple. This time, though, it lingered long enough for him to grab it with both hands, and loop the tether through one of the rings on his belt.

The line went taut, pulling him away from the wall. But Marcus had other plans, and as soon as he had his boots back on the deck, he shot a glance back up the corridor at the troopers trying to reel him in.

The female lieutenant was about halfway between him and the former supply cache, belaying the tether with her hard suit and pulling him to her hand-over-hand. Keeping the carabiner in his right hand, Marcus waved at her furiously, signaling first for some slack on the line, then pointing at the trooper behind him with a nasty crease running down the side of their helmet and a slowly spreading crack in their faceplate, desperately clinging to the catch ring with just one hand.

The lieutenant motioned to the troopers behind her, two of whom were standing by the catch rings on either side of the corridor. The tether was threaded through one and attached to the other, with just enough slack between them for Marcus to execute his plan.

I think.

Trusting they understood what he wanted, Marcus turned and clomped over to the trooper he'd saved once already, straining against the line for the last few centimeters as the trooper pulled against the current at about the same rate. Marcus snapped the tether to a hardpoint on their suit just as they lost their grip, then gathered the trooper in his arms while they regained their feet.

With the extra leverage provided by two pairs of boots, a strength enhancing hardsuit, and the lieutenant hauling hard on the tether, the pair rejoined the other troopers in just a few seconds. Marcus handed off the trooper to the lieutenant, then sagged against a catch ring, turning his head away from the blast and taking big gulps of thinning air before he remembered the concentrator he'd scavenged just minutes before.

Okay, first problem solved. Saved myself, saved the Martians, and—wait, weren't there ten of them before?

Marcus' quick count only came up with four, a number which went down again when the two manning the catch rings turned and clomped up the corridor.

Marcus pulled the concentrator away from his face to shout at the lieutenant, but she was already in a conversation with the other trooper, helmets pressed together and faceplates cleared. Marcus couldn't make any of it out, but could see the one he'd saved was also female, and visibly terrified by her experience.

Before he could address the pair, the lieutenant waved the other trooper ahead and turned her attention to Marcus, lips pursed and eyes uncertain. In the dim glow of the emergency lighting, he couldn't make out either the color of her eyes or skin inside her helmet. Then she blanked it, and Marcus saw his bloody and battered face reflected in her visor.

Damn, I wouldn't surrender to me either.

The escaping air was whisking drops of blood away from his forehead and down the corridor at an alarming rate, though the most concerning part about his new look was the swelling on the right side of his face. Without any real direction to work with, his head was starting to balloon outward in the reduced atmosphere.

Not sure I like this new look, but what am I going to do about it?

In an unexpected move, the nameless lieutenant grabbed the fabric of his jumpsuit with one hand, and the tether still attached to his belt with the other. With a single tug, she pulled Marcus off his feet and swung him over her shoulders, then started running after the rest of her squad.

With each power-assisted stride, Marcus was sure she was going to slam him into the top of the corridor. He thought he heard something from inside her helmet as they passed out of the emergency lamp's cone of illumination, but he didn't have long to think about it before they came bounding up to another one around the curve.

The scene here was much more intense, as was the rush of air blasting past them from an emergency hatch. There were four troopers, two on each side of the gap, slowly failing to keep the blast doors open. With emergency lamps flashing on either side of the hatch and an alarm blaring as they approached, Marcus gave up calculating the time he had left somewhere between "not enough" and "please-pleaseplease."

The lieutenant stopped running just as they reached the hatch, launching him unceremoniously forward as her arms slammed into the inside edges of the blast doors. Marcus felt the tether whip through the loop, tearing away his control belt as it snapped back way they came. He tumbled to a stop on the deck plating a few meters away, adding even more bruises to his collection in the process.

Marcus heard, rather than saw what happened next, as a banshee scream rose from either side of the hatch mechanism as it fought against her efforts. Boots pounded past him in time to the flashing lights, and he turned his pounding head to see almost the entire squad grab some piece of the surprisingly strong officer and yank her through in a move so coordinated he'd swear it was practiced.

The hatch slammed shut with a dull thud, cutting off both the venting atmosphere and the last bit of light in the corridor. Marcus' ears popped so hard he thought his eardrums had exploded, until the painful ringing started and he forgot about everything else in the universe.

He didn't remember when he started screaming, but he stopped abruptly when someone grabbed his jumpsuit and hauled him roughly to his feet. Faceplate lights flared to life all around him, and he blinked away tears and sweat and blood as a ragged shout died in his throat.

The last faceplate to light up was just centimeters away from his face—the lieutenant who'd nearly died saving his life, and the lives of her entire squad.

Marcus had several thoughts pop into his oft-abused head at the same time. One, having just survived an explosive decompression, for the first time since he'd woken up he was under the effects of a gravity field, and he really, *really* had to pee.

And two...

Jesus Christ, those are the coldest eyes I've ever seen in my life.

The owner of said eyes had an equally cold smile, and her next words were just about as terrifying.

"Okay, Commander. We surrender. But if we don't find your miracle workers before this floating deathtrap runs out of air, I swear you'll be the first one to die."

Marcus' jangled nerves supercharged what was left of his brain, rifling through his repertoire of pithy responses and coming up just this side of empty.

"Lieutenant, you've got yourself a deal."

DEMARCO

SAM DEMARCO WAS FINDING it hard to keep his Captain Face on while dealing with an officer who was not only out of his chain of command, but didn't really want to be an officer at all. The young woman seated across the desk from him was rage incarnate, and his own temper was rising with each of her monosyllabic responses.

I'm not even sure what I want to say to her. A dozen years ago it was me in that chair, and it was Ykaterina saving my career. But I don't think a dressing down is what Andreison needs right now, though I'm not sure she really needs a friend either.

Despite the sobriety meds, Andreison didn't seem fully present, and Sam had the distinct impression that if his borrowed office had windows, she'd probably be looking out one right now instead of forcing herself to meet his eyes.

Sam had instructed his aide to pull a hardcopy of Andreison's file while he went to collect her, and it was waiting for him on his borrowed desk when he returned. It was ridiculously thin for a serving officer, though he already knew what was in it.

At least, right up until her life got blown apart.

First she'd lost her eyes saving the lives of hundreds of people, including his own and that of then-Fleet Captain Maranova. He didn't think she'd remember him shaking her hand before she went up in the trainer, but he'd never forget the amazing aerobatics she'd executed to land not only her own damaged aircraft, but that of another pilot incapable of landing on his own.

I thought I was going to die that day—alone, and on a planet. She gave me back the sky, at the cost of almost everything she loved. We took away her wings, put a shiny medal on her chest, and then forgot about her.

Well, mostly. The rest she did herself.

The inquest following the accident was a brief one, and after a year of learning to do everything again, she returned to the academy and graduated with top honors. Sam had specifically requested her for his permanent staff, but then came her court-martial and subsequent imprisonment.

Looking at her now—after seven years of bad postings, missed or denied promotions, and a series of disciplinary notes in her file—he wondered what, if anything, was left of the promising officer she'd once been.

He didn't have a good enough read on the woman she'd become since then to start in on the big questions, so he defaulted to interview mode, reading her record aloud from the hardcopy.

"Sub-Lieutenant Marya Elaine Andreison. Born on the Andreison-Proctor collective station 2612 OER, entered the Colorado preparatory academy on special dispensation as an emancipated minor in 2625, formally sworn in as a Cadet First Class during the winter term of 2627."

Sam paused for a moment to look at Andreison's reaction, and was happy to see her sitting up straighter. But before he continued, her reply made it clear it wasn't respect she was showing him.

"McCallister, sir. Technically, it's McCallister-Andreison-Harlan, but Records refuses to make the change despite me filling out dozens of forms, and BuPers won't issue me a uniform with anything but my birth name on it. If you're going to drum me out, I'd prefer you do it under my legal name."

One, two, three, four...

Sam rarely got to ten with a junior officer, but he'd made it to fifteen several times since meeting Andreison. She knew she was getting to him, and that he knew what she was doing. But having already blocked her resignation, until he could figure out what to do with her, he was earning every bit of her anger.

"Understood. I'll see that your file is updated by end of day. Shall I continue, or do you finally have something to say to me?"

"What do you want to hear, Captain?"

"I'm not sure I like your tone, Sub-Lieutenant."

Sam knew the words were a mistake as soon as he said them. Andreison's artificial eyes widened, and he dropped his gaze momentarily in an attempt to de-escalate the conversation. He was losing points with her all over the place, and running out of ways not to be angrier with himself than with Andreison.

McCallister. Fuck. I need to remember that. And to say something right, for a change.

"Frankly, sir, I'm not sure I care. But if answering your questions gets me off this station and out of the Fleet, ask away. I appear to have plenty of time."

Sam took a deep breath, wishing he had a real chair to lean back in instead of the bench he'd had them install behind his desk. Something poked him in the side, and it took him a second to realize it was his command baton. He exhaled, took the baton off his belt and placed it next to her file, and stared at her for a few more seconds while he searched for the right words to bring her back in line.

"All right, Ms. McCallister. If that's how you want to play it I'm going to be completely honest with you. I don't know why you're on this station, but I do know why Chief Rivers called me when he realized who you were. You have a reputation for disruptive behavior, but out of respect for what you've done, he didn't want you back in the brig.

"Your record, such as it is," said, waving a hand at her file, "tells me your last posting was at the Pacific Deep Space array, but that was over two years ago. Yet there's a letter of commendation here from the commander of the Arecebo facility dated last month, indicating that in your six months there you were 'the finest young officer he'd ever had the pleasure of serving with,' and he was sorry to lose you to the Home Fleet. And now you're sitting in front of me, after flying in a packed shuttle full of confused officers and crew from *City of Lights*.

"Care to explain?"

McCallister's expression softened somewhat, but her body language was still defensive, and Sam wasn't sure how to put her completely at ease. Her reaction had to be to his rank, not to him personally, and if prior commanding officers had singled her out for abuse, he had to know that too. Even by Fleet standards, her records were a complete mess, and Sam wondered how much of his meager political capital it would take to straighten them out.

I owe her that much, at least.

McCallister gave a half shrug, shifting a bit in her chair so she could rest both hands on the desk.

"I get new orders, I move on. After a few years you get used to it, just like the rest of the bureaucratic nonsense that happens to you. The only things that ever seem to stick are my medical and disciplinary records, which are always waiting for me when I arrive. I was hoping *City of Lights* was my last stop for a while, but I guess that just wasn't meant to be."

Sam detected actual hope in her voice, so decided to press on.

"And why was that, Ms. McCallister?"

"Do I really have to say it, sir? You're going to ask me about the trial sooner or later, right? What version of events are in there now?" McCallister waved a hand at the hardcopy, but Sam didn't need to consult it, and he kept his focus on her face. He'd been there in the gallery when she was sentenced, only narrowly avoiding serving on her panel by a couple days of seniority.

But McCallister had opened a door for him, and Sam wasn't about to let her slam it in his face.

"I'm trying to help you here, Marya. I could write you up as AWOL, conduct unbecoming, and half-a-dozen other minor infractions you've committed since we started talking. As far as I can tell, exactly two people outside this room know you're on this station, and both of us know they called me instead of station security.

"So yes, I'd like to talk about why you tried to kill Doctor Thomas Watson in 2633, and why you refused to testify at your own disciplinary hearing and subsequent court-martial. A lot of people went to bat for you, back in the day, and..."

Marya sat up abruptly, taking her hands off the table and jamming them under her legs. Her voice went straight back to "angry short-timer," and her strange eyes were fixed and wide as she spoke.

"With, respect, sir, my feelings about that waste of skin have not changed. He raped my wife and beat her mostly to death, and if I had it to do over again, I'd have finished the job. Mira would probably have done the same thing if she was planetside, and her history with that bastard is a lot more direct.

"So no, I'm not sorry. No, I haven't moved past that chapter of my life, and also with respect, why the hell do you care?"

Finally, a question I can answer.

"Because, Sub-Lieutenant, before all that anger you're carrying around landed you in prison, you were scheduled to report to me aboard *City of Lights* when she was mine. I stayed in that courtroom for three weeks waiting to testify on your behalf, but thanks to your silence I never got the chance. You went to prison for contempt, not assault, and six months later when you got out on a technicality, I was too far past Jupiter to swing back and pick your dumb ass up.

"So, yes, I'd like to know if the reason they couldn't call Watson to the stand was because you killed him when no one was looking and hid the body somewhere. Because I believe in second chances, and third ones; because for some damn reason, someone once tried to help me out of a bad situation, and I'd like to think I turned out okay.

"So consider your next words very carefully, Marya. If you want to go back to prison, tell me now. If you're still set on resigning your commission, there are four other senior officers aboard L6 who might approve your request. Or, they might decide the first option is a better place for you after all.

"But before you go down that route, I feel I should warn you that one of them is Commodore Ykaterina Maranova. And if you think I'm upset by your actions, imagine what *she'll* have to say when I pull her out of a Reclamation Council meeting so you can say hello."

McCallister's face went slack sometime around "Jupiter," and completely pale by the time he got to "Maranova."

Gotcha.

"So tell me right here, right now, what really happened to Thomas Watson. Because I'm due to leave this station for EFS *Clarke* in a few hours, and I'm in need of a personal pilot."

Several minutes passed in silence, with McCallister fidgeting in her chair and almost talking while Sam stared. Her expression moved between resolve and the verge of tears and back again, but to her credit she kept his gaze the entire time.

"I...I can't. I mean, I don't know where he is. Mira went looking for him when she got back, but the last anyone saw of him was some Fleet officer rolling him out of the hospital into a ground car. And as for the job, I'm not really flight-rated. My eyes. These are," she said, moving her left hand up to touch the flight wings pinned over her DSM, "honorary."

Like hell they are. I've seen you in action when you couldn't see a damn thing, and...

Wait, did she say Mira?

Sam ran their conversation back in his mind, hoping he'd somehow heard her wrong. He checked her file again, then remembered what he was looking for wasn't there, by her own admission.

McCallister-Andreison...Harlan.

Shit. And I'm the only one who can tell her, because I'm the only one that knows she's here.

"Marya, I don't know why, exactly, but I believe you about Watson. The job is real, and yours if you want it. I don't need a Shrike jockey, or even a drone operator. I need someone for point-to-point runs, who can keep my shuttle on course while I deal with Fleet business. And the one thing that *is* in your file is that you've got the comms experience to keep my private business private."

Sam paused as she took in his words, preparing himself for the very uncomfortable conversation that came next.

"But there's something else we need to talk about right now, and it's not going to be easy for either of us."

"Sir?"

Sam opened his mouth to tell her that her wife, and the rest of *Valiant's* crew were dead, but his wrist comm chimed three times in rapid succession, this time with Commodore Maranova's ident code.

>>*Pod's in>Ch2>Not good>*

>>*K has proof>M traitor>*

>>*War*

Without thinking Sam swiped the message towards the desk's holo emitter, then activated Channel 2 as instructed. The air between him and Marya filled with a chaotic firefight in a half-destroyed transfer bay, but two things caught his eye immediately.

The first was *Valiant's* registration code at the bottom of the image, and the second was Captain Aloysius Martin being thrown to the deck by a fully armored trooper, who then knelt on his chest and began firing a pair of induction pistols at similarly outfitted attackers.

Five opponents went down in as many seconds, and then one of the pistols appeared faster than the eye could follow on the trooper's chestplate, barrel glowing cherry red. Captain Martin was then dragged across the deck and thrown behind a piece of machinery, with his apparent savior firing the entire time with their remaining weapon.

Martin wasn't wearing a helmet, and the holo was soundless, but he appeared to be shouting something at the trooper while he was being dragged, even though the micro-sonic booms of an induction pistol would have drowned out anything short of a full shuttle launch. The trooper fired for another second, then discarded the remaining weapon and leapt over the barrier Aloysius was hiding behind.

The blaze of red across the trooper's shoulders marked them as Operations group, and the full combat kit of the armor was comple-mented with some components Sam had only seen in formal Fleet reviews. He reversed, then slowed, the playback until he could see the unit coding on the armor's left chest, just over the barrel of the overheated pistol. The desk's pickups registered where his eyes were focusing in the holo, then pulled up the trooper's personnel file before he could stop it.

Now hovering unasked for over the somewhat degraded holo image of the heroic trooper was her name, rank, and picture, and the almost forgotten Lt. McCallister-Andrieson-Harlan on the other side of his desk spoke it aloud a half-second before it registered in Sam's mind.

"Mira?"

The creamy brown and freckled face in the image matched the one in Sam's memory, especially the hair pulled back in a severe bun and ice-blue eyes he'd seen each of the last five years as he awarded her and her ship the Clarke Cup during Fleet exercises.

This just keeps getting better, doesn't it?

"Marya, there's something you have to know about this image. There was an accident aboard *Valiant*."

I can't tell her anything about the original holo. She shouldn't even be seeing this new one. But she has to know her wife is dead, and I...

"Looks pretty intentional to me, sir. Can you show me who she's firing at?"

Sam moved to the side of the desk, trying to draw her attention away from what might be the last image ever taken of Mira Harlan. But her eyes were darting all over the holo, mechanical irises zooming in and out independently of one another and calling up dozens of personnel files. He took a step forward, raising his right hand to touch her shoulder in what he thought was conciliatory gesture.

McCallister spun away from his hand with a move he hadn't seen since basic training, still intent on something deep inside the holo. Before he even registered what she'd done, she was two meters away at the other side of the desk, trying for a better view.

"Marya, she's dead. They're all dead!"

Sam's almost shouted response finally gave McCallister pause, but instead of shock, or grief, or any emotion he was prepared for, she simply took a step back from the holo, and asked, "Who told you that, sir. And when?"

Sam didn't quite know how to react to her statement, and suddenly conscious of his hand held out between them, raised it to scratch at the side of his neck.

What the hell is going on, here?

"There was an accident. A rogue planetoid hit *Valiant* amidships, roughly..." Sam moved his hand forward to get the exact time from his wrist comm, still not fully comprehending why she was asking.

"...four hours ago relative. This footage just came in from one of the rescue ships, and..."

"Then she's not dead. And this holo has been edited."

What?

"What?"

"The holo. It's been altered, and it's not just the normal compilation process, or even FTL compression lag. There's things missing, more happening than we're seeing. And also, I've loved that woman since the first time I saw her, and if she's really gone you need to send me to prison right now. Because this time I'm definitely going to murder a lot of people until I find out why."

What?

McCallister continued speaking as if she hadn't confessed her intent to commit capital crimes to a senior fleet officer, as if this was just another day at the office for her.

"For example, it's not showing Mira reloading, but I can see her spent canisters on the decking here, here, and here."

If McCallister had any inkling of how absolutely insane her statement sounded, she gave no outward sign. Instead she maintained her attention on the holo, pointing to sections that appeared perfectly normal to Sam's eyes. Obviously her implants were showing her something he'd missed, but she was back in that same distracted place as when they'd started talking. Then she bent her head, tapping furiously as the holo moved beyond the borders of the desk, expanding and magnifying across the compartment until they could both view it unobstructed.

Sam was so intent on trying to figure out what she'd seen that it took him almost a minute to realize the thing she was tapping was his command baton. Before he could comment on what a bad idea that was, red splotches appeared in the middle of the holo, then resolved into outlines of spent canisters, exactly as she'd predicted.

"The time codes are altered as well. At this point it's twenty seconds ahead of what I see in the helmet visors here, and here. Where did this recording come from? The time codes match generally with what you're talking about, but *Valiant's* are way out of sync with those from *Indomitable*? What were they even doing there, if a planetoid destroyed the ship? And the compilation is only about forty-five minutes old. Who sent it?"

Marya's question—*no, questions*—hung in the air between them, with Sam still processing both her quick competence and the incredulity of what he was watching.

My god, that's your wife in that image committing treason, firing on fleet personnel in apparent collusion with the Outer Colonies, and you're providing commentary on the evidence against her? With technical details that half of—no, most—of the people who'll see it will never understand?

Marya walked into the holo until she was face to face with the image of Mira Harlan crouching over Aloysius Martin. Sam moved to next to her, holding out his hand for the baton.

If Marya registered his unspoken request, she gave no sign. Instead, she twisted her wrists, and the holo advanced until Harlan and Martin were both behind the barricade. She then set it on a frame-by-frame repeating loop, something Sam didn't even know his baton could do.

"Here, sir, look. That section of bulkhead behind them, it's not right. And here," she said, waving the baton at a point in the air in front of the bench, "they've scrubbed something out. Really sloppy work."

Sam stared at the loop for a few repetitions before he realized McCallister was waiting for a response. Other than calling in a team of experts to explain her explanation, all he felt competent to do was repeat—and expand on—his earlier offer.

"Sub-Lieutenant McCallister, you are to consider yourself a member of my personal staff until further notice, effective immediately. I'll see about getting your records sorted out when we get back to *Clarke*. And as my first official order, I must insist that you hand back my baton, before in your zeal you accidentally activate a weapons system and kill us all."

McCallister stared at the baton in her hands as if it she had never seen it before, tapping one more button to create a hovering menu in front of her before handing it back. Sam wasn't exactly sure what the new menu would do, but given that his baton seemed to still be transmitting, he also wasn't sure he'd be comfortable knowing. He made a point of shutting it down completely before placing it back on the desk, but McCallister continued entering commands as if he hadn't said anything at all.

"Sorry, sir. But it's all right here. Whoever did this was skilled, but she rushed the job. Thinking two-dimensionally, probably trying to impress the boss. It's Captain Kołodziejski commanding *Indomitable* now, right? Why are his troopers shooting at Mira? What's his part in all this?"

Sam's mind was about to shut down from the constant barrage of questions. He almost preferred her silent hatred to this unexpected, entirely inappropriate reaction to news of a personal loss, which she'd dismissed with a seditious—no, *mutinous, given who we're talking about* —statement so casual that he was beginning to doubt he'd heard it at all. To keep himself sane, he focused only on the questions he knew how to answer, hoping that sooner or later what she was saying would start to make sense.

"Yes, Captain Kołodziejski is in command of that vessel, and yes, he sent this to us via FTL pod a little over an hour ago. But how in the worlds do these images tell you that it was a woman who created this record?"

This finally got a reaction out of Marya, a tight-lipped smile with the right corner of her mouth drawn up.

"How long have you been in the SDF, sir?"

Thankful for another easy question, Sam's response came about a second before he thought to wonder why she'd asked.

"Forty-one years, T-standard."

Marya's was equally fast, as if she'd prepared it in advance.

"And how many male comms officers have you served with in that time?"

It wasn't exactly insubordination, or even sarcasm *per se*, but try though he might Sam couldn't remember a single one, so he allowed it. McCallister took his raised hands and sheepish smile as an apology, and continued.

"A standard holo-recorder combines images from three different lasers, each scattering out to around thirty meters before the signal loss is too great to overcome. So something like this," she said, as her hands "pushed" the image out to, and apparently beyond the bulkheads, "is a combination of multiple streams, adjusted and compiled by specialized algorithms.

"Your eyes don't see the overlaps and duplications, because at any given time humans are only really focusing on what's in front of them, and what's at the extreme periphery of their vision. A good holosuite like this one reads those eye movements, and extrapolates to show a seamless image.

"I don't have that problem, so when someone kludges together..." Marya tilted her head again, as if looking at something only she could see, "...this many feeds, the algorithms have to work overtime to compensate. It leaves seams behind for the next core to interpret, and I guess they weren't expecting someone with my kind of processing power to take a close look at this."

Processing power? What in the worlds is she...

Marya was tapping the side of her head, where a nasty scar led from her eyes back into her hair. Her mechanical irises were fully open now, and Sam nodded in understanding at the additional cybernetics necessary to control her eyes.

"Can you show me?"

Marya pushed a hand through her floating menu, then started flicking away small cones of light, each with its own identcode. Sam stopped her when she had forty floating in front of them, with no end in sight.

"Okay, so as plainly as you can, what does this mean? Can we trust this holo?"

"No, sir, not as presented. Everything they've told you about it might be true, but this," she said, indicating the floating cones, "this says they tried really hard to *not* show you something. The time codes are all wrong, and if what you said was true, they were still beaming data to the pod in transit."

Sam leaned against the desk, wondering how he was going to explain this to the commodore. Then he remembered where she was at that exact moment, and started tapping out a message of his own while McCallister continued her explanation.

>>StopVote>Hv witness>

"Look here, and you'll see what I mean. There's a projectile of some sort, or at least, there should be. Microslugs move too fast to show up in holos as anything other than a blur, but whatever this is moves slower and hits a hell of a lot harder. This area," she said, indicating a section of bulkhead, "has been revised using earlier footage. The reflections are all wrong, and Mira motions toward it with her pistol here, here, and here. Captain Martin looks up at it, then the vid jumps forward several seconds until Mira's shooting at something out of frame."

>>Bullshit>

>>Who>

"Slow down, McCallister. I'm not following you."

>>K's lying>StopVote

"It's sir, I'm sorry. It's okay to say Andreison. I was angry, and I keep expecting to see Deb over my shoulder every time you say her name. She doesn't care that we kept our careers, and in a crisis, using the whole name takes too damn long."

"We? We who?"

Marya stared at Sam as if he'd grown a second head. The passion in her eyes made him want to check his shoulders just to make sure, but just about the time he remembered she had two wives, she'd moved the holo back to an earlier point.

"Someone on *Valiant* is using a weapon that can blast a 1.2 meter hole in a bulkhead in a single shot. And whoever sent you this footage has been systematically erasing them from the record. Nothing we have can do that, it's as if..."

Andreison trailed off, staring at the image. Now that he knew what to look for, Sam was sure saw something moving inside her eyes, but at this point he'd believe just about anything.

"As if what, Lieutenant?"

"Sir, the reason I left *City of Lights*—the reason I had to leave—is because I discovered an encrypted gennie transmission buried inside a naked hyperspace signature. That's tech way beyond Earth's current capabilities, even in the Home Fleet.

"If they can do that they might be able make weapons like this, or worse. Someone tried to bury that information—and me, for that matter—just the way they're trying to erase them from this firefight at the same time they're framing my wife.

"Can't you see it, sir? They're back. The gennies. They're really back!"

Sam crossed his hands behind his back, and began pacing circles around the room. After a second circuit past Andreison, he sat down on his bench and studied both the officer across from him and the featureless, holographic bulkhead she swore was really destroyed.

In less than five minutes, she's almost stumbled onto a secret myself and the rest of Maranova's hand-picked conspirators have been trying to keep for years, and even without all the information at hand has added more complications to an already impossible situation.

What have I gotten us into with this one?

His comm chirped again, and he could also hear someone knocking at the compartment's hatch.

>>VoteCancl>WHO>

There's no way this ends well, and I still don't know where it begins.

"Walk me through it again, Marya. Slowly. And after you tell your story, I've got one of my own you need to hear."

KOŁODZIEJSKI

"AND THAT'S about the size of it, Mister President. We had them ready to declare war, and then Maranova invoked privilege and canceled the vote. If we want to proceed with our plan, you'll need to make a formal defense of sovereignty declaration, and we'll have to defend our footage in open session, not just before the Council."

Horace had been dancing around the provenance of his doctored holorecords throughout his call with Victor Darbin, ever mindful of any prying eyes or ears. Lt. Monahan had scrubbed all record of the originals from *Indomitable*'s central core, and there was no telling what other repercussions there would be on the ship's systems from her quick and thorough deletions.

She's good people, almost at the level I need on my permanent staff. Depending on how this all shakes out, I may extend her an offer, once I have a cure.

If I get a cure

An actual gennie invasion had never been part of Horace's plan, merely a series of Separatist attacks against high profile targets, culminating with a massive outbreak of a modified Transgenic virus on

Earth. But true to their nature, the colonials' untimely arrival had destroyed that plan in the most chaotic way possible, and he'd been forced to improvise a new one. Discovery was inevitable now; all that mattered was putting the proper spin on things.

I didn't think I could hate those genetic mongrels any more, but here we are. And since my carefully engineered bioweapon is killing me, instead of the Reclamation Council, I'm running out of time to get this war started—and ended—the right way.

"And you still believe this is truly necessary for our survival?" Victor Darbin's weak, reedy voice was especially annoying today. Horace's nerves were already on edge with every small sound or smell he encountered demanding immediate attention, but the strange feeling of Thomas Watson's artificial blood substitute coursing through his veins made every waking moment intolerable.

Of course it is, you pompous toady. And need I remind you who pulled the strings to get you where you are today?

"Yes, sir, Mr. President. It's only a matter of time before one of these gennies slips through our blockade and infects the whole planet. We have to stay the course, until Admiral Worthy returns with reinforcements and some kind of technological edge. Our only hope against the gennies is to strike hard, and strike fast."

Darbin's face in the holo was pensive, and his head tilted slightly to the side as if he was listening to something. Like Horace, Darbin was using a simulation for their conversation, inhabiting a virtual avatar that responded to his every move, but didn't really require him to be present. Horace needed one in case he had to vomit up the tiny amount of food he'd eaten today, but Darbin usually used them to make himself appear more presidential.

Too bad he never looks at his own images. With his weak chin and tiny eyes, all it really does for him is make him look like a child dressed in his father's clothes.

Was there really no one else we could pick to warm the seat until I retire?

After a conversational delay that seemed to stretch on for hours, Darbin sat up straighter in his chair, and forced a smile.

"I trust in your judgment, Captain. I know you would never do anything against the interests of Mars. I just wish there was some other way. What you're proposing I've never been comfortable with this, and we still need time to generate good sentiment for the war in the domes."

"Sir, my people can handle that. Keep your focus on appropriations and the Council, it's where you can do the most good for our planet right now. We'll get through this, I promise. Mars, together and strong!"

"Together and strong." Darbin's response was a bit slower than Horace would have liked, and he fought to keep his contempt for the man off his face. The Darbins were a founding family, and even though the current scions had about as much in common with their ancestors as trees and turnips, their name still meant something among the proles.

For now, anyway.

An abdominal spasm hit Horace just as he was about to speak, causing him to pitch forward in his chair. Darbin's avatar didn't react, but Horace had to roll away from the pickups and curl up against the pain, while Darbin kept prattling on.

"And how are things going for you personally, Horace? Iselda and I would love to have you and Caroline for dinner when this is all over."

I just bet you would, you obsequious lickspittle. You'd take any chance to reignite your falling star.

Horace tried several times to crawl back into his chair, but even the slightest movement only intensified his pain. He dragged himself into a sitting position with his back against his bunk, and took a deep breath before responding, not caring about how Darbin perceived the delay.

"Things are fine here, but let's not make any plans. Commander Annahko and I are colleagues and crewmates right now, nothing more. But I will give her your wife's regards; I know the two of them are close."

Below the pickups, Darbin couldn't see his predatory smile. Caroline hated Iselda Petrovina, and Caroline's mother had more than once suggested her daughter kill the hapless prole over one of her numerous social gaffes as an object lesson to any other social climbers.

Yes, that would be an interesting meal, just not one any sane person would want to attend.

"Well. Yes. Of course. Just let us know when you return home, Captain. I'll arrange something so that we can all catch up. I—"

"I'm sorry, Mr. President, but something has come up. I'll have to cut our time short."

"Is there anything I can—"

Horace ended the call with a tap on his wristcomm, not caring about any political repercussions. The Kołodziejskis—and the Annahkos, for that matter—were so far above Victor Darbin and his puppet government's reach that he probably could set Caroline loose in the Capital Dome with a knife and a smile, with full vid coverage of the massacre, and the pair would come across as planetary heroes by the time her mother was through spinning it to the masses.

Thinking about Caroline, and her exquisite physicality, gave Horace both pleasure and regret. He would marry her, when the time came. The inevitability of their pairing was an established fact, and had been for most of their lives. Ever since their families signed a contract for a shared heir over forty T-years ago, their union was the bedrock on which he'd formed all his plans, including the one that would eradicate the Transgenic virus from the known universe.

But it all falls to ruin if the virus kills me first. Hopefully, the new gennie test subjects Caroline salvaged from the Valiant *wreckage will help Watson develop a cure.*

Hopefully, it won't be worse than the disease.

Horace fought through another spasm to drag himself onto his bunk, where he lay, wasted, for some time until his wristcomm chirped.

Raising it just enough so that he could see who was requesting access, Horace smiled when he saw it was Andrew Collins.

Along with Daniel Tepes standing guard outside his door, Collins was the only one of Horace's operatives who knew the truth of his condition.

And I specifically told him not to contact me unless…

Horace accepted the request, resting his arm high enough on his chest for the comm to pick up his pained whisper.

"Good news, Andrew?"

"Yes sir. The techs say they have found a way into the container. It won't be easy, but they're ready to breach on your mark."

"Excellent. We'll be there momentarily. And Andrew?"

"Yes, sir?"

"I don't want to be disturbed while we examine our new arrivals. I'm tasking you to handle all my incoming calls until further notice."

"Of course, sir. I'll make the arrangements." Collins closed the channel on his end, and Horace let out a deep sigh of relief. It would be many hours until *Indomitable*'s arrival at Echo Base, time he intended to make the most of. And no one, not even Caroline, would stop him from his revenge.

For Bob, for myself, and for everyone we've lost to this alien assault over the centuries, Transgenesis must end, no matter what the cost.

ANNAHKO

CAROLINE DODGED LEFT, then right, as a pair of robotic arms came swinging at her from above. The fabric of her gi slid over the fine hairs on her arms and chest, teasing her skin to life with every movement as she fought. But even this small pleasure wasn't enough to make her forget the events of the day. Mindful of her heavy-G workout's unexpected audience, she spun and launched a high kick into one of the armatures, spinning it away and drawing a chorus of appreciative signs from the gathering crowd.

Only scant hours after their discovery—and subsequent abandonment—of SDF *Valiant*, the gymnasium was packed with confused crewmembers. When none of them stepped forward as a sparring partner, Caroline had selected a high-level workout from the gymnasium's automated systems, and so far the Class 5 rating was living up to her expectations.

Plus, it looks like yesterday's demonstration of force was effective after all. They all know that I'm the one to come to with their problems, instead of gossiping amongst themselves. And although none of them were willing to take a beating like Bob Calas was, they're still here looking for answers.

Answers I don't have.

Caroline couldn't explain what had happened to *Valiant*. She didn't know whether Captain Aloysius Martin was alive or dead, who else might have escaped the ship's destruction, or even why *Indomitable* was hunting *Valiant* in the first place.

All I know for certain is members of this crew, loyal Marsborn, are dead. Murdered by gennies, aboard a ship I used to call my home. I didn't even like Bob Calas, but the moment of his death is burned into my brain, blown up by a gennie girl who had no business even being in this system, let alone hiding out on a cargo container attached to a giant hunk of space rock.

She slammed a fist into the nearest armature, imagining the gennie's bloody-toothed smile as she did. The blow disabled it for a few seconds, and it hung loosely from the ceiling while she unleashed a quick series of follow-up attacks to make sure it was "dead," punctuating each one in her internal monologue with the only question that mattered.

Why?

Why?

WHY!

Unlike the holographic opponents presented by other gyms aboard *Indomitable*, Caroline preferred the programmable armatures installed here in CF-3. Not only because it was the closest gym to her quarters, but because she could use her full strength when fighting. Once one of the ceiling mounted armatures was defeated, it didn't disappear into nothingness, but instead went dormant for a few seconds while the gym's data core reprogrammed it with a random attack pattern and put it back into play.

For a fighter as skilled as Caroline, it was the closest thing she could get to a real, thinking enemy, and she didn't have to worry about its health, its feelings, or any ulterior motives.

Yesterday, I nearly killed a man in this very room, only to have the gennies finish the job for me a couple hours ago. Bob Calas may have been an opportunistic pig who wanted into my pants, but he didn't deserve to die like that.

And at least I felt a real connection between us while we were fighting.

No one else on this ship has even come close to doing that in a long, long time.

Caroline grabbed the overhead arm and pulled, tearing it off the mounting in a shower of sparks and swinging the twisted metal at a second armature sporting a cluster of ropy tentacles. But instead of breaking apart and letting the attack pass, the tentacles seized her improvised club and tried to pull her off the mat.

That's new. I wonder what else the core has in store for m—

Something slammed into Caroline from behind, forcing the air from her lungs. She lost her grip on the broken armature, but the tentacles seized her wrists and kept her in place while whatever had ambushed her continued moving down her body, rolling her out until she was suspended nearly horizontal above the mat.

With the tentacles pulling her backward and her head facing the wrong way, Caroline couldn't formulate a counter until the object rolling down her body got to her legs. She bent her knees in an attempt to gain some leverage, but all she achieved was a moment of excruciating pain as two irresistible forces played tug-of-war with her body. Caroline gasped for air as she let her legs relax, and then again in pain as the mystery object slammed into her heels and kept moving forward.

With her arms still trapped, Caroline swung backward, now able to see her "attacker." A pair of armatures had fused together as a sort of trapeze-mounted battering ram, which was now reaching the end of its own arc and ready to come back for a go at the front of her body.

FuckfuckFUCK! Something is seriously wrong with this exercise.

Caroline tried to shout out her override code, but couldn't manage more than a tortured squeak. So instead of fighting against her backward motion, she swung with it, adding enough momentum to slam herself into the ceiling. The tentacles registered this as a successful attack and let go of her arms, tearing the skin of her wrists as they retracted into their housing.

She dropped fast in the simulated 1.2 G she preferred for her workouts, and had just enough time to tuck into a roll before she hit, slapping the mat and changing direction as another arm reconfigured itself into a piston and slammed down into the mat in front of her with a solid WHACK.

Caroline was moving on pure instinct now, senses alive and adrenaline flooding her system. Another slap stopped her roll as she pivoted into a spinning heel kick with enough force to dent the piston arm. The arm squealed as it tried to retract, but the damaged section kept it planted in the practice mat.

She heard motion behind her, and dropped from her ready crouch into a forward roll. The joined arms passed over her on a collision course for the immobilized piston, and Caroline came up punching.

Her hands slammed the fused bar hard enough to break it in half against the piston, dealing even more damage and littering the mat with sharp-edged debris. A second later the piston sparked and died with a small explosion, and Caroline threw her arms up just in time to shield her eyes.

The explosion knocked her on her back, and she felt several sharp impacts along her skin. Head ringing, she struggled to her knees just as she heard the whir of another armature coming online. She wasted no time in rolling away from the destruction she'd caused, grabbing a piece of jagged ceroplast from the mat as she went. A salvo of riot bullets savaged the already ruined mats a moment later, and a jumble of gasps, shouts, and screams rose from the crowd.

Caroline kept rolling, racing the line of fire and attempting to reach to the edge of her pre-defined encounter area and hopefully stop the runaway exercise. She paused briefly at the edge of the mat to throw the fragment at the nearest control panel, shattering both as she tumbled to a stop against the bulkhead, arms up to protect her face and curling her legs in to protect her body.

She stayed there for a few terrifying heartbeats as the minigun on the ceiling spun down and whined to a stop, then slowly got to her feet to survey the scene. The mat was a total loss, but luckily none of the destroyed armatures were on fire. A cheer went up from those few crew who hadn't already run for help, while Caroline sagged against the bulkhead, head spinning, pulse pounding, gasping and trying desperately not to puke.

Well, I certainly felt that.

"That's enough!" Caroline's ragged shout stopped their cheering, unwilling to let them celebrate their inaction. Any one of them could have tried to shut down the simulation when it started to go wrong, a matter she'd address later when her body wasn't primed to kill something.

She stalked over to the nearest intact control panel, which also happened to be the one where she'd left her carryall and comm. It took her several tries to pull up the gym's training protocols, as not only were the panel's holo-interface and touch controls slow in responding, but she was having a hard time focusing on either.

When she did gain access, Caroline found a completely different sequence of attacks on record, and that the safety overrides had been disengaged remotely by the central core as part of a system reboot and recalibration.

What the hell is going on on this ship? I programmed a training exercise, not a suicide room. And why the hell is the system rebooting right after we made a combat drop? I didn't order that, and...

Caroline shuddered, both at the implications of an autonomous system only she and three other people on *Indomitable* could reprogram trying to kill her, and as her body renewed its production of adrenaline in response to a new threat. She dove for her carryall and hurriedly extracted her command key, dumping out most of its contents in the process. She then hurried back to the panel and jammed the key home, quickly shutting the system down, along with every other gymnasium onboard.

She felt instantly lighter as *Indomitable*'s Mars-standard gravity took over from the gymnasium's systems, but her head and heart were still pounding. After a couple deep breaths, she shouted, "I need an engineer over here. Now!", and started searching the floor for her wristcomm.

"Ma'am, are you okay?" The voice was familiar, but in her current state Caroline couldn't place which of the dozens of male crew members aboard it belonged to.

"I'm fine. Get me someone to look at this panel," she snarled, finally locating her comm. There were several message indicators on the display, the last of which was flagged urgent, but her head was still spinning from the attack and she couldn't make out the names.

"I tried to reach you earlier, ma'am, but I guess you were busy. I heard you might be here, so I came up to talk to you directly about—"

Caroline snapped her head around to see who was speaking, and his features resolved into a burry outline of Cadet Kurt Currano, her distant cousin Illyana Tepes' flight crew partner and lover.

"Whatever it is can wait, Cadet. We have a more pressing problem. Can you run a diagnostic on this panel, or not?"

Caroline struggled back to her feet as a fire control team entered the gymnasium, followed by a stream of non-coms and officers attracted by the commotion.

"Yes. ma'am. Of course, ma'am. I...uh, your key is...um, are you sure you're okay"

One of the armored troopers working their way across the room was shining a hand light in her direction, and holding an emergency medkit in the other. Whoever the woman was, she carefully skirted the destroyed area of the practice mat while her teammates were carefully peeling it off the deck square by square, brushing the ceroplast shards and smoking circuitry of the ruined armatures into hazard bins as they worked.

"Commander, are you okay?"

Why do people keep asking me that, I...

Caroline held up her left hand against the brightness of the hand lamp, and almost stabbed herself in the eye with a piece of debris embedded in her palm. She lowered her hand, noticing for the first time that the sleeves of her gi were soaked in blood, and pinned to her skin in several places by additional shards of ceroplast. She sat down hard on the deck, attended instantly by both the fire team medic and Cadet Currano, as all the voices in the worlds rushed in at the same time.

"Ma'am, I..."

"Just hold still, Commander, I..."

"...you see that? She's incredible..."

"...in a million years..."

"...should tell the Captain that..."

Caroline felt the compartment close in around her until there was only a single point of light in a universe of darkness, growing dimmer as it moved ever farther away.

Horace, I...

"...losing her! Cadet, hold her arms. And whatever you do, don't..."

Horace, where are you? I need you...

Help...

Caroline's body was a distant memory as she floated away, a cold, unhappy place full of confusion and doubt. Where people she loved could be ripped away with the stroke of a pen, while others slowly died in front of her, rotting away from the inside.

The light was nearly gone when she remembered her mother's voice, calling out to her from her childhood.

"He's a good boy, from a good family. Easily molded, and you'd do well to cultivate him sooner, rather than later. We didn't pay a fortune for your genes so they can go to waste on an in-family match, so you should just forget about your childish notions of 'love' and start thinking about—"

Caroline screamed as the needle pierced her heart, born again into a universe of light and pain. Something hard and sharp was pressing down on her shoulders, keeping her from moving her arms. Her neck was also immobilized, and in addition to the burning pain from the injection site, her chest was cold and wet.

"Wha...what..." Opening her eyes, Caroline had an excellent view of Cadet Currano's crotch, chest, and chin as he leaned over her to hold down her arms.

What?

"We almost lost you, Commander. Please, don't try to move yet, I need to administer a general sedative and a beta blocker, or you might have a stroke." Caroline couldn't see the speaker, but recognized the voice as the medic who'd approached her before her blackout. She felt an injector hiss against her neck, then a slow tugging on the skin next to her left breast as the trooper withdrew a large needle from her chest.

"get...get..." Caroline was having trouble breathing, and still couldn't move her arms. She tried to kick free, but her legs wouldn't obey her either.

"Okay, Cadet, you can let her up now. Slowly, if you would. You can take the neck brace off as well."

The pressure on her shoulders and arms disappeared, as Currano retreated from view. She felt hands fussing at her throat, but she batted them away to remove the brace herself. A quick surge of pain from the cut on her palm helped to clear her vision, and the room around her fell into sharp focus as Currano helped her to a sitting position.

She touched a hand to her bare chest, fingers coming away with a smear of bright green fluid she dimly remembered being described in an emergency medical class at Marsforce Academy as being "for last resort only." Her torn and bloody gi was a few meters away at the edge of the practice mat, and her compression bra was hanging in tatters at her sides. Someone had cleared the compartment of all non-essential personnel, and from the lack of crowd noise outside, possibly the corridor as well.

"What happened?" Caroline's voice was more ragged than she'd have liked, and her mouth was dry.

The trooper kneeling in front of her shined a light in her face, one eye at a time, before clearing her faceplate and popping her helmet seals so they could speak directly.

"You went into shock, Commander. Your heart was beating way too fast, and the rest of your body just couldn't keep up. Most people would have died permanently, but you've got good genes."

Best that money could buy, or so they tell me. The thought came unbidden, but Caroline couldn't deny the truth of it. Something about the woman's statement didn't quite track for her, but the trooper kept on talking.

"I just needed to jump start your system after you coded, and now you're good as new. Well, mostly. I wouldn't recommend any more

Class 5 workouts for a while, and we are absolutely taking you to Medical as soon as my team clears the room. You're lucky we were here, and that Currano here can keep a cool head in a crisis."

Caroline turned her head to look at the cadet supporting her back, who was trying very hard not to stare at her exposed breasts.

"Thank you, Kurt. I...wait," she said, directing her comment—and attention—to the trooper. "I died?"

"Just a little bit. One of the shards in your arm nicked an artery, and as soon as you stopped moving it finally had the chance to bleed out. You're all sealed up now, but it's a temporary fix. Nothing an hour or so in an autodoc can't handle."

Confident that her patient wasn't going to die permanently, the medic smiled at Caroline. Her features looked high dome, but it was hard to tell through the duraglass.

"I'll stay with you until we get there, though. Us girls need to stick together. No offense, Cadet."

"None taken, ma'am."

"Don't 'ma'am' me, son. I work for a living." Currano stiffened at her back, but Caroline had heard some variation on the trooper's statement many times over the years, and smiled in return.

Definitely not high dome; a woman with her skills, from a good family, should have started her career as an officer. Which means she's never had a proper patron.

Until now.

"What's your name, trooper?"

"Senior Technician Ariel Amagosa, ma'am." The trooper was busy reassembling her medical kit, but stopped when the import of Caroline's next words fully registered.

"Ms. Amagosa, consider yourself a part of my permanent retinue, effective immediately. You too, Cadet, and you might as well extend the same invitation to Ms. Tepes when you see her. I have a few projects that need immediate attention, and I find myself in need of some extra hands."

Caroline held up her scarred and bloody arms as emphasis, and almost fainted at the sight of them. Her perfect olive skin was marred with nasty red scars, highlighted by shiny nuskin bandages. But Currano and Amagosa were able to get her up on her feet, wrap an emergency blanket around her shoulders, and carefully walk her over to a trauma chair just outside the gymnasium.

And while neither had officially accepted her offer of patronage, she could tell they were standing just a little but taller as she walked.

Mother would be proud. I'm finally using our family name the way she intended. Now, I just have to...

Once she was seated, and the trio were rolling down he corridor, Curanno pressed something hard and rectangular into her hand. Looking down at her command key, Caroline flashed back to what she was doing just before she blacked out, and grabbed Currano's arm. In her excitement, she'd forgotten about her cut, but whatever sedative Amagosa had given her kept the pain down to a dull roar.

"Kurt, I need a full diagnostic on that control panel—and all the training programs throughout the ship—as soon as you can get it. Now, what were you trying to tell me earlier?"

The cadet was still trying not to look directly at her, a proper show of respect she almost admired.

But if I'm to be the next captain of this ship, I need people who can not only handle me at my worst, but do so with grace and professionalism.

"Spit it out, Cadet. We don't have a lot of time."

"I...uh...I finished that analysis you asked for, ma'am. On the..."

On the black space rock that killed Valiant. *No wonder he was so insistent earlier.*

"Have it delivered my quarters, Kurt. And if you've stored any copies in the core, remove them as soon as possible."

Because if I can't trust the ship's brain with my life anymore, I certainly can't trust it with my secrets.

"Yes, ma'am. Right away, ma'am!"

Currano almost skipped down the corridor to comply, and Caroline had a hard time imagining herself ever so eager to please a superior officer.

Except one. And I have some serious doubts as to whether that particular relationship is still viable.

MIRA

MIRA PICKED HER WAY ACROSS A BROAD FIELD OF SUN-WARMED GRAIN. She'd heard this part of North America described as "rolling fields of gold," but she and the gennies had done more than enough rolling for the day.

We're alive. That's all that matters. I'm just hoping the miracles continue and we can find some sort of shelter before too much more time passes.

Jantine was watching the sun set from atop a broad rock. Even dressed in shapeless brown coveralls, the gennie had an air of command Mira had tried to present for years. Out of her suit, out of her uniform, Lt. Commander Harlan was a rapidly fading memory, one being replaced by Mira the gennie-come-lately.

Mira reflexively squinted against the yellow brightness of the sun, and discovered another benefit of her changing biology. There was an extra layer of moisture sitting on her eyes that counteracted the harsh light, and though it was still a bit painful to stare at, she could now make out details on the surface that were hard to see even in space.

Despite the chaos of their escape, and the knowledge that she was fast becoming Fleet Enemy Number One, Mira found the open field around her very relaxing. For a change, the only thoughts buzzing around in her head right now were her own, instead of those the Omega had jammed into her brain. But like the shuttle at her back, there were things about the current situation that needed to be addressed.

As she approached Jantine, she could "taste" the uncertainty lurking underneath the iron barrier of control the young leader maintained. She didn't know if it was a reaction to Mira's presence, or that the girl never really relaxed. But the group had had all the downtime they could afford; it was time for Jantine to make her decision.

One of Mira's new memories suggested that Jantine preferred people just start talking instead of announcing themselves first. It was paired up with an image she's always associated with authority; that of her father sitting behind his big desk with a stern look on his face.

"Janbi says it will fly. I have my doubts, but after his display in orbit I believe he means it."

A tiny smile played at the edges of Jantine's face, but her mind was full of pain and loss. Jantine's record of today's events was written in blood, and although she'd brought most of her people down alive, she was agonizing over those she'd failed to save.

Part of Mira wanted to smile at the gennie's discomfort—she was the enemy, after all. But the extra memories in her head were pushing her to project a feeling of well-being, even though Jantine had made it abundantly clear that she did not welcome such efforts.

Not from me, anyway.

Jantine kept staring at the horizon. A deep layer of blue sat above a band of orange framing the distant tree line, and the clouds above were painted in purple. Evenings at flight school in Colorado had offered similar vistas, but Mira could now compare them to memories of a dozen different horizons on as many planets.

The original is definitely better. And she's seeing it now for the first time. I just wish she could enjoy it.

"Katra?" Jantine's question was terse, but the sense of concern behind her words supplied all the context Mira needed.

"Better. An hour in the shuttle's bio-bed dealt with most of her internal damage. We had to tweak it a bit to handle her particular attributes, but the system worked just fine in the end."

Mira held back the words she wanted to say next, unsure of how Jantine would take them.

We Gammas heal fast, it seems.

Instead, she brushed her fingers across the smooth line of her now-healed nose, and waited for the proud girl from another planet to collect her thoughts.

Even while dealing with her pain, Jantine's mind was remarkable. The Gamma memories told her she shouldn't be able to sense whole images or thoughts, but Mira watched as Jantine replayed the frenzied action of the team's journey through *Valiant* over and over again, searching for anything she might have overlooked, any opportunity she'd missed to save a life.

In Mira's opinion, there weren't any, but Jantine's unspoken pain was that her friends had died while she was paying attention to other things. Jantine was too new to command to understand that she couldn't fix everything, a lesson Midshipman Harlan had learned when Jantine was still in the crèche.

Doesn't mean you have to like it, though.

Mira wished she could share this understanding with the girl. Tell her how it was okay to be afraid, or uncertain, as long as you understood what the right thing to do was and stayed the course. She'd had no mother or father to tell her these things, no older brothers to rub dirt in her hair or whale the tar out of some boy dumb enough to break her heart. Everything was new for Jantine, so everything hurt.

She decided to try a new tactic. If Jantine didn't want a shoulder to cry on, perhaps she could use a friend. Mira walked up and sat beside her on the rock. From Jantine's mind came an intense image of spikes shooting out of the gennie's skin, and a cold mask fell across the girl's face as Jantine put a wall up around her thoughts.

I should probably stop using that term. Never liked it much anyway.

"I don't think we got off to a good start, Commander. My name is Mira, Mira Harlan. I was born about twelve-hundred kilometers over yonder," Mira gestured off to the left in a generally southwestern direction, "and until a few hours ago I was a Lieutenant Commander in the System Defense Force. My life was primarily occupied with running training simulations for a crew just a little older than you are, and fixing whatever broke aboard *Valiant*."

When Jantine didn't interrupt, she continued, intentionally trying to distance herself from the Colonial's guarded emotions.

"I'm not going to apologize for what happened to your people centuries ago. There really aren't any words. What we...what Earth has done is monstrous. But I can promise you that there are still good people here. I don't understand fully why you're here, or what's really going on with that little girl in the sleeper unit, but we can't stay here forever. Sooner or later someone's going to come looking for us, and I don't think they'll like what they find."

A smile spread across Jantine's face. If anything, the setting sun made her even more beautiful, and Mira smiled herself at the thought of her brothers going ga-ga over the exotic off-worlder.

She'd probably kill Jim and Adam as examples to the others, but Sean might be able to keep up with her for a little while. Although come to think of it, Deb or Mar might be a better fit...

"You don't talk like a Gamma. Most of them would be afraid to sit this close to me, and they certainly would never speak their minds without permission."

As Jantine said the words, Mira's new memories confirmed them. The genetic caste system in the Outer Colonies was ruthlessly insular, and all of the voices in her head were trying to get Mira to show proper the respect to her "better."

From what Mira had learned at the Academy, Betas like Jantine were exceptionally rare. Mainly because of the low Beta birthrates, but also due to the difficulties involved in taming new worlds. Only a handful of gennies made the cut—in general, the Colonials were just a better variety of human being, one adapted carefully to their planet of birth on a world-by-world basis.

"Carlton said much the same thing. He's not sure I am a Gamma, not really. Thanks to my new best friends the Omegas, I'm transgenic like the rest of you, but for the most part I'm still a baseline human. I mean, I've got these crazy empathic skills, and dozens of lifetimes of memories telling me how to do just about everything. It's like reading a book while someone else is speaking. I can't concentrate any one voice well enough to understand it, but I still have a basic idea of what they're saying. I can almost hear your thoughts, but every time I try to project mine, I get a massive headache and an even bigger scolding from a bunch of people who don't even exist.

"From what Carlton says, there's no real precedent for what's happened to me, and it's tearing him up inside that he can't nail down a proper classification. Besides, he's been pretty busy with Katra and the…"

This time, she couldn't shut out Jantine's spike of annoyance. It had flavors of anger, frustration, and fear, and for good reason.

As uncertain as Mira's position was in the Colonials' group dynamic, Jantine's was based entirely on the fact that she was the best genetic fit to lead her people to Earth. Her life so far had been spent training for a mission to reunite the human race, with the full knowledge that she wasn't expected to succeed.

In a way, Captain Martin's plan has destroyed her life just as thoroughly as it has mine.

A kilometer behind them, just outside their mostly dead shuttle, was an Alpha. A little girl locked into a centuries-long, dreamless sleep, who would become their undisputed leader the moment she woke up, invalidating everything Jantine's people had fought and died for.

If Captain Martin's intel was correct, it was entirely likely that the sleeping child had no leadership training whatsoever, but short of waking her up and asking some questions, Mira had no way to confirm that. Her surface mind, the only part Mira could reach, was a blank slate. The prolonged hibernation seemed to have caused no damage, and it was equally likely that when fully conscious, she'd have just the intelligence and personality of a normal eight year-old girl.

But Jantine doesn't know one way or the other, and her life is one of absolutes.

While Mira was thinking about what to say, Jantine turned her attention to the ground in front of her. Mira could see that she'd been poking at the soil, but didn't know why until Jantine's right hand darted out and came up with a tiny, wriggling figure cradled between her thumb and forefinger.

"What do you call this?"

Mira started to squint again, but her new eyes knew how to adjust their focus on small things as well as distant shiny ones, even if her brain needed more time to adjust to her expanded visual range.

"It's an ant. There must be a colony nearby."

Jantine nodded, and gently placed the insect back on the ground. It took a moment to orient itself, and then raced away as fast as its six legs could carry it.

"This was supposed to be us. A colony. Hidden inside the Earth until we were strong enough to venture forth. But like the ant, we are subject to forces beyond our control."

Mira didn't need transgenic powers to know Jantine was building to something. She was far more intelligent than any Earth girl would be at her age—certainly smarter than Mira herself had been.

"Think about what stories it will carry back to its fellows. Of the great pink thing that held it in place. Of the rushing wind that carried it from one pebble to another. Will it even have a vocabulary for what happened?"

Mira saw where Jantine was heading, and decided to ease the Beta's mind.

"Ants work together. They're never really alone. Even if an individual worker has a problem, the colony survives. They also have a queen, who works to protect them."

Well, that's about as ham-fisted an analogy as I can come up with, isn't it?

"I don't know. We don't have these where I come from. About twelve-hundred light years, yonder."

Mira laughed as Jantine waved her arm toward the darkening sky. But then the young woman's thoughts took on a decidedly different flavor, and Mira regretted her earlier word choice.

"But we do have queens. And their rule is absolute. It's what they're there for."

The pair sat in silence for almost a minute. For Mira, the wait to speak was an eternity, but Jantine had said her piece, and was waiting for whatever the universe brought next.

She may have said it, but what has she decided?

Mira let the silence continue, wishing she had enough real experience as whatever it was she'd become to help Jantine. Implanted memories were fine as a guideline of what she was supposed to do, but those same memories told her the knowledge she had right now would fade in time, sinking to the lowest depths of her mind until it was time to pass them on to someone else.

The extra lifetimes she'd received had only survived by associating themselves with her own life experiences, and were for the most part inaccessible until something triggered one. It was just her dumb luck that she was two decades older than most Gammas were when a transfer was made, and had more memories to match them up to.

An empathic Gamma child was born with the ability to reach another's mind, and was trained for years by other Gammas in how to hone that ability. Mira had the lessons they received over a decade crammed into her skull all at once, and the Builders were as surprised as she was that the process had worked.

They just wanted someone to talk to. Lucky me. And if I can't get a soldier like Jantine to open up, I've got no hope of cracking open one of those big orange skulls without a hammer as big as a mountain.

"We should get back. Janbi and I were able to salvage part of the data core, but he figures we've lost about half the information. And the Omegas are impatient for your decision."

It was Jantine's turn to laugh. The Beta stood up, folding the wrapper of a ration bar into a pocket and then brushing dirt and crumbs off her coveralls with quick, efficient motions. Watching her, Mira was sure it would take an ultrascanner to find any particles she'd missed.

"Now I know you're not a Gamma. One of them would have started the report with the Omegas. But you're right, we need to get back."

Jantine started back to the shuttle, and was a few meters away before Mira rolled to her feet and went after her. As she drew even with the Beta, Mira could feel the walls the Jantine had erected coming down, and chanced sending her a wave of encouragement. She felt, rather than saw a smile widen in response.

"What do you want to be called?"

Unsure of how to answer the question, Mira searched the memories for some clue as to her meaning. Finding none, she quickened her steps to try and get a reading from the girl's face. Jantine's rare smiles had a mischievous quality, and for the first time she seemed truly happy.

"We choose our names in the Outer Colonies. The designations don't really matter unless you're ready for a pairing, and only traditionalists insist on them. But 'Lieutenant Commander Mira Harlan of the System Defense Force ship *Valiant*' is going to break Artemus's mouth. And among friends, we speak as equals whenever possible."

The last rays of the sun had turned the shuttle into a beacon of reflected fire. Mira's enhanced eyesight could pick out the Omegas and Artemus gathered around the bulky sleeper unit, with Carlton and a now-upright Katra watching them through a smoothed and widened hole in the vessel's side.

"Mira. Mira will be fine."

Jantine stopped walking, and Mira was several steps past her before she realized what had happened. Turning back, she saw a hint of the uncertainty and fear Jantine had worked so hard to master in her eyes. Mira walked back to stand at her side, and was surprised when Jantine took one of her hands in her own.

"Mira, I don't want to open that sleeper unit, not until we find out what happened to the others and are someplace safe. Can we trust the people of this Harrison Institute? Really trust them?"

Mira didn't need help from any borrowed memories to answer this one.

"I have no idea. I can only tell you that the captain trusted them. The names of his network were in that data core, and who knows what we'll be able to salvage given time."

Jantine held Mira's hand for a few more seconds before continuing.

"Then what am I supposed to do?"

Now Jantine looked like a frightened teenager was supposed to, and the Gamma part of her was appalled at the lack of confidence the Beta was displaying. But Mirabelle Agnes Harlan from Roswell, New Mexico, thought it was a good thing, and did what any big sister would do.

She lied.

"I can only tell you what Captain Martin told me, when I first came aboard *Valiant*. The ship was so big, you see, and I'd never been part of a command team before.

"He took me aside, and said, 'Harlan, I'm about to give you the most important piece of advice I've ever received, but I'm only going to say this once. So listen carefully. You're going to screw up. You're going to make a lot of bad calls, and some may even get people killed. You'll stay up at night trying to figure out what you could have done better, but the answer is always going to be the same.'

"'Absolutely nothing. You're in command now. You're the one with the answers, even when they're wrong. Feel free to listen to other people's opinions, but your first instincts are going to be right pretty much every time. You're going to fight it, you're going to hate yourself, but the decision you know has to be made is always the right one.'"

Mira paused for effect, trying to summon up the twinkle in the Old Man's eye when he talked. She'd used her best approximation of his voice, but the smile was the real key.

It made the lies that much more believable.

"Now personally, I thought he was full of crap. It was my job to keep people alive, no matter what the regs said. But you and I both know that's not always an option, and, as officers, the only thing we're ultimately responsible for is keeping ourselves alive as long as possible, so that the people who look to us for leadership know what they're supposed to do."

I fired that first Geyser salvo at your cargo slug. It was the right thing to do, even though it ultimately killed your friends Malik and Doria and Harren. Jarl died rescuing me from my own people, and Crassus is dead because I put that Alpha on the shuttle. And I'd do it all again, because it was the right thing to do.

"I can't tell you what to do, Jantine. You're in charge. But I can tell you one thing that the rest of them won't." Mira gestured at the shuttle. The warm caramel flavor of Carlton's thoughts spiked in her mind, as did the icy peppermint of Katra's disapproval.

"And what is that?"

"On Earth, we pick who to follow by their actions, not their looks. No matter what happens, you've earned their respect, and no one can take that away from you."

Jantine nodded, and Mira could feel the wall around her mind going back up again. Carlton and Katra were coming closer, and as she turned to look at them, Jantine's hand slipped out of her grasp as the last emotional bricks fell into place.

Do what you think is best, Jantine. But the real truth is that thing in there terrifies me, and I hope it never wakes up.

JANTINE

Jantine looked past Mira to the captured shuttle, and didn't like what she saw. It wasn't the damage to their escape craft, or the concerned faces of Carlton and Katra as they walked to meet her. It wasn't even the Omegas standing next to the sleeper unit with Artemus watching over them.

It was the sinking feeling that one of them was about to give her some more bad news, and there was nothing she could do about it.

Carlton spoke first. Now that they'd reached the surface, the Beta was much more himself than he had been aboard *Valiant*. How much of that was having a puzzle to solve, or patients to treat, she couldn't say. Mira said they'd been talking, so his mood must have softened some from their initial encounter.

A lot of things have changed in the last few hours, for all of us.

"Commander. There's something you should see."

"What is it?" Jantine was surprised to hear Mira ask the same question, but not so much as Carlton. The civvie's mouth pumped soundlessly for a few seconds as he processed both their faces, trying to decide if Mira actually outranked him.

Katra had no such qualms. She stared Mira straight in the eyes as she spoke, though the words were meant for Jantine.

"Transmitter in the unit. Started pinging when we moved it."

Jantine cocked her head toward Mira, noting that Carlton was now studying all three women's features for some clue as to who was in charge.

Or, he could just be staring at Mira.

The virus was still changing Mira's face. The odd spots on her skin were already gone, and her eyes were changing color. She would never look like a true child of the stars; she was too tall for one thing, with hard muscles formed and refined on the home planet. Plus, no amount of genetic restructuring would change the way she acted. Her culture promised her she could have anything she wanted, provided she had the will to take it.

And just what is it you want now, Mira?

At the moment, she had her hands in the air, palms out, shaking her head in denial.

"Don't look at me. I saw that thing for the first time just a few minutes before you did. But a hidden transmitter would definitely explain..."

Mira chewed her lower lip, seemingly unaware of the three mods waiting for her to finish her premise. The unguarded expression was an odd thing to watch, especially in an otherwise disciplined person. Jantine wondered how many other foreign mannerisms she'd have to learn before she could fully understand her new team member.

That's definitely the direction we're heading in, at least if I still have any say in the matter.

"Mira, what is it?"

The verbal prompt shook Mira out of whatever reverie she'd slipped into. Jantine felt a touch of embarrassment brush against her mind; despite her growing skill in empathic communication, Mira was having a hard time keeping her inner feelings a secret.

"Oh, sorry. I was thinking about whoever fired that last Geyser salvo. Until you crashed into us, *Valiant* was, for the most part, completely undetectable. A transmitter on the sleeper unit would explain how they found us; Captain Martin and I had just finished stowing it on the shuttle when Captain Kołodziejski's capture order came through."

Mira's face took on a more serious expression, and her projected embarrassment shifted to urgent concern.

"Jantine, if it's active now, Janbi's trick about covering our tracks up there may not last much longer. Carlton, do you know where it is?"

Carlton raised his hands and gave a small shrug. He turned back to look at the sleeper unit before talking, and his voice had the same sort of distracted quality Jantine found so annoying in JonB.

"I've got a fair idea, but the Omegas won't let me touch it. After we got it out of the shuttle, they pushed me aside and started well, whatever it is they're doing now."

Jantine stepped forward out of the impromptu huddle the others had formed around her. The Omegas were sitting on the ground, backs to one another. One was facing the sleeper unit, and the other was looking in her general direction.

"Carlton, how did you detect the signal?"

"It was the Omegas, Boss. That thing they do when they swing their heads, like on the ship. When they started again, I checked my handheld and found an RF signal just outside the range of both the scattercomms and the ones the humans normally use. I'm sure they can detect it, but I haven't seen anything like it before."

Carlton's explanation reminded Jantine of something, a half-remembered lesson from the crèche regarding the early days of the colonies. Of how ships sometimes would go missing on long voyages, only to be found waiting on the surface of an inhospitable planet years later by another expedition.

We didn't know the galaxy so well then, but we had no choice but to go on looking.

Jantine looked at the Omega facing her, trying to find some clue as to which one it might be. They were intentionally vague in that regard, letting the rest of society see the Gammas as their "faces."

Well, you haven't got one now, have you? And I need answers.

"Mira. Will you help me speak to them?" Jantine wanted to make it an order, but still didn't know how to treat Mira.

"Of course. They've been pounding on the inside of my head since we started back. I can't promise I'll get it right, but it seemed to go well enough earlier when Janbi asked."

And what has my civvie scientist been up to that he needed the Omegas? Perhaps I was out in the field for too long.

But it was the other part of Mira's statement that troubled her.

"You have to tell us right away when they want something. They don't ask us for that many things, but when they do it's usually important."

"I'm sorry, I didn't know." Mira's face fell, and the embarrassment came back, underlaid with tastes of regret and fear. "I thought you were working something out on your own, and you didn't seem that interested in talking to me."

It was Jantine's turn to be embarrassed. She had treated the human poorly, resenting her new status and shifting some of the blame for what happened to her team onto Mira.

It's not like she's the one who killed them. And she's one of us now, sort of. We have to learn to work together.

Putting the matter aside, Jantine moved forward until she was close enough to get a good look at the Omega's face. Mira came up to stand behind her, and Jantine assumed the flicker of fear coming from the human meant Katra was nearby.

I'm going to have to deal with that, too.

Jantine readied herself. Her last two conversations with the Omegas had not gone well, but she thought she understood part of the reason why now.

Hopefully, this one won't end in violence.

Burying her fear, she began.

"It's a distress beacon, isn't it?"

"Of course!" Before the Omegas, or rather, Mira could answer, Carlton's exclamation ruined the somber mood Jantine was trying to create. The Beta rushed toward the unit, but the Omega facing away from her raised an arm to block his path. Carlton stared at it with a shocked expression, and Artemus hurried over to pull him aside.

Then Mira started speaking, and the words had a distant quality to them Jantine recognized.

Here we go.

"Why have you not awakened the Adept? Wait, that can't be right. It's... the thought concept they're using doesn't make sense Jantine, I'm sorry."

The unfamiliar word didn't bother Jantine, she knew what the Omegas meant. And she felt a bit guilty; not that she'd delayed her decision, but that she took some pleasure that Mira wasn't quite as far advanced in her communications as she thought she was. Ignoring Mira's commentary, Jantine continued with her questioning.

"It's not safe here. Whoever she is, we can't expose her to needless dangers. And our priority is the mission. We need to find the rest of the sleepers first."

"No."

No?

Jantine hadn't heard that word in some time, and having the Omegas finally voice their disobedience didn't make her like it any better.

"The distress call. What does it say?"

"S-A-198 must be awakened. You will instruct the others."

Jantine did her best to keep her temper under control. Nothing in her training had prepared her for this kind of insubordination, and the Omegas were the last members of her team she expected to give it.

"I give the orders on this mission. Tell me about the distress call."

When Mira did not answer right away, Jantine turned and looked at her. The older woman's face had a puzzled expression, and when she did speak, it was clear to Jantine that she was using her own words this time.

"I'm not sure they understand it either. But one of them is more agitated than the other. The memories...I've got nothing to work with for this situation."

"Just do your best, Mira. What do they want you to say?"

Mira nodded, and her voice again took on a detached tone.

"Cold. Cold star rising. Fire and death. S-A-198 must be awakened. It has been too long."

Jantine wanted to look Mira in the eyes, even if the other woman wasn't the one really speaking. Doria usually stood between the Omegas and whomever they were speaking to, and Mira had assumed a subordinate's position behind her. But Jantine's gaze was locked on the Omega's black eyes, and she felt if she looked away, something bad was going to happen.

"And do you have any idea at all what that means?"

Mira's reply was a bit tentative, and as she spoke the differences between her and Doria became even more evident.

"Nope. They not really using words to communicate; it's more like they're suggesting meanings and letting me know when I've got the right ones. The extra memories help, but the images they're sharing with me don't make any sense at all. I'm seeing a sky full of stars, some mountains maybe. Also, when you mentioned the sleepers, one of them was happy and the other one was afraid."

Eyes still locked on the Omega's broad face, Jantine nodded. Delays in communication were common with Omegas, but Mira's different worldview was both helpful and a hindrance in this situation. When she thought of the right words to say, Jantine used her best command voice.

"I told you, it's not safe here. That distress signal will bring our enemies to us. We have to find a way to turn it off, and then we need to get to a place we can protect her."

"No danger. Safe here. S-A-198 must be awakened. They're—Jantine, he's lying!"

"What?"

"The one facing the unit, he believes you. But the other one...I think something is wrong with him. I think he's not just scared, he's terrified."

Jantine's world was coming apart, one piece at a time. Not only was she on the verge of losing her command to an unknown, but now the Omegas were actively working against her. Lying to her. There were always things they did that didn't make sense, but this...

The Omega in question was on its feet before she could finish her thought. It was almost twice her height, and just one of its arms massed more than her entire body. In the dim light of the setting sun, shadows drew dark lines on its face, and Jantine felt Mira's fear pulling at her own.

She took a step back, chiding herself for the unconscious gesture. After seeing the Omegas in action aboard *Valiant*, she knew there was nothing she could do to stop them if they really wanted to hurt her. Artemus couldn't possibly get to her in time, and even if he could get past the second Omega, it would only be to collect her corpse.

Then her fear was gone, replaced by a wave of support and confidence. Whatever it was seemed right, and as the feeling wrapped itself around the base of her mind, Jantine stood a little bit taller.

"I've made my decision. We must find a way to disable the transmitter, and once we are in a secure location, Carlton and JonB will—"

A hand touched her shoulder, and Mira's whispered words came from right behind her.

"Jantine, let me talk to him. I think I can get us out of this."

Angered by the interruption, Jantine shrugged the hand off.

"No. Don't do anything else. It won't hurt me. It can't."

"Are you sure about that? Because he's not."

Jantine didn't have any time to consider the implications of Mira's statement before a new voice added an unexpected complication to the situation.

"Commander, a word?"

The Omega spun its head to stare at JonB, who paled a bit under its four-eyed scrutiny. The scientist was standing just inside the hole leading to the cargo area, holding himself steady by gripping a protruding piece of conduit. He still had a few drops of Katra's blood on his face, but otherwise looked fine.

"What is it, JonB?" Her words sounded a lot more confident than she felt, but Jantine refused to back down.

"Uh, not you, Boss. Her." Without loosening his death grip on the conduit, JonB doubled up his right arm, pulling his wrist almost level with his shoulder and pointing at Mira.

"He's awake. Captain Martin, that is, and he wants to talk with you. If you can spare the time."

And now you're starting to do it. I'm still in charge here, JonB. Not the Omegas. And certainly not Mira Harlan!

"I think we're good, right? Everyone's said what they have to say?" Mira stepped forward in front of Jantine, staring down the Omega with steely eyes. Jantine felt a fresh wave of confidence as she passed by, one with familiar undertones.

But then she did something Doria would never have attempted; Mira reached up a hand and made a snapping noise with her fingers until the Omega turned away from JonB. Behind it, the second Omega rose to its feet, and Jantine thought she saw something like concern in its eyes.

The sound of her fingers wasn't loud enough to be painful, and even with her muscular build Mira didn't appear to be a real threat to the Omega. But her intent to scold was apparent to everyone, and she didn't let it go with just the one gesture. She pointed a finger up at the Omega's face, and shook it several times for emphasis while she spoke.

"It's not nice to ignore someone when they're talking to you. Commander Jantine has very real concerns for your safety, for all of us. I know you're frustrated, but this is not the way." Lowering her finger, she nodded in JonB's direction.

"And you leave him alone; he's only trying to help. I'll be gone a few minutes, but we're not done talking about this."

Mira spun on her heel and walked over to the shuttle. Jantine's jaw dropped, and almost fell off her face when the Omega followed Mira to the side of the ship and then gently boosted her up through the hole. Jantine heard her say "thank you" before she leaned out over the edge of the hull and kissed the top of the Omega's orange head.

The Omega stood there with its hands spread out on the hull for almost a minute after JonB and Mira made their way further into the ship, just watching the space where she had been. When it turned around, its tiny mouth was pressed tight in something approximating a smile. It could have been the last sliver of sunlight painting everything with warm colors, but Jantine could have sworn its skin was a deeper shade, almost red in places.

Carlton started to say something, but Jantine waved her hand without looking at him, not wanting to spoil the moment.

Just then, work lights strung along the hull warmed to life, bathing the area in the broad-spectrum light of Colony A's secondary star. After so many hours basking in the warm yellow radiance of Sol, it was like gray paint had been splashed over everything.

By the time she could distinguish colors again the Omega's face was back to normal. It walked over to the sleeper unit to rejoin its companion, but instead of turning to stare at Jantine, it raised its hand to the spot Mira had kissed. The second Omega did the same thing, and Jantine wondered how much of Mira's scolding had been delivered mentally so the Omegas could save some face in front of the other mods.

Whatever she's becoming, it's definitely not a Gamma. And the rest of us are going to have to change almost as much just to keep up with her...

MIRA

"Is someone going to tell me what all of that was about? Or should I just stay terrified until my heart explodes?"

Janbi's question made Mira smile. He'd been busy since she last saw him, restoring grav in the corridors and completing an amazing clean-up job. The walls and floors no longer dripped with gore, and she wagered he'd done a better job than any middie work detail could have managed in the same amount of time.

Give this one another few hours, he'll probably come up with something to patch the hull as well.

In regards to his question, she could still feel the Builder's seething confusion behind her, a deep well of frustration that wouldn't be satisfied until the universe returned to the way it used to be. Mira's Gamma memories told her that most mods had difficulty distinguishing between one Omega and another, but she didn't need to see them to know who was who.

There was the one who'd changed her, and the one who thought doing so was a bad idea. The angry one, who still wanted to punch something with those big hands.

"I'm not exactly sure, Janbi. The Builders are…complex."

The boy's laugh was like a warm shower, setting her mind at ease. There was a small spike of annoyance when she'd spoken, but it faded quickly into the general aura of unshakable confidence he was projecting.

Oh, boyo. If you weren't half my age, Mama Harlan's little girl would be in trouble right now.

It wasn't just his looks that Mira found fascinating. Janbi's whole outlook was as different from the other mods as Artemus was physically from Carlton. He seemed out of place among the dour and brooding Colonials, though the longer she talked with Jantine the more she suspected the young leader was also a breed apart.

Maybe it's a Beta thing. Carlton seems fairly normal, but he can still get pretty intense at times.

"Well, if you figure it out, let me know. I never want to be on the wrong end of those two."

Nodding her agreement, Mira thought about the perpetual dark mood the one she'd taken to calling "Grumpy" was in. Both Builders had experienced significant emotional trauma in the last few hours, but it had changed them in very different ways.

When "Happy" forced her body's transformation it was more of an accident than anything else. At first he'd just been curious about the different taste of her thoughts. But one he'd seen her up close, he acted on instinct, giving her both the Transgenic virus and the Gamma memories.

Including those of Doria, their last facilitator. Wherever I go with these people, they're always going to be thinking of her. I don't even know what she looked like, and I feel like I'll never match up to their memories.

It seemed silly to be jealous of a fifteen-year-old girl she'd never met, but that's definitely how it felt. Having a selection of Doria's memories wasn't the same as talking with the Gamma or experiencing her thoughts, something every other personality fragment bouncing around in her head had done before passing on their knowledge to Doria.

Mira reached out a hand to Janbi's shoulder, and a wave of raw desire rolled off him when they touched. Images that could make a courtesan blush flashed through his mind, and Mira couldn't help but be flattered.

Well that's good to know. They're not completely indifferent to sex after all.

A memory fragment bubbled up—a private conversation between Doria and Malik—and Mira felt a touch of shame. It wasn't her fault the Gamma had assigned such an important meaning to the encounter. But it was something personal, something intense that was never meant to be shared with another. Mira was pretty sure the Builders didn't know about it either. Happy had just been carrying the memories; he didn't have the emotional vocabulary to understand them. But Mira did, and their meaning was clear to her. The Betas on this mission *were* different. Very different than those back "home."

"Janbi, tell me something. Why were you selected for this mission?"

Confusion warred with curiosity and passion in his mind, but the analytical ability that was his greatest strength trumped them all. Janbi considered her question carefully before answering, and she detected no doubt whatsoever in his response.

"Actually, it's...never mind. I was chosen because I am the best."

"Best? Best at what?"

"Everything."

Janbi's confusion mixed with pride, and the combination twisted his face into something she wanted to stare at forever.

Oof, those eyes.

Pulling herself back to task, Mira pressed for more.

"Surely, there has to be more to it than that?"

Thinking about who in the Colonies would have made that decision, Mira was more afraid than ever of waking up S-A-198.

"My entire crèche was tested. I was selected, trained, and prepared to be a civilian adjunct to Jantine. Specifically Jantine, to answer your next question. One of the sleeper Betas is...was Malik's match."

Something in the way he said the word made her want to know more, but Janbi's brain was already moving on to another topic.

"We should continue. Captain Martin—"

Mira pictured the captain as she'd last seen him, breathing uneasily in his cabin with Carlton removing a scanner from his head. She'd felt the pain he was in since re-entering the shuttle, but so far it was manageable.

"He's dying. I know, Janbi, and so does he. But this is important. I need to understand Jantine if I'm going to work with her. With all of you."

"My training tells me you are enemy combatants, but what I've seen—what I've learned since meeting you—tells me a completely different story than the one our leaders have been feeding us. I have to know more."

The concern on Janbi's perfect features was real, and most of his salacious thoughts receded as he studied her face. Carlton had done something similar outside, and now that she'd tasted it again in his mind she understood the feeling for what it was.

Pity. He knows I can never fully understand him, and that there's nothing he can do about it.

She could feel the captain down the corridor, managing his pain with thoughts of duty and how he could best make his death serve the human race. She might not agree with his decisions so far, but she could at least *understand* them, and that was a feeling she knew she'd have less and less of during her time with the gennies.

"I'll help you if I can. But you're not one of us. Not yet. You're still an Earther at your core; you believe everything's going to work out for the best. It won't."

Janbi's stark acceptance of a futile universe seemed at odds with his deep curiosity as to how it worked. She knew his mind was always seeking alternatives, and that he was capable of incredible intuitive leaps. But underneath it all was the cold certainty of his inevitable failure, and he was okay with that.

"But, we still have to try, Janbi. It's what makes us human."

"Are we, Commander? Are we really? What do you think those people on the ship thought when the Omegas tore them apart? I've lived my entire life with them, and I still can't believe what I saw them do. Think about when you first saw the Deltas. Did you think they were human, or monsters?"

Mira was about to say "human," but realized it would have been the Gamma memories talking. Janbi was right, they *were* monsters at first, and she'd recoiled from the Omega too until he'd shoved a couple dozen lifetimes of tolerance into her brain. Part of Mira wanted to believe she was a better person than that, but she'd been an officer long enough to know that people don't really change.

They just get better at fitting in.

Janbi took her silence as an invitation to continue.

"I don't think we are human, at least not what you mean by the term. We're something else. Something better. And until you accept that you're not one of them anymore, you'll never understand Jantine."

Mira detected nothing but honesty in Janbi's mind, and wondered if she could do what he said. The longer she talked with any of the mods, the more her universe expanded. And locating her exact place in it was getting harder to do.

"We really shouldn't keep Captain Martin waiting."

As much as Mira wanted to talk to the captain, there was still something she needed to ask Janbi. And given how much he'd altered her worldview already, she wasn't entirely sure she wanted to hear his answer.

"In a minute. This is important. When I asked you earlier why you were chosen for the mission, what I really meant was, why are you different from the others? None of them want to talk about this, or accept me without question the way you do."

Janbi's mind went into overdrive, but Mira detected no particular emotion from him. It was a refreshing change, but she was a bit apprehensive about what kind of response required such intense contemplation.

"I don't think it was me in particular, although out of all my crèche I am the best suited for the mission. It was the combination of myself and Jantine that made me the only choice. We are compatible."

The nagging feeling was back. Janbi was saying more with the word "compatible" than she was hearing, and it was more than just a Beta vs human thing.

Or is it? Match. Compatible? It can't be. They're just kids!

"Janbi, are you married to her?"

Things that he'd said, that Jantine mentioned in passing, that Mira had seen but not understood in the Gamma memory dump started falling into place.

"I don't know what married means, but your context is correct. We are paired, or we will be if we can complete the mission and establish a colony. Our children, when it's safe to have them, will be of this world, and their children will be our ambassadors to humanity.

"Your other question is more interesting. I like you, Commander. I like you because you're <u>not</u> one of us. Not Beta, not Gamma. You're something different, something new, and I enjoy speaking with you. You almost make me believe I can change our fate, and that makes you a puzzle worth solving."

Mira knew he meant it, and as much as she hated herself for asking, she had to know for sure.

"Are you sure that's all of it? You have no other motives?"

Right on cue, all the boy's salacious thoughts resurfaced. And the knowledge that he knew she could sense their content was both embarrassing and very attractive. What's worse, she felt herself respond, if only as a courtesy to his wonderful smile.

Trou-ble.

"Oh, that. We will have sex, you and I. And our children will be even more impressive, I think, than those I will have with Jantine. But we don't have time for that right now. There are more important things to worry about than your pleasure."

Janbi took her hand from his shoulder, and raised it to his lips for a kiss. Mira felt her cheeks redden, embarrassed not only by the fact that she'd left it there throughout their conversation, but at the electric charge she felt when his breath touched her skin.

He was several meters down the corridor when the full impact of what he'd said hit her.

Wait, my pleasure? Why you little...

"Captain Martin, I've brought Commander Harlan as you requested. Do you need anything else?"

A wet, hacking cough preceded Martin's reply, and his pain banished all thoughts of Janbi from Mira's mind. She ran to the open cabin door, and saw the captain sitting up in bed and wiping blood away from his mouth.

"No, that's okay, son. Thank you. Just wait outsi—"

This close to the captain, his pain was almost overpowering. But Mira's mental companions knew a few tricks for dealing with it. She tugged on his memories until one from childhood popped up, and she massaged it into a warm, soothing blanket to wrap around his mind.

MARTIN

Aloysius's pain subsided, and the warm feeling that replaced it was more than a little nostalgic. He smelled something spicy that reminded him of cold winter afternoons, watching the snow pile up outside while his great-grandfather explained how in his day, life was simpler, and "you boys best not forget where we came from!"

Opa. Haven't thought about him since...

Gerolt Maarten was one hundred and forty-seven years old when his great-grandson had entered the Academy, and almost lived long enough to attend his graduation. He did get to see Aloysius wear his uniform one time, on a visit home that also involved snowdrifts and hot cider.

Now, where did that come from, I wonder?

Martin opened his eyes, and saw Mira Harlan sitting beside him. For a second, she was framed by a sky full of stars and an old oak tree, but then the familiar confines of his cabin surrounded them both. She was wearing a set of ship blues, but the last time he checked her name wasn't Marcus Callaway.

Apparently my pilot's clothes made it aboard, even if he didn't.

"You're out of uniform, Harlan."

Harlan's smile made him feel almost as good as whatever drugs the gennies were pumping into him. There was something about her face that seemed off, but his head was still fuzzy.

"Yes, sir. It was these or your formals, and I didn't think them appropriate at the time."

"Well, you'll get your command soon enough. Might as well get used to people calling you 'Captain.'"

Maybe it's her eyes. Were they always that color?

Admittedly, Martin hadn't spent a lot of time in Harlan's company, but there was something different about her. She was softer somehow, as if some of her hard edges had been knocked off during their escape.

"I'm not so sure about that, sir. Since the last interaction I had with the fleet involved missiles and a bit of treason, I don't think either of us is in their good graces right now. Sir, Janbi said you wanted to talk to me?"

Martin grunted, then wished he hadn't. A fresh round of coughing brought up more blood, and Harlan had to ease him back into a sitting position. A fresh wave of warmth washed over him, and he had the distinct impression it originated from her. He still didn't know what was bothering him about his new second-in-command, but she was right. There were things to discuss.

"So that Carlton kid, he told you what's wrong with me?"

"Yes, sir. Vasogenic cerebral edema. Your brain's getting too big for your skull, thanks to all the hits to the head you took. I'd tell you that you should have kept your helmet on, but we were both pretty help-less by the time the mods captured the shuttle. But you also got shot and didn't tell anybody, and that's what's killing you."

Martin nodded, glad the pain in his head was finally gone.

"Wrong tense there, Harlan. I'm dead already. Only question is, what can I do to help you and those kids before I check out completely?"

Harlan squeezed his hand, and when she did, something like feathers tickled the back of his head. Her smile was infectious, and he was about to laugh when he remembered what happened the last time he tried it.

No sense making things worse. Didn't she used to have freckles? Maybe that was one of the others, it's hard to think straight right now.

"Sir, I need you to tell me about the Alpha. Specifically that sleeper unit. Where and when you found it, and what kind of shape it was in."

Martin attempted another nod, and when the pain didn't blind him, chanced a look around his cabin. Most of his effects were back on *Valiant*, but this shuttle had been his real home for a while now. Four months of detached duty with Horace Kołodziejski and his black hats while Bill Williams built him a crew he could trust, and then a month hiding out with the gennie on the other end of a hyper tunnel while things cooled off enough for him to return to *Valiant*.

It seemed a reasonable enough place to die. His books were here, as well as his chess set. Gerolt claimed he'd carved it from a fallen tree after it was split by lightning, but when one of the pawns was damaged a few years after the old man died, he'd found an identical replacement in an Amsterdam flea market.

"Sir?"

Harlan. Right. There was something I was going to tell her, something important.

"Sir? The Alpha?"

"I stole it. Off the *Tribune*. Horace was moving it around the system as an insurance policy in case our people found out about it. He was right, of course, but at the time he thought I was working for his side. When I saw my chance, I corralled a couple techs I could trust and we grabbed the thing and ran."

Harlan nodded, but her eyes were still fixed on his face. The feathers tickled him again, and her look of concentration intensified.

Is there something on my face?

"Anything else, sir? Did you detect any signals maybe when you moved it?"

Martin tried to remember what it was he needed to do. It was hard to think, when all he wanted to do was sleep.

"Did I ever tell you about my opa? He was full of crazy old sayings. My brother and I could predict which one was coming after a while, based on his mood. But his favorite of all was, *'de eersten zullen de laatsten zijn.'*"

Gerolt loved working with wood, but Martin never had the patience. The carved chess set was his favorite, and he always praised the boys on their skill at the game.

"Sir? Sir, I don't speak Dutch. You asked to see me, sir. Was there something you wanted to tell me? About the Alpha? The shuttle's computer core is damaged, and most of the proof you said was in there is corrupted."

Harlan? When did she get here? There was something I wanted to tell her, something important.

"Captain? I feel you slipping away, and I don't know how to help you. Is there something you want to tell me? Something important?"

Mira Harlan, that's her name. Top of her class. One of Maranova's "bright stars..."

Martin smiled. Harlan was a good kid. Bill Williams said she had potential, and kept her on when he re-staffed *Valiant*.

"We should probably bring her in, don't you think Bill? She's got brains, and a good heart. She'll know what to do when the time comes."

Martin looked to his left, but Commander Williams was missing. He thought he heard someone talking, someone yelling, and then his world caught on fire. It was hard to breathe, and when the coughing started again something tore inside him. Strong hands held him up, and wiped something warm and wet from his face.

"Captain? Can you hear me?"

"Ha-Harlan, is that you?"

Martin blinked his eyes, but he couldn't make out where she was. Everything was white and gray clouds, and the pounding in his head wouldn't stop.

"It's me, sir. Don't try to talk. If you can, just think about what you want to say, and I'll try to translate it into terms I can understand."

"What's...what's happening to me?"

"You've been injured, sir. You're dying. I can take away your pain, but when I do it clouds your mind. You called me in here to tell me something. Was it about the Alpha?"

Martin took in a breath to speak, but doing so sent pain throughout his chest. After another round of coughing he decided just to nod, and try doing what Harlan suggested.

Yes. The Alpha. You have to get it to safety.

Harlan's hand squeezed his, and the warmth in his mind went up a notch. Martin wasn't sure what exactly was happening, but at least the pain was getting easier to handle. Harlan's voice came from floating down from somewhere above the clouds.

"I know sir, we're trying. There's a signal of some kind coming from the unit. I think it's what let Captain Kołodziejski locate the *Valiant*, but I don't know enough about what you were planning to turn it to our advantage. Can you tell me how to turn it off?"

Connect it to a power source. Damn. You have to get out of here. How long has it been transmitting?

Martin tried to get up, but his arms refused to do his bidding. Harlan squeezed his hand again, and then continued speaking in her far away voice.

"I'm going to go with too long. And things here are…complex. The Colonials are debating what to do about the Alpha, but your contacts are the most important thing right now. We found a course in the core for someplace called the Harrison Institute; near as I can tell it's about a thousand kilometers northeast from here.

"The shuttle will fly, but it's in no shape for a fight and these kids don't know the first thing about space warfare. They're smart, and lucky, but our people have been training for this a long time. They'll— we'll be picked off as soon as we break atmosphere."

A fresh round of coughing doubled Martin over, and set his head to spinning. He could feel Harlan's arms around him, but he couldn't summon the strength to do what had to be done. When he could breathe again, he put everything he had into three words.

"I'll do it."

"Sir, no. We can figure out a remote…"

"Only play. Sacrifice knight, save queen."

Martin felt a small cold spot on the back of his neck, then another. Harlan started to speak several times, but for some reason, never finished. When he heard her voice again, this time it had undertones of sadness and resignation.

"What do you need me to do?"

DEMARCO

2140 SHIP TIME, SHUTTLE **CX-1**

SHUTTLE FLIGHTS in near-Earth space always took far too long for Sam's taste. With so many man-made objects flying around, even the relatively simple trip back to EFS *Clarke* was subject to delays: be they from supply runs between the satellite ring stations, avoiding emergency transits, or unscheduled idiocy from private pilots thinking they owned the space lanes.

But today Sam had instructed the autopilot to take an intentionally oblique approach to the Home Fleet's flagship, to give them enough time to both rendezvous with an FTL communications beacon, and convince Marya Andreison of the righteousness of their cause.

And from the look on her face, I'm not doing that great a job of it.

"So that's our story, Andreison. That's what we're fighting against, and with the analysis you've provided directly contradicting his sworn testimony, we have to move quickly to counter Captain Kołodziejski before he can convince any more members of the Council."

The Admiralty compartment was a stripped down version of the council chambers, with overstuffed chairs for six people surrounding a small holotable. None of them were large enough for Sam, though, and it didn't feel right for him to pace the small space as he explained things to Marya. So he sat leaning forward over the small center console, with the two women one chair away from him on either side.

Watching Marya process his words, he almost felt like he was the one who needed convincing rather than the junior officer who still wanted nothing to do with her uniform. The commodore had both heard and delivered this speech many times, but it was the first for Marya, and she was intelligent enough to know what would happen to her if she picked the wrong side.

Marya's strange eyes gave him no clue as to her mental state, but they were dilating rapidly, as if she was looking at something he couldn't see. Her posture was still ramrod straight, sitting on the edge of her chair in stark contrast to Ykaterina's relaxed sprawl.

"So what you're telling me, sir, is that you're part of a secret cabal, one that's actively committing treason while at the same time trying to prevent another war, and Captain Kołodziejski heads a different cabal dedicated to starting one. That my wife's entire battlegroup has been hijacked and sacrificed to determine the fate of a centuries-old gennie child, and that Kołodziejski's people are convinced that the only possible explanation is that Mira and her captain are gennie sympathizers. Specifically, gennie sympathizers in collusion with an unknown force of super-stealthy gennies who travel the universe in big black rocks with high powered weapons that can blow holes in things that will outlast the solar system. Did I miss anything from the recordings, or should I explain them to you one more time?"

I should get her to write my after-action reports. That's a summary even an oversight committee could understand.

But Marya wasn't done talking yet, and Sam knew from their brief association that if she was ever going to join them, it had to be on her own terms.

"Other than the possibility that Captain Maddsen may have ordered my death to cover up any gennie involvement—which, as you say, definitely runs counter to the narrative Captain Kołodziejski is selling to the Reclamation Council—I don't see why your shadow war needs me in particular. Why I can't just go home to my family while the rest of you important people figure this out for yourselves?"

Marya wasn't aiming the comment at Sam directly, but Ykaterina seemed content to let him take the lead on this one. Taking a deep breath, Sam prepared himself for the same hard sell he'd given Marcus Callaway a few months back.

His delay in answering was answer enough, so Marya got up from her chair and pulled up the holo of Mira Harlan and Aloysius Martin hunkered down behind a workbench, pacing around it and occasionally reaching in to peel away layers until all that was left were the two officers and the bulkhead behind them. She waved something at the taller of the two, and Sam saw that she'd somehow swiped his command baton when he wasn't looking.

Again.

"Sir, ma'am, this is my wife. I know her better than anyone, and if Captain Martin gave her the same speech you just gave me, she'd probably have believed it. I'd almost believe it myself, if this stitched-together holo wasn't just another shit sandwich I'm supposed to swallow with a smile. Ask yourselves a question: who is Mira shooting at here?"

Sam started to answer, but Marya was still building up a good head of steam, and Ykaterina was now leaning forward with a gleam in her eyes.

"The clear implication here is that she's shooting other troopers, but why she would shoot at Fleet personnel—her own people to boot—isn't supported by the facts at hand. And the second reason I'm almost ready to believe your crazy space ghost story is because whoever's on the other end of her sights is conspicuously absent from any of the footage we have. The footage we've been *given*, carefully curated for little minds with big fingers poised above doomsday buttons.

"The three of us know the gennies have returned, and from their transmission we know they're not inclined to talk. But what I can't believe is why you keep telling me that Mira is dead. You've shown me no proof that SDF *Valiant* has been destroyed, nor any proof that your gennie-in-a-box is even a gennie. If this footage survived the supposed destruction of a Redstone dreadnaught, Mira would have survived as well, with Captain Martin in tow.

"It's one thing to offer me a pilot's berth aboard your ship, but quite another to ask me to join your crusade. So my questions for you are: if I do join, what are we doing to find her; and, what are we going to do about this?"

A time index floated into view, and the holo started advancing a fraction of a second at a time. Marya did something with the baton that outlined something small and fast moving across the frame and impacting the bulkhead, leaving behind a shining crater that Kołodziejski's comm techs had done their best to erase.

"We—the Fleet—can't defend against these gennie weapons unless we're going to escalate to tactical nukes. Gennie weapons, not ones developed by humans on a secret research base. If Captain Kołodziejski's faction had them, they'd have used them by now, and if your spies inside his organization are as good as you say, they'd have brought you some prototypes. So unless you've got a plan for dealing with pissed off gennies who don't care that not all humans hate them, your resistance is doomed from the start."

Sam's head was spinning from her rapid-fire responses, and all he could think to do was hold out his hand for the baton again. When she gave it back, Sam gripped the handle as tight as he could, still marveling at her ability to take it from him seemingly at will. He still had no answers for her, so he looked over to Ykaterina in the hope she had something better to offer.

He didn't have long to wait.

"Are you dictating terms, Sub-Lieutenant, or presenting facts?"

Ykaterina was sitting up straight in her chair now, every inch the commodore.

"Because either way you look at it, you're going to have to come to terms with Mira Harlan's death. Death by SDF *Indomitable* or death by gennie aren't any different in the long run, and that's the plain truth of it. I'm sorry for your loss, but this is the way things are right now.

"As to the gennies, we're of the opinion that this is a small force, somewhat depleted by the action aboard *Valiant*.

"As to what *I'm* going to do about it, the first step is having you reconstruct all the available footage back aboard *Clarke*. You are correct in that we've been silent—and secret—for far too long, and what I'm offering you is a chance to help us bring it all out into the open. To be in control of your life for once, and able to make a real difference.

"So if that's something you want, I believe the right place for you is with us. Samuel here has been your biggest supporter for years, and the cadet I remember was ready to take on the universe. That's what I'm offering. No conditions, no expectations. Just a chance to do what's right."

"Are you through, ma'am?"

The coldness of Marya's response matched her earlier tone from Sam's office, and knowing that she'd just pushed one of the commodore's big red buttons, he stood up in an attempt to de-escalate.

"That's enough, Andreison. We're only trying to help you."

"No, Samuel, let her finish. Best to have it out in the open now. Please continue, Sub-Lieutenant."

Ykaterina—no, she was pure Commodore now—had locked eyes with Marya and was using the same expression she'd had earlier when negotiating Fleet appropriations.

All business, no bullshit. And no way out for the person on the other end.

"What I was going to say, ma'am, is that I'll take the job. I'll join your faction, not only for the reasons you listed, but to bring my wife home to our children, one way or another.

"Because if she's willing to risk her life for what you believe in, then so am I."

The two women exchanged silent stares for a while longer, and Sam found the room growing smaller and hotter with each passing second. Then Maranova started laughing, and it took all of his resolve not to let slip a nervous chuckle in response.

"Fair enough, young lady. Fair enough. Samuel will see you situated in the command structure once we're aboard, but I want a thorough analysis of all the *Valiant* footage before 2800 shiptime. Send it straight to the captain and myself, along with any questions people may have about what it is you're doing. Will that work for you, Sub-Lieutenant?"

"Yes, ma'am. Thank you, ma'am."

Sam detected a hint of humility in Marya's reply, but couldn't praise her for it just yet. Twice in the last few hours she'd committed serious breaches of etiquette towards flag officers, and Ykaterina's coded message to get her "situated" meant the commodore was keeping count as well.

If Marya's ass lands back in the fire, so will mine. And since it will take most of my existing favors to get her set up proper as a real officer again, how much does that leave for me?

On the other hand, she did save my life once, and whether she knows it or not, the information she's brought us may put her in a position to do so again very soon.

"Samuel, we've been at this a while, can you see if the steward can fix something up for a late lunch? And check on our flight time while you're at it. Ms. Andreison and I have some more talking to do."

From the look on her face, Marya was not at all interested in talking, but part of being commodore was getting what you wanted from junior officers, and that applied to captains just as much as sub-lieutenants. Sam made his way aft to talk to the steward, and tried to convince himself for the thousandth time that he was on the right side.

KOŁODZIEJSKI

1900 SHIP TIME, **SDF** *INDOMITABLE*

WAITING HAD NEVER BEEN Horace's strong suit, and despite Collins' assurances, the techs tasked with opening their captured cargo container were nowhere near ready to do so.

Due to the container's size, getting it—and its precious cargo of sleeping gennies in suspension units—aboard had been no easy feat. In fact, it had involved two shifts of pilots moving shuttles and maintenance frames in and out of transfer bays all over the ship, while Caroline and her crew waited out of visual range to tractor it in. She and her crew ultimately docked on the other side of *Indomitable* before reporting for debriefing and decontamination.

He hadn't heard from her since, but to be fair, that was by his own design. Once she was back aboard, they'd set course for Echo Base on Luna with what was left of *Valiant*'s battlegroup in tow, and he'd begun his negotiations with the Reclamation Council for a formal declaration of war.

I don't need her to be a part of this, any more than she already is.

And as for these idiots, I gave them one job. One! And this is how my faith is rewarded.

"I'm sure it won't be much longer, sir. We know we can cut through in no time, but your orders were to preserve the container's integrity at all costs. Is that still what you want?"

Andrew Collins was head and shoulders taller than anyone else in the transfer bay, and when he talked, the jumpsuited crew members huddled at the container's hatch stopped their own conversations to listen. It didn't hurt that Collins was broadcasting his question using his armor's omnidirectional speakers, and that he had a well-deserved reputation as Horace's enforcer.

Daniel Tepes, however, was by far the deadlier of Horace's two primary bodyguards. He'd trained under the same tutors as Caroline, and had spend much of his time since joining Clan Kołodziejski wearing—and fighting—in suits of custom powered armor and the best weapons Horace's labs could turn out.

Whether the techs knew it or not, from his station at the container's hatch Tepes controlled more than half of the transfer bay with his slugthrower, and could hit any target Horace specified in less time than it took him to name it.

My left and right hands. And either one would gladly kill the other were he to betray me.

"Let's give them a little more time, Andrew. No sense rushing things if we don't have to."

"That's the spirit, Horace. Plenty of time to kill them all."

What? Who said that?

Horace stalked over to the techs, spinning one of them around by the shoulder.

"What did you say?" Horace was angered more by the casual familiarity of the speaker, but the sentiment was also bothersome. As far as he know, none of the four proles messing about with scanners and repair kits knew his plans for the gennies inside the container, or even what was inside.

"S…Sir?"

"Are you deaf, as well as stupid? I asked you what you said just now. Or was it one of you? Hmm, speak up!"

The faces of the techs were blank slates, all bland, low dome disasters in the making. The one he was holding by the shoulder was sweating profusely, his mouth opening and closing soundlessly as he thought of another lie to tell his captain.

Horace fixed the others with a piercing stare, daring them to challenge his authority.

"It's no use, old friend. They can't hear me. I'm here just for you." The voice was naggingly familiar, but had an odd resonance, as if spoken in an echo chamber.

"What did you just say!" Horace's eyes went wide, and his voice rose to a near shriek. He grabbed the tech's jumpsuit with his other hand and tried to pull him to his feet, but his wasted arms had only a fraction of their former strength. The resulting action was more a mild shaking rather than intimidating, which stoked Horace's rage even further.

"Daniel."

Horace heard two booted steps behind him, the whine of a slugthrower spinning up, and then saw a shadow fall over the tech's face when the muzzle of Daniel's weapon appeared out of the corner of his eye.

"Speak up, Specialist. I don't think he'll ask again." Tepes' words had the effect Horace's did not. All blood drained from the man's face, and he sagged in Horace's arms. The sudden weight was too great for him to bear, and he dropped the unconscious crewman to the deck.

"Well? Let's have it. Say it to my face!" The repair crew edged away from Horace, who was now shouting loud enough to hurt his own ears. His hands were shaking, fingers tingling, and he was finding it hard to breathe.

"It's ok, Horace. Just relax, it will all be over soon."

Horace put a hand on the container to steady himself, still not certain where the voice was coming from. The metal was shockingly cold, an icy, burning sensation that quickly spread throughout his entire body. He tried to pull away, but his palm was stuck to the metal —*no, that's not right, it's more like it's pulling me in. Like it...wants something from me.*

"Don't fight it, Horace. Let it happen. It's the only way you'll see how this all ends." This time, the voice was a lover's whisper directly into his ear. Tantalizingly familiar, someone who knew all his secrets, and how to push all his buttons.

Horace could see the techs stumbling to their feet several meters away, could see Daniel approaching from his right side, but there was no one close enough to speak those words. His hand was on fire now, and the container started thrumming under his palm, a slow, regular vibration that quickly built to deck-shaking rumble.

"Well, this *is* exciting. What happens if we give it a little push."

This time there was no separation between Horace and the voice, and he heard it undistorted for the first time inside his head.

"And here I thought you'd forgotten all about me. After all, it's been a whole five hours since you sent me to my death. In a container just Like. This. One."

Each word was punctuated with a slap, a phantom hand pressing down, and through, Horace's. The container answered with a rapid fire sequence of clunks, as unseen machinery inside responded to the man had once considered his closest friend.

Bob Calas. But…you're…

The smiling form of his former second-officer shimmered into view in front of him, ear pressed against the container only centimeters away from his trapped hand and eyes wide with anticipation.

"Dead? Such a droll word. I like to think of my self as—you know what? Dead works. You did kill me, after all. But it's all for the best, since now everybody gets to know your little secret!"

No, no, no…this can't be happening. This isn't…

"Real?" said Calas, "of course it's not real. We're just taking a little time out inside your head, while the rest of them catch up. See?"

Calas's phantom hand reached up and caressed Horace's cheek, sending a wave of revulsion through him. It was an intimate gesture, one the two men had never shared in real life. But this…whatever it was wasn't really his friend. It was something else, something…evil, and it had Horace so thoroughly trapped that he couldn't even blink.

"That's right. I'll do all the work. Oh, look, it's your boy Collins, coming to your rescue. He knows you're sick, right? Do you think he's made the connection yet? Do you think he'd still love you if he did?"

The Calas apparition turned Horace's head, pushing his field of vision far beyond what he could normally see with his real neck. Collins did indeed appear to be coming to save him, gauntleted arms outstretched and running full tilt across the transfer bay.

"Now this one," it said, swinging Horace's head to the right to reveal Daniel a few steps away from the container, with his slugthrower trained on Horace, "This one knows the monster inside you better than anyone. He's watched it grow and fester for decades, even before your ambition sealed your doom."

Horace's eyes went wide, or at least, he thought they did. Daniel would never betray him—the fate of his family was riding on his willing service.

"But that's the thing, isn't it, H? Things are different now, aren't they? You're different, inside and out. You just opened up a *gennie* container with just the touch of your hand. Your *gennie* hand, full of all sorts of happy extraterrestrial plasmids just itching to turn you into one of them."

Horace's hand *was* itching, and he snatched it away from the container. He thought he saw a glowing outline where his palm had been, but a second later Bob Calas was standing there, laughing.

Horace tried to take a step back, tried to run, but Calas was on him in a second, wrapping him in an embrace so tight he could neither breathe nor speak.

"You can't escape what you are, Horace. Who you are. Daniel can see it; Caroline's beginning to suspect it. And before you try and deny it, think about who's really talking right now. Because it's certainly not—"

The universe snapped back into motion as Andrew Collins' strong arms grabbed Horace just under his shoulders and pulled. Horace screamed as the skin of his palm separated, leaving behind a wet imprint on the container's hatch. But a second later the pain was gone, and as Collins dragged him to safety Horace lifted his hand and saw pristine, unblemished skin, though he could feel his artificial blood pumping through it with every beat of his heart.

Horace snapped his attention back to the now open hatch, where a thin, white mist was billowing out of the container and disappearing under the deck plating.

"Let me go. Let me go! I have to get in there!" Horace struggled against Andrew's superior strength, but the burly bodyguard would not budge.

"No, sir. You have to let Daniel do his job. He's been ready to kill anything that comes out of that container from the moment you stepped up to the hatch, and neither of us is going to let anything happen to you. Not now, not ever."

Daniel was indeed at the ready, moving quickly in front of the hatch and ducking into its dark interior. The techs hurriedly collected their gear and started to withdraw, dragging their unconscious companion with them.

"Andrew. No witnesses." Horace's whisper was all Collins needed to leap into action. Denied the support of Andrew's strong arms, Horace dropped to his knees, from where he watched Collins club all three techs into submission. His blanked faceplate turned in Horace's direction, waiting for further instructions.

What if they didn't see it, Horace? What if they didn't make the connection? What if it only took a second for the hatch to open, and you just ordered Collins to...oops, too late.

Horaces eyes went wide as Collins' hand came down four times, neatly breaking the necks of each tech in succession. He felt his hand unclench, let it fall numbly to his side.

Okay, to be fair, that one's on me. But who am I, Horace, if not you? The real you, the one you're trying so hard to suppress with your Earther drugs and your hope for a cure.

Collins stood up with a body in each hand, casually draping them over his left arm and moving easily inside the container. When he returned moments later his arms were empty, and moved toward the other two.

Tepes followed him out, taking a step away from the hatch and turning his head to watch his partner collect the remaining bodies.

He knows, Horace. He knows what you've done, what you're becoming. And he's making a choice. Right now, he's deciding to...

Daniel tightened his grip on the slugthrower, slowly turning his body until he was facing Horace, then taking slow, measured steps toward him. With every pace, Horace saw himself grow larger in Daniel's mirrored faceplate, watched himself reaching to his waist for a sidearm that wasn't there, heart pounding and head spinning and...

"The container is secure, sir. The mist we saw seems to have vanished, probably just an environmental interaction of some kind. Like Mr. Calas reported on the first container, there's gravity and atmosphere inside, both at safe levels, with no trace of...alien toxins."

Did you hear that, Horace? No alien toxins inside. Shall we bring some in with us, or maybe open up some gennie coffins while we're there?

"It should be safe to explore, sir. Is there anything in particular you'd like to see?"

Go on. Say it. He'll probably blow off his own head, if you order it. Just one word from you, and another problem just disappears.

"No, Daniel. I'll be fine. Our real work begins when we bring these...these test subjects back to Echo Base. I just want to look around a bit, make sure this container is worth the price we paid for it."

Ooh, that's a good one, Horace. I almost believe you myself.

"Shut. Up." Horace wasn't aware he'd spoken the words aloud until Daniel reacted by tilting his head slightly. They were a hissed whisper at best, barely loud enough to escape his clenched teeth, but the Daniel's suit pickups were probably still set to maximum sensitivity from his scouting mission

Here it comes. He'll be so polite, all 'Pardon me, sir? Did you say something?' You should just kill him now and be done with it.

"Did you say something, sir?"

The air in the transfer bay seemed much cooler than before, and Horace crossed his arms across his chest, rubbing his shoulders. It wasn't that he was particularly chilled, but he needed to be in control of something, anything, right now. Whatever dark part of his soul was acting out through the guise of Bob Calas, it was only a part of him, not the real Horace Kołodziejski.

"No, Daniel. I'm just tired, is all. It's been a long day. Why don't you go get some rest—it's a long haul back to Luna, and I'll need one of you on guard here at all times. Andrew here..."

Both men needed to step aside as Andrew carried the second set of bodies into the container, but it was Horace who stepped through after him.

"...will keep the first watch with me. I'll be in safe hands, never fear." Horace smiled, keeping his jaw tight and lips closed, lest his unwanted delusion do something else he'd regret.

Daniel's helmet stayed fixated on Horace for some time, mirrored faceplate betraying nothing of the man's feelings or intent. After what seemed like an eternity of silence, the suit's speakers crackled to life, amplifying Daniel's soft words enough to echo off both the container, and the rear of the transfer bay.

"Of course, Captain. Comm me if you need something. I am at your command, as always." Daniel finally lowered his slugthrower, fingers moving away from the firing studs and pointing the weapon at the deck. Horace's heart was still pounding, and he worried for a moment that Daniel's suit could hear that too.

Of course he can, you fool. You're an open book to him. Collins can read you too, but at least he has the good sense not to get personally involved. You're really going to have to make a choice between them. It's the only way you'll survive.

"I will, Daniel. Thank you. Sleep well, old friend."

Daniel was already turning to leave when Horace spoke, and paused for the briefest of moments before continuing his slow walk to the out hatch. Horace followed him with his eyes the entire way, not sure if what he was feeling was pride, or fear. Daniel opened the hatch and stepped through, and Horace watched the indicator panel cycle from red to green as Daniel sealed it from the other side.

"Do we have a problem, sir?" Collins' voice at his back was both menacing and reassuring, but it was the former Horace needed right now.

"No, Andrew. No problem, just an opportunity to explore. I need you to finish cleaning up here, and then stand guard at this hatch. No one—and I mean no one—is to come down here unless I give them express clearance. That goes for comm access too," said Horace, unfastening his wristcomm and handing it to his hulking guard.

"I understand, sir. I will keep you safe, always."

Did you hear that, Horace. Did you hear that! He's ours, always. He's seen the monster, and he doesn't care. Everything is working out so well!

"Quiet!"

"Sir?" Asked Collins, head swiveling to find some target he'd missed.

"I just want...I need quiet for a while, Andrew. See to it that I'm not disturbed."

Aw, that's sweet. But you'd better take your own advice, and rest for a while. I'll take things from here. You said it yourself; you've hard a hard day.

No, wait, that's not what I meant. I...

Horace smiled, a broad grin that made his eyes almost disappear, and pulled his lips into thin lines displaying his well-maintained teeth. It had been some time since he was truly free to act, and he was definitely going to make the most of it.

"Okay you gennie freaks. It's time to even the score. Are you coming, Bob?"

Whistling to himself as he stepped through the hatch, Horace pulled it closed behind him, and inhaled a double lungful of sweet-scented air.

"Yes, I absolutely agree, Bob. This is going to be fun..."

ANNAHKO

2200 SHIP TIME, *SDF* INDOMITABLE

CAROLINE EASED herself into her workstation's chair, then decided against it in favor of her bunk. She was still sore from her near-death experience in the gymnasium, even though the auto-doc and *Indomitable*'s actual doctor had pronounced her fit for duty.

Shows what they know. I feel like shit. I need a good drink, a good screw, and someone to share them with.

Fighting killer robots is a younger woman's game, for sure.

Instead of indulging herself, Caroline propped herself up against her headboard and started reading the first of Cadet Currano's prepared reports, the one having to do with the strange rocks—or rather, rock, as he insisted it be called—that had destroyed *Valiant*'s battlegroup.

Caroline was a combat officer, and a fair pilot, but her last engineering refresher course at Marsforce Academy was a relative decade before Currano was born, and she was woefully under-qualified to understand what he'd written. Thankfully, the cadet had also compiled a one-page summary in plain language, for which she was eternally grateful.

Of particular note was the last paragraph, which even when simplified had her head spinning.

"In essence, the rock is a single, distinct mass, operating in thousands of discrete instances. Each sample is entangled with all the others on a quantum level, and exists in both 'charged' and 'hungry' states simultaneously. Even the smallest piece can absorb tremendous amounts of energy, and discharge the same amount at any point along its personal continuum. Moreover, it 'wants' to 'infect' all other nearby matter, invalidating every known law of practical and theoretical physics."

Well that's just great. If he's right, a microgram of this stuff could explode with unparalleled destructive force, or properly managed, power a Redstone dreadnaught for a thousand years.

And the gennies have enough of it to waste a few billion metric tons delivering cargo containers across the known universe, for reasons known only to themselves.

The container!

Caroline scrambled back to her workstation, sending the hardcopies of Currano's report flying in her haste to inform Horace. She keyed in his personal comm channel, adding her private encryption key.

To her surprise, instead of the captain, it was Andrew Collins who answered Horace's comm, his face lit up by a hardsuit helmet's numerous internal displays.

"This is not a good time, Commander. He'll be ready for you in about an hour. Until then, please stop sending him messages."

Caroline fumed at this disruption of *Indomitable*'s chain of command, and the massive lack of respect Collins was showing her. As the ship's first officer—not to mention its next captain—she should have total access to anyone on the ship at all times, especially the captain. But as part of Horace's personal staff, Collins was completely outside the ship's command structure, and as such was not subject to Fleet protocol.

The fact that he's illegally slaving Horace's comm to his own means he's either committing treason, or faithfully carrying out Horace's orders.

But only Horace can tell me for sure…

"This is an emergency, Mr. Collins. I need to speak with the captain as soon as possible."

"Which will be in roughly an hour, Commander. I'm sorry, but my orders are clear on this matter. I will let you know if and when Captain Kołodziejski is available, but I expect he believes whatever it is, you can handle it on your own."

Collins terminated the call, and Caroline slammed her fist into the workstation's surface in frustration.

Lowborn trash! How dare you address me in this manner. How dare you!

Normally, Caroline would correct Collins' behavior immediately, and publicly. But only a few hours removed from massive physical trauma, and given what she knew of his combat training, she could only calculate a 50% survival rate for either of them should their conversation come to blows.

And even if I come out on top, I'll still have to deal with Daniel if Horace truly doesn't want to be disturbed.

The thought of her cousin always stirred up mixed feelings for Caroline. Their time together officially ended the day her mother sold off his line to the Kołodziejskis, but it was a lot easier to put him out of her mind when he was one or more star systems away. Working in close proximity these past few weeks had added many complications to her relationship with Horace, especially since Daniel's slip of the tongue the previous day outside the captain's quarters.

"I'm sorry," he'd said. "But I think…I think if something's going to happen, it has to be soon. We may not…no, I've said too much."

Too much? Not enough by far. And as soon appears to be never, I think we should have this out right now.

Caroline keyed Daniel's comm ID into the workstation, but received "channel not in network" as a response. Furious, she slotted her command key and tried again, this time with an override code and her personal encryption key. When she got the same result, she angrily jerked her command key from the workstation, and was halfway across her quarters to the out hatch when the rational part of her brain kicked in.

He either can't respond, or doesn't want to. And marching down to his quarters to demand answers probably wont get me what I want anyway.

Caroline clenched her fists, then stepped forward to place her hand on the cool metal of the hatch. She wondered what exactly it was she did want, and apart from her earlier wish for a strong drink and an even stronger man, she couldn't think of anything. Her perfectly ordered world was coming apart at the seams, and try as she might she couldn't summon up the Iron Princess to force it all back into line.

I have nobody to talk to, no one who'll understand. My new retinue are virtual strangers, and everybody else on board are Horace's people, beholden to him as I once was.

Caroline took a step back, and her foot slipped on one of the flimsy sheets of Currano's report. Half a century of physical conditioning kept her from falling on her ass, but as she dropped into a perfect three-point stance, her eyes came to rest on a page from Currano's other dossier regarding the corrupted training program that nearly took her life.

"...conclusion that the central core has been intentionally manipulated so as to remove specific files generated between ship times 1329 and 1426, roughly correlating with the activity of SDF *Indomitable* personnel aboard SDF *Valiant*, the result of which is a catastrophic corruption of all predictive algorithms and autonomous systems..."

Did you do this, Horace? Did you make the gym malfunction? Is that why you haven't answered any of my calls?

Caroline leaned back on her heels, reading page after page of Currano's conclusions. And while she was no theoretical physicist, she did know Indomitable's central processing core inside and out, and what her new retainer was outlining was nothing short of treasonous.

Treason. I'm using that word a lot lately, and I definitely do not like it. Am I on the wrong side of this?

Was I ever on the right one?

Caroline had the sudden urge to talk to her mother, but both the physical and emotional distance between them made her discard the notion almost immediately. News of her incipient promotion would certainly be welcomed by the family, but apart from any familial bond she might share with Anastasia, all the Annahko matriarch really cared about was Clan Kołodziejski's money, and how soon Caroline could lock it in for the family's future endeavors.

Horace promised me that things would get back on track when this was over, but I almost died today, and he didn't come to see me in Medical. He hasn't sent a response to any of my messages, and he set his attack dog between us to monitor my calls.

What are you doing with our lives, Horace? It's as if there isn't even an 'us" any more. There's barely even a me and you, outside the chain of command.

And what am I, exactly, without you in my life? Who will I be when this ends?

Caroline realized with a start that she already knew the answer, and that knowledge set her universe spinning in a completely different direction. It felt like she was dying all over again, but this time Ariel Amagosa was not on hand to restart her heart.

The last few days had pushed her relationship with Horace to the breaking point, and beyond. She still loved him, and probably always would. But she was no longer *in* love with him, and she didn't see any path back to who, and what, they once were.

Why, Horace? Why did you push me away, and for what? A mystery cargo container? Some crazy vendetta against Aloysius Martin, a man who until recently we both called our friend?

How many more people are going to die, Horace, before you finally decide to share your secrets with me?

Caroline's stomach rumbled, reminding her just how long it had been since she'd had any solid food. Deciding to leave her quarters as they were for now, she grabbed a mess tunic and pulled it over her uniform, fastening the straps down tight around her bruised ribs before she left her quarter and headed down the corridor to the elevator farthest away from compartment CF-3.

Autodocs can handle cuts, breaks, and contusions, but the nanites always stopped just short of a full cure. They'll heal on their own in a few days, but in the meantime they hurt like a sonofabitch.

The pain distracted her from her emotional trauma, but like her ribs, it would be a while until it was gone. Every step she took was another reason to cry, but Caroline refused to let the bastard ruin her reputation any more than he already had.

The officer's mess on the command deck was quiet, sparse, and most importantly, empty this time of day. It also had the advantage of being only a few steps away, but the common room she'd visited the day before had been full of sound and energy and happiness, things Caroline needed more of in her life right now.

Let's do it. Let's find someone new to talk to, someone who hasn't lied to me for decades.

Who knows, maybe they'll smell nice and I'll give them a night to remember. Anything's better than living with this pain.

Once she was in the elevator and had fewer choices to make, Caroline sagged against the support rail for a few seconds before keying in her destination. She didn't really want to fuck a random crew member —that sort of hookup always had negative consequences. But she wanted someone, anyone, to make her feel wanted, and she could count the people serving aboard *Indomitable* that didn't make her feel like punching something—or somebody—without running out of fingers.

Hell, I'd even give Allie Martin another tumble, if I could find him. He was always nice to me when we were just starting out in the fleet, and every negative thing I've heard about him in the last few years has come from either Horace or Admiral Worthy. If they've been lying to me about his motives, I'd sure as hell like to hear it from the man himself.

Besides, he never left me uncertain about his intentions when we served together, which is more than I can say for...

The elevator came to a stop, opening its doors on an unfamiliar corridor. Caroline took a cautious step out, wondering if this was another random software error caused by whatever Horace's little cabal had done to the central core.

Before she could read a corridor marking and determine where it was she'd ended up, Caroline heard someone shouting from down the corridor.

"Hold the lift. Hold the lift!" The voice was one she recognized instantly as the author of her quarters' newest decorations.

But what's he doing on C-Deck? And why run for an elevator when there are so many...

Caroline turned her head from side to side, but couldn't find a corridor marker anywhere. By the time Currano reached her, the doors were closing, so she stepped back inside to reset the sensor long enough for the cadet to join her in the car.

"What deck, Cadet?"

"Uh, yours, actually. Command. I was just coming to see you, and you said not to use the core if I didn't have to."

I did? Perhaps not in so many words, but given what you've already uncovered, it's a reasonable extrapolation.

"Well, here I am, Mr. Currano. What's on your mind?"

"I...uh, I mean, how are you feeling, ma'am? I...we...Illyana was wondering if..."

Caroline fixed him with a withering gaze, urging him with an arched eyebrow to get to the point.

"Right. Illyana always says I talk too much, but that's exactly what we have to do. Talk, that is."

Caroline sighed, wondering if extending patronage to a cadet this tongue-tied was the right decision after all.

No matter how talented he is, if he can't talk to me directly, he's no good to me in the larger scheme of things.

"We are talking, Cadet. Or rather, I'm trying to listen, but you aren't really saying anything. Should I call Cadet Tepes for the real story, or can you figure it out while you get us back to Command deck?" Caroline waved a hand at the control panel, which Currano attacked with rapid-fire tapping before speaking again, cheeks burning and eyes facing the elevator doors.

"I found the signal we were chasing in the debris field, ma'am. The one from that shuttle we thought was destroyed. I still don't know what's causing it, but while I was reviewing some of the file fragments in the core, I found a search subroutine specifically tasked to look for it. The signal that is, not the shuttle.

"The parameters looked familiar to me, so I ran it through a navigational program for verification. I just got the results, and it matches a pattern we were running a couple days ago, distributed...distributed by Mr. Calas, ma'am."

Bob Calas' search parameters. But those are for Valiant, *not...*

"Where is the signal coming from, Cadet?"

"That's the thing, ma'am. It's coming from Earth. Right in the middle of the North American Reclamation, to be precise, but I don't think anyone else can hear it. I only discovered it because I spliced a shard of black rock into a sensor array to boost a Fourier—"

"In Standard, Cadet. Not engineer." Caroline felt her spirits lift for the first time since her favorite gymnasium tried to murder her, and any more of Currano's technobabble would seriously kill her mood.

"It's moving, ma'm. Somewhat erratically, in fact, like it's running an evasion routine of some kind, or maybe the signal is bouncing around communications satellites in an attempt to hide itself. But I know where it is, and if you'll authorize a quick hop over to one of *Valiant*'s missile tenders for me and Illyana, I can use their drone rig to capture it. They're a lot slower than we are under tow, and they'll still in be range for another few minutes. But we have to move fast."

Caroline stabbed a finger at the control panel, bringing it to an abrupt halt. She then input her command override, sending the pair directly to Transfer Bay 7, where they'd left their shuttle after tractoring in Horace's mystery container.

"Call Illyana now, Kurt. I'll run preflight while you collect whatever gear you'll need."

Currano finally turned and looked her in the eyes, beaming youthful inspiration from every pore. Caroline allowed herself a smile, but as soon as the doors opened on the hangar deck, she was all business.

"Get moving. Your mystery signal could disappear at any time, and if you two don't bring me something to take to the captain, I'm going to be very disappointed in my favorite pair of cadets."

Currano was shouting into his wristcomm as he ran for the transfer bay, and Caroline couldn't help but laugh at the sight of him.

But the Iron Princess was back as well, and already working out how best to turn this to her advantage as she followed.

Let's see you wave this one away, Mr. Collins. Because this time, I'm not taking no for an answer.

JANTINE

JANTINE STARED AT THE SLEEPER UNIT AS CARLTON AND AN OMEGA fussed over its controls. It hadn't taken long to move their remaining supplies outside the shuttle—and the bulky machine back in.

A warm night breeze came in through the side of the shuttle and exited past her down the ramp. The image of Crassus sailing away into the open sky kept playing in her mind, and she was only half-listening to Mira speak.

"...should keep him conscious long enough to get far away from here, but I can't say for sure. I've used a technique on him that will handle most of the pain, while keeping him lucid. He's still going to die, but he can at least provide a distraction and help us get away."

From what Jantine understood Captain Martin's plan was a good one. And if Carlton said the captain was sound enough to pull it off, she believed him.

The bigger problem was what Carlton was doing right now. The choice to revive the Alpha was out of her hands entirely. Before discovering the distress signal she could delay it indefinitely, and maintain command of the mission. Now that there was no other option, she worried that the Omegas would be even harder to control.

The Omegas were getting easier to distinguish, just by the way they stood. One had its arms folded across its broad chest, glowering at the delay. The other was helping Carlton input the final wake-up commands, shoulders rounded and pointing at various readouts as they worked.

The team was back in their encounter suits, and Jantine had to admit she felt a bit more secure dressed for action. Artemus and Katra stood with weapons at the ready, watching the sky for attackers but still keeping an eye on the imperious Omega.

I'm not sure which bothers me more: a threat from above, or the one standing in front of us.

Knowing she could do nothing about either, Jantine turned her attention to the newest member of her team. Even with her faceplate open, the sight of the woman wearing the white hardsuit reminded her of all the humans she'd had to kill to get to this moment.

And also of the one she hadn't killed quite yet, hopefully the last casualty of their arrival in the home system.

"Mira, can I talk to Captain Martin?"

The human nodded, and Jantine detected a hint of sadness in the gesture.

"I think he'd like that, actually. He has a lot of respect for you, for what you were able to do aboard *Valiant*. As soon as Carlton and Jon*B* are finished, I'll take you up. By the way, were you ever going to tell me I was saying it wrong?"

Jantine smiled at the light rebuke. Mira was beginning to understand mod humor, though it was doubtful she'd ever grasp the full reasons behind JonB's obstinance and the others' response to it.

"I was certain you'd figure it out, eventually. Which one talked?"

"Carlton. I asked him what S-A-198 meant, and then it all fell into place. Are you really going to marry him? You have to know you have a choice in the matter."

Jantine shook her head. While any distraction from the Alpha's imminent awakening was welcome, this particular topic was not among her favorites.

"Whether I do or not, that's a matter for another time. And you mistake my meaning. I don't want to see your captain, I want to *talk* to him."

Jantine raised her right hand, tapping the side of her helmet with a finger. Mira's eyes widened, and Jantine felt the human's soft touch in her mind.

"You're getting better at that."

"Thanks. It's not easy, believe me. There's nothing in the Gamma playbook that covers this, and I'm not sure I can do what you want. It it doesn't work that way."

Jantine lowered her hand, and turned away from Mira.

Carlton pulled on a handle, gave it a half-turn, and pushed it back almost all the way. The Beta's expression was equal parts excitement and concern, and when he looked back at Jantine for approval the other Omega stepped forward to block his view.

"On board your ship I discovered that our main communication methods were vulnerable to interference. If we could harness your abilities tactically, it would give us an unparalleled advantage. Empathic Gammas are not combat trained, and you are. And we're not going to have a better chance to practice than now."

Jantine took a step to the side and nodded at Carlton, who pushed the handle home. The sleeper unit started shaking, and after a few seconds she could feel the vibration in her bones.

"Mira? Anything?"

"I'm sorry, Jantine. The words are there, but I can't make them work."

"It's not a problem. We'll revisit this later. For now, we'll just use your radio, and later I'll teach you how to use the scattercomms."

The bay became noticeably hotter, and despite herself Jantine couldn't take her attention away from the sleeper unit. What she was about to see was the most important event in the colonies, and she had only one chance to do this right.

A ring of lights strobed around the face of the unit, casting alternating shadows on the child within. Suspension fluid drained away from her face, and her pale skin almost glowed when the lights stopped moving. Then the duraglass cover unlocked, sliding back with a series of warning chimes and another set of flashing lights.

A cloud of scented steam escaped the chamber, and Jantine's breath caught in her throat. She had to see, had to know, and when Mira turned on her radio Jantine nearly jumped out of her skin.

"Captain? Can you hear me? Commander Jantine wants to speak with you."

"I can hear you, Harlan. Is she listening now?"

"Yes, sir. Jantine?"

There was an odd buzzing sound accompanying each of Captain Martin's words, as if the tension she was feeling was interfering with the transmission. It felt wrong to be talking right now, but the feathery comfort of Mira's mind that accompanied her words set her at ease.

"Commander?"

"Yes, I can hear you, Captain. I wanted to thank you for your sacrifice. You will be remembered well for this."

Carlton stepped up onto the sleeper unit, assisted by the less aggressive of the Omegas. Jantine moved forward herself, ducking under the orange arm that appeared in her way and very aware of the sound of five pulsers whining to life.

When she arrived at the base of the unit, "Carlton's" Omega offered her a broad hand while at the same time looking back over her shoulder.

Jantine floated off the floor up to Carlton's side. The Beta was removing sensor pads from the Alpha's skin, and staring at her face. Up close, she looked even more delicate, not at all like the shadowy figures who'd dictated the course of her life over viewscreens since her earliest memories.

S-A-198's hairless head was oval in shape, and absolutely symmetrical. From her wide forehead to her tiny, pointed chin, she was a miniature vision of perfection. Even her almost translucent skin was flawless.

The sound of Captain Martin's voice over the radio made her scowl momentarily. How dare he distract her from such beauty?

"Thank, you, Jantine, is it? But you have to know I'm not doing it for you. Despite what's happened, Harlan is one of my people, and she's the best chance we've got of getting your Alpha away from here and into the hands of those who can help."

Mira gasped: "Her mind, oh my God her mind!"

The Alpha's eyes snapped open, and the child's liquid brown eyes scanned both Jantine's face and Carlton's before fixating on the former.

Jantine was scared and alive and worried and delighted. Despite all her earlier concerns, she smiled, and her emotions doubled in intensity when the Alpha responded. The child's lips were plumping up, and her skin seemed to be thickening over her cheekbones.

The words were out of Jantine's mouth almost before she thought of what to say.

"I am JTN-B34256-O, commander of Expedition Force SS7. This is CRN-B34310-T. How do you want to be called, S-A-198?"

The sleeper unit gave one last chime, and fell silent. A broad pair of orange hands inserted themselves between Carlton and Jantine, who were both still entranced by the Alpha's delicate face. The Omega gently moved them aside, and S-A-198's tiny hands stretched feebly toward those of the hulking giant's. The Omega lifted her from the suspension chamber, and then stepped back with the child gently cradled in its arms.

To her surprise, Jantine saw that it was the angry Omega who'd come forward to claim the child, rather than the one who had helped Jantine and Carlton climb up. The Alpha's head flopped toward Jantine, and her skin took on a more healthy color as blue-green suspension fluid poured from her mouth and nose. The Omega's chest compressed, and a white mist came out of its mouth and flowed over S-A-198's face.

For several terrible seconds, Jantine thought the child was going to die, until her chest started to rise and fall in a regular rhythm.

"Commander, it's so wonderful. Her mind is like sunlight, and she's, she's..."

Jantine heard the buzzing sound again, but before she could ask what Mira meant one of the Alpha's arms came up, and beckoned her forward. In her haste to comply she almost stepped straight off the sleeper unit, but Carlton and the Omega were there to help her down. Jantine was dimly aware that Artemus, Katra and JonB were staring at her, but she only had eyes for the Alpha.

She took a tentative step forward, then another, until she was standing just half a meter from the Omega. The mod crouched down until S-A-198 was at eye-level, and the child opened her mouth to speak. Her voice was barely above a whisper, but the sound of it sent a thrill through Jantine's body.

"Serene. I am called Serene. Where is J-A-197?"

Before Jantine could answer, the shuttle's gravity drive powered up. Artemus and Katra were already halfway down the ramp, and Carlton and the Omega were hastily checking that the sleeper unit was fully secured. JonB was staring at the Alpha, but Jantine's swiveling head drew his attention away.

The face of the Omega holding Serene was also on a level with hers, and Jantine swore its small mouth twisted into a snarl. The orange giant spun around and pounded its way down the cargo ramp, and once she could no longer see Serene's eyes a deep sense of loss settled in her heart.

"Jantine!" Mira's shout brought her back to reality. "Captain Martin says we have hostiles inbound at three hundred kilometers Zulu and falling. It's now or never, Commander, let's go!"

Jantine looked down at her hand weapon, wondering when she'd drawn it. Looking up, she saw Mira using one hand to close her face-plate, and waving a weapon of her own in the other. A lifetime of training kicked in, and she gave the order to abandon ship.

"Move out, go, go, go!"

She was down the ramp in less than a second, pausing at the base while Carlton, the Omega, and JonB exited. When the civvies were all on solid ground, she ran after them to the pile of supplies several hundred meters away.

The shuttle's maneuvering thrusters fired, and it rose unsteadily on columns of twisting air. Jantine could see internal lights shining through the hastily patched hole in its side, and when the cargo ramp closed the shuttle spun around and accelerated into the night sky.

Die well, Captain Martin.

Jantine followed the shuttle's course with her eyes. She'd spent some time outside the shuttle earlier memorizing and admiring the visible stars. As a new one rose to join them, she saw several other shining points of light race toward it.

"He knows, Commander. The last thing I got from his mind was that he wishes he'd had more time with you, and with her."

Mira's words were like a punch in the stomach, and Jantine took several long seconds to consider her options. Not wanting to see the end result of Martin's last act, she turned to follow the rest of the team.

What she saw was another emotional hammer blow, and Mira sent her a wave of warm, if misplaced encouragement. Most of the other mods were racing away in pursuit of a tall jumpsuited figure holding a tinier one. Only JonB and Mira were waiting for her, and the enormity of her loss was staggering.

"No, Mira. It's just Jantine now. I'm not the Commander anymore."

Jantine moved past JonB, and the Beta reached out a hand to her shoulder. She batted it away, and felt a tinge of regret at his hurt expression. He likely meant no offense, but she was in no mood to be comforted, especially by him.

But Mira Harlan was not so easily dismissed. Her faceplate was transparent and illuminated from within, and Jantine saw the same expression on her face that she'd used earlier to chastise the Omega.

"Like hell you're not." Jantine didn't like Mira's commanding tone one bit. It wasn't that the human was in a position to use it on her, but that like JonB, she was right. "Assuming the Omega puts her down sometime soon, that little girl may well be the most wonderful thing that will ever set foot on this planet. But there's no way she could ever do the things you've done today, and the others will see that soon enough. You're their leader, damnit. Act like it."

JonB was carefully avoiding Jantine's personal space as he moved into a position where he could see both hers and Mira's faces at the same time. Jantine wanted to tell him she was sorry, but she knew he'd never look for or expect an apology from her.

"You don't understand, Mira. You can't. It's like I told you earlier, this is who we are. Alphas direct, Betas serve. Gammas support, but I think the three of us can admit that's not who or what you're becoming. And that uncertainty is what will save us in the end."

Jantine was confused by JonB's words, but then she realized what the civvie was working up to. The cold brilliance of his plan was astounding, and once again she was impressed with his analysis of the situation.

Perhaps you and I really are compatible after all.

MIRA

"Wha...What?"

Mira wasn't sure what JonB was saying, but his thoughts had the same rock-solid certainty he'd had when announcing how he'd spoofed the Geysers, and then again with his certainty of their children together.

He really believes whatever he has in mind is going to work, and she's on board without even hearing what it is.

"You're going to have to break it down for me. You two think a lot faster than I do, and I haven't got a clue as to what you're planning."

The three of them were alone now, and far enough away from the rest of the mods and their acute hearing for a bit of privacy.

"I told you before. You're not a Gamma, and you're certainly no Beta." Mira wanted to slap the smug smile off his perfect face, but the certainty of his thoughts made her more curious than angry.

"But you are definitely a mod now, and completely new variety at that. From what we understand, spontaneous expressions of the T-Virus among humans are exceedingly rare on your planet, and as a soldier—with your level of training—you are potentially more important than any Alpha. *Your* empathic abilities will revolutionize the order of battle, not to mention the advantages we'll have in dealing with outsiders. You, not S-A I mean, Serene, need to be our leader."

Mira searched JonB's thoughts for any trace of humor, but found none. Both he and Jantine were convinced that his ridiculous plan had merit, even though Mira couldn't for the life of her figure out why, or even when they'd come up with it.

Looks like it's time to be the grown-up in this relationship.

"Let me get this straight. A couple of hours ago, Jantine had a weapon trained on me. Not long after that, you, her super-genius fiancé, blithely announced that not only were *we* going to have sex, but that our children would be the stuff of legend. And now both of you are telling me that—oh, come on, really?

In another universe, the expression on Jantine's face would be priceless comedy. Her nod, her smile, and the pleasantly surprised look in her eyes would leave a tri-vid audience in tears. But Mira could see past the mask the Beta wore and into her soul, and Jantine wasn't offended by the idea in the slightest.

In fact, she approved.

"Excellent thinking, JonB. We must lock in her variant as quickly as possible. You are fertile, correct? When did you last ovulate?"

"I am not having this conversation. Not now, not ever."

To punctuate her feelings on the matter, Mira sent a wave of disapproval into both the Beta's minds, wincing as it created an answering spike of pain in her own.

"Fascinating. How long has she been doing that?"

"Since before we landed. It's remarkable, isn't it?"

Mira couldn't believe either her ears or whatever sense carried their emotions into the deep parts of her brain. Not only was JonB revisiting some of his more exotic fantasies, but Jantine had her own imagination in overdrive on the same topic. And all the while, the Betas were calmly discussing both Mira's mental abilities and over-throwing the political structure of the Outer Colonies.

"What is wrong with you two? First, neither of you is my type, and I've a mind to give you both a psychic cold shower. Second, haven't each of you told me that crossing the Omegas was the last thing you wanted to do? They'll never agree to this, and once they discover your plan, what then? Kill them?"

The confidence JonB and Jantine had been projecting vanished in an instant. The Betas each took half a step back, as if even standing next to her would incur the Builders' eternal wrath.

"I'm sorry, I'm sorry. I didn't mean that. But you have to agree this is a ridiculous proposition."

"What do you mean, you didn't mean that? Why would you say such a thing?"

Jantine's voice was a quivering whisper. JonB moved to her side, and this time she didn't push him away. It took Mira almost a minute to figure out why they were so frightened, and that in itself was another condemnation of Colonial society. The two of them were shut down so completely that Mira couldn't get into either of their minds to put them at ease.

The Gamma memories gave her clear examples of what happened to mods that went rogue, especially those who threatened revolution. And while JonB wasn't really advocating an overthrow, the distinction was fine enough that when she'd pressed the point what appeared as a logical plan to the Betas was completely undone by a simple exaggeration.

Can they really not know how to lie?

"It's just the way we talk here, " she continued. "No one wants to hurt the Builders—me especially. It's to prove a point, that's all. Everything's fine, really. I'm sorry. Please, I'm sorry. I just don't want you two to give up hope. Hope is all we have, in the end."

The platitudes seemed to be working, at least on Jantine. Her face regained its customary composure, but it was JonB who let his mental shields down first. Concern, uncertainty, and happiness were his immediate goals, and Mira was pleased to see that for once, his thoughts were directed outward.

"How will we do it?"

It was Mira's turn for shock. Whatever internal crisis it was that nearly shut her down, Jantine had made it through to the other side and was prepared to reclaim her position. Her words were spoken in a carefully neutral tone, and Jantine disengaged herself from her...

Just what am I supposed to call him now, intended? Betrothed? They seem to have made up their minds, at least about each other.

Whatever else JonB was to Jantine, he was still the hyper-intelligent civilian scientist whose advice was meant to support her decisions.

Or does that change too, now that Serene is awake?

"As I see it," he said, "were Jantine or I to act directly, the others would have no choice but to lock us down. But you, Mira, have no official status in Colonial society. If you were to demonstrate sound leadership, and appeared to have support from the Betas, the others might well assume that Serene blesses your actions as well."

Mira studied JonB's face, wondering how smart the boy really was. His plan wouldn't stand up to any intense scrutiny, but from what she knew Gammas and Deltas cared more about carrying out orders than questioning them. Katra wasn't her biggest fan, but Artemus had "adopted" her almost as completely as had JonB.

Hopefully, not for the same reasons. If this works, we can keep things together long enough to locate the institute, and possibly get us some help.

"Mira?"

Her name hung in the night air. Jantine's voice wasn't yet back to its normal confident tone, but her mind was. With the question came a sense of urgency, and with a little concentration Mira could feel Katra's eyes scanning the plains for them.

"The plan has holes. Big ones. But so did Captain Martin's, and I signed on for that with even less information. We'll need to recruit Carlton for sure—I'll leave that to one of you. I like him and all, but he doesn't trust me. And Katra ..." Mira looked in the direction where she'd last detected the Gamma's thoughts. "If we're going to do this, we'll need to figure out if I—we—really can use my abilities as a secure communication network."

Despite the collected wisdom of the Gamma memories telling her it was impossible, Mira opened her mind to the two Betas, letting their emotions mingle with her own. Oddly enough, despite the time she'd been working with Jantine, it was JonB's thoughts that were easier to decipher.

≈Oh, this feels wonderful! It's like holding hands, but without the hands.

What happens if we...≈

Mira regretted opening her mind to him almost instantly, but Jantine gave JonB a mental punch in the arm that pushed most of his thoughts of "experimenting" aside.

It would be a lot easier, though, if I didn't get all his thoughts at once. He really needs to...No. Not thinking about that. Definitely not...

Mira waved the Betas forward, taking point on a leisurely walk into friendly territory. Katra was indeed looking for them, and the pulser in the Gamma's hands was a chilling reminder of what could go wrong if any of them slipped up. She put on her best smile, and continued with their internal war council.

It was much harder for Mira to insert her thoughts into another mind than to decipher what they were thinking, and the pain it caused her was unlike anything she'd experienced before. To make it a bit easier, she imagined herself whispering the words directly into JonB and Jantine's ears.

≈One thing at a time, young man. And never, understand me? Not. Ever. I need you focused on keeping us alive, not your sexual fantasies.≈

≈If it would help, JonB and I could copulate tonight. It is perhaps too early for us, but it would seem natural to the others.≈

Mira wouldn't have believed Jantine was serious if she wasn't reading her mind. JonB was certainly interested in the plan, but before he could speak up Mira made another attempt to control the situation.

≈I don't think that's necessary, but thank you. I think. But we're going to have to spend tonight recruiting, not relaxing. Whatever you do, don't talk about your plan to make me your leader. Instead, talk about what good advice I've been giving you.≈

≈But that's not the plan...≈

JonB's words carried a mixture of doubt and annoyance, but as far as Mira could tell he was willing to "listen."

≈It is now. Hold up.≈

"Jantine. Is anything wrong?"

Katra's question was half challenge, half concern, and Mira felt more than a little panic at how suddenly the Gamma had appeared in front of them.

Katra's eyes had a cold, calculating look that left Mira no doubt as to her feelings.

Betas may not be comfortable with telling lies, but Gammas are, and do. This is going to be harder than I thought.

"No, Katra. Mira was telling us about life on Earth."

Smooth. You're learning. And you hardly flinched at all when she didn't call you Boss.

"JonB, Carlton has found some machinery on the other side of the hill. I will take you there."

Mira's blood went cold at Katra's report. There were reasons this part of North America was uninhabited, and although the chances of a pre-Reclamation war machine being intact and operational in a Kansas wheat field was slim, it did exist. But before she could explain her fear Jantine brought up another pressing matter.

"Good. The Omegas?"

Katra shrugged, indicating their location with her weapon. Mira knew where they were already; in her mind she could feel the cool summer's day of Serene's thoughts thirty meters to her left, and close at hand the swirling pools of doubt and adoration that were the Omegas. With her new eyes, she saw a soft glow behind some trees in the same general direction.

There was a shift in Jantine's mindset which Mira read as a sense of determination before she shut her emotions down completely. It was a habit that as an officer she understood, but her extra lifetimes of Gamma experiences found it rude and a bit selfish. Examining those memories brought her a new realization about the Outer Colonies, one she filed along with the other things that made her want to scream.

The Gamma facilitators aren't there to help, not really. They're the thought police, and none of the other mods realize it.

"What kind of machines?"

JonB made no attempt to hide his pleasure. As instructed, he'd returned his fantasies to "storage," and applied himself to the more pressing business of survival. Like Jantine, he only wanted what was best for the group.

Katra gave another shrug. The starlight favored her long lines, and

Mira's new eyes couldn't help but count the healed scars on the Gamma's encounter suit.

She's still hurting, but won't let me see it. Can't, and still remain herself. Out of all of them, Katra will definitely be the hardest sell.

"He did not say. There are several buildings, and some odd containers in the area."

JonB nodded, and made to move ahead before Jantine grabbed his arm. There was a brief flash of pleasure from him, then curiosity.

"Leave your pack, JonB. I need to do an inventory of our supplies. Whatever it is, Carlton's equipment will be enough."

After speaking, Jantine turned her eyes to Mira and formed a question in her mind. Despite the pain, Mira opened her mind again.

≈What is it, Commander?≈

≈Please relay to JonB: I don't think Mira's plan will work, but it has a better chance of success than yours. Start thinking of more alternatives. Do not attempt to initiate contact with me about any of this without approaching Mira first. Avoid scattercomms at all costs.≈

Mira thought about the few items in her own bag, mainly rations drawn from the shuttle and a few of Captain Martin's personal effects. Everything else she "owned" was affixed to the outside of her hardsuit.

Jantine took JonB's pack from him, then snapped her head to the side. There was a brief flash of alarm from her, then appreciation. Katra's eyes flicked in the same direction, then returned to stare at Mira.

Mira felt Artemus approach long before hearing the Delta. The ease at which the big mod moved through the trees was impressive, and she was curious at what had tipped Jantine off.

Artemus slid out of the shadows and approached the impromptu conference. For a change, his lower hands held several dead birds instead of weapons.

"Scout Katra. Scientist JonB. Lieutenant Commander Harlan."

The Delta paused. It was slight, but the confusion in his mind told Mira more than any words could. A second later, he completed his deliberation and addressed Jantine.

"Governor Jantine. I have set up a two kilometer perimeter line. Support Technician Carlton is very interested in his discovery, which he believes will allow us increased mobility."

Mira wasn't sure Jantine was comfortable with the new title, but sensed that she at least accepted it. Maybe it was because there wasn't really a colony for her to govern, but Artemus still wanted to follow her orders. And despite Serene's new status, Jantine was still the senior soldier present.

Well, that's somewhat debatable I guess, but I have even less interest in commanding these people than Katra does.

"What are those?"

Katra pointed her weapon at the dead birds.

"I believe these small animals may be edible. Lieutenant Commander Harlan, is this so?"

Mira remembered turkey hunts with her family as a child. Prairie chickens and pheasants weren't exactly the same, but she still knew how to clean and dress a bird. And since Artemus had apparently captured and killed them with his bare hands, when she was done there would be no annoying pellets to pick out of the final product.

"Yes, Artemus, thank you. I can show you how to prepare them if you wish."

Mira held out her hands for the birds, wondering if any of the mods had ever hunted before. Thankful he hadn't brought back a deer, she smiled and accepted them.

"I would appreciate that, but another time. There is still work to do to establish our camp."

"Artemus," said Jantine, "take JonB to Carlton. I will continue your patrol."

Artemus looked between Jantine and Katra, who gave him a small nod. Despite her efforts at control, Mira felt Jantine's annoyance spike, but the Beta didn't let it reach her face. It faded quickly, though, and the three Colonial soldiers split off in different directions, with JonB trailing after Artemus.

Mira called out to them while they were still all in hearing range. "JonB—all of you, really—please be careful with any machinery you find. Try to avoid activating anything without knowing what it does, and if you feel threatened, run. And if you can find a transport of some kind, remember that it has to be large enough to carry the Omegas."

"Of course. How long will it take to prepare the small animals? I wish to eat them as soon as possible."

"JonB, this is not our priority. There are enough ration packs for all of us."

One benefit to her new mental abilities was that Mira could "hear" the Betas bickering as they walked away, and knew they were doing so more out of habit than annoyance. Something had happened between the two of them while comforting one another, and despite the stress her earlier comments had caused Mira was happy they were getting along better. During their first encounter on the shuttle, Mira wasn't entirely sure Jantine wasn't going to shoot him.

She felt them move out of range, noting the distance. In time, she might be able to extend her abilities, but for now a two hundred meter radius seemed to be a hard limit.

"Do not get comfortable here, human. You are tolerated, nothing more. You are not one of us."

Katra's words matched her thoughts, both equally uncompromising. Mira had thought Jantine's mind inflexible at first, but Katra's was etched in stone. It wasn't hard to reconcile the sight of the warrior in front of her with the image of the Gamma fighting to breathe while she was bleeding out on the deck. Katra would never stop fighting until she was dead, and would kill anyone who threatened her comrades.

A group that, as I am continually reminded, does not include me.

Mira shrugged, and held up the birds.

"Does this mean you don't want dinner? I think I saw some lemongrass earlier. Should be able to get something ready in about an hour."

Katra grunted, narrowing her eyes slightly. Though she didn't have Jantine's level of control, the Gamma's emotions were still difficult to isolate. Her anger was easy enough, but there was enough curiosity to give Mira some hope that Katra might eventually accept her.

That, or she's waiting until I finish cooking to kill me.

"It's fairly easy, once you know how. I remember my first time, though. Even though I wanted to be treated the same as my brothers, when Daddy handed me the bird, I didn't understand what he wanted me to do with it. Once he showed me, I was sure I'd never be hungry again."

Mira filled the short distance to the mods' temporary camp describing her brothers' faces when she finally tried to clean the bird. As she talked, Katra's interest grew, and Mira was very pleased to feel the barrier between them coming down.

You're all so good at making hard choices, but not so much at making friends.

Her earlier assessment of the Omega's positions was correct. "Happy" was sitting near the small pile of supplies that had survived the damaged shuttle, while "Grumpy" was acting as a pillow for Serene. Mira felt the Alpha's attention on her as soon as she entered the small clearing, as well as flares of recognition from both the Omegas.

As before, Happy was relieved to be in her presence, and the mod's need for companionship was as powerful as ever. But Grumpy was a different matter entirely. He made no attempt to communicate with her, though Mira thought she could sense activity on that level in his mind.

Serene looked up into the Omega's face and smiled. Of all the mods Mira had seen so far, the child's face was the most alien. Shadows from a salvaged emergency light made her strange face seem even longer, and in the dim illumination her big brown eyes appeared nearly black. Grumpy certainly had no qualms about them, and from the way he was looking at Serene, Mira was certain she wasn't the only one in the clearing who could talk to the Omegas.

Oh, dear.

A snippet of Doria's conversation with Malik rose from her borrowed memories. She'd mentioned to him how few empaths there were in the Outer Colonies, mainly because only a handful were necessary depending on the size of a community. But Mira was starting to think there might be a different reason, and wasn't sure of the best way to ask Happy about the capabilities of a mature Alpha.

At her side, Mira felt Katra's defenses soften, and tasted love and devotion aimed at the strange child. Mira felt a touch of embarrassment for the abrupt way in which she'd ended her story, but the Gamma didn't seem to care. This "softer side" of Katra seemed somehow appropriate, and Mira had to admit that it would be nice to love someone that much someday.

Just as long as it's not JonB. Trouble, trouble, trouble, that one.

Katra finally noticed the lull in conversation, and Mira sensed she was about to ask a question. One she'd been working up to for a while now, from the feel of it.

"This family you speak of. Father. Brothers. Uncles. Where are they now? Were they aboard the ship, the *Valiant*?"

Mira wasn't sure which question Katra was more interested in knowing the answer to, so she settled on the easy one.

"No. It's been a few years since I've seen them in person, but they are here, on Earth. There are Harlans spread out all over the place, actually, but most of our kin are still here in North America."

Katra nodded, and Mira thought she detected a bit of sadness behind her eyes.

"These words are old ones for us. Families. Kin. In the first days of a colony, they are necessary until the crèches are set up."

"And how does that make you feel, Katra?" Mira couldn't believe she'd used the clichéd words of a psychoanalyst, but they seemed appropriate to the moment.

Katra was silent for almost a minute, still looking at Serene lying back against Grumpy's legs. Happy repeated his request for communication, but Mira felt there was something here she should know, something important. She opened her mind to him, noting how much easier it was to do than sharing herself with the Betas.

≈I need to speak with Katra now. Can you find me some water, and something to cook with? I promise, we'll talk soon.≈

Mira did her best to imagine her mother's tall-sided stew pot, and also sent along the image of carrots and potatoes in the vain hope that there might be something similar in the pile of supplies. Happy sent a feeling of understanding, just as Katra's mind let go of the sadness she'd been holding back.

"Jarl is dead, human. There will be no family for me. And unless the Betas can find the sleepers, there are no more Gammas within a thousand light years."

The pain in Katra's voice was unbearable, and Mira wanted to pull her into a hug and never let her go. But two things stopped her. One, she was still wearing her strength-enhancing hardsuit, and Katra might well interpret the gesture as an attack.

And secondly, Katra wasn't through speaking yet, and her sadness shifted into cold anger.

"So to answer your question, I do not have time for feelings. I must protect those of us who still live. I do not think you are my enemy, but I do not wish to go to Harrison Institute. And if your presence here threatens Serene, I will kill you."

As the Gamma stalked away, Mira tried to remember waking up with only one person in her head. Of just being Lieutenant Harlan, who was a lot more like the woman walking away than either of them would ever admit.

She's right: I don't belong here. But right this moment I don't belong anywhere else either, and until we figure out who I really am, this will have to do.

Mira heard a crashing sound, and her induction pistol was out before she had time to process the sight of Happy holding up a large metal container in one hand, and several brown things in the other. Her smile was something she didn't have to hold back, and she sent it to the Omega along with her thanks.

Wondering what she was going to use for firewood, Mira set the birds down and began taking off her hardsuit. If they were going to be here for a while, someone else could stand guard.

Besides, it's like Daddy said: "Grab hold, little girl; bird's not going to skin itself."

ALOYSIUS

2220 SHIPTIME, SHUTTLE EFSC-II

As SUICIDE MISSIONS GO, thought Captain Aloysius Martin, former commander of SDF *Valiant*, former double agent, and current Colonial collaborator, *this one can end any time now.*

There was only so much more he could do with a damaged shuttle and a dying pilot, and he'd been flying the mission long enough now to have forgotten not only exactly where he'd started from, but what in the worlds his mission was.

Have to keep moving. Can't disappoint what was her name again? I had it just a minute ago before before...

The shuttle rocked from a portside impact, and Aloysius spun along its primary axis to foil any follow up shots. Proximity and collision alerts were blaring all around the flight deck, but Aloysius paid them no heed, executing a four second burn from both the shuttle's main engine and the port maneuvering thrusters that exhausted most of his remaining fuel and kicked him into a slightly higher, north-south polar orbit.

I always liked Argentina. Maybe they'll bury me there when this thing finally crashes.

Something rocketed past the shuttle on an attack vector along his former course, and Aloysius remembered with a smile what had changed about his mission.

Drones. Never saw the point of them, really. All those fancy communications linkups and predictive algorithms. Why, all you have to do is—

Aloysius fired his braking and maneuvering thrusters hard enough to stand the shuttle on its nose, spilling more of the improvised chaff whatshisname had spread throughout the shuttle's corridors out the hole in the cargo section. A pair of not-so-smart drones lost their targeting locks and exploded in his wake, and Aloysius smiled at the brilliant flash of golden light marking their demise.

He's a nice kid, that whatshisname. All of them are, especially nope, lost it again. Hope I remember before I run out of air.

The young man with the nice smile had sealed Aloysius in the flight deck hours ago, with as much oxygen as they could cram into the walls to keep him going. But it was running out now, and Aloysius didn't have all that much time left either. He checked his board for how much propellent remained, noting that the forward, port, and aft jets were completely dry, and that there was just under 8% in the primary fuel cells.

What was it he'd said? Something about "spoofing pursuit" on their way down to where they were going. Sounds like fun. Wish I could remember it.

Wish I could remember a lot of things, really.

Starboard maneuvering thrusters were still at 50%, so Aloysius gave them little nudge. The burn was supposed to last half a second, but a violent, hacking cough pulled his hand away from the holo-control, and by the time his vision cleared, the shuttle was floating free with an empty board, and fresh globules of blood were hovering around his mouth and beard.

Well, it was fun while it lasted. Time to hit the primary target.

What was that again? There was something about a button, I think.

Aloysius blinked several times to clear his vision, but the shuttle kept on spinning anyway. Earth moved left to right across his forward windows every few seconds, a bright, beautiful beacon he wanted to reach out and touch. Extending his right hand to do so, he saw something written on his sleeve in yellow Elac, which his mind translated back into standard as he brought it closer to his face.

Push the Red Button.

Well, that seems simple enough. Let's do that, shall we?

Aloysius scanned the board for a Red Button to Push, finding one a few seconds later just past the fuel gauges in the center of the panel. He pushed it, and a second later a new holo filled the entire panel, showing an older man with a close-cropped beard strapped into a chair.

"Hello, Aloysius," the man said. "I thought you might like a reminder of what's at stake here."

Thanks, mister. Who are you again?

"I'm you, of course. The old you, not the hero you've become. I don't know how much you'll remember by the time this holo plays, but whatever mental whammy Harlan put on me to keep my brain working is supposed to wear off in a couple hours, right about the time your oxygen runs out. So I wanted to say goodbye while I still could, and thank you for what I've done.

"There's some very special people down there on that planet, Aloysius. People who are counting on you to draw away pursuit and buy them some time to escape. One of them I can't even describe how important she is, but I've risked everything—my career, my friends, and now my life—to keep her safe.

"But more important than that, there's bad people chasing her, one very bad man in particular who simply cannot be allowed to find her. Which is why we've programmed this shuttle to home in on the nearest Reclamation communications satellite, and destroy it.

"Janbi calculates that overloading the shuttle's grav drive on impact will simulate the effect of a massive solar flare, and since he's far and away the smartest person I've ever met, I think there's a fair chance he knows what he's talking about.

"I wish we had more time with the gennies. I wish we'd met them under better circumstances, and could introduce them to the world as the brave pioneers they really are. But wishes don't end wars.

"Heroes do. So this is goodbye, old friend. Goodbye, and thank you."

The holo started again, but Aloysius had already fallen asleep, slumped forward in his acceleration harness with a thin line of blood undulating away from his mouth. He didn't wake up when the satellite's automated defenses began firing at his shuttle and its drone escorts, nor when the shuttle's explosion lit up the night sky for hundreds of kilometers in every direction.

"...oodbye, old fri—"

JON-B34726-S

JON-B34726-S STUDIED THE GROUND IN FRONT OF HIM, MEMORIZING THE path ARS-D59007-C was taking. The Delta would have already selected a route free of obstacles, and it made sense for him to benefit from that experience.

JTN-B34256-O's last words to him were troubling, as they represented a definite change in their working relationship.

"Be careful."

Even in the middle of the battle aboard *Valiant*, she had maintained a certain distance. But now that S-A-198—Serene—was awake, JTN-B34256-O's attitude toward him had definitely shifted, and he wasn't at all sure it was for the better.

"It is just ahead, Scientist JonB."

JON-B34726-S set his mouth in a tight smile. The other mods had been corrupting his name for nineteen days, two hours and five minutes now, and it still rankled. At least the Delta had the excuse that he was following orders, but the others were laughing at him every time they did it. Even Mira Harlan's mistaken pronunciation of "Janbi" was preferable, but since she'd shifted to the form the others were using, someone must have told her.

There are some things that should not change. We must be better than the humans, not the same. Isn't that the point of this mission?

"Are you experiencing discomfort, Scientist JonB?"

"No, it's all right, Artemus. I'm fine. What can you tell me about Carlton's discovery?"

Instead of answering, the Delta pointed through a gap in the trees with a lower hand. Just down a small hill was a landscape completely different from the grasslands. The ground itself was a different color: gray spotted with black instead of rich brown soil.

There were several buildings, one of which glowed from within. The area between was covered with long bars of metal, either laid down in lines on the ground or stacked in rusting piles. There were large, rectangular boxes made of metal as well, some lying flat on their sides and others with wheels attached to their bases and fitted onto the metal bars.

Even in its dilapidated state, this was the first sign of civilization he'd seen on Earth, and JON-B34726-S wondered how he'd missed it while they were descending from orbit.

I must have been distracted by all the screaming. But if this is an indication of their society, how did they ever launch a ship like Valiant?

Mira Harlan said she was from this planet, and seemed familiar with this continent in particular. She would know what this was, but Carlton had been here for some time already, and would likely have a more scientific explanation for what he was seeing.

Increased mobility? From this collection of rusted garbage?

"I see. Is it safe to go down there?"

"There is a substantial amount of hydrocarbon residue on the ground and most surfaces, but limited exposure will not be hazardous. I recommend you maintain suit integrity at all times."

"Understood, thank you."

A crumbling dirt path led down the hillside, one which JON-B34726-S suspected was not made by human feet. Artemus descended rapidly, kicking up dust and rocks as he went. The Delta then did a quick spin, checking for enemies at the base before lifting a top hand and motioning for JON-B34726-S to follow.

Let's see...it's about fifteen meters down, angle of almost fifty degrees. If I fall, I likely won't live long, but he would have carried me down if he thought I couldn't make it.

Trusting the Delta's earlier pledge of protection, he checked his helmet seals and placed a suited foot on the path. Easing himself onto the slope, JON-B34726-S saw several ledges along the path, and their irregular shapes suggested buried roots or rock outcroppings.

Well, if it will hold his weight…

JON-B34726-S took a moment to calculate the smallest number of jumps he could make to reach the bottom. Given his size and conditioning, he didn't trust himself to slide the entire length. But at the same time he was a Beta, and took pride in his capabilities. Satisfied he'd chosen the optimum path, JON-B34726-S skipped down the hill in four uneven jumps, timing the last so that he landed right behind the Delta.

As soon as he reached the bottom, Artemus started moving toward the lit structure. JON-B34726-S followed, searching the area for possible signs of more advanced technology.

The metal bars he'd spotted from the top of the hill were of various compositions, and up close he could see that most of those on the ground were in better condition. There was a faint odor in the air he could not place—it reminded him of pre-exile artifacts he'd handled as a child.

Tires, if memory serves.

There was nothing resembling the textured black fragments he remembered, but he did notice more of the metal bars, including some arranged in a line leading into the illuminated building. JON-B34726-S kneeled down near the entrance, taking advantage of the extra light to conduct a closer examination.

The bars were spaced approximately 1.4 meters apart, and set into a slabs of hard stone. JON-B34726-S ran his hand along both the metal and stone, and found the latter to be a composite material of some kind.

I remember this from the museum as well. They made buildings out of something like this in the early years of Colony C. Crushed stone mixed with a binding agent. This site could be centuries old!

JON-B34726-S stood, and looked back over the metal-filled plain. From ground level, he couldn't see the other end, but the line of bars and stones ran roughly a kilometer from where he stood, intersecting with multiple smaller angled sections of bars. When nothing else triggered a recollection, he turned and followed Artemus into the structure.

The interior was reminiscent of the launch bay of the *Valiant*, with dozens of scaffolds, machines and work spaces. The tire smell was much stronger here, and several of the machines were surrounded by piles of black dust.

There was dust everywhere, in fact. Unlike the Earth vessel, these machines appeared abandoned and incomplete. Carlton had cleaned an area next to the largest of the machines.

The Beta was examining large wheels on the side of the machine when he noticed JON-B34726-S and Artemus enter. He had unpacked most of the gear they'd salvaged from the *Valiant*, including several of the power generators, with which he'd also installed work lights on either side of the big machine.

"JonB, come look at this!"

Whatever it was, was certainly impressive. It was tall, multi-colored, and had handles and steps leading into an enclosed section at the far end.

JON-B34726-S walked the length of the building, marveling at both its new and old aspects. There were no comparable structures in the colonies; so much refined metal would have been re-purposed long before it could reach this state. Massive tools meant for human-sized workers were everywhere, and behind glass panels mounted on the wall he could see where Carlton had used his hands to reveal fading images. Not all the panels were intact, and like the large object many were coated with some brightly-colored pigments.

"What is it, Carlton?"

"It's an engine of some kind. They maintained it here, but look at this."

Carlton came forward and showed him a handheld. The image displayed was a scan of one of the glass panels, depicting a machine very like this one attached to a long line of containers, also on wheels.

"It's part of a transport system."

"Yes! And according to this," Carlton exchanged the image for another, displaying a series of lines drawn across the continent, "there's an interconnected network of these things all over this region. I think if we can get this one operational, perhaps some of the others as well, we can use them to get to Chicago and the institute."

JON-B34726-S nodded, appraising the condition of the machine. He walked around it, noting that though it was covered in dust, from the outside the engine appeared intact. He pulled himself up a ladder into the enclosed area and used a hand lamp to examine the control surfaces. After memorizing the positions of the machine's controls, JON-B34726-S joined Carlton in examining its underside. The engine's wheels each had a flange which rested snugly against the inner surface of the metal bars, with a large gear assembly joining each wheel to its duplicate on the other side.

Most of the bare surfaces on the machine were covered with an oily residue, and exhibited none of the oxidation he'd seen on the metal outside. Reaching up and drawing a finger down a dust-caked panel, the resultant smear indicated the same coating had been applied to the entire machine, most likely as a preservative.

In fact, everything inside the structure appeared to be in very good shape, as opposed to the crumbling and rust-laden containers outside.

JON-B34726-S considered the implications of everything he'd seen so far, and as a scientist the condition of the machine was encouraging. But Carlton was a support technician, and though his knowledge of contemporary equipment was extensive, he was no theorist.

"Carlton, what makes you so sure this machine can be restored? It may have been inactive for some time, perhaps centuries."

Carlton smiled, and moved over to the salvaged equipment. But instead of selecting something from the pile, he leaned down and picked something thick and rectangular up from the floor. "Is that…?" JON-B34726-S couldn't complete the question. Such things hadn't existed in the colonies for centuries.

"Yes! It's a book! And it's not the only one I found."

Carlton nodded over his shoulder to a metal cabinet. His smile was bigger than ever, and JON-B34726-S couldn't help but share it. Carlton deposited the book on a workbench. Leaning in, JON-B34726-S saw that an image of the same machine that rested behind them was visible on the cover.

With the proper reverence due such an ancient treasure, JON-B34726-S moved forward and opened the book. The pages were thin leaves of plastic bound together by heavy plastic rings, and the script was a bit hard to read at first. But after tracing the lines of text on a few pages with his finger, he came to a diagram showing the wheel and gear assembly he'd just been looking at.

The letters above the diagram were much larger, and as he scrutinized each one the meaning of the text below it became clear.

Ex 1450: Asynchronous traction motor and distributed power couplings.

Adjust the resting generator's main power output until all connected cars register a base charge of 1200v. Maintain output for a minimum of one hour to calibrate drive stems, then increase voltage until initial motion begins.

JON-B34726-S closed the book, resting his hand on the monochrome image of the machine on the cover. He looked at the open cabinet, noting crumpled sections of the door panels approximately the same size as a Delta's hands. He began tapping his fingers on the book, and looked over at the power generators they'd seized from the dead repair crews aboard the *Valiant*.

Yes, it should work. Assuming the bar path is still intact, of course, and we can find something big enough to hold us all...

"Scan it. Scan all of them, just in case. Make sure we've got a complete set of operation and maintenance instructions."

JON-B34726-S smiled. It wasn't ideal, but finding the engine was a promising development that gave the mods something they hadn't had before.

Hope. It looks like Mira Harlan may have had the right idea after all.

Thinking of the Earth woman made him remember his other objective for the evening. And a few long term personal goals, but as far as he knew Carlton couldn't help him with those.

"Carlton?"

"Yes, JonB?"

"Mira wants us to make sure and select containers in which the Omegas can rest comfortably. I'm not sure she knew something like this was here, but so far I have found her counsel to be remarkably insightful. Wouldn't you agree ?"

MIRA

MIRA HUMMED TO HERSELF, KEEPING THE IMAGE OF HER MOTHER WEARING her favorite apron in the kitchen at the front of her mind. Whatever alien root vegetable Happy had given her was surprisingly fragrant, and as she peeled the last one she could almost hear her mother's pleasant drawl.

You have to be happy when you cook, Mirabelle. What you're doing keeps people alive, and people can't live on sadness. Put a little heart into every-thing you do, and there ain't nothin' or no one can give you troubles 'less you ask for it.

Annamarie Weston-Harlan was forty-three years old when she died, the mother of four sons and one precocious teenage daughter. The loss of her eldest boy put lines on her face that betrayed just how sick she was, but Mira remembered her mother best like this. Happy, alive, and full of down-home joy.

She worked the knife across the whatever it was by the light of a bed of coals, scraping off the skin with quick, sure motions. Seconds later it was cubed and into the pot, joining the others alongside some crushed lemongrass, salt, and a can of evaporated milk drawn from the shuttle's stores. The smell of the improvised sauce was heaven, and she turned her attention to the birds.

The Gamma memories were devoid of tasks like this, and she

enjoyed the feeling of being her own woman again. To do something with her hands, with no other lives offering suggestions as to how to do it better, made her feel—for lack of a better word—human. Happy sat nearby, watching her cook in an eerie echo of Mira's own kitchen education. The Omega was basking in the happy glow she projected, drinking in the rich emotions thoughts of her mother always summoned up. It was another area untouched by the Gamma memories, and Mira was determined to keep it that way.

Taking up one of the birds, Mira was keenly aware of Serene's attention, as well as Katra lurking in the trees. The Alpha child was sitting up on her own now, staring at her from across the clearing. She was wearing one of Marcus Callaway's uniform blouses as a belted dress, and in addition to foodstuffs, Mira was glad she'd had the foresight to take as many of the absent pilot's clothes as she could fit into a duty bag.

She didn't quite know what she was supposed to feel about Marcus. Their relationship was really only beginning, and may have been purely physical. But the smiling pilot's embrace was another memory that the Gammas couldn't touch, and one more thing the mods had taken from her.

I'll need to be more like Jantine in this regard. His loss is something I'll have to deal with, just like the deaths of the rest of my crew. But until we can find some help, there's nothing I can do about it.

The sleeves were far too long for Serene's small arms, so Mira had done a quick bit of combat tailoring and cut them off at the elbow while Happy was collecting cooking supplies. Other than her first words to Jantine, Serene had yet to speak aloud, but Mira could feel her mind working behind those large, expressive eyes.

Mira had to admit to curiosity about what the Alpha was thinking, but the one time she'd attempted contact she slammed up against a mental barrier much stronger than the one Jantine maintained. The resulting headache was almost as bad as her first minutes as an empath, and Mira resolved to wait until Serene was ready to talk.

Plus, it's hard not to notice Grumpy crouching behind her, broadcasting a silent challenge to the universe: "Mine!"

Mira ignored the pair as best she could, focusing instead on the meal she was preparing. If Artemus had come back with turkeys, she'd have plucked and filleted the birds for grilling by now and called everyone for dinner. The process wasn't onerous, but even given how tired she was and the lack of both time and spices, she was thankful for the chance to improvise with these smaller birds.

Conscious of her audience, Mira stood up, positioned the first of the birds on the ground, and got to work. With pheasants there was less usable meat, so there was no need to spend a lot of time worrying it off the carcass. She spread the wings and placed her feet on either side of the breast, grabbed the feet together, and gave an exploratory tug. She felt the wing under her left foot shift slightly, so she placed a little more weight on that side, bent her knees, and pulled.

The bird separated cleanly, with the backbone and entrails coming with the half still in her hands. She set it aside, savoring the surprise in her spectators' minds at how fast it had transformed from a recognizable animal shape into a collection of parts. Katra's attention was completely focused on Mira's actions, and Happy was equally rapt as she cut away the wings to expose the bird's breast meat.

Thirty seconds later Mira had it washed and sliced into finger-sized pieces, and then dropped them into the sauce. She repeated the cleaning process on the other two birds, this time setting the breasts aside for grilling. She almost asked Katra to come over and pull the last bird apart; her desire to do so was at the front of her mind and easy to read. Despite herself, the Gamma was impressed with Mira's skill, and Mira chalked the positive thoughts up as a point in her favor.

Looks like I can do something right after all.

The otherwise capable Gamma was completely out of her element here in the most boring part of North America. Katra's hyper-vigilance was getting a hefty workout from crickets, night owls, and other small animals sharing the tree line with them, each encounter adding another sound or motion to her list of "things that won't kill us, yet."

It was odd to think of a trained assassin as a "city girl," but the label fit Katra better than anyone Mira had ever met. Jantine tried to hide it when she thought about the Gamma, but every time the two mods met, Jantine was thinking of ways to get Katra to both relax and think outside the box.

For her own part, Mira was glad Katra was the way she was. Like herself, Katra was a training officer, and the secret to earning her respect was to demonstrate competence. Plus, despite her overt hostility, Katra was always curious about the world around her, and that constant need for information gave Mira something to work with.

An owl took flight, and Mira sensed Katra's pleasure when she recognized and accepted the sound of its wings as a non-threat.

At least you didn't shoot at it this time. Before we leave here, the squirrel and field mouse populations will have even better stories to tell than Jantine's ant.

Happy noted it as well, but for the most part both Omegas ignored the sounds of the night. Mira knew their hearing range was far wider than even what her suit's pickups could detect; with four ears and a much larger brains, it pretty much had to be. But in general, the Omegas seemed immune to the trivia of normal existence, focusing instead on their projects and philosophies.

Builder is a good name for you two. Everything you do adds to the world, and you like making long-term plans.

As if sensing her interest, Happy's thoughts shifted into a pattern Mira recognized as "I want to talk to you." She nodded, fitting the breasts onto a wire frame suspended over the coals by the gauntlets of her hardsuit. She wasn't sure what the frame's intended use was, but the Omega brought it to her with a sense of satisfaction as she was setting up her improvised kitchen, and Katra hadn't objected.

Sitting back on her heels, Mira opened her mind to the Omega while the food cooked. She let her mother's smile fade back into memory, and let the "others" rise to the surface. The hurricane inside her head was getting easier to tame over time, but Mira had doubts she'd ever come to accept the Gamma memories as her own.

≈*I am here with you. I am listening.*≈

Happy's thoughts were chaotic at first, until the Gamma memories took over and she was able to assign meaning to the concepts he was sharing. She felt ethereal fingers roaming around her thoughts, and an image of the Omega standing in a white room inside a glass case came to mind.

With the aid of those same memories, Mira partitioned herself, leaving enough awareness in her own body to keep an eye on the meal she was preparing. Across the camp, starlight and shadows framed Serene's odd face, who was still looking in her direction.

In the Omega's mind, his self-image was reduced in size until he was just over two meters tall. Mira found herself standing just on the other side of the glass, looking into his eyes. A wave of sadness poured into her, and she felt several other presences nearby.

Several meters away, Grumpy and Serene were sitting cross-legged on the floor. The other Omega was also reduced in size to a near-match for Serene's small form. Mira's mental eyes widened when the pair began playing patty-cake, and while neither spoke she recognized the memory as one of herself and Deb as little girls in a sandbox.

With her own mind now supplying the scenery, the white room faded into green trees and a summer's day. Happy remained in the case, looking out at the other mods with his hands pressed up against the glass and still radiating sadness. Mira was at the side of the case now, and imagined it expanding out to enclose her.

Inside, the sadness was much more intense, and she shared Happy's feeling of isolation.

≈*You're wrong, though. It doesn't have to be this way.*≈

Mira put her own hands on the glass, and a third child approached the pair as they played. At first it had little Debbi's face, then the image shifted into a young Mira, and finally a small Happy. The combined child sat down and the sandbox melted away, replaced by a sidewalk covered in chalk drawings. When small Happy started bouncing a red rubber ball, Grumpy and Serene turned and smiled at him, the latter pulling a handful of jacks from a shirt pocket and scattering them on the ground.

≈*Go to them. I'm sure they won't mind the company.*≈

Happy shook his head, pressing even harder on the glass. Grumpy and Serene continued playing with the jacks, passing the ball between them and ignoring the other child. The young Happy stood up and started to blur around the edges. It faded from view, and then a group of adult Omegas walked into the scene.

The newcomers came up to the seated pair one by one, and Serene looked up into each of their faces and smiled. The Omegas started sitting down in circles around them, and no matter how many orange faces approached, Serene greeted each one with warmth and affection. All except for the last one, a stoop-shouldered, elderly version of Happy to whom Serene gave no greeting at all.

≈*Now that's not fair. Everything is new to her; you just have to give it time. Here, let me show you.*≈

Mira imagined a handle on the glass, and opened the door to lead Happy out and into the main hall of the Academy. Bright-faced cadets filed all around them, and Mira remembered and shared the pain and isolation she'd felt her first weeks there before she'd met Marya.

Dream Mira was thin and gangly and everything she'd tried so hard not to be over the last decade. The young girl raised her hand to wave before being carried away in the press of bodies, and Mira painted a few of the faces orange for effect before letting the scene focus on her father, standing proud and tall in his uniform as he waved goodbye to his only daughter.

Brian's death had hurt him too, but instead of wasting away like Momma, he'd buried himself in duty until one day it was all he had. Four years later, his remaining children were grown and living their own lives, his wife was dead, and he took his own life. Mira and Happy stood by his casket as Shrikes thundered overhead, accepting a folded flag with numb fingers and saluting then-Captain Maranova with tears in their eyes.

≈*But it didn't have to be that way. He could have asked for help, told people how much he was hurting. I did, and so did the boys. We got through it together, and so will you.*≈

Mira's brothers raised their glasses and cheered as Happy went to fetch another round of drinks. When he came back, she pulled him into a hug, letting the joy she felt being part of a family soak into him and force out all the unhappy thoughts. Her brothers joined the embrace, which then turned into a laughing wrestling match that came to rest next to the campfire.

Mira turned the improvised basket over, and gave the pot a quick stir. Katra had moved on, but she could feel Artemus and Jantine coming closer from opposite sides of the camp.

≈*You have a family too, a good one. I'm the one looking for a place at the table.*≈

The Omega sent her another image of the cemetery, but this time it was Mira handing the flag to Happy, as they stood next to five graves of assorted sizes.

Mira countered by envisioning a sunrise, distracting Happy until Carlton came up to lead him away. She tugged on his memories of plans for the Earth colony, highlighting all the places where he and Grumpy had indicated other hands doing the work.

Mira realized she'd taken the analogy too far when Happy's memory of sealing the sleepers into their container came to the fore, and with it an even greater sense of loss. She was unceremoniously dumped out of his mind, and the sudden disconnect left her unprepared when Serene's consciousness brushed up against hers.

If joining with Happy was like navigating a choppy sea at night, Serene's mind was being caught in a hurricane on a small raft. Instead of a feathery touch, Mira felt sharp claws digging into her brain, searching for answers and casting aside anything that didn't relate to life in the Outer Colonies.

≈*Slow down, you're hurting me!*≈

If the Alpha heard her mental cry, she gave no sign of it. The onslaught continued, starting with Doria's memories of the mission briefings and then focusing on Colony B and the mods that lived there. Feeling herself slip away, Mira imagined a tall pillar of stone, and chained a mental image of herself to its base. The pain lessened, but the rummaging continued unabated.

Though she was terrified, Mira sensed something familiar about the way her mind was being peeled back. It was almost the reverse of the process Happy had used to give her the Gamma memories, and true architect of her situation was revealed.

She's got help, and Grumpy likes me even less than Katra does.

Not knowing what else to do, Mira imagined an ear-splitting emergency klaxon, and sent out a mental mayday with all the strength she had left. She felt Jantine, Katra, and Artemus respond to her call for help, but it was Happy who got to her first.

Mira felt a broad hand slide under her shoulder blades, and the hurricane was gone. But Serene's mental talons were still ripping away the parts of her life attached to the Gamma memories, and Happy had even less of an idea of how to stop her than Mira did.

But there was one thing the Alpha couldn't get at, because she'd never had a mother of her own. The warm smell of the stewpot rose in her mind, and eight year old Mira climbed up on her stool and reached for the metal handle to raise the lid and check out what they'd made. Momma's warning came too late, and Mira jerked her hand away and fell backwards to the floor.

Howling at the pain of the burn, Mira opened her eyes to the night sky just as Jantine entered the clearing. The waffle pattern of the wire frame was seared into her palm, and the smell of her own flesh combined with the roasting pheasant filled the air. The meat was resting directly on the coals now, and blackening around the edges.

Happy was a warm presence at her back, and across the clearing Serene was sprawled unconscious against Grumpy in similar fashion. The Omega's cold hatred came off him in waves, but for the moment he was more concerned with Serene than any thoughts of revenge.

The pain of her burn was pure agony, but it was nothing compared to losing so many parts of herself at once. There were holes in her life now, empty spaces where her childhood used to be. Any memories not directly related to her family or the Academy were just gone, and the words were out of her mouth before she knew what she was saying.

"She took them. The Gamma memories. They went into my mind and just took them!"

Thanks to her new and improved biology, the burn on her hand was already healing, and Mira felt a slight rush as her body flooded with endorphins. But while it helped to dull her physical pain, it only magnified the feeling of being in two places at once.

Part of me is over there now, locked up in that little girl's head. Is what's left enough to make a whole me?

Jantine's face had turned to stone, and the light of the coals made her expression even more dramatic. But it was nothing compared to the storm brewing in her mind, and Mira sent her what she thought was a wave of comfort and acceptance before the Beta acted on any of her murderous thoughts.

"It's all right, Jantine. It's all right. They weren't mine anyway. Don't do anything rash until I figure out how bad it is."

"This is not done. Ever. She must be held accountable."

The logical consequences of what she was thinking hit Jantine like a landslide, and the Beta shut herself down so completely that Happy's other hand had to reach out to catch her before she fell into the fire. The Omega drew both women into a tight embrace, but as he did one of Jantine's feet bumped the pot, knocking it over. A wave of scented liquid spilled onto the burning pheasant breasts and extinguished the coals.

Years of therapy after Brian's death had taught Mira a few coping mechanisms for impossible situations. One was to shut down all emotion until she was in a safe environment, and another was to turn pain into laughter.

Mira started laughing, drawing a puzzled stare from Artemus as he crashed through the trees. The sight of the Delta's expression and a weapon in each of his four hands only made her laugh harder, and sensing Katra rushing toward the camp in a similar state of alarm only added to her amusement. The sheer absurdity of the scene was just too much, and she leaned back against Happy's broad chest and sighed.

Dinner's served, everyone. Come and get it!

The laughter helped Mira push back feelings of outrage from the mods around her—an emotion she was ill-equipped to deal with without the Gamma memories. Only Happy knew the true extent of what Serene had done, and he did his best to shield her from their feelings.

Jantine recovered quickly, and pushed her way out of Happy's arms. That she was furious with Serene and Grumpy didn't make Mira feel any better. If anything, Mira could sense Jantine's emotions even stronger than before.

Despite Happy's help and her endorphin rush, Mira's head was pounding. She knew she had only one chance to stop Jantine from starting a fight she couldn't possibly win, even though the Alpha deserved everything Jantine was thinking about doing to her.

"Jantine, stop. We can get through this. Just don't push her right now, Grumpy's right on the edge and I don't know what he'll do next."

"Grumpy? What is 'grumpy'? Another Earth thing I am required to learn?"

Mira stood on shaky legs, grateful that Happy was there to keep her from falling. "It's what I've been calling the Serene's Omega. Just to keep them straight in my head. Happy is this fella here."

Jantine stared at her, and Mira could feel a mental message forming in the Beta's mind. Unsure of what that might feel like, Mira waved her off.

"Just let me handle this. And keep the others back. It's hard to be around you all right now."

Mira pushed gently on Happy's arm, then took a tentative step toward Serene. Jantine's anger was a bonfire behind her, one that kindled in Katra and Artemus as well as she explained what had happened. But Mira only had eyes for the strange alien child and her hulking guardian.

Out of habit, Mira reached for the Gamma memories for some clue as to how Grumpy would react to a confrontation. The cold emptiness in her mind was almost as frightening as the Omega scowling at her. She should be angry. Furious. But although she knew the words, and understood the general concepts, her emotions were savaged as badly as her memories. All she had left was happiness, pain, disappointment, and fear—and a headache that would not go away.

After a few more steps, she stared into the eyes of the seated Omega, and spoke from her heart.

"That can never happen again. I would have given them to you gladly, if you'd asked. But you hurt me, very badly, and now I don't know how, or even if, I can help you."

Mira could feel Grumpy's anger, and tried to replicate it in herself. But it faded too fast, and she was about to continue her harangue when she realized why; Serene was awake, and every bit as upset as Mira. But the Alpha was more direct in her disapproval, and whatever she was doing to him went from subtle to sadistic in a flash. Even without a full connection, Mira could tell he was in agony, and she had to do something to stop Serene from seriously damaging his mind.

"What are you doing? Stop that, it's not helping anyone! We have to learn to work together, or it's going to go very badly for us."

Grumpy's pain vanished, though he was visibly shaken. Mira's knowledge of the Omegas was spotty at best, but she could still remember all of her interactions with Happy, and Jantine's reaction to Serene's mental assault gave her an idea of how serious the matter was for them.

Serene stood and looked up into Mira's face. Mira's first instinct was to kneel down and talk to her as she would a child, but was unwilling to cede any advantage to the Alpha she didn't have to.

"I am sorry. O-6913 told me no harm would come to you, and I believed him. You have been kind to me, and I see in your memories the kind of person you are. You should not have been made to suffer."

The thought of an alien child being able to remember things about her life she could not was agonizing, but Mira forced herself to remain calm.

Serene stepped forward and took Mira's burned hand in both of her own. The Alpha's skin was much warmer than Mira's, and her palm stung for a second. But in Serene's touch, Mira felt an echo of the electric charge JonB's similar gesture had imparted.

Despite herself, Mira smiled. Serene did too, and Mira could sense genuine regret in her mind. Remembering how it had felt to have other people's lives forced upon her, Mira knew Serene had to be more than a little out of sorts right now, and hadn't meant to hurt Grumpy.

Then she felt it, and all Mira's sympathetic thoughts vanished in a heartbeat.

The Alpha's level of control was amazing, much more subtle than Mira's blundering efforts. But even though Serene was using the Gamma memories to guide her efforts, Mira's empathic ability was far stronger. Making note of her technique, Mira started building a wall to keep her out, while at the same time planning a verbal response. Putting aside any ethical concerns about what she'd done, Serene was still a child, and not quite in control of her actions.

Of course, now she's got a few dozen lifetimes worth of memories in her head telling her what to do. Including mine. How much longer can she really be considered a child?

"It probably would have been fine, with a Gamma. Not right, not by a long shot. But I'm different, and what the two of you did is considered a serious crime on my planet."

Or it would be, if we had any telepaths of our own.

"As you say. I will think on how to make proper restitution. You and I are linked now, and harm done to you is harm to myself. As you say, we must do better in the future at expressing our desires."

These last words came with an empathic rebuke for Grumpy, and Mira couldn't let Serene have the final emotional word. She let go of Serene's hands, reaching out instead to the Omega's face.

Mira was impressed by how steady her fingers were. Grumpy's skin was much cooler than Serene's and Mira sent as focused a burst of forgiveness as she could muster.

She was still upset, and she let him know it. But while they touched, Mira could sense all the confusion she'd suspected Grumpy was feeling regarding their very long, very stressful day. He honestly hadn't intended to hurt her, but at the same time he really didn't care that he had.

That, more than anything, made up Mira's mind to go forward with JonB's plan. She and the Betas would have to stay alert at all times to prevent any further mishaps, especially now that Serene had demonstrated an ability to enter their minds uninvited. The Alpha was too unpredictable to leave unsupervised, and Grumpy was far from an effective counselor.

Mira walked back to the extinguished cookfire, leaving Serene and Grumpy to work out their differences. Happy was still sitting there, staring at the remains of dinner with a sigh in his heart. Mira sent him a smile, and the memory of her mother's gumbo. She got one in return along with an image of herself, Carlton, and Happy walking along a path eating ice cream.

It took her a moment to realize she was looking at one of her own memories, recovered and translated through the Omega's eyes. Skipping along the river with Debbi and Tommy Watson after a revival meeting, making plans for their future. Tommy didn't want Mira to go to the Academy, and that was the day Debbi realized he was never going to marry her, because he was in love with someone else.

Love. I can remember love!

The bittersweet memory of three friendships ending forever wasn't exactly appropriate to the situation, but Mira thought it was the most wonderful gift she'd ever received. Not trusting her emotions, she crushed herself to the Omega's chest for almost a minute, savoring that long-ago day she'd just had ripped from her when her world was simple and small.

Though it must have looked ridiculous to the other mods, she moved her hands up to his cheeks, then leaned in and kissed Happy on his lipless mouth. She sent him her thanks, along with an image of her mother's last family dinner, with him in the guest of honor's chair.

Stepping back, Mira thought about the scenes Happy had shared with her just before the attack. With only memories of her memories of what Colonial life was like, it was hard to be sure but Mira had a strong sense that there was no real concept of privacy in their worlds. With Gammas and Alphas able to root out any secrets, it was no wonder that Jantine maintained such strong mental discipline. Even now, in conversation with Artemus and Katra, the Beta was pointedly avoiding looking in her direction, allowing her to deal with the Omegas in her own way.

A thought struck her, and she was about to share it with Happy when an image came into Artemus's mind. JonB and Carlton were in a building, working on a—

Oh, you clever, clever boys. That's perfect!

"Jantine?"

Jantine's conversation with Katra and Artemus died abruptly, and all three turned to look at Mira.

"You should ask Artemus about what the other Betas are doing. I think you'll be pleasantly surprised."

A few seconds later a flash of annoyance mixed with laughter slipped past her shields. Apparently, Artemus hadn't yet told her what the boys were up to, and Jantine wasn't sure how to react to the news. But building a train solved a lot of their travel-related problems, and Mira was happy for any good news she could get.

We're all feeling our way blind today, and today just keeps getting longer.

Jantine and Artemus set off into the trees without Katra, with the former set on seeing the engine for herself. Mira could tell Katra was upset that the meal she'd been preparing was ruined, and Mira resolved to cook her another one as soon as possible. Turning to the Omega, she smiled and opened her mind to him. Without Doria's direct experience as a guide, it was a little rough at first, but Happy supplied the missing mental steps for her. This time, instead of entering his mind, she held out her unburned hand, palm up.

"I'm Mira, Mira Harlan. What's your name?"

Happy simply stared back at her, mind in neutral. It wasn't until she repeated the words a second time that he understood what she was asking, and his reaction was not at all what she expected.

The Omega jumped to his feet, hands out and head shaking. Mira brushed aside his refusals, sending the concept of an introduction and a handshake again. Then she sat on the ground, and patted the space next to her.

"This is Kansas, my friend. You're not in the Colonies anymore. And among friends, we speak as equals. So what's your name, or do you want me to pick one for you?"

Happy didn't respond at first, but after a minute or so of silence he eased himself down next to her, and looked up at the sky. Mira followed his gaze, and started pointing at the stars.

"That one? It's called Vega. But if you look at the stars around it like so"—Mira made a drawing motion with her finger, adding lines of light in her imagination—"you get the constellation Lyra. The ancients thought it looked like a lyre, a kind of harp the god Hermes gave to his brother Apollo."

Mira could tell that Katra was listening to her every word as well. Without openly acknowledging the Gamma's presence, she raised her voice slightly so the other mod could hear her better.

"And that one over there is Rukbat. It's the knee of Sagittarius. Most of what we can see of the constellation from here are actually clusters of more distant stars, but in the ancient world they had no way of knowing that. There are a lot of stories about how it was named, but my favorite involves..."

Happy did something to his eyes, and Mira's voice trailed off in wonder. She'd been happy just to look up at the stars and talk, seeing them now with her improved transgenic vision as if for the first time. But instead of the slightly better defined blobs she was enjoying moments before, through the Omega's eyes now, she saw Sagittarius A in all its multi-spectrum glory. The burning black hole at the center of the Milky Way galaxy was sending out radio waves across the millennia, to find two lost souls on an insignificant planet at the edge of everything.

Oh, wow.

It was several minutes before Happy returned the universe to an understandable state, during which Mira simply watched in silence. There were no words to describe what she'd seen, colors unknown to even the most sensitive instruments and rolling waves of energy dancing across the sky.

Happy sat beside her, truly content for the first time since she'd tasted his thoughts. He saw the universe like this all the time, but only through her eyes was it magical.

There was something else new in his emotions. Curiosity. Not how she understood it, but something much deeper. He wanted to see everything through her eyes now, and experience the world he knew in a different way.

But more importantly, he wanted to hear the story she'd started. Mira leaned into his arm, closed her eyes, and remembered her father's voice.

"It was a long time ago, before humans sailed the stars or even understood what they were. In a land where gods walked the earth, a group of ordinary men set out on a quest aboard a ship called the Argo..."

CALLAWAY

MARCUS GAVE the jets another nudge, carefully aligning the grab arm as they approached the last pod. It was still tumbling in space, and the open tear on the side told them all they needed to know about its inhabitant. Matching spin and rotation with what was essentially space junk wasn't his first choice for how to spend this last trip, but every pod they recovered was another data core to add to the stack back on Valiant, and possibly more propellant, generator power, and components to add to their ridiculously small supply.

Besides, it's not like we've got anywhere to go.

"You ready, Alonso? We're damn near bingo on propellant."

"Just keep it steady. I'll have it this time for sure."

Flying a maintenance frame was an entirely different experience than a Shrike or a shuttle, and not just because he and Ramirez were one micro-meteoroid away from certain death. If the extra rads they were picking up from unshielded space hadn't already cooked their DNA into an unrecognizable mess, the frame itself might fly apart if he pushed it too hard, and they were way too far out from *Valiant* for anyone else to come get them if he fucked up. But the general principles were still the same. Propellant vs. Mass; spin vs. velocity.

And most important of all, luck vs. skill.

So far they and the other teams had retrieved twelve of the pods launched during what the crew was calling "the Incident," but only five of the pilots. One hadn't made it back to the dreadnaught, and the others…

Marcus felt the arm impact the pod through the feet of his suit, and gave the jets the tiniest of pushes to maintain contact while Alonso worked the grab. A second later, it locked into place, and Marcus started worrying about the massive debris field they were in, instead of the small piece of it they'd just risked their lives to recover.

He hadn't been lying to Ramirez when he said the frame was almost out of propellant. Even the minute amount he was using to stabilize their improvised vessel while Ramirez worked his way down the gimbaled arm to the pod was too precious to waste, an expenditure he was only willing to make on the off chance they could get more from the pod itself.

With the pilot inside dead, there was no need to bring the whole thing back to *Valiant*. In fact, with what propellant they had left there was barely enough to get the two of them close enough for one of the other teams to toss them—or more accurately, their cargo—a rescue line.

Fucked, fucked, and more fucked. The Marcus Callaway Story. Coming to a destroyed starship near you in 2641.

Alonso was opening the pod's outer hatch when Marcus saw the fragment spinning toward them. A conjunction of Sol's radiance, *Valiant's* ever expanding shadow, and the frame's running lights revealed it just in time for him to flip the frame out of the way of a jagged piece of hull that would have put all of Marcus' worries permanently to rest.

In the seconds as it passed by his faceplate, he learned some very inventive new phrases in Elac from Ramirez. The new language of the Reclamation wasn't in wide use just yet, but Fleet maintenance workers were definitely putting it through its paces.

"Sorry, man. I figured you'd want your pilot to still have a head for the trip back."

"A little warning would have been nice. Next time, I'll swing you around with your ass hanging ...aw hell."

Even after years in space, Marcus hadn't rid himself of the habit of swinging his head around to see when something odd happened. The motion was enough to introduce a new wobble to their flight path, which took a few more precious seconds to correct. By the time he had it back under control, Alonso was inside the pod, and the sound of his panicked breathing over their comm channel was not encouraging.

"What is it? What's going on in there?" A few more seconds listening to Alonso hyperventilate had Marcus ready to unhook and head over to drag him out, but then Alonso pulled himself together enough to reply.

"It's nothing, really. I just I know this guy. Lucas Garza, head of Comms division. I ordered him to launch his pod, even though we both knew it was damaged."

Well, shit. Had to happen sooner or later.

"Ramirez, can you complete the mission, or do you want to switch places?" Marcus knew exactly how much worse Alonso's day had been than his, if only because of the way they'd met.

Hell, it didn't take that much convincing to get Hatchet-face Horace's own troopers to come around, once they knew how bad the bastard had screwed them. But Alonso...

Alonso had been In Charge, and every dead pilot they'd found added another stone to the load he was carrying. And Lucas Garza's was bound to be the heaviest of them all.

"No, sir. I'm good. Lucas was injured when he launched, and from the looks of things the pod ruptured soon after. He apparently had enough time to shut down his bottles, so we've got maybe another fifty kilos of O2, and half of his batteries intact. Give me twenty minutes; I can get it all."

Damn, son. You're learning a bit too fast what command really means. And since me and my command key are technically your superior officer right now, I'm officially enrolling you in the Marcus Callaway School of Shit Happens.

"All right, Alonso. Do what you have to do. I'll keep my eagle eye open for any more transients, but just to be safe I'm going to point us back at the Hull."

"Roger that, sir. I'll make the transfer as fast as I can."

There really wasn't much point in describing the half a ship they had left as a Redstone dreadnaught, but to the people who'd served aboard her, she'd always be SDF *Valiant*. In the hours after their abandonment, Marcus and Alonso had engaged in half-a-dozen negotiations to form the sixty survivors living inside her now into something approximating a crew, who were now affectionately calling the almost functional derelict they inhabited the Hull.

Marcus didn't care one way or the other, but as its titular commander he was more than happy to accede to the crew's wishes.

We're all dead in twelve hours anyway, if we can't get the scrubbers back online. And the solar arrays, and the core. And...

Marcus tapped the stick, and the frame/pod assembly rotated around an axis somewhere aft of his body until the Hull was fully in view. Another two seconds of thrust emptied the propellant tanks, but set them on a three meter-per-second collision course with the biggest clusterfuck he'd ever seen.

Valiant was more than dead; she was extinct. Only her forward decks were intact, and the ragged midpoint that connected her with an ever-expanding debris field was still studded with black rocks of unknown origin, which Alonso was certain were the reason they had no power. The mess Marcus was dead-sticking through now was comprised of smaller chunks of the same material, plus what was left of three missile tenders and a corvette that once had names, but were now referred to collectively as *Unattainable Parts*.

If we can get a shuttle functional, maybe we can thread our way out to the other wrecks and commit some proper piracy. Until then, they're just points on a plot, and reasons to keep on working.

Over the Hull's rim was the shining disc of Sol, and behind it, and a few million kilometers of declination down, was the omnipresent, tantalizing shape of Earth. Marcus was one of the few people in this section of the Home System that knew why most of this had happened, and why no-one was coming to rescue them anytime soon.

Doesn't make this shit any easier, but at least I can point to why we're all going to die.

Marcus used his gauntlet thrusters to avoid some potentially life-threatening collisions as they fell steadily towards the Hull, though for one slow-moving piece he just flicked it away with his fingers. Alonso more than delivered on his promise while they flew, exiting the pod with a spacesuit-shaped bundle in tow, surrounded by a train of equipment modules that couldn't have been easy to extract in under fifteen minutes.

Once he was back aboard the frame and strapped in, they released the pod and performed a double gauntlet burn to move past it. Eight minutes and a fresh bottle of propellant later, they were within comm range of the Hull, and a few more after that were being gently reeled back in to the worst day of everyone's lives, ever.

Okay, then. What's next?

RAMIREZ

ALONSO SCANNED the room for threats, but even accounting for the twenty armored troopers from *Indomitable* who'd grudgingly joined the crew, all assembled fleet personnel were eagerly awaiting the words of the ranking officer aboard, which thankfully was now Commander Callaway.

And he's welcome to it. I couldn't have done a worse job in command if I'd tried, and even though a couple of the pilots we rescued have more time in service, only Callaway had the authority to relieve me.

Even though I was flat on my back and surrounded by enemies who used to be friends, Valiant *was still my ship, to the bitter end.*

Even with all but one of the tables removed, the wardroom was crowded. Nervous sweat and sickness and too many hours of suit smell made a room designed for forty people even smaller, and packing in more made it especially hard to breathe.

From a starting compliment of two hundred, *Valiant* had thirty-nine officers and crew left, several of whom were barely hanging on. The troopers abandoned by Captain Kołodziejski could have overwhelmed any resistance, but despite being Marsborn, they were just as angry as the rest of the assembled survivors.

Bastard left us to die, without even so much as an explanation.

Callaway had scrounged up a mess tunic from somewhere, and looked extra heroic in the wardroom's hastily installed emergency lighting. He lingered a moment to make sure everyone was paying attention, then stepped up onto the remaining table and began his long-delayed "first" speech.

"So, we're pretty much fucked. This isn't exactly news to any of you, but I wanted to say it up front, so you'll understand what comes next."

Having it out in the open let everyone give a sigh of relief, and looks of resignation gave way to grudging smiles. But the brief puffs of clouded breath in front of everyone without a suit on reminded Alonso of just how true that statement really was.

"We've got battery power for another fifteen hours, if we go with the assumption that Ramirez and the genius squad can't get the forward generators online. If they can, we've got enough O2 for another ten after that, at which point we'll all suit up for three more and contemplate our lives. I'm not going to sugarcoat our chances after that, because without communications or propulsion of any kind, the only people with any inkling we might be here are the ones who left us to die."

Callaway made a show of looking around the room, and Alonso found himself doing the same thing. He still wanted to make a long push for one of the wrecked tenders for more salvage, but the cargo frame had only enough propellant for one short trip, if its pilot didn't care about getting back to the Hull afterward.

And we all know who's going to be in the second seat. Better to die trying, than waiting around for someone to save us.

"So, fuck those guys," said Callaway. "Fuck 'em hard. Because I'm going to live. We've got three mostly functional shuttles in transfer bay three, but at this point none of them has anything more than a maintenance charge left.

"If we pour everything we've got into one of them, I think we can get it operational and fly it close enough to Earth to send a distress signal. We could maybe do it—send the signal, I mean—from here, but right now we're spinning out into interstellar space the hard way, with nothing to show for it but some cool stories nobody is in the right position to ever see or hear.

"So here's the deal. A launch will take ninety percent of the power we've got left, but that's not all the bad news. I'll also be sending as many spare oxygen bottles as we can scrounge up for the flight crew, which means I'm proposing some of us die a lot sooner. But if we do this, we can at least get our story moving back towards home instead of spiraling out to nowhere."

The room was still silent, and even the Marsborn were nodding in agreement. They'd done the math hours ago when they'd cast their lot with *Valiant*'s survivors, and it wasn't going to improve anytime soon.

"So I'm asking you for options. Any tricks you know, any secrets you're keeping, now's the time to share them. Because the launch has to work for any of what we've been through to matter. And the longer we spin out into a forever orbit, the less likely it is the shuttle will have enough power to get back into transmission range.

"And since I'm sitting on the biggest secret of all, I'm going to go first."

Finally. Tell them all what we're dying for, Commander.

Alonso turned his full attention to Callaway, who despite his bandaged head still looked a lot more In Charge than Alonso had felt since this whole mess began.

"I don't know what Horace Kołodziejski told you kids in the back, but the reason *Valiant* was out here in the middle of nowhere is because we were hiding from him. You see, a while back, Captain Martin and I stole a sleeper unit from a ship attached to a secret base under Kołodziejski's command. After laying low for a while, we brought it aboard this ship, and then moved the whole battlegroup up here where nobody might think to look for us."

Well, almost nobody. We sure as hell got hit with a big fucking rock out here, and Kołodziejski wasn't that far behind.

Callaway gave the room another slow look, pacing his revelations for maximum effect.

"We did this, because what Captain Kołodziejski was planning for it was flat out wrong. There is—I mean, was—a gennie child inside, and he wanted to experiment on it. Just like he'd already experimented on her traveling companion, a little boy he woke up just long enough to watch him die.

"I can't tell you his reasons, or even where he got two sleeping gennie kids in the first place. What I *can* tell you, with Mister Ramirez's help, is what happened to the one we saved after *Valiant* got hit with a big fucking rock that nobody saw coming."

This was the cue Alonso was waiting for, and he tapped a command into his suit's control panel. There was no need to dim the emergency lighting for the edited holo—in fact, the wardroom's projectors were bright enough that several people near where Callaway was standing had to shield their eyes when it started up.

Commander Callaway narrated only the basics of what they were seeing, letting the facts play out for everyone to see.

"Captain Martin and Lt. Harlan left Alonso here in Command at 1308 shiptime, and made their way down to where we'd stashed the gennie."

"Lieutenant Commander, sir. Captain Martin made her the XO before they left. I logged it myself."

The correction was out of Alonso's mouth so fast it seemed like part of the narrative, and Callaway wasn't alone in staring at him after he'd said it. Alonso was glad he'd kept his faceplate sealed and mirrored, so no-one could see him blush at the extra attention.

"Did he, now? Well, all right then. Lieutenant Commander Harlan it is. You can see here" said Callaway, "the sleeper unit itself, being disconnected and prepared for transport."

Alonso had to admit that Callaway's strong, confident voice lent a lot of *veritas* to an otherwise unremarkable recording. A bunch of troopers in hardsuits milling around while a few techs unhooked power couplings wasn't exactly hard evidence, but so far no one was questioning his narrative.

Or even why Captain Martin would be willing to abandon his command over a gennie, of all things. Sure, we were doomed from the time the rock hit, but if he'd surrendered, gone peacefully, we would have probably left with Indomitable *and the other ships.*

We'd be imprisoned as mutineers—most of us, anyway—but at least we'd be alive.

"Hold it here, Alonso."

Alonso paused the holo, and realizing what Callaway wanted, backed it up a few seconds until the sleeping gennie's face was visible.

She doesn't look real, inside that unit. Almost like a drawing of what a little girl is supposed to be. Is this what we've been afraid of for three hundred years?

"I don't know who she is, or where she came from. I just know what Captains Martin and DeMarco told me. That girl, that sleeper unit, is hundreds of years old, from a time not long after the exile. She and her partner were found on a planet so classified it doesn't even have a name, and with my back against the wall and a map of the universe in front of me, I couldn't even begin to tell you where it was."

This did get a reaction from the crowd, some of whom were now voicing the same thoughts as Alonso. Callaway waited a minute, then called on one of the many people who had questions.

To Alonso's surprise, it was Carson, the engineer who'd brought them the first report of the object lodged in *Valiant*'s hull. Given the orders Mira Harlan had given him to investigate further, Alonso was amazed he'd lived through the explosion that tore the ship apart.

"Can you at least tell us why, sir? Why the captain was trying to get *her* off the ship, and not any of us?"

Callaway's eyes tightened up a bit, and he hopped down off the table before answering. With his feet on the ground, he was still impressive, but he seemed much more human.

"I'll be honest with you, son, I haven't got a clue. But if things had gone differently, I'd have been one of the people walking with him there, and what we're going to see next probably would have done me in.

"Best guess, I think he couldn't stand to see her get hurt, especially if she could possibly put an end to the madness between our two peoples. Alonso, show us the transfer bay."

Advancing the holo didn't take much time, and the crew was soon pressing forward to watch the techs glide the sleeper unit up into a shuttle. He paused it again as Martin and Harlan came back down the shuttle's ramp, and a couple of the techs started in on pre-launch preparations.

"Now, you all heard Captain Kołodziejski's announcement earlier, just like most of you heard Alonso's own transmission from the command center. But what you don't know is that shuttle there is mine, and the reason why I'm wearing only half my own uniform is that the rest of my kit is in one of the compartments aboard her, along with all the answers to your questions.

"I wish now I'd disobeyed orders and read them for myself, but I trusted Captain Martin, who in turn was under orders from Commodore Maranova."

Everyone but the Marsborn straightened up a bit at the War Witch's name, and even they had to give her respect, if only for her rank. Callaway gave the crew a few seconds to process the chain of command, then continued.

"But he was willing to leave me behind too, if it meant getting that gennie to safety. And considering what happens next, I'm kind of glad he did. Mister Ramirez?"

Here the holo got a bit hectic, but Alonso kept the focus on the captain and Harlan. There was round of murmurs when Harlan started shooting, and another one when bulkheads started exploding around them.

"Hold it there, please."

Alonso froze the image on Harlan pushing the captain down behind some machinery, while a bright light outlined them from behind.

"About this time, the first squads from *Indomitable* encountered resistance in the corridors. We've got some of that vid too, and I'd like for Lieutenant Olvrsdóttir to walk us through it. Astrid?"

One of the armored troopers moved forward to stand next to Callaway, and set her faceplate to clear. Her thin, angular face was typical of the Marsborn officers Alonso had encountered since leaving the academy, including the extra shadows and strange pallor added by suit lights.

In actuality, Alonso had never seen a Marsborn face to face, only over screens. So far, the Marsborn troopers in the Hull were content to draw scrubbed and sanitized air for their suits from *Valiant*'s stores, but they still didn't like to share actual atmo with Earthers. So much so that the one trooper who'd cracked her helmet when *Valiant* broke in half stood a bit apart from the rest, even though she'd affected repairs without ever breathing unfiltered air.

Olvrsdóttir requested access to the projectors, and Alonso keyed her into the system. She could have used her own codes—Alonso was still trying to figure out how they'd shut him out during the attack—but it was nice to be sharing now, instead of shooting.

She brought the transfer bay holo down, and put up one of a dimly lit corridor, a black wall of rock, and a handful of dead crew scattered amongst unfamiliar crates. Alonso knew what he was looking at, but Carson was seeing it for the first time, and jumped to the same conclusion as a few others in the crowd.

"You fucking dusters! You murdered them!"

Alonso stepped into the holo, both to obscure the image and move forward to talk to Carson. But Commander Callaway stepped away from the table and got there first.

With his hands on the Carson's shoulders, Callaway spoke softer than he had when projecting from the top of the table, but his words still carried across the room.

"No, they didn't, son. Watch with me, and you'll see for yourself."

Callaway stepped to the side, and motioned to Olvrsdóttir. Alonso moved to the other side of Carson, and turned around just in time for the Marsborn's lightly accented words to come over the wardroom speakers and kill any other conversation.

"At 1408 shiptime, Lt. Calas discovered the scene you see here, and his squad entered a manufactured compartment inside what we are calling the Rock. The compartment had an independent power source, gravity, and its own atmosphere.

"After examining their transmitted suit recordings, and correlating with footage from *Valiant*, we can now show you the full record of this cowardly attack."

Alonso grimaced at this, but inside his helmet no-one could see his reaction. Callaway, on the other hand, went completely stone-faced, and crew members around him straightened up a bit.

If this is how she's got to spin our Big Lie to her troopers, fine. But she's not winning any goodwill talking down to the rest of us.

Olvrsdóttir either didn't notice Callaway's reaction, or didn't care, and kept on talking.

"As Lt. Calas moves inside the structure with Lt. Martinez here," she said, indicating the holo with a gauntleted hand, "you can see them begin a standard search pattern. And at this moment, they encountered the enemy…"

Bobbing lights played across two bloodied forms wearing black bodysuits, one of whom looked like his head was smashed in. The other had him cradled in her arms, with a device of some kind in her free hand.

"…just as across the ship Lt. Ross and his squad encountered a gennie strike team."

This did get a reaction, as did the abrupt appearance of a third holo, this one also composited from suit cameras. Crouched at the entrance to a transfer bay were seven figures, ranging in size from merely human to truly monstrous. The first five were wearing the same form-fitting black bodysuits as the pair from the first holo, as well as dark visors. The other two, oddly enough, wore simple cloth coveralls.

Of course, the fact that they were huge, orange-skinned, and had wide, broad heads fixed them forever in the minds of the assembled crew as what they really were.

Gennies. They're the ones that killed Valiant, *both with their space rock, and their actions afterwards.*

Alonso had no idea why the gennies had attempted such a

perilous journey inside the Rock, but he and everyone else in the wardroom could figure out their goal was to get a real ship for the rest of whatever their mission was.

Suicide mission is the kindest way to describe it, and their day doesn't get any better from here. They had no idea "our" gennie even existed. Or did they ?

The orange giants were setting down crates of the same kind stacked outside the Rock, and the other gennies were firing weapons of some kind into the bay.

"The ones with four arms are designated Deltas, combat infantry specialists. We cannot determine the mod types of the smaller ones, but the larger, orange ones are called Omegas. Our intel had tagged them as pacifists, but what you are about to see proves just how dangerous they truly are."

As *Indomitable*'s troopers approached, one of the orange giants stood up and advanced into the bay, micro-slugs tearing through the cloth of its coveralls. But instead of injuring the gennie, the slugs flattened against its skin and fell to the decking as it walked.

Eyes widened around the wardroom as the gennie moved forward, even more so when it picked up a workbench and threw it at a firing line of armored troopers. Then the squad in the corridor started shooting, and the second giant walked into the line of fire as if it wasn't there.

"With their strength and seeming invulnerability, the Omegas are an unparalleled threat. And as you can see here..."

The first giant followed up his initial attack by grabbing one of the troopers in front of it and swinging them like a club. Olvrsdóttir re-enabled the initial holo image, which was no longer showing Mira Harlan and the captain, but instead two black-clad gennies blasting their way across the bay, every shot taking down another trooper until they raced up the shuttle's ramp.

A second later, the holo of Lt. Calas took center stage, just long enough for the female gennie to smile and drop the device in her hand. The holo went bright white in an instant, then dead black.

"...we cannot underestimate the others either."

Back in the transfer bay, the image shuddered as the four larger gennies made short work of *Indomitable*'s troopers, with the holo degrading further as each suit camera died. *Valiant*'s feed took over now, tracking the gennies as they made their way quickly to the shuttle.

"Stop it there."

Alonso knew Callaway's words were for him, but Olvrsdóttir was a microsecond faster in pausing the holo as a human-sized gennie with no obscuring visor came down the ramp and embraced one of the others.

"And that's about all the information the worlds have right now about what's happened here, assuming Captain Kołodziejski even reports it. And before anyone starts quoting regs at me about respecting the chain of command, remember that right now I'm it, and Kołodziejski left us here to die.

"And, we know something he doesn't. There's more to the story than what *Indomitable* carried away with her, and we're the only ones that can tell it. Alonso, the next holo, please."

Alonso felt every eye and faceplate in the room on him as he walked through the embracing gennies to the corner of the table where Olvrsdóttir and Callaway were standing. Turning to address the crew, he fought down his fear and keyed up the next sequence.

"By the way, all the records we have of the incident are available for review—we're not trying to hide anything from you. It's just that we've got a limited amount of time before we're all dead, and you need to see this part of it to understand the urgency of our task. After we're done here, if you think it's a good use of your time, please feel free to check out the entire archive."

Alonso waited a few seconds for the crew to think it over, then ran the telemetry scans of the shuttle's flight through the debris field while he talked.

"What happens next was captured by one of our deployed sensor pods. The records I just mentioned show the gennies board the shuttle and launch it, but telemetry from *Indomitable* shows them either destroyed by a Geyser spread, or from a collision with a big chunk of the Rock.

"But thanks to all the extra rads the commander and I picked up on our salvage runs, we found a sensor log that tells a different story. A log from a pod too far out to transmit to the rest of the sensor net, so the data you're about to see also didn't get transmitted to *Indomitable*."

Alonso put up a dim, but clear image of the debris field as it looked right before the explosion. It was pure chance that the pod was even pointed in the right direction at the time, but longshots were the only bets they had to play right now.

He zoomed in on the aftermath of the explosion that ended the chase, held it there, then switched to a negative color index. The blackness of space became a million shades of white, filled with tiny black stars and the outline of an intact shuttle coasting alongside a tumbling chunk of rock. Alonso shaded it gray for the crew, so they could better make out what was happening.

"The gennies survived, and unless they were killed when the gennies took the shuttle, there's a good chance that Captain Martin and LtCdr Harlan are also on board. So you see, we have to..."

A dozen voices started talking at once, as all the frustration the crew had been holding in finally broke loose. While they'd been content to listen to Callaway and Olvrsdóttir give detailed summaries of an ongoing story, they apparently weren't willing to let Alonso tell its end.

I don't blame any of you. I'm just as pissed as you are, and in your position I'd have questions too.

Alonso paused, then flattened the holo, letting the image rest on the wardroom's ceiling. The space where it had been immediately filled with shouting people, and forgetting where he was—and that none of them could actually hurt him inside his hardsuit—Alonso took an involuntary step back and tripped over one of the legs of the table. Arms and legs flying, he crashed to the deck, and decided to stay there for a while.

Yeah, this is nice. Definitely officer material.

A piercing whistle rose above the noise of the crowd, followed by Commander Callaway's voice.

"All right, that's enough!"

A few murmurs persisted, but from his position on the deck couldn't tell who or where they were. But when Commander Callaway spoke again, his was the only voice in the room.

"Our timetable hasn't changed any, and you can see now why I want to take a chance on a shuttle. Simply put, the threat these invaders pose to the home system overrides any plots or politics. We don't know how many more rocks are flying our way right now, or what they are intending to do with them when they get here.

"And before you start in on what I was doing trying to save that sleeping gennie from being experimented on in the first place, I'm going to share another fun fact with you, something else Captain Kołodziejski was trying to keep from the Fleet.

"That little girl is what they call an Alpha. She's one of their leaders, and if you think the other ones are full of surprises, we've got no idea at all what she's capable of."

A gauntleted hand moved into Alonso's field of view, palm outstretched, and he followed the arm up to see Olvrsdóttir smiling down at him. He took it gladly, and with both suits working together he was back on his feet in an instant.

"So we have to warn Earth that the gennies have returned, no matter the cost. That a handful of them just outfoxed some of the best officers in the Home Fleet—which to be perfectly honest scares the living shit out of me—and they've probably already landed on Earth."

Olvrsdóttir's smile hardened slightly at that, but she turned away to look at the rest of the room before Alonso could get a good read on her mood. Alonso did the same, and the faces he could see were a mix of anger, confusion, and fear.

Pretty much sums it up for me.

Message requests were flashing all over Alonso's visor, but he blinked them away. Callaway was still talking, and something about the flattened holo was bothering him.

"Whether or not I, or any of us, are alive when that happens depends on what we can do in the next few hours, after which I'm ordering one of our remaining shuttles prepped for launch. Mr. Ramirez and I will answer any questions you have for exactly one hour, after which time he'll report to me in transfer bay three to begin checks on the shuttles.

"Dismissed, people. Let's get to work."

The murmurs became a dull roar, as the crowd pressed in on Commander Callaway. Alonso braced himself for an hour of angry questioning, but was entirely unprepared for Lieutenant Olvrsdóttir to step between himself and the crew.

He heard her boots lock in place with her back to the crowd, and his eyes widened in shock when she removed her helmet, then pulled off her inner hood. An impressive set of braids fell down her back as she took a deep breath of the Hull's unfiltered air, swaying a bit as her ears adapted to the lower pressure.

"Much better, I think. No more need for rules, when we are all going to die, yes?"

Alonso smiled, then removed his own helmet for the first time in over a shipday. His first breath was cold and sharp, and he added a suit maintenance check, and one for the wardroom as well, to his already overflowing schedule.

"Yes, I agree. Welcome aboard, Lieutenant. Sorry we can't give you a better reception, but it's been one hell of a day."

Olvrsdóttir smiled, and held out a gauntleted hand.

"It is Astrid to my friends. And you are Alonso, yes? I have seen you fight. Very impressive."

For a moment, Alonso's mind shut down as he tried to parse her words. Part of it was the pressure adaptation, but the only response he could offer was a mechanical handshake.

Then the memory of his brief battle in the command center came back to him.

Of course she reviewed the footage. In many ways, she's my opposite number, and if it had been Indomitable *floating lifeless, I would have been the in the first squad aboard her to offer assistance.*

Still, my actions are nothing to be proud of. I killed members of my own team trying to stay in command, and sooner or later I'll have to pay for that.

"So, Alonso. Which will you choose? Die slow, or die early on the shuttle?"

Alonso dropped her hand like it was on fire, but Astrid's smile never faltered. Over her shoulder, he could see dozens of people he knew by only by name waiting to talk to him, but this strange Martian woman had crystallized all their questions into the only one that mattered.

Do I really think Callaway's plan will work, or is it only a way to make our deaths seem more worthwhile?

"I..."

Alonso stopped himself before voicing his fears, and pulled himself away from Astrid's ice-blue eyes to look at the flattened holo on the wardroom's ceiling. The silhouette of the shuttle still hung beside a chunk of space rock, but beyond it, at the edge of the field, something else was visible in the negative image. Something tantalizingly familiar, yet still alien enough not to register as a "real" thing.

"I don't know, Astrid. I'd like to think I can still save us all, but I'm willing to admit I can't do it alone. I don't know if that helps, but it's what I've got for now."

Astrid released the maglocks on her boots, and took a step forward and across the space between them, ending up close enough for Alonso to smell cinnamon, sweat, and a hint of flowers as she passed.

"Good answer. Come find me when you are done with them," she said, nodding at the approaching crew. "I think we should talk."

She slipped away before he could respond, leaving Alonso surrounded by shouted questions. He caught a glimpse of her over the crowd as she rejoined her troopers, half of whom had already followed her example and removed their helmets.

Yeah, I definitely think we should talk.

"Okay, okay. One at a time, please. I haven't got a lot of good news for you, but if any of us are going to live through this, I think we should all be on the same page. Um, Karen, you're first. What would you like to know?"

ANNAHKO

CAROLINE WASN'T sure exactly what she was looking at, and the strange look in Horace's eyes made her question if she'd done the right thing in salvaging the gennie container. The soft light emanating from rows and rows of suspension chambers was a sight unlike anything she'd seen before, and Horace was looking at them with a passion he'd once reserved only for her.

Much like the one they'd found lodged in *Valiant*, the container had its own environmental systems: the gravity was slightly higher than that of their home planet, and the atmosphere was rich with heavily oxygenated air. There was a strange smell to it all, a mix of lightning and spices she couldn't quite identify.

And cold. So very cold.

She'd found Horace moving from unit to unit—studying the frozen faces within—rubbing his fingers over bronze plates with numbers and letters on the front of each one. He was muttering to himself in nonsense syllables, making quick side-to-side glances as he explored the container.

The odd shadows and highlights cast by the units made his face look almost skeletal, and standing beside him made Caroline more than a little nervous. He was still Horace, still the man she'd loved for most of her life, but something about these units, despite the apparent joy they brought him, had transformed him, and not for the better.

"Do you see it Caroline? Do you understand what this means?"

She didn't, but at least he was talking to her.

"I'm not sure, Captain. What do we hope to accomplish here?"

Horace's head snapped around, and he fixed her with an almost manic glare.

"It's life, Caroline. For me, for Mars, for all of us. With this many test subjects, we can end the gennie menace forever. We can avenge Bob we can..."

Whatever Horace was about to say died on his lips, replaced by a tittering giggle she'd never heard before. In the time it took her to process her feelings about that, he was off to the next unit, repeating the process of discovery.

"What about this one, Bob? How do you think she'd look on the table? How about it, GIL-B29760-A? Are you the one with the answers? Do you want to come out and play?"

Not knowing what else to do, Caroline followed him for a few more minutes, listening to him read off more nonsense numbers, all the while talking to a dead man who'd met his end in a container just like this one.

I didn't know Calas all that well, but he clearly wanted to know me. I don't even think Horace would have minded the dalliance, but now we'll never know.

Even as he is now, even with what's changed, Horace is still my friend. He's in pain, that's all. Grieving for his friend, with the weight of our entire planet on his shoulders. If only there was some way I could help. Something I could...

"Horace?"

Horace was standing in front of a container with a truly monstrous gennie inside, tall, with gray skin and extra arms. He appeared contemplative, and for a moment Caroline thought he had something profound to say to her. But when he did speak, her blood ran cold.

"No, not this one, Bob. Too far gone, not much human left in there. Best that I put it out of its misery, yes? We don't want another accident, now do we?"

Caroline's eyes went wide as Horace did something to the unit's controls, and the lights inside winked out. A second later, the small monitor on the side of the unit powered down as well, but not before the suppressed life signs it displayed flatlined. Horace was already on his way to the next suspension unit, peering intently at the male gennie inside.

"Yes, this one will do nicely. Congratulations, mister gennie, you get to live, for now."

I have to stop this. I have to do something.

"Horace!"

When he didn't acknowledge her, Caroline took two quick steps and grabbed his shoulder. Horace spun around at the contact; his pupils shrunk down to nothing and fixed on something far away.

"What's that, Bob? Are you back already? Well come on, let's pick the next one."

Caroline's heart sank, but she wasn't done trying to reach him just yet.

He's still in there, I know it. He just needs a reminder of what he's got to live for.

Caroline closed the distance between them and grabbed Horace's face in both hands. She bent her head and kissed him, but the second she did she knew it was the wrong thing to do. Not only were his lips cold and unresponsive, but instead of the electric charge she remembered from their last embrace, her stomach lurched as her mouth and nose filled with the smell of rot.

Oh, God, Horace. What have you done to yourself?

She ended the kiss, but did not let go of his face. Caroline searched his eyes for some sign the man she once loved was still inside, and a second later she got her answer.

Horace shoved her roughly to the floor, screaming something she didn't understand. The shoulder seam of her uniform blouse tore, and she brought her hand up to protect herself from…

Horace?

"Talk to me, Horace. Tell me what's wrong. I can help you. I can..."

"No, no, no! You don't get to do that. Gennie filth, you've ruined everything. Get out. Get out, get out, get out!"

Caroline looked up at him from the deck, watching him pound his fists into his stomach as he ranted. She recoiled in horror, scrambling back until she fetched up against the deactivated suspension unit. Cold from the glass and residual heat from its base sent competing fear signals through her back, but all she could do was stare at Horace as he continued his manic episode.

Horace had turned his aggression towards another active unit, punching the glass until his hands bled, then ran off into the near darkness, still screaming, "Gennie filth, gennie filth!"

Caroline got to her feet slowly, hurt more by his rejection than the fall. She approached the bloodied unit, hand trembling as she reached out. Horace's blood looked strange in the dim light, far darker than it should have been and smeared in an odd, decidedly un-fistlike pattern.

Unable to stop herself, her fingers touched the glass, and came away covered in an oily residue. Holding them up to her nose, she didn't smell anything, but her fingertips itched, as if she'd dipped them in pepper sauce.

But the thing that sent her running from the container was when the blood left on the glass ran together into a single dark spot, and the tiny amount on her fingers moved in sympathy.

Caroline didn't stop to talk to Andrew Collins at the container's entrance. She couldn't chance losing her composure any more than she already had, and when she got to an elevator, she punched in an override code so she could return to her quarters quickly, and in privacy.

She tried very, very hard not to look at the strange brown residue her fingers left on the keypad, or how it kept vibrating even when the car came to a stop.

Caroline was out of the car in a flash, momentarily confused at the unfamiliar corridor she found herself in. The doors closed behind her, and she spun to look at the legend on the grating.

4>A-1. But that's not what I...

Caroline's—and Horace's—quarters were on the command deck, three levels further down in the heart of the ship. This deck was assigned to general crew, and it wasn't the first time she'd been here today. Her heart sunk even lower when she realized what she'd done, and why.

Or rather, what I'm about to do.

Praying no one would see her as she walked, Caroline moved mechanically down the corridor, wiping her soiled fingers on her trousers and trying very hard not to cry. When she found the hatch she was looking for, she pressed the call button in a pattern she hadn't used for almost forty years.

Three short, two long. And once more after a few seconds had passed.

Damn you for making me wait. This is a mis—

The hatch snapped open, revealing a half-dressed, bleary-eyed Daniel Tepes.

"Commander? I...what is it?"

Caroline stepped into his quarters and arms, slamming a fist into the control panel to close the hatch. Her other arm pressed him to her so tightly she could hear him struggle for breath, but with her eyes shut tight and face buried against his chest, she didn't care. The smell of him filled her nose, chasing away the nightmare odor of whatever it was Horace had become inside.

"Caroline, what happened? What can I do? Did Horace do something?"

Her eyes snapped open, and the tears she'd been fighting flowed freely. Her head came up, and she saw Daniel looking down at her, his own eyes wet and full of life.

Caroline spun him around, using both arms to pin him against the hatch. His face was too far away, so she pulled it down roughly to her level, stretching up to meet his lips as his arms pressed her close. Her body ached for him, for the love they'd shared so long ago, and she could feel in his kiss that he remembered too.

When their lips finally parted, Caroline shuddered, panting against his neck and drawing in the scent of his sweat with each ragged gasp. One of his hands found the small of her back, the other cupped her bottom and lifted her easily from the deck. Her heart skipped a beat as he nibbled at her ear, his warm breath teasing her hair as they moved toward his bed.

"Is this what you really want, Carrie? I don't want to…"

Caroline bit down on the skin of his collarbone, putting an end to any further objections. In response, Daniel slammed her down on the bed, fully tearing her sleeve open in the process. Her skin was alive, nipples instantly hard and desperate to break free of her undertunic. She kicked off her left boot hard enough to send it flying into the bulkhead, and she pulled him down for another savage kiss as he hurriedly worked the buttons of her uniform.

"No more questions, Danny," she gasped out between kisses.

"Just…love me."

DEMARCO

SAM HUNCHED FORWARD in his chair, trying to keep his face level with the holo recorder. When Ykaterina suggested he use her equipment to make his calls, he thought she'd meant the Admiralty compartment, not her private quarters.

Unfortunately, just like the rest of the Fleet the workstation was built more for someone like Andreison than a man of his size—or a woman of the commodore's small stature.

And after too many hours wedged into this damned chair, I'm considering cutting off my legs rather than stretching them out when I'm done.

"I can't say for sure what did or did not happen, Anya. But my comms expert tells me the footage has been altered, and from what she showed me it was towards a very specific goal. Just try to keep an open mind about it, and we'll talk more once you arrive."

Sam stopped the recording, and signed it with his personal code before forwarding it to Marya on the flight deck for transmission to SDF *Nelson*, along with her latest analysis on the data itself.

For all the good it will do us. Anya Goro isn't accepting calls today, though Marya did confirm that Nelson *received my initial hail, and the two that followed. But we can't wait out by this FTL beacon forever, so it's time to start pushing rocks up another hill.*

After Horace, Anya was the most hawkish captain in the Home Fleet. Sam's appeal to reason probably wouldn't do anything to change her mind, but although she hadn't officially thrown in with Kołodziejski, she hadn't exactly come out against him either.

We need more allies if this is going to work. And it's not like I can just tell people the truth, can I? We are technically committing treason.

Well, counter–treason, but treason nonetheless.

Sam sat up straight and rolled his back, feeling the vertebra pop as his spine relaxed. He threw in a few head tilts for good measure to sort out his neck, then carefully unfolded himself from the work-station.

Since accepting Ykaterina's patronage, Sam had spent most of his time in Earth-normal gravity, and although fleet-mandated workouts made it easier to cope, the constant toll on his joints was something no amount of physical therapy ever eased.

After the first hour of recordings, Sam considered having Marya kill the shuttle's grav while he worked. But on a vessel this size that was an all-or-nothing proposition, and the commodore liked her tea from a cup, rather than a bulb. Although both scenarios were self-indulgent, Ykaterina's preferences were the deciding factor here, and she was far more comfortable at simulated Earth-norm than the Mars-norm used aboard most vessels.

I suppose I could have had Marya work the recorder for me while I sat in comfort, but she's got her own tasks for Ykaterina, and there are things I need to do today that she can't be a part of.

Yet.

A quick turn around the commodore's quarters worked a few of the kinks out of his legs, and after a second go-round he gratefully settled into the overstuffed couch Ykaterina insisted follow her onto any shuttle in lieu of a standard-sized bed. It was just wide enough for her to lie down on for a quick nap, or for a certain over-sized flag officer to sit and rest his legs for a few minutes. It creaked slightly as he leaned back, but he knew from experience the sturdy frame would accept his weight.

This thing's probably older than both of us put together, and has supported a lot of privileged asses over the years.

The couch was a lot like the commodore: old, comfortable, and one hundred percent impractical. Everything about it screamed excess, but no one—especially not Sam—dared call her bluff and refuse to transport it. Moving it on and off shuttles was never quite an order and certainly more than a request, and after a few months Sam and his crew just got used to dealing with it several times a week.

In contrast to the antique couch was the second object he'd loaded in for the commodore before they left EFS *Clarke* for L6 station, a low ceroplast table crafted to look like a solid block of aluminum. Few visitors knew it contained one of the most advanced data cores in the Fleet, or that its surface also disguised an unhackable, touch-interface desk suite keyed to her, and her alone.

Currently, its incredible processing power was extravagantly employed in supporting a mess tray with a synthbeef sandwich and a sealed cup of imitation au jus, along with an unlabeled bulb of something to drink.

Curious, Sam bit off the nipple, and took a cautious sip. The rich, fruity flavors of a planetside red wine activated all his senses, and he indulged himself in a second sip.

Never a dull moment with the commodore and her staff. Knowing Ykaterina, this bulb, or rather, the bottle it came from, is probably an extravagance most people on Earth will never enjoy. The flavors are completely wasted on me, but given how little arable land is left down there, it's likely one of the best ones left.

Another thing we need to fix once this shadow war has ended.

Sam put the bulb down, and started in on the sandwich. The first bite was a bit bland, but having never tasted the real thing, Sam thought the now-cold sandwich was adequate, if a bit underspiced. The faux jus added a lot to the flavor of his second bite, soaking the bread and protein in a tangy wetness.

Better than normal Fleet fare, for sure. Probably tasted different when first served.

I'll have to try that, someday.

Sam ate mechanically, eyes resting on a point somewhere beyond the compartment walls, searching the imagined blackness of space for purpose, if not answers. He dipped his sandwich as necessary, chewing each bite to near liquefaction before he swallowed and took another. It was a ritual he'd perfected over the years to minimize his body's problems with standard rations, and one of many reasons he preferred to eat alone, and in silence.

When the sandwich was done, Sam was no closer to a solution to their problems than when he started. Another sip of wine didn't add anything more to his analysis, leaving him to his initial assessment of his—no, their—situation

Fuck. Andreison's right, we are being assholes about all this. Too wrapped up in our fake virtues to realize how full of shit our entire situation is.

Marya's revelations had changed everything, and it was now his job to keep her alive—and cooperative—long enough to build a case against Horace Kołodziejski that even Admiral Worthy's patronage couldn't sweep under the rug.

At the same time, he had to admire Horace's audacity. His position was a populist one, shared not only by the majority of the uninformed citizens of the Reclamation, but also the entirety of Mars.

The gennies are "not us" in every way possible, and have been gone long enough that they're an easy target for resentment.

But they're back now, and it's time for us to end this pointless feud. There's no way forward as a divided species, and it's our job to pave the way for a new understanding.

Although he wasn't much of a drinker, Sam took up the bulb and gave it a hard squeeze, filling his mouth with the wine and then swallowing it in one big, burning gulp. Warmth spread throughout his chest, and he savored the feeling for almost a minute before he surrendered to his relentless work ethic and returned to the commodore's workstation.

"Marya."

The station's pickups dutifully connected him to Andreison on the flight deck, and her prompt response was one more point in her favor.

"Sir. No response from *Nelson* as yet. I've instructed the beacon to send another transmission at 2830, and again whenever *Nelson's* transponder is in alignment. Will there be anything else?"

How in the worlds did you let them bury you in obscurity, Andreison? You're every bit the professional—a perfect officer, really—when you set aside your ego. When I think of what we could have done, where you'd be if you'd just...

"Yes, thank you, Sub-Lieutenant. I need a secure channel to EFS *Clarke*, and set course for her as soon as I'm finished. We've been gone long enough."

"Aye, aye, sir. I'll ping you when we're ready. And you might want to check in on the commodore when you have some time. The Admiralty compartment's pickups are registering a very interesting chanty, and her steward's having problems with the harmonies."

Sam's own abilities in that area had been tested early on in his relationship with the commodore, and found lacking. He could only imagine what Mr. Curtis was going through at the moment.

Then again, there's probably at least three more of these wine bulbs floating around...

"Understood. I'll check in on them as soon as we're finished."

"Yes, Sir. I have Commander Salisbury for you now."

Well, that was fast. One more reason to keep her around, I guess.

"Put him through, Marya. And thank you. I'll let you know as soon as we're ready to fly."

Andreison closed the channel as soon as he was done speaking, and opened up a red blinking indicator for his next conversation. So far, she'd done everything he'd asked of her and more, while at the same time powering though the analysis of the *Valiant* data for the commodore.

I hope you're right about Mira Harlan being alive, Marya. Because if you ever focused your full attention on revenge, I'm not sure there's anyone in the worlds that could stop you.

Sam opened the channel, and the anxious face of his second-in-command filled the display.

"Fleet Captain DeMarco. It's good to see you, sir."

"Thank you, Kent. Did you get the packet I sent? We're on our way, and it's somewhat time-sensitive."

Salisbury hesitated before answering, and Sam had a feeling he knew why. What he was asking was not an easy thing, but all the same a thing that needed doing.

"It's important, Kent. She's been dealt a bad hand, no matter what you may have heard about her. This is the very least she's due, and I want this taken care of before we arrive. Will you be able to handle this, or should I call BuPers myself to straighten things out?"

Sam wasn't particularly looking forward to that conversation, but was definitely prepared to have it should the need arise. His hope was that Kent could take care of things without his intervention, thus mitigating the impact of a Fleet Captain throwing his weight around the already complicated bureaucratic nightmare that was Marya Andreison's career.

"No, sir. I can handle it. Is there anything else you or the commodore will need on arrival?" The implied promise that Sam would use his influence to smooth things over should Kent encounter any difficulties softened his subordinate's demeanor somewhat, but he was still visibly uncomfortable with his task.

And it's not going to get any easier going forward.

"There is, in fact. I'm having some compartmented analysis sent over that that will need dedicated core space. My pilot..." he said, avoiding saying Marya's name aloud to ease the situation, "...will send an authorization code to go along with it. This is a request straight from the commodore, so please prioritize accordingly."

"How large a file, sir?"

"She'll give you the relevant details. And Mr. Salisbury?"

"Yes, sir?"

"Try to keep an open mind. I have a feeling you two are going to be talking quite a bit in the next few days."

Kent's apparent discomfort ratcheted up a notch as he put all the pieces together, eyes widening and sitting up a bit straighter in his chair. Though they were many millions of kilometers apart, Sam wanted to put a hand on his shoulder to reassure him.

"I'll...I'll try, sir. I'll route a secure packet if I run into any difficulties."

"That's all I can ask for, son. We'll talk more when I arrive. DeMarco out."

"Aye, sir. Over and out."

As the holo winked out of existence, Sam pressed down on the table with both hands, shoving back against the too-small chair and savoring the friction of his palms against the smooth surface. He held himself there for almost a minute, letting his back and shoulders tense until the feeling moved all the way down his arms to the heels of his hands. He took a small breath, then blew out a much larger one until spots danced in front of his eyes.

When he finally let himself slump, the feeling of release was almost orgasmic. Blood and oxygen and relief spread outward from his core, mixed with the pleasant warmth of Ykaterina's wine. Tiny moments of victory like this were hard to come by, and discharging at least some of his unspoken debt to Marya lightened his load enough to justify the briefest of smiles.

Okay. What's next?

18 JULY, 2640 OER

JANTINE

"How much longer will the repairs to the track take this time, JonB?"

Jantine looked past the civvie towards the east, a seemingly unending expanse of green hills and blue sky. Sol was climbing high in the sky when they arrived here, and it had moved several degrees while the train sat idle.

JonB's face was smudged with some black substance different from the dirt on his jumpsuit and forehead. He appeared not to notice, and Jantine had to admit she liked the way it looked.

"It depends on whether the tracks are intact under the soil. They should be, the foundation blocks are sunk deep into the ground. But we won't know how much for sure until we dig it out. Katra's forward survey found intact tracks coming out of the ground half a kilometer ahead."

Jantine nodded. Katra had already relayed this information through the scattercomm, but the longer the team stayed in one place, the more exposed she felt. Not being in control was becoming the norm rather than the exception, and she didn't like it.

Working through the night, JonB, Carlton, and Mira had constructed a working transport, attached several empty containers to it, and got them moving toward Chicago before dawn. Mira had mentioned in passing that she used to repair things aboard *Valiant*, but when the three of them got to work, the woman's skill was truly impressive.

Another thing she's better at than the rest of us. Perhaps JonB's plan was not too far off the mark after all.

"Are we going to have to lay down new tracks again?"

Although the engine was running fine off the converted power cells, several kilometers from their starting point they'd had to stop when the rail line ran out of metal tracks, and again a few hours later when fallen trees blocked their path.

"Most likely not. But then again, we weren't expecting to do it the last two times either. The system is in very good shape overall, but after four hundred years, I'm just happy we've made it this far."

JonB's words encapsulated everything about their mission to date. No amount of planning could have predicted they'd stumble onto the one ship in all the universe that had a sleeping Alpha aboard, or that during their chaotic arrival, they'd find an ally so perfectly suited to their predicament.

We would never have come to this point without Mira Harlan. Our escape from the Valiant, our improbable landing, all of it happened because she was with us.

And the greatest miracle of all is that she did not abandon us when Serene betrayed her.

Although Mira had reached her own peace with the Alpha, what Serene had done, or at the very least allowed to happen, still made Jantine uneasy. Mira seemed to be adapting well enough to yet another change in her status, but having a project to work on certainly helped.

In fact, Jantine had had to order her and the Betas to take a rest period before they started traveling, but after they'd slept a few hours it had not taken much more work to make the engine fully operational. The adapted power cells required frequent recharging, but Sol had energy to spare.

"In answer to your first question, I think an hour, maybe two, if we, as Mira Harlan says, 'put our backs to it.' Possibly sooner, but I can't say for sure."

There was hesitation in JonB's voice, and Jantine could tell he wanted to ask her something else. Ever since Mira had joined their thoughts, she was more understanding of his peculiar mannerisms. At times, Jantine almost sensed what he was going to say on her own, but the rational part of her brain knew that couldn't be true.

We are what we are, nothing more. To expect more from life is to court disappointment and failure.

She let the silence linger, hoping he'd bring up his question without any prompting from her. His eyes focused on something over her shoulder, and she saw his jaw clench slightly as he made up his mind.

"Of course, this would go faster with an additional pair of hands. Jason and Artemus can only do so much..."

Jason. One more unwelcome change initiated by Mira Harlan's strange ways.

Jantine wasn't really upset that the Omega had taken a name, or even that Mira had started telling her people stories of ancient Earth. She was as surprised as the rest of the team to hear the Omega announce his choice through Mira before they boarded the train, and although she did not fight the change, Jantine had needed a private explanation from Mira to truly accept it.

It did solve one of her problems, that of how to tell the Omegas apart. From where she stood, Jantine could see that Jason had painted a red stripe on his head, and was playfully throwing dirt at Artemus as they worked to clear the tracks. Carlton was with them as well, smiling and laughing as he dodged head-sized clumps of packed soil. It was the happiest she'd seen the Beta since the death of his crèche-sib Harren, and if this was the ultimate result of Mira Harlan's meddling, it was a livable outcome.

Then again, the pendulum swings both ways.

Jantine turned and followed JonB's gaze to the other Omega, walking along the tracks at the rear of the train of transport vehicles with Serene. O-6913 was leaning down to offer support to Serene, who was holding one of his fingers in her hand as she walked.

Serene was adapting well to Earth, gaining color and strength by the hour. She was still the most beautiful being Jantine had ever encountered, and her heart ached for harboring its thoughts of betrayal. But despite the additional lifetimes of experience she'd stolen from Mira, she was dangerously naïve, and not fit to lead their expedition.

As Jantine and JonB watched, Serene let go of O-6913's hand, and went tumbling down a low hill out of sight. She was alarmed at first, but then she heard the Alpha's sweet laughter, and saw her race back up the rise only to throw herself down it again. The Omega was too far away for Jantine to make out its expression, but she knew it had to be one of amazement.

"Will our children do that too?"

JonB's question was an interesting one. No matter how distasteful the thought of natural births was to both of them, until he could build gestation chambers and crèches, the colony's children would most likely run unfocused and wild just like Serene.

We'll have to find the sleepers first, and resolve our issues with the humans. But maybe...

Leaving the question unanswered, Jantine started walking toward the Alpha and her hulking escort. JonB did not follow her, for which she was thankful.

What I have to say is not for him to hear.

Serene repeated her tumbling fall one more time as Jantine approached, then spent time examining something on the ground. Wondering if she'd found an ant, Jantine waited patiently to be acknowledged. O-6913's glare wasn't the recognition she desired, and Serene would have to deal with her as senior military commander, if not as an equal.

"Jantine! Look what I found!"

Serene's smile was radiant, made more so by several spots of dirt on her face. Her borrowed clothing was similarly soiled, but as with JonB, on the whole Jantine found the imperfections pleasing.

What she wasn't expecting was for the child to run at her full speed, and wrap her arms around her waist in a tight embrace. O-6913 started forward, but then stopped as a glow of pure happiness enveloped all three mods.

Serene disengaged, and held up a brightly colored plant for her inspection.

"Isn't it wonderful? It's called a *daisy!* Mira used to pull the petals off and sing a song about her friend Tommy. He loves me, he loves me not. He lo-oves me. Here, you can have this one, there are lots of them!"

Not knowing what else to do, Jantine took the plant from Serene, and held it while the child began to twirl in place.

"I love it here. It's much better than the train. How long can we stay?"

Jantine searched O-6913's face for some clue as to how she should react. Serene's transformation was something she had no referent for, and her behavior was entirely at odds with the Alphas she'd interacted with during training. It was almost as if she'd suffered some sort of injury, and when the girl spiraled in for another hug, Jantine used her free hand to search Serene's head for a contusion. She could feel none on the surface, and the short stubble now forming on Serene's head scratched her fingers.

"JonB thinks it will be several hours. He would like to shorten that time if possible."

Jantine kept her eyes on O-6913, willing him to follow her unspoken order. Serene's head moved under her hand, first to Jantine's face, then turning to look at the Omega. The emotions she was projecting changed subtly, and Jantine thought she detected a sense of urgency combined with determination.

The Omega's face seemed to tighten up, and it wasn't until Serene repeated whatever mental instructions she'd given aloud that Jantine understood.

Grumpy. Mira calls him Grumpy...

"Go. I will be safe with Jantine, she is my friend, too. The others need you more than I do right now."

From anger to frustration to cruelty, Jantine had seen a lot of expressions cross O-6913's face in the last day. But she never expected to see total shock. Even when Doria was dying, the Omegas were stoic. It wasn't until they'd detected Serene's distress beacon that they started to change, and Jantine wondered yet again what might have happened if the mission had proceeded as planned.

Her next thought was both surprising and unexpected.

We would all of us have become ants. Smaller than we should be, and hidden from the world.

The Omega lowered his gaze and walked forward to join the other mods. She followed him with her eyes, and saw JonB still standing where he'd left him. The Beta was gesturing to O-6913 as he approached, but the Omega ignored him and plodded on to the front of the train.

"Will you walk with me, Jantine?" Serene's voice against her stomach was muffled, but Jantine could still hear her well enough. "We can pick more daisies, and talk."

Jantine looked down into the Alpha's big eyes, and knew that despite her reservations she could deny the child nothing.

"Of course."

Serene gripped Jantine's left hand firmly and pulled the Beta after her as she started walking. Jantine kept her eyes moving, scanning the vegetation for the snakes Mira had warned about and wondering what she was supposed to do with the daisy in her hand.

"I am sorry, you know," Serene said.

The words took Jantine by surprise, mostly because the cloud of happiness that had surrounded Serene vanished abruptly as she spoke.

Keeping her face and thoughts neutral, Jantine erected her mental defenses. "About what?"

Since Malik's death, she'd come to miss his casual way of pulling the truth out of people. It was a skill she had trouble mastering, mainly because unlike Malik, she trusted everyone to say what they meant the first time.

"About Mira. It was wrong, what happened. I wanted you to know that I understand that."

All Jantine could do was nod. This was certainly no child of the colonies, and she had no protocols for speaking to an apologetic Alpha.

"But despite the pain it caused her, I'm not sad it happened. I understand so much more now, especially how hard this must be for you."

Serene let go of her hand, and flopped down on her back in the tall grass. Jantine crouched beside her, still uncertain as to what exactly was going on.

"In what way?"

"There's so much I still don't know about the current Colonies, and my memories of life before I went to sleep are not all that clear. But the ones I have now are very complimentary of your abilities. O-6068 in particular has a great deal of trust in you."

"Jason. O-6068 is called Jason now."

When it hit her that she'd just reflexively and openly challenged an Alpha, Jantine felt dizzy. She sat down, fighting to keep control of her emotions and prepared for the worst. While none of the other mods could see them, Serene was well within her rights to discipline her.

"That's a nice name. Do you know what it means?"

Swallowing, Jantine forced herself to answer. Something was not right here, but the only way to determine what it was was to continue this bizarre conversation.

"As I understand it, Jason was an explorer on ancient Earth. He led a team of warriors on a variety of missions, eventually returning home to seize control of a kingdom from his half-brother."

Serene nodded, and closed her eyes before speaking.

"It means 'healer' in the language of that people. It's an old name, but the origin of yours is even older. It's from the same part of the world, but religious in nature. It means, 'God is gracious.'"

Where is this coming from? We do not teach these things in the crèche...

The answer came to Jantine in a rush, and she was glad she was sitting down when it did. Serene's eyes were open now, and her head was turned to look at Jantine with an expression she'd come to know very well in the last day.

Mira Harlan learned different things as a child than we did. And probably spent her time picking flowers and playing in sunlight.

"I see that you understand. I don't mean to pry, but I had to know. Yes, Mira's memories are very strong in me right now, and they tell me more than anything that I need your help. O-6913 keeps waiting for me to tell him what to do, and is so convinced something bad will happen to me that he's pushing the rest of you away. Especially you, but we both know why."

Jantine nodded. There never was much hope that they could seize control of the group from Serene, but something in the way she was speaking made the Beta think that perhaps it wasn't necessary.

"I'm not upset, or mad, as Mira would say. Especially not after what I've done, however well-intentioned it was. But it's precisely that mistake that lets me understand why you are plotting against me."

"We didn't want…you shouldn't blame…it was for…for…"

Jantine couldn't make the words come out. She felt her control slipping, and years of conditioning told her what was going to happen next: Serene was about to kill her.

But for some reason, she did not, though how Jantine felt now, staying alive was worse. Instead, the Alpha crawled over and laid her head in Jantine's lap and started to cry.

Jantine put her hand on the Alpha's head again, fighting to keep her own emotions in check. Between her sobs, Serene was still speaking.

"I don't know what to do. All of them are in my head, telling me you need to be punished. But Mira's there too, and Doria, and they keep asking me why.

Jantine felt even worse.

"Why, Jantine. Why does it have to be this way?"

Jantine didn't know the answer, but from her own time listening to Mira, she knew what to do. She pulled Serene up from her lap into a hug, and kissed the crying child on the top of her head.

Serene hugged her back with surprising strength, and for a

moment Jantine thought she'd decided to kill her after all. But she kept on crying instead, until her sobs were replaced by long, wet sniffles.

Jantine felt the urge to start rocking, and the motion made her feel better. Serene's happy aura returned, and Jantine could make out two words whispered into the folds of her jumpsuit.

"Thank you."

"It's all right. It's all right. If you have to do it, I understand."

Serene's head shifted under her cheek, and Jantine pulled her own head back to look into her eyes. The child's face was puffy and red, but Mira Harlan's smile was firmly in place on her tiny lips.

"Don't be silly. If I kill you, who's going to help me find the sleepers? Also, I think JonB would be sad if you died, and I'm done hurting people. It's not very nice, and I want to be a nice person from now on."

Jantine couldn't help smiling herself. But before she could thank the Alpha for her life, Serene did something with her fingers that made Jantine give out a very un-leader-like shriek. She tried to roll away, but Serene's grip was secure, and her laughter was infectious.

Oh, child of Earth and sky. What have you done to me, and what strange creatures are we becoming...

MIRA

"MAY I SPEAK?"

Katra's voice was strained, as if the words cost her something to say. Mira wasn't sure what she wanted, as the Gamma's arrival in the train's control cab was wholly unexpected.

After last night, Jantine's instructions were that all the mods should practice and maintain mental shields. Katra's military mind had taken to it much faster than the others. After only a brief demonstration of what Jantine wanted, Katra nodded and vanished completely from Mira's perception.

It had been fun to track her movements during the train's frequent stops by how frightened JonB and Carlton were by her frequent mock ambushes, but over time Mira had found it necessary to close off her perceptions and do her best to minimize her interactions with the others. Something was wrong, and without the Gamma memories to guide her, the pain in her head was getting worse as the day went on. Now Katra wanted to talk, and so far her conversations had been full of nothing but strong emotions.

But it's not like I can say no, is it? If she genuinely wants help with something, I have to at least listen. And until we get the tracks dug out, we're not going anywhere.

"Of course. Please, sit down."

The train's cab was easily twice the size of their escape shuttle's flight deck, and was set up more like living quarters than a working control center. Mira was sitting at a small table that folded down from the compartment's wall, on a small chair that did the same. She waved Katra toward the one on the opposite side.

The Gamma wrinkled her nose as she unfolded the chair and sat, and Mira was reminded of how long she'd been hiding in here.

Katra looked around the otherwise shining compartment, searching for hidden enemies. Once her visual survey was complete, she focused her attention on the table itself, and Captain Martin's chessboard.

Mira had voiced reservations about taking the carved wooden set with her from the shuttle, but the captain had insisted that she have it. "You need to have something non-regulation about you, Harlan. It gives people a reason to stop and talk."

Looks like you're right again, sir.

Mira savored the memory of Aloysius Martin's voice in her head. It hurt to remember how he was at the end, half-blind and most of the way dead. But once Jason had helped her rewire his brain a bit, he was as alert as ever.

"You do not want me here. I will leave."

Katra made to stand up, but Mira sent her a mental apology to go with her upraised hand. The effort sent fresh spikes of pain into her brain, and she closed her left eyelid tight against the flashing stars.

"No, it's all right. A painful memory, that's all. Please, stay. What can I help you with?"

Katra looked uncertain, but settled into the chair anyway. She was still nervous about something, and Mira chanced another probe of her mind. The Gamma's shields were still in place, and the resulting pain in her own head let her know what a fantastic idea it was to stop trying for a while.

Now if I can just get the others to stop thinking so darned loud, that'll work out nicely.

"Do you play this game?"

It seemed an odd question to ask someone sitting in front of a chess set, but from her limited experience of the woman Mira knew Katra took nothing at face value.

"A little. This belonged to Captain Martin, he thought I should have it when he..."

Mira couldn't finish her sentence. It was one thing to know her commanding officer was dead, but all the training in the worlds couldn't make her like it.

"I am sorry to have killed him. Jantine says he was an honorable man."

Katra's words left her a different kind of speechless. Even though the mods' arrival in the solar system had killed dozens, if not hundreds of Mira's crewmates, it was an accidental encounter. And the Gamma had no way of knowing that Mira was directly responsible for the deaths of at least three of her friends, and bore a large share of the blame for the others.

And she's apologizing to me?

"Captain Martin used to say that apologizing was a sign of weakness. We used to say belowdecks that he was full of crap, but what I think he meant instead was 'if you didn't do anything wrong, don't worry about it.' Also full of crap, but it's a bit more honest."

Katra reached out her hand and collected two pawns from the board. One white, and one black.

Oh. Okay, here we go. She's found a way to kick my butt and leave no marks.

Katra closed her fists around the pieces, and held them out for Mira to choose. The Gamma cocked her head as if listening to something, but Mira's brain already hurt too much to go looking around where she wasn't wanted. Tapping Katra's left hand with her finger revealed the white pawn, and the two women cleared the board and reset the pieces.

Mira didn't care too much about the outcome, so she selected a standard opening from memory and moved a pawn forward.

Katra did not hesitate in her response, and moved one of her own. She stared at the piece for a while after letting it go, but gave no indication she was unhappy with the move.

No fear. Good. At least, I think it is.

"It is a warrior's game. We learn to play in the crèche, but we do not have boards of this type."

Mira advanced her queen's knight, and Katra moved her pawn a second time, giving the piece a longer look.

"It was a gift from his grandfather, I think. The captain didn't talk about family in the wardroom much, but I do know he was a very old man, with very strong views on honoring one's past."

Mira moved her knight to the center of the board, and Katra advanced a second black pawn to meet it.

"Your commander was a very wise man. It is important to honor traditions."

Mira advanced a second pawn of her own, which was quickly captured by Katra's first.

Oops.

Katra was studying the board intently now, keeping the captured piece in her right hand instead of setting it down on the table.

"When he did mention him, it was fondly. Some of his last words were about his 'opa,' a favorite saying of some kind."

Mira's queen took the field, capturing the black pawn that had invaded her side of the board. Mira set it aside, and noticed Katra's eyes following the motion of her hand before returning to the game.

"Do you remember the words?"

It was Katra's turn to move a knight, and Mira deployed one of her bishops.

"I think so. It was in Dutch, an old Earth language the captain tried to get us all to learn. I don't know what it means, but it was something like *'dursten zuln de latsen jin.'*"

Katra smiled, and Mira had the distinct impression it was the expression a wolf used when cornering a rabbit.

Then her bishop came out of nowhere, placing Mira in check.

"I think you mean *'de eersten zullen de laatsten zijn.'* It was a favorite saying of Hendrik Trajectinus, Count of Solms, Commander of the *Garde te Voet.* A general in your seventeenth century."

Mira stared at Katra, uncertain she'd heard the mod correctly. Her accent was flawless, a near copy of the captain's, but to her knowledge Katra had never been to Earth before, especially not to the European Reclamation. Despite the fact that her king was in jeopardy, or the alien warrior woman's has a better understanding of Earth's military history than she did after top marks at the Academy, all Mira could think about was the feeling in Captain Martin's mind as he'd said the same words, knowing he was about to die and trying to share something important with her.

"What does it mean?"

"It is a religious proverb, but also a military one. 'The last will be first, and the first last.' It speaks of service to the greater good, and of pride."

Matthew, 20:16. The parable of the workers in the vineyard. But why would the captain choose that as his last message, in a language he knew I didn't speak?

"It is your move, Lieutenant Commander."

Mira numbly slid her bishop up to protect her king. Katra pressed the attack, taking the piece offered and sacrificing her bishop to Mira's knight on the contested space. Katra followed the move by castling, and then in a completely unexpected gesture tipped her king on its side before standing up.

"You are weary, we will speak another time."

Mira was out of her chair as well, but was tired enough that she hadn't noticed her left leg had fallen asleep. She stumbled forward into Katra's arms, who took her weight easily and steadied her on her feet.

Instead of thanking the mod, Mira simply held on, wanting to know more about what had just happened, and why.

Katra eased Mira back into her chair, and sat down herself. Mira made a show of massaging her leg for a few seconds while she tried to get a read on what Katra was thinking. Her shields were firmly in place, but her body language indicated she was definitely uncomfortable.

"You...Katra, what did you want? When you came in here, you wanted to ask me something, didn't you?"

Katra nodded, and took a few seconds to compose her thoughts. There was something about the Gamma's smile that pulled at Mira's heart, but she couldn't quite put a finger on the feeling.

"Last night, I was wrong to threaten you. I found your transformation unsettling, and did not know what the future would bring. After Jarl, and Crassus...Jantine, Artemus and I are the only soldiers left. They have accepted you as one of us, but I needed to know more.

"When you were assaulted by the Omega, it was your right to claim both their lives. Jantine could never act against an Alpha; Betas are born to serve. When she told us what had happened, I stood aside and ordered Artemus to take no action as well. We would have killed you afterward, of course. But it was your right to try."

"I...Katra, I never..."

"But then you did something we still do not understand. You repaid horror with kindness, something no warrior of the Colonies ever does. And in a moment when you had every right to be vengeful, you turned enemies into allies."

She doesn't know. Can't know, if I want them to see me as a whole person. But I have to try and explain...

"You have to understand, Katra. It's...it's not our way to seek vengeance. It's not *my* way. I have fought battles before, and I've taken lives. Some of the people I've killed were men and women I trained myself, who at the time believed *they* were the ones doing the right thing. I even took a few shots at you in the transfer bay if I'm not mistaken.

"But that's war, not vengeance. I don't hate you for what happened on *Valiant*, and I don't hate Serene or Grumpy for what they did. It was an accident, nothing more. That proverb, do you know what it really means? It says that it doesn't matter what happens to you in life, but how you respond to the challenges it gives you *does*. It's about fairness, and compassion—"

The Gamma was the one now who looked like the wolf was coming for her, and was halfway to the door in a heartbeat. Mira wondered what colonial taboo she'd blundered into this time.

"No, Katra, don't go..."

Katra froze in place, then fell easily into a ready stance. It took Mira a few seconds to realize that, however indirectly, she'd given Katra an order, and the Gamma had followed it.

She addressed me by my rank earlier, not as "human..."

"Katra, I'm not sure what to do here. I don't remember what I'm supposed to say, not anymore. Tell me what you want, and I'll try to help you. But you have to talk to me, please."

The Gamma only smiled, and moved to the ladder leading down the side of the train. But she paused before leaving, face as composed and flawless as ever.

"I came to tell you, Mira Harlan of Earth, that I acknowledge you and your accomplishments. I look forward to fighting at your side, as does Artemus. We are at your service, until the end."

Did that just happen? How the heck am I supposed to respond to that?

"The black pawn. It is six grams heavier than any other piece of the same size. If you are studying the chessboard for a message from your captain, you might want to start there."

Mira looked to the two black pieces on her side of the board, and out of the corner of her eye saw Katra slide down the ladder. She was almost afraid to pick up the pawn she'd captured, slightly smaller but from this angle almost identical to the bishop next to it. Part of her was in awe at how skillfully Katra had manipulated the board to put it there, and the rest of her wanted to know what might be hidden inside.

She reached out and took the piece in her hand. Her eyes widened as she confirmed Katra's statement. It was hard to see, but there was a seam inside the carved groove on the pawn's base. It resisted her attempts to twist it open, and also did not budge when she pulled on it.

Well, I'll be. Aloysius Martin, you old fox.

Whatever the captain had hidden inside, it meant enough to him that he'd altered or replaced one of his "opa's" custom pieces to keep it safe. And Mira knew of one secret in particular he was willing to die to keep...

RAMIREZ

ALONSO LAID BACK on his bunk, head swimming with details from dozens of personnel files and even more images captured from *Valiant*'s now defunct pod network.

There has to be a way to add this all up. There has to be... something.

So far, hours of research and in-depth analysis had provided him with no clarity. Worse yet, so far no one inside the Hull had any way to extend their lives but Alonso, and despite his best efforts to keep it running, *Valiant* was still dead in space.

At least I got our spin stabilized, and the data core back online. And eighteen more hours of heat, oxygen, and light, but so far every single member of the crew has told me personally, that they're willing to sacrifice all of it on a mission I designed to send a message in a cosmic bottle towards cislunar space.

Sometimes, this job really sucks.

Even the troopers from *Indomitable* had grudgingly volunteered their remaining oxygen bottles and power cells, though they'd done so by messenger, not even giving him the courtesy of a comm.

The Martians as a whole were ciphers, with personnel files

scrubbed clean of any personal details or character. All but two of them were non-coms, with Lts Petrovina and Olvrsdóttir having the most informative files. And of the two, only Olvrsdóttir had even bothered to acknowledge him as second-in-command to Commander Callaway, or even communicate with him directly.

"I think we should talk," she said. But she also asked me to come find her, and I clearly haven't done that yet.

Idiot.

Alonso didn't know why he hadn't contacted the prim and proper Martian officer, other than he was more focused on squeezing every last erg and milliliter from the ship's stores. He wasn't really a people person, and though her offer of collaboration intrigued him, when he'd received the message about the Martian stores, he'd just assumed she'd been involved in extending it.

It was certainly the right call to combine their resources, but after that brief contact he'd heard nothing more out of any of them. In fact, other than sharing body heat to warm the Hull's air, the Martians hadn't contributed much at all to their continued survival.

And unless I can manufacture another miracle, we'll be huddling together to survive soon enough.

Alonso's wristcomm chirped, but he canceled the call without looking. He'd already heard everything the crew had to say, and Commander Callaway had told him not to make contact until the miracle was real. Instead, he turned his attention to the image projected onto the compartment's ceiling, of a tiny shuttle hiding behind a chunk of space rock, and an indefinable *something* at the edge of the field.

The comm chirped again, and this time Alonso answered it.

"This is not a good time. Send me a file with what you need, and I'll review it." Alonso closed the channel, regretting the words as soon as he said them. But if he was going to solve the mystery of the phantom object floating above him, he needed to concentrate.

What are you, out there? And why are you there in the first place? You're not Fleet, but you also don't match any...

The comm chirped a third time, followed by an alert from the hatch control panel. His composure shattered, Alonso sat straight up, raised the comm to his face, and shouted, "I'm. Fucking. Busy!"

"It's ok. I can wait. But please open the door, it's cold out here."

Alonso's eyes widened as he scrambled to his workstation to pull up a holo of the corridor outside his quarters. Olvrsdóttir was standing at attention in front of the hatch, freshly scrubbed and wearing a jumpsuit drawn from *Valiant*'s stores. She looked softer than she had at the briefing, but Alonso could tell from her bearing that underneath her borrowed clothes she was all angles and hard muscle.

Alonso had no idea what she wanted, and a wave of panic shot through him. He'd smoothed his hair down twice before he remembered the comm channel was still open.

"Astrid I...I'm sorry. Give me a moment to clean up in here."

Olvrsdóttir smiled, and took a step back from the hatch.

"You may have three moments, but only because I like your eyes. It's very cold out here, and I..."

Alonso leapt across the compartment and opened the hatch before she could finish, his mouth pumping several times before his voice caught up with his brain.

"Of course, come in. Please, I mean. I... "

The Martian lieutenant flowed past him into his quarters, and Alonso forgot everything he'd planned to say. All thoughts of crew manifests and resource allocations were replaced with the scent of wildflowers and honey that she left in her wake.

What the hell is wrong with me? She's...I...

Once he convinced his fingers to seal the hatch again, he leaned forward to rest his forehead on the cool metal.

Stupid, stupid, stup...

"Yes, this bothers me as well. So much mystery, these gennies. So many unknown variables."

What?

Alonso turned to see Astrid lying in almost the same spot he'd just vacated, staring up into the holo image and pointing with a long finger at the mystery object he'd highlighted while gesturing at the shuttle with her other hand.

"But we have other things to discuss now, yes? It has been many hours, and I am the one finding you."

What?

Alonso stumbled back to the workstation, barely avoiding a collision with his hardsuit standing at attention on its frame and falling hard into the chair with an audible THUMP.

Olvrsdóttir put both her palms flat on the bunk, and effortlessly floated up to a seated position. Her lips were pursed, and her eyes fixed him with a knowing stare. Desperate to avoid stammering out another nonsense response, Alonso drug himself away from her ice-blue eyes only to notice that her normally braided hair now hung loose, falling down in waves past her shoulders.

"Now, tell me. What bothers you so much you cannot talk to me all this time?"

Other than we're all going to die out here in space since your former commander decided we weren't worth saving?

"It's not any one thing, it's all of them at once."

"Pick one. We'll solve it together." Astrid's tone was playful, but he could tell she meant what she said.

"It's not that simp—"

"Yes it is. Everything is. So stop worrying. If something breaks, you fix it. If an enemy presents itself, you defeat it."

Astrid looked around the compartment, and Alonso watched as the corners of her smile turned down. Whatever survey she was making of his quarters finished in seconds, and she resumed her end of their conversation before he could respond.

"We all die, Alonso. Stop worrying about things you can't change, and focus on the time you have left. Maybe some of us live, but that's ok too. Either way, it's not your fault."

Alonso slumped forward, head bent and supported by his hands. He let out a deep sigh, then spoke to Astrid without looking up.

"I really wish it was that simple, Astrid. But it isn't. This situation is like nothing we've ever faced, and there's certainly no training manual for 'abandoned for death during an undeclared civil war.'

"There's no way I should be the person dealing with this. I'm just not the guy. And all these people, they're counting on me. You don't understand, I—"

Astrid was off the bunk and standing over him before he could say another word. She took his hands away from his face, forcing him to either look up at her or fall completely forward.

"Stop talking, Alonso. You are killing the mood. And if you don't stop tearing yourself down, I may have to take drastic action to set you straight. So for the next few minutes, I just want you to listen, understand?"

Alonso nodded, even though he really only understood half of what she was saying. It was enough for Astrid to release his head and return to the bunk, where she was now she perched on its edge, leaning forward until their faces were uncomfortably close.

"You are from Earth, correct?"

Alonso nodded again, though his pride forced him to correct her.

"Oaxaca Station. I went to the Academy on Earth, but I've really only spent a couple years on the surface."

"Close enough," Astrid said. "All that air and sunshine, free for everyone at any time. No labor riots, no rationing. Nothing to worry about when you wake up except how you will contribute to the greater good today."

Alonso sat up straight, taking a breath to rebut Astrid's oversimplified view of the Reclamation. While it was true that basic necessities were guaranteed for all citizens of Earth, there were still struggles on the surface, and even after a hundred years, the Reclamation was far from complete.

But Astrid was prepared for his answer, and cut it off with a wagging finger.

"No, you listen now. You can argue later, once you hear my story. Or rather, that of my family."

Alonso had skimmed her file, such as it was. Most of the text was redacted, and what was left mainly consisted of names and dates. He knew she was a year or so older then he was, that she'd graduated with honors from the Fleet Preparedness Center, and that her extra year in service meant she technically outranked him.

I would definitely like to know more about her, but I don't think this is the time.

Or is it? It's not like I'll have many more chances to make new friends.

"On Earth, my family was from Ukraine. A small country in Eastern Europe, when such distinctions were still observed. Not many cities of note, few resources worth fighting over other than its geography.

"It was almost ignored in the wars. Almost."

Alonso tried to keep as neutral an expression as possible, but the emotion in Astrid's voice ranked somewhere between pain and nostalgia. His own family had been forcibly removed from their land during the Reclamation, and although the evacuation was centuries past, as a fellow descendant of refugees she'd earned any listening time he could give.

"After the wars, after the evacuation orders, our family put in for emigration like everybody else. They walked for days to the nearest spaceport, but the prime berths filled up before we even left home. Corporations snapped up the orbitals, Luna had no megacities at the time, and Mars closed its borders as soon as the first ships lifted. The oceans rose and died, earthquakes destroyed what was left of Europe, and once the plagues started, no inner colony would take us.

"After years of trying, we finally got a berth outsystem on a slow-ship. But while we were in transit, the New Kiev colony was ceded to the gennies as part of the Exile. All ships from Earth were turned back on arrival without ever waking the sleepers, adding even more years to their journey. By the time our vessel returned to the home system, Juno was only place left for us to go."

Juno. Shit. That wasn't in her file. Of all our in-system colonies, the Juno mine complex is the closest place to Hell we've ever settled, and the hardest by far to escape.

Olvrsdóttir kept talking, eyes fixed on some point far beyond the walls of Alonso's quarters.

"Of course, the dome was already full when we got there. So our community crowded into corners and corridors and any space we could claim as our own, and still stay ourselves. Now we were

Earthers instead of Ukrainians, but the word meant the same thing to those who spoke it.

"Papa's father was a Doctor, so he had work. Papa himself was sold to the medical guild before he was born, and spent his whole life moving us closer to the surface. But Juno is not for humans, and the virus does not care for caves, yes?"

Alonso moved his hand across the gap between them to take Astrid's hand in his own. She grabbed it and squeezed, surprising him with her strength.

Legs and arms I can understand, powered armor isn't easy to wear. But her callouses are as thick as mine, and her grip is even stronger.

Why is she telling me this, and what am I supposed to do with her story?

Astrid was silent for almost a minute, lost in the past. Her lip was trembling, and Alonso didn't know if he was supposed to move closer or farther away, and uncertain whether the iron grip she had on his hand would let him do either.

"They tell me I had brothers. That they lived full lives, had little Ukraine babies, and died within meters of the surface. But even after many, many years of crowded quarters, missed meals, and carefully applied bribes we were still refugees. Still small people. And there was only one way out. For any of us."

Astrid squeezed his hand again, then released it. She bowed her head just enough for him to lose sight of her eyes, hair spilling over her face while she dabbed at the corner of her eye.

"Mama was dead, Papa almost so, when the Mars Central Authority came to call. He was all out of sons, but he had the only thing they still cared about—a virus-free, old Earth genome."

Alonso's eyes went wide at the implications. If the Martians were harvesting genes from offworld, it explained a lot about how they were able to sustain themselves with no immigration.

"So he sold it to them. Sold me, or the concept of me, anyway. And to make sure I grew up with all the advantages of a true Marsborn, he entered into a long-term harvesting contract."

Alonso was dumbstruck, unable to do anything more than hold still and listen to Astrid's story. Her life was so different than anything he'd even encountered, or ever would again. But her next words almost broke him.

"They kept his body alive another sixty years. His genes spread out among the Domes for whoever could afford to pay, with half the credits going into a special fund to buy me a better life. And even then, it took seventy years for that fund to buy me a place at the table.

"When I was twelve years old, they showed me the message Oliver Janics left for his true genetic children, painstakingly assembled from whatever bits of his wife's DNA they could recombine. He'd intended for us to build a new family together on Mars, to keep the dream of Ukraine alive into the future.

"But I am the only one, Alonso. The Central Authority used Oliver's genes to build a better Mars, never intending to honor their promise. I was the last viable embryo, the last legal descendant of a man who sold his soul and genetic legacy almost two hundred years ago."

Astrid straightened up just enough to meet his meet his eyes straight on, fixing him in place while she delivered the final blow.

"It wasn't easy to turn away from my people, Alonso, even though I am not really one of them. I'm better, faster, stronger. Painstakingly designed to be the perfect human, without any nasty transgenesis to get in the way.

"But being better means I have to make better choices, and siding with you and Commander Callaway was the right thing to do, and saved the most lives. That is why we do this, why we wear the uniform, and why you have to be the man you think you aren't.

"You can talk now. But no more worrying. It does not suit you."

Alonso couldn't come up with any words appropriate to the moment other than, "I'm sorry. Truly sorry."

"It is what it is. That is my past, and I'm here to talk about the future."

What?

"The future? I..."

"Alonso, I want a better life than my parents had. I don't want to live on spaceships anymore, and I certainly don't want to die on one. I want to grow old and die in open air, with the sun on my face."

"I I don't know what I'm supposed to say."

Astrid let go of his hands and shrugged, a sinuous motion which stole away what was left of his heart.

"Really, Alonso? I've been here twenty minutes now. I've told you my life, held your hands, breathed your breaths as my own, and you still haven't figured it out?

"I...Um..."

Astrid stood up, drawing Alonso to his feet with her eyes. She reached out and took his shoulders in her hands, then pulled him closer until her lips brushed his ear.

"Do you not like girls, Alonso? Or do you just not like Martians? Because as I have patiently explained, I am neither."

Alonso's breath caught in his throat, and his heart raced as her words tickled his skin.

"You are smart, Earth boy. But at the same time, not so smart." Astrid took a step forward, pushing Alonso against the bulkhead. "I like you very much, and once you stop feeling sorry for yourself, I have new orders for you. It's time to stop thinking about dying. Time to..."

Alonso stopped her next words with a kiss, which Astrid returned with enthusiasm. She tightened her grip on his shoulders, spinning him around until he sat down hard in the middle of his bunk. He raised a hand to her face, but she slapped it away, sliding her hands down his arms and pinning them at his sides. A second later, Astrid's legs were wrapped around his waist, one hand cupping the back of his head and the other working at the straps of his mess tunic.

"Turn off the lights, Alonso. Save some energy for more important things."

KOŁODZIEJSKI

I hate this place.

The office Horace had commandeered was as sterile and unimpressive as the regolith around it, but it gave him an unimpeded view of the gennie suspension units now connected to the Echo Base power grid.

Once he'd come back to himself, crumpled up against a cold metal tube with Andrew Collins looming over him, Horace immediately got to work on the next phase of his plan.

The first part of which was to start a heavy regimen of anti-psychotics. I can't lose control like that again, not with so much at stake.

And the second, well, apologies are better delivered in person. But in this case, not necessarily by me.

Getting all three hundred units out of the salvaged container and into a secured chamber hadn't been easy, and getting Dr. Watson to relocate to an adjacent laboratory had taken three direct orders and an armed escort.

And that was before we even got here.

Horace had spent his last shift aboard *Indomitable* purging both it and Echo Base of all non-essential personnel, which included what was left Aloysius' captured battlegroup. They were technically prisoners of war, and he'd let the Martian courts deal with them once this was all over. When *Indomitable* arrived at Luna, the corridors were clear, and there was a fleet of rock-hoppers waiting to take people to a secure facility in Argo City.

The process wasn't unusual for an active command, and allowed him the perfect cover to sequester the Earthers. The displaced personnel would be in Martian quarantine for the next hundred hours —long enough for a Loyalist vessel to arrive during moonshadow and ferry them all away to Mars.

Normally he'd just use *Indomitable* for the trip, but the dreadnaught was now completely invisible to other parts of the Home Fleet command loop, and he intended to keep it that way until he could once again command her. The rest of his battlegroup, and the ships he'd "inherited" from *Valiant*'s, were powered down on the far side in the deepest crater he could find, safe under the simplest camouflage possible—the stygian darkness of a Lunar night.

Handing over his command—one of them, anyway—was a lot easier to do knowing that Caroline Annakho was the one taking it on. He'd left her a full briefing packet with the modified truth about Captain Martin and the events aboard *Valiant*, some of which would become public knowledge anyway when Victor Darbin's people leaked it onto the datanets, along with the official Loyalist response.

Yes, the truth is a dangerous thing right now, and something I can't share with anybody outside my immediate circle. That imbecile Watson has twenty hours to cure me before Caroline becomes the executor of my will. And the gennie cargo we've got on ice down there is our only chance for a happy ending.

Still, I've made preparations for the other kind, should it come to that.

He hated putting Caroline in this position, but if he couldn't trust his own mind, the deception gave her plausible deniability. And after their last encounter, he had even more reasons to keep her at arm's length. Even a small distortion of the truth was better than entangling her in his true plans for the gennies.

She should have known better than to try and stop me. These fucking gennies are the enemy—they aren't even human! I'm right, and I've got an entire planet to back me up.

That fool Harrison is right as well—we're still too dependent on Earth to completely ignore the Reclamation Council, and without a proclamation we're not officially at war. But until I can plant our flag here, we need to at least pretend to follow their laws.

Other than the fact that he was dying, Kołodziejski's one remaining problem was Watson himself. In any other scenario, he'd be the first one on the list for reassignment. The Earther was too volatile to keep around Horace's secrets for much longer, and so far Watson's efforts at a cure had done him more harm than good.

I've already seen to your end, you groveling worm. If you can't find me a cure, there are plenty of Martian scientists who'll be more than happy to continue your research.

On you, if need be.

Looking down on neatly spaced rows of sleeping gennies, Horace offered a silent prayer that it wouldn't come to that. Somewhere in those alien suspension units there had to be a cure, one that could also protect his people forever.

As if the Earther could read his mind, Horace's comm buzzed with a message alert.

>>I've established a quarantine, and Subject 3 is ready.

Watson can't even send a proper message. Useless.

Resigning himself to participating in another of the Earther's fruitless experiments, Horace straightened his uniform tunic and locked down his desk terminal. Even with his own people on guard, even with the base on total security lockdown, the secrets he could access in this room were worth the lives of a hundred Watsons, and certainly those of a few hundred gennies.

His current physical state was well-matched to the base's construction, and despite feeling completely hollowed out, Horace was able to walk unassisted to, and through the office's door.

Collins and Tepes came to attention, each giving him a quick glance to determine his current condition. Horace saw a hint of a smile on Collins' face, while Tepes' slight frown was the perfect reminder of the other thing Horace needed to deal with today.

"Lab 7, Andrew. We're apparently to be witness to greatness. Again."

"Yes sir. Follow me, sir."

"I'll catch up in a moment. Daniel, a word?"

"Of course, sir." Reading his tone, Tepes popped his helmet seals for a direct—and off the books—conversation. Horace approved, though he wasn't particularly pleased with its subject matter.

"I've had some papers prepared for your cousin, Daniel. If something happens to me—"

"Sir," Daniel interrupted, taking a half step forward and dropping his voice to a near whisper, "you can't think like that. Things are going to be—"

"I have to think like that, Mr. Tepes. It's my job, and yours is to deliver the parcel in my desk drawer to Caroline should the worst happen. You know the one, yes?"

Tepes nodded, and swallowed hard before speaking.

"Yes sir. I remember."

"Good. Now you're probably right, but just in case the drawer is coded to your key. I'll be back in a bit, unless Watson's miracle happens ahead of schedule. Wait here for our return."

"Of course, sir. And if you'll permit me to say it, it's been an honor to serve you and your family."

There was something in Daniel's voice that didn't quite ring true to Horace. It wasn't that he was insincere—Horace had heard that sentiment from him many times over the years. But today it wasn't the absolute declaration of loyalty he was used to, and he didn't have time to figure out why.

"Thank you, Daniel. I've enjoyed our time together as well."

Tepes stiffened slightly, giving Horace even more reason to question his previous statement. But Collins was waiting for him, and no matter how long they'd been together, Tepes wasn't a true friend, just an exceptionally talented servant.

And there are plenty more Tepeses to choose from, if he oversteps his bounds.

Horace turned without exploring whatever was bothering Daniel, quickening his steps to catch up to Andrew twenty meters ahead. Collins said nothing about the delay, falling into step with his hands at the ready in case some threat magically materialized out of the shadows.

There we were several reasons Horace preferred the company of Andrew Collins to that of Daniel Tepes right now. Not only did the man have a complete lack of empathy—*something Daniel is increasingly blessed with of late*—but he was a Simak with an even higher rating than Horace; his enhanced perception might catch some aspect of Watson's test Horace was too emotionally invested to comprehend.

If there's anything to be learned from this encounter, one of us will see it. And if there isn't, we'll see that too.

The lab where Watson was testing his latest serums was close by, and a quick walk down a sloping ramp brought them to a set of double quarantine doors and an observation window through which they could see both the Earther, and the gennie test subject he'd chosen.

Watson was pretending to be a real officer, wearing a borrowed Fleet medical uniform complete with an encounter belt. The force field it generated protected against anything short of small arms fire, a necessary precaution when dealing with something as insidious as the Transgenic Virus.

His subject, however, was something else entirely. Stripped of his gennie-issue coveralls, he was a nearly perfect specimen of what they called a "Beta." With flawless skin and symmetrical features, he was a veritable recruiting poster for the benefits of Transgenesis, and every-thing Watson wanted to inflict on Horace in the name of science and the greater good.

The fact that Watson intended to strip all that away from him made Horace smile, and there was no time like the present to prove the Earther wrong. Horace shuffle-walked over to the intercom, and pressed the send button.

"Whenever you are ready, Doctor."

Watson nodded, then began attaching a series of devices to the gennie. Most of them were diagnostic, but Watson was also draining off gennie blood for use in his next formulations. When he was done, he looked up to a securecam inside the lab, and began his documentation.

"This is Doctor Thomas Watson, attempting Transgenic cure formulation Y19 on gennie subject 3. Male, approximately 17 T-years of age. No prior injuries, designation," Watson paused, looking down at something below the window line mouthing something before he read it aloud, "DRN-B34316. Administering the formulation now."

Watson pressed an injector to the gennie's neck, then stepped back to watch the monitors. Horace had no idea what the Earther was waiting for, but when the steady beeps he could hear through the intercom were replaced with a shrill alarm, he pressed against the glass to get a better look.

Horace didn't have long to wait. Black veins spread across the gennie's chest, and it sat up screaming. The screams were cut short when the gennie's forehead split open, and tentacles of some kind started waving around through the wound. A second later, the gennie's chest ripped apart, and its internal organs rushed out at the end of a twisted pillar of black flesh.

Both the screaming and the alarms stopped a few seconds later, and the gennie slumped over. The body twitched as the skin of its shoulders cracked, dark fluid oozing down what was left of its chest. The head tentacles grew milky eyes at their tips, several of which turned to stare at Horace.

Rage building, he stabbed a too-thin finger at the intercom.

"What the hell was that? This is your cure? You've got the greatest research facility ever built at your disposal, unlimited power, and complete freedom to experiment. And your grand plan to save my life is to kill me?"

"I can fix this. I swear. Just a little more time and I-I-I c-c-can d-d-do it." Watson was plastered against the quarantine room's back wall, and for a second Horace thought the sputtering fool was going to wipe his face with ichor-splattered hands.

"Clean this mess up, and meet me in your office. It's time we have a long overdue talk about your future, Mister Watson."

Horace cut the audio, with Watson still pleading with him on the other side of the glass. He signaled for Collins to follow, then screamed in pain as an abdominal spasm sent him to his knees.

The polished steel floor was cold on the palms of his hands, and the blue veins visible through his papery skin were eerily reminiscent of the black-blooded gennie. Skin on fire, he closed his eyes tight against the pain, and his stomach tried its best to rid him of the gennie poison flowing through his veins.

What's wrong, Horace? Was it something you ate? Or maybe I gave you a little something extra to deal with when I was in charge. Guess we'll find out soon, eh, old friend?

Collins put a steadying hand on his shoulder as he dry heaved, and Horace grabbed for the front of his armor. Another spasm hit, and his bowels loosed, one more indignity added to an ever-growing list.

"Andrew..."

"I'm here, sir. I've got you."

"Don't let him do it, Andrew. Don't let him put that...filth...in me."

Don't worry, Horace, I won't.

The room spun around him, and Horace felt Andrew's strong arms pick him up. It was hard to focus on any one thing as they moved, as the faces of the sleeping gennies passed by like a sick parade, down a long, darkening tunnel.

Yes, everything's going to be just fine from now on...

ANNAHKO

CAROLINE STOOD IN HER OFFICE, noting with approval how well the cadets were cataloging and packing away her things. A slow train of boxes and bodies stretched between the XO's suite and the Captain's suite, where in a few minutes she'd supervise the assembly of her new workspace.

In the hours since she'd assumed command, she'd been primarily occupied with the fallout from Horace's personnel purge, and the subsequent mountain of paperwork it had generated. She now had a shift and a half of seasoned officers and a dozen loyal cadets at her beck and call, and little else. It would be another day before *Indomitable* could lift again, leaving her restless, alone, and unexpectedly horny.

She hadn't yet to moved into Horace's quarters, nor did she intend to. She was still processing their encounter in the container, and everything that happened afterward. But what made things worse was that Horace seemed to have no memory at all of his manic episode.

At *Indomitable*'s formal change of command ceremony, she kept her face neutral, forcing herself to meet his eyes instead of looking at

Daniel standing behind him. But if Horace knew, or even suspected their renewed relationship, he gave no sign of it. He made a short speech, congratulated her, and then disappeared into the warrens of Echo Base.

I hate this place. Now more than ever. I hate the secrets it contains, and what it's done to Horace. And he took Daniel with him, complicating our strange geometry even further.

She didn't really love Daniel, not the way she did—*no, had*—Horace. But she also didn't fear him, and even after decades apart, he still knew how to please her in all the right ways.

I know he'll keep Horace safe, but is the reverse still true? Will the others protect him if Horace finds out?

Do I really care?

She hated herself for using Daniel like this, but she didn't want a full partner right now, just someone to scratch her itch. Whatever they dreams they had as children ended the day her father sold his line off to the Kołodziejskis, and he belonged to Horace now, body and soul.

And yet, he makes me feel alive. And for some reason, I need that now more than I ever have.

Putting aside her personal difficulties had never been hard for Caroline until she came aboard *Indomitable*. There was always a handy lover to use and discard, and there was always Horace to come back to. But this time it was him doing the leaving, and there was nothing she could do about it.

He's making all the moves in a game I know nothing about, and sooner or later I have to decide whether or not I want to keep playing.

Case in point, after the last box joined the parade of cadets heading down the corridor, there was one more item to move out: a handheld maglocked to her desk and displaying the Captain's seal. The cadets had cleaned around it in silence, not wanting to incur any disfavor from either of *Indomitable*'s captains. But now that she was alone with the thing, she wanted nothing more than to smash it to pieces and blow it out the nearest airlock.

He says it will have the answers I need. But after last night, I'm not even sure I want to know.

Sitting down in a chair that was no longer hers, she slotted her command key into the desk and released the lock. The handheld activated as soon as she picked it up, playing a basic audio message from the one voice in the worlds she didn't want to hear from right now.

"Caroline, I know right now you are upset and confused. I know you want answers, and as the Captain of this vessel, they are your right. I'm sorry I've had to keep things from you. I'm sorry that our time together has not been everything you wanted. I can only hope that after you review the files on this handheld, you'll come to understand my position, and why I've had to keep you at a distance for your own protection.

"The next time we talk, things will be different. I'll be a new man, one you can be proud of, and a hero to our people."

The message cut off abruptly, and Caroline spent a few seconds waiting for more before exploring the handheld as Horace wanted her to.

Her desk picked up the handheld's content, and once it was loaded in began indexing and organizing the files. When she agreed to join Horace's crew, one of the things she insisted on was that both of them have independent, non-Fleet workstations, separate and secure from their quarters. She wasn't sure where her mother had found them, but the pair of antique desks had some of the best processing cores in the worlds, and could be keyed to voiceprints, biometrics, or secure identifiers like her command key.

Whatever portion of his secrets Horace is finally willing to share is safe with me.

For now.

Caroline had a plan for getting at the rest of them, but for now she shut the desk down and began reviewing the handheld. The story it told was one she already knew. Most of it, anyway. Both versions of the death of the *Valiant* were meticulously documented, as were Horace's efforts to find her in the first place. The revelation of a previous pair of gennie test subjects complicated matters, but Admiral Worthy's seal on the transfer orders kept everything on the right side of legal. Some heavily redacted documents followed, describing in general terms where they'd been acquired, and what had been done with them since.

The death of the male gennie wasn't particularly disturbing to her —technically gennies were non-human, enemy combatants, and had been for four hundred years.

Gennie filth, he called them. And now he's got three hundred more to experiment on. But why? Mars is virus-free, and so are we.

Aren't we?

Caroline thought of Horace's strange blood, and the fundamental wrongness of his kiss. How desperate he'd been to find Aloysius, when in fact he wanted his little gennie girl all along.

He kept pushing me away, "for my own protection," when all I wanted to do is get closer.

You fucking bastard. For this, you sent Bob Calas to his death? For this, I defended you? I crippled a man in your name, and nearly broke another.

For a fucking gennie, pretending he's a man.

Caroline felt a scream building in her chest, one powerful enough to make the whole ship vibrate in response. The handheld buckled in her clenched fists, then shattered in a sparking cloud before breaking into jagged pieces of crystal circuitry-infused display glass.

"Caroline?"

Caroline's head snapped up, a snarl on her face and muscles tensed and at the ready. Daniel was standing just inside the compartment, armored up save for the helmet he cradled under his left arm, with a duty bag at his feet most likely stuffed full of all the keepsakes from home she'd admired in his quarters when she woke up this morning.

"Where is he, Daniel? No more lies. I want to talk to him. Right. Now."

"Caroline, I...I have to tell you something."

Caroline surprised herself with how fast she was out of her chair and around the desk. She hit Daniel at a full run, lifting him up and carrying him through the hatch to slam his armored form into the bulkhead across the corridor.

"No. More. Lies."

The fear in his eyes was intoxicating, affecting her on an even deeper level than his passion from the night before. She could do anything to him right now, and he would let her.

And he'll give me anything I want in return. Anything but the truth.

"You can't see him, that's the problem. He's in quarantine. It's..."

"The fucking T-virus, I know. How long? How long have you two morons been keeping this from me?"

Caroline pressed harder on Daniel's chestplate, willing it to crack the same way she'd destroyed the handheld. She wanted to scoop him out of his armor and either beat the truth out of, or fuck some sense into him.

Or maybe both.

"Six months. But he's had it for over almost three years, in one form or another. There's a doctor, an Earther who's been helping him. But it's gone too far now, and he's in a coma."

Three years. You've been planning this for three years, you sick bastard. You wanted me here, now, to clean up your mess. And you didn't even have the decency to tell me yourself.

And how many times did you fuck me before I joined your command, Horace, knowing you had this filth inside you the whole time?

Caroline stepped back from Daniel, desperate to get away from the horror her life had become. But she tripped over Daniel's duty bag and went down hard to the deck, sprawling very un-captain-like half in, half out of the hatch.

"I wanted to tell you. I did. But he swore us to secrecy. Specifically about you. My family...I couldn't. Please understand."

Daniel took a step forward to help her up, but Caroline batted away his hand. She kicked his bag away, savoring the confusion in his eyes as she clambered to her feet.

"Our Family. Daniel. Ours. Whatever legal fictions took you away can be undone. Mother and I could have protected you, protected you all.

"But this, this deception, will not stand. I won't have it. Not on my ship, and not in my life!"

Daniel rose from his half crouch slowly, hurt and fear and confusion warring on his face. She could almost smell his emotions wafting off him, melding together in her mind with the taste of his sweat and the feel of his hands on her body as they rediscovered each other after so long apart.

No. No more! I'm done playing these stupid games.

"Carrie, I…he…"

"It's Captain, Mr. Tepes. Captain Caroline Fucking Annahko. And if the next words out of your mouth aren't the absolute fucking truth, they'll be the last ones you ever say to me. Do you understand?"

In lieu of a response, Daniel reached down and opened his bag, withdrawing a thick beige envelope bearing the official seal of the Mars Confederation.

"He left you these…"

"Do. You. Fucking. Understand?"

Caroline hated herself for torturing him in this moment almost as much as she hated Horace for making her do it. But she'd allowed both men too far into her life, and it was time to start playing the game by her own rules for a change.

"Yes, Captain Annahko. Captain Kołodziejski left these instructions for you, in case…in case the worst happens."

Caroline waved away the envelope, not wanting any more "gifts" from Horace today.

"I know all about his fucking instructions. Take that garbage with you when you go."

Daniel's eyes were now pure pain, displaying a spirit broken down and melted by her righteous anger. He pressed the envelope into her unwilling hands, using both gauntlets to cover her merely human appendages.

"Not these, you don't. Please, take them. They're important."

Caroline kept her anger close to the surface, not wanting to give an inch to this man who'd made love to her knowing the emotional torment she was going through, and how to end it with a word. Two days ago he'd stood beside her in this same corridor, stoic and strong and everything she wanted in a partner, except that he wasn't Horace fucking Kołodziejski.

And he fucking lied to me then, too.

When Daniel pulled his hands away, she let the envelope drop to the deck. It hit with a solid smack, the noise echoing up and down the corridor. She couldn't bear to look at his crestfallen expression any longer, so she grabbed the collar of his hardsuit and dragged his face down for one last savage kiss, filled with years of regret and anger and missed opportunities. She poured everything she had into it, only breaking away when she couldn't bear another second without him in her life.

Eyes closed, head down, she released him.

"Goodbye, Daniel."

She heard him step back, heard him collect his helmet and bag from the deck. She felt him press the envelope into her hands again, and this time she took it, gripping the semi-solid bundle with the same strength with which she'd snapped the handheld.

Heard him walking away, and his whispered reply.

"Goodbye, Captain."

When she opened her eyes, he was gone, and it took all her strength not to run after him.

She stormed back onto her old office, securing the hatch and activating the privacy filters she'd installed the day she moved in. She brushed away the remnants of Horace's handheld, and slammed the envelope down on her desk.

Tearing the packet open, she dumped out its contents onto the smooth surface, which obediently lit up when she sat down. There were three thick packets of paper, each with a data chip affixed to the first page.

The first two she recognized immediately as the executorship documents she and Horace had drawn up a decade ago, the second time their almost marriage almost happened. She'd assigned him most of her liquidity and a third of her shares in the Annahko shipyards, with the rest reverting to the family trust. She recalled inserting an escalating rider of 5% for every five years of marriage, with an ultimate cap of 70% ownership should she pass before him. He'd laughed it away at the time, assuring her that he'd never die, and he'd make sure she lived forever with him.

How many lies in were you at that point, Horace? Had Worthy already corrupted you, or were you still the man I used to love?

She'd never read his will, assuming it had like provisions. But after the second page, as his byzantine list of entanglements, sponsorships, and holdings unfolded, she opted for the data chip version instead. Slotting it into the desk's reader, she was surprised to see that the document had been updated within the last month, and that—on paper, at least—he'd finally fulfilled his promise to her mother that she'd never have to work another day in her life.

But the third document was the one that finally did her in. The tears she'd been fighting won through, and she had to wipe them away quickly lest they stain the intricately watermarked pages that formally transferred control of Clan Tepes back to Clan Annahko, under her personal directorship.

And I sent him away, maybe forever.

Caroline wept in silence, until she had nothing left to give. She quietly cleaned up the destroyed handheld and disposed of it in the recycler, then collected her command key, the data chips, and the hardcopies into a loose bundle before releasing the room.

She hurried down the corridor to her own quarters to freshen up, but also to secure the physical documents in her personal safe. She then took an extra few minutes to erase all signs of weakness from her face, transforming herself once again into the Iron Princess, and the undisputed Captain of SDF *Indomitable*.

Examining herself in the mirrored surface above the sanitary sink, she judged herself once more fit for duty.

All right. Let's do this.

Crossing to her regular workstation, she keyed up one of the comm ids she'd memorized as she assembled her new crew.

"Mr. Currano. Meet me in the XO's suite in five. If you're not there by then, I'll come find you in six."

Not waiting for a reply, she took her time tidying up her quarters, and arrived at her former office four minutes and fifty-nine seconds later to see the hastily dressed and breathless cadet waiting for her outside.

"Thank you, Mr. Currano. Follow me, please."

She opened the hatch and ushered him inside, closing the hatch behind him.

"Ma'am?"

Caroline held up a finger to her lips, and made a show of activating the privacy filters. When she was sure he understood the process, she disabled them and motioned for Currano to do it himself. As soon as the light was green, she tapped the desk and spoke aloud for the first time since she'd summoned the clueless cadet.

"Computer, reconfigure secure access. Authorization Annahko 3-2-7."

The emotionless, pre-programmed response of the central core came back immediately, and she kept her face impassive as her mother's no-nonsense voice spoke at her with words recorded before she was born.

"Workstation unlocked. Please enter new authorization code."

Caroline waved a hand in front of Kurt Currano's glazed eyes, then pointed at her mouth, making a circle with her index finger. It took him a moment to understand what she wanted, and when he did speak, his voice cracked in true middie style.

"Uh, Cadet Kurtis J. Currano. *Ipsum Lorum No Decorum.*"

Interesting.

"Authorization accepted."

The desk powered down, leaving the two officers "alone" for a moment.

"Uh, ma'am, what just happened?"

Caroline stepped away from the desk, waving him to sit down in the chair. It took her two tries to get him there, with the second requiring her to move him physically to the chair and plant him in it.

"Congratulations, Cadet. You're officially on detached duty. Do you know what this is?" she said, indicating the desk.

"Yes ma'am. I'm familiar with the specs, but I haven't seen one before today."

Caroline had seen as much in his file, but it was nice to hear it aloud

"As of this moment, this room is your one and only duty station. You are responsible for everything that comes in and out of it, and you will speak to no-one but me about what you learn here. Do you understand?"

"Uh, yes? Yes Ma'am, I mean."

"Good. As your commanding officer, I want you to use this workstation and the information it contains to find every fucking secret hidden in, or about, Echo Base. Do whatever it takes, but I want it all, and I want it yesterday. Do you understand?"

Currano swallowed hard, nodding as he reached for the desk's controls. The surface came alive at his touch, recording his biometrics and finishing the authorization process. The joy in his smile as he explored its functions was the most genuine thing she'd seen in days.

Finally, someone who doesn't have their own fucking agenda. And if I have to have a completely green crew to rid myself of this web of lies, so be it.

"Then I'll leave you to it. Sub-Lieutenant Currano. Keep me informed as to your progress after every shift."

"Cadet, ma'am." The correction was reflexive, and with the zeal with which he was accessing the desk's controls, he may not even know he'd said it aloud.

"Who's the captain on this boat, Sub-Lieutenant?" Caroline kept her voice neutral, but she couldn't help but smile as she repeated his brevet promotion.

Currano stopped tapping, blinked, and looked up at her with a smile of his own.

"You are, ma'am."

You're goddamn right I am.

CALLAWAY

MARCUS HAD COMPLETED both the pilot and copilot preflight checklists, marking them off on physical pads for later verification. Shuttle V-12 was as ready as it would ever be, and all he needed now was a count of how many people were willing to sacrifice their remaining hours of life to stock the ship with O2 bottles.

By my count, we need to reduce overall consumption by half, assuming we can launch at all.

Marcus was still upset he couldn't get V-10's maneuvering thrusters operational. If he could, he'd have installed the targeting computer from V-9 and the communications array from V-15, and flown a second shuttle remotely until his air ran out.

Maybe then I could have saved the rest of the crew. As it is, I'll be lucky if I get myself, the bottle, and whatever fool draws the second seat anywhere near a transit lane, much less a communications buoy.

Maybe. Always maybe.

He'd been trying not to laugh at the absurdity of their situation for most of a shipday, and now that he was too tired to do so, Marcus wished he had. They'd been out of stims for hours, and even with the forward generators back online they couldn't formulate more.

The Infirmary stores were aft of the Rock, and who knows where they are now.

So now, with their one mostly functioning shuttle charging and the crew recording their messages for home, all he could do was wait.

The watchwords of my first, and only command. Great job, everyone. Now let's wait and maybe see if I was right.

Marcus heard footsteps behind him, and turned to see Lieutenants Ramirez and Olvrsdóttir walking up the passageway. Neither was wearing armor, and their jumpsuits appeared particularly rumpled.

Marcus smiled, and most definitely approved. For a second, he thought they were holding hands as they walked, but by the time they reached the pilot's compartment, Ramirez was all business.

"Sir, may we have a moment?"

Oddly formal of him, but I'll go with it. Today has sucked for pretty much everyone.

"Absolutely. How goes the count?"

Ramirez turned to look at Olvrsdóttir, and Marcus knew something was wrong.

"The count is finished, sir. Unanimous. We can move the supplies in as soon as you're ready. But that's not why we're here."

"Spit it out, son. It won't get any easier if you sit on it."

"Sir, I—we," he said, looking again at Olvrsdóttir, "don't want to run the bottle."

"That's okay, Alonso. I'm sure there's someone else who can sit second seat for me. You've done enough already."

Ramirez took a step away from the Martian lieutenant, who now definitely looked like she was blocking the passageway.

"No, sir, you don't understand. I don't think anyone should run the bottle. I have another plan."

Oh, this should be interesting. Two mutinies in one day? Alonso, you're such an overachiever!

Marcus had a spike of anger, but he'd been expecting something like this since the wardroom.

Just not from Alonso.

Marcus reached under the pilot's chair, and took hold of the induction pistol he'd stashed there for just this sort of situation. Olvrsdóttir had her own out in a heartbeat, but it didn't stop him from smiling back at her.

"Now I've been expecting this from her and her people since they came aboard, but not you, Alonso. What changed your mind, or do I even need to ask?"

The corner of Olvrsdóttir's mouth turned up, but her aim didn't waver at all.

"It's not like that, sir. I mean, it is, but not the other thing. I finally figured out how the gennies did it, traveled through hyperspace I mean. If you can not shoot me for a minute, I can show you."

Instead of an induction pistol, Ramirez had a holo-emitter in his hand. The sheer absurdity of a diplomatic mutiny was almost funnier than their whole fucked-up situation, but so far everyone was still alive.

"Okay, go. You have sixty seconds."

Like time means anything right now anyway.

"The Rock wasn't just a rock, sir, it was a vessel. We theorized it was a cargo slug early in the game, but it just didn't make any sense until we saw the footage from *Indomitable.* The compartment they explored was too regular, and far too large for the number of gennies we encountered.

"So I ran a projection for its entire volume, based on the Rock's speed after emergence. And in the simulation I found two pieces missing that I couldn't account for, which got me to thinking about how it got here in the first place."

Alonso's pause didn't make any sense when Marcus had a weapon drawn on him, and especially with the clock ticking like it was. And since he'd yet to use the holoemitter, Marcus was wondering if he really had a plan at all.

"And?"

"So, a cargo slug is usually covered in containers like the one we found. The mass of the rock is the only significant factor for acceleration, which evens out on cost when it's mined at its destination. But with this black stone and its strange properties, one container just didn't make any sense, unless we weren't supposed to find it at all."

"Time's up, Alonso. Start making sense or get out, and take your new girlfriend with you. I've got a mission to prep."

This time, Alonso turned on the emitter. It was a familiar image, *Valiant* tumbling madly with a giant rock lodged amidships. But Alonso had it rotating much slower this time, and paused it just as it eclipsed some bright star.

"There, sir. Do you see it?"

"It's a space rock, Alonso. There are a million pieces of it floating around outside, and you're not making your case."

"Look harder." Olvrsdóttir's smile never wavered, which made her command voice even more impressive. She also showed no sign of dropping her aim, so Marcus resolved to do just that.

"Fine, play it again. But this time, tell me what I'm looking at or for."

Alonso fiddled with the controls, then set the emitter down. *Valiant*'s slow tumble repeated, but this time Alonso circled a section of black space with his thumb and forefinger, until the rock moved in front of him. The same lensing effect happened, and afterward there was just Alonso and his hand standing there.

Marcus stood up, pistol in hand but no longer pointed at anyone.

"What the hell is that?"

Alonso ran the holo again, this time even slower, and with narration.

"Was that, sir. I think it was a second container, shielded from our sensors by the Rock. There were more gennies on the cargo slug than the ones that took the shuttle, and at least some of them got away. But that's not all. Have a look at this."

This time, Alonso inverted the colors, just like he had in the wardroom. But on the much smaller holo, the Rock had a few features Marcus wasn't prepared for. He stepped forward, pushed his finger into a "black" section, and said "This?"

"Exactly, sir. It's an attachment point. For a hyperdrive module.

Specifically," Alonso paused while he pulled up a second inverted image, with a black, spidery shape slowly spinning against a white starscape, "this one, and you're right that we're running out of time."

Marcus stared at the image, trying to make out exactly what it was. It never got any clearer, but with every rotation his mind generated new possibilities.

"Where is it, and what will it cost us?"

Both images disappeared, and were replaced by a schematic of the Hull and its current outbound velocity.

"Time, mainly. Time, and reaction mass." Alonso added a new vector, one almost perpendicular to their current path. Whatever he'd found, it was leaving the solar system even faster than they were, and no amount of wishing would make it slow down or reverse course.

Marcus did the math in his head, then flipped over one of the preflight checklists and did it again by hand. He noticed Olvrsdóttir move over to Alonso's side and take his hand, but he was too consumed by his calculations to spare the couple much thought.

When he was done, he sat down hard in the pilot's seat, and let his pistol fall to the deck so he could take his head in both hands.

"If we miss, everybody dies. You know that, right?"

"Yes sir. But if we don't, everybody lives. And I think that's a chance worth taking, don't you?"

Marcus looked up and saw worry on Alonso's face, but also hope. Olvrsdóttir was half shielding him with her body, biting her bottom lip and waiting for Marcus to make his move.

What do I think, Alonso? I think you're out of your damn mind, and you've got me halfway there with you.

But maybe. Maybe.

"Run it for me again."

JANTINE

"I STILL DON'T UNDERSTAND WHY WE CAN'T USE THE BRIDGE." CARLTON'S question was a fair one. In the Beta's mind, if JonB hadn't raised concerns about the structural integrity of the bridge, they may have been in Chicago by now.

The bridge in question was a narrow span across a wide river, one which the maps and Mira Harlan had named Mississippi. There were ruins on both sides of the bridge, but across the river the crumbling piles of stone and rusting metal were slightly taller. The setting sun looked much different here than it had on the grasslands, and the shadows formed as it peeked through the remains of the city were edged with fire.

Unlike other bridges they'd crossed during the long day's journey, it was barely wider than the train, with just enough clearance for the engine to pass without incident. There were small islands of some sort paralleling the bridge, but Jantine didn't understand their function.

JonB and Mira had performed a quick survey of the structure, and returned with some unsettling news. Not only was it decrepit, but it had been mined. JonB's quick thinking had saved them all, again, and Katra's perimeter survey had uncovered another problem.

The track system split into two paths several dozen meters in front of the ancient bridge, with the second spur traveling into the ruined city. While scouting for another path across the river, Katra fond deep scratches cut into the metal of the tracks, and more leading into an underground tunnel.

"Carlton," Mira said, "do you remember what I told you about the Reclamation zones?" Mira's casual tone reminded Jantine again of the easy way Malik handled this aspect of the mission for her, but she suspected the explanation was more for the wide-eyed Serene.

"What is this Reclamation?" Serene had been sleeping when Mira gave her pre-dawn history lesson, and was understandably curious. Carlton blanched at the memory, and thinking about what might be down in the tunnel made Jantine's blood hot.

Mira turned and looked at the Alpha. For some reason, the Earther hadn't been broadcasting her emotions for many hours, so Jantine had only visual cues to go by in determining her mood. Mira's expression fell somewhere between sadness and embarrassment, but she seemed willing to tell the story a second time.

"It's a dark period of our history. Earth history, about half a century before you went into suspended animation. So far, there's been enough track for us to avoid the cities, even if it meant going a good distance out of our way. Most of the smaller towns and communities between Old Kansas and here were already abandoned when the war started, but the cities...I don't want to be sitting here all night if I can help it."

"What kind of war?"

Jantine saw Katra and Mira set their jaws, and imagined each was thinking the same thing she was.

There is only one kind of war. The weapons may change, but the end results are always the same.

Mira crouched in front of Serene, face carefully neutral. Despite her statements of forgiveness, Mira still had to feel some resentment over what was taken from her. But having heard this story herself, Jantine knew that Mira was trying to put the best possible spin on an even greater atrocity.

"A bad one. One that should never have happened, but in hindsight most scholars believe it was inevitable. Earth was a much different place, then. We'd used up many of our resources, and were surviving by taking what we could from the rest of the system. Mars and Titan had only been settled for a hundred years, and we'd already cut off contact with the Outer Colonies.

Serene nodded. There was no need to rehash the Exile, she knew more about it than anyone else present.

"But here on Earth, there were problems too big to ignore. The World Congress had dissolved, and nation-states were arming themselves with whatever they could buy, invent, or steal. Those who already had access to space could take whatever they wanted, and only a few were willing to protect those who could not.

"So what happened?"

Mira smiled, and lowered herself all the way to the ground. Face half in shadow, she looked up at Jantine before continuing her explanation. Jantine nodded, and thought a simple question at her.

≈*Who will you need to scout the tunnel?*≈

≈*Katra, and Jason. Carlton too, if you can spare him. I need someone with no military training.*≈

≈*Not JonB?*≈

≈*No, he's more valuable up here with you. If something happens to us...*≈

≈*Understood.*≈

"You have to understand," Mira said, "everyone was so afraid. If you didn't have a weapon, you were an easy victim for those who did. And once you had one, before too long someone else would get a bigger one. But there wasn't just an arms race, there was a knowledge race as well.

"Corporations were nearly as powerful as governments, and sold their inventions to whoever had the most money. Most often one another, but there were enough spies on all sides to render any advantages moot in short order."

"I still don't understand. Why? And what's wrong with the bridge?"

Mira's smile was a brittle thing that threatened to crumble if she pressed her lips any tighter together. Jantine looked up and caught Katra's eye, tapping her left cheek with her forefinger. The Gamma acknowledged the signal for communication and moved back from the rest of the group.

Jantine placed a hand on Serene's back, and leaned down to kiss her on the forehead. The Alpha stared at her with a confused look, until Jantine gestured toward Mira by wagging the fingers of her left hand. Mira patted the ground next to her to complete the message, and Serene moved forward to sit next to the reluctant storyteller.

Jantine stepped away from the assembled mods, and she frowned when JonB tried to come with her. He narrowed his eyes and cocked one eyebrow, but when she mouthed "later" at him, he resumed his position against the train and simply watched her walk away.

Trust me, JonB. You don't want to know about this just yet.

"The weapons kept getting more and more destructive. Air superiority was still a deciding factor, so the great powers for the most part ignored what was going on down here on the surface. If one of them took a side in a corporate conflict, there's no telling what might have happened. But they didn't stop building their own weapons, and in the end all it took was one mistake to set the world on fire."

Jantine walked around the back of the train to the other side. The three cars attached to the engine were tall enough to block her sight line to the mods gathered around Mira, and as she descended a small hill toward the ruins she could no longer make out Mira's words. There was nothing she could do about the Omega's acute hearing, but she was satisfied there was enough distance between her and the others to use the scattercomm undetected.

She ran a finger down her jawline, and heard two clicks in her ear.

"How big would you say it was?"

Katra's whispered reply was short and to the point.

"Possibly as large as the train engine, but more likely half that size. The marks were fresh, not weathered. No more than one day. If it's one of Mira's war machines, it's still active."

Jantine didn't have to ask if Katra was sure—she wouldn't have brought it up in her scouting report if the Gamma didn't consider it a threat.

"Mira will lead. Yourself, Carlton, and Jason. Priority is to secure a clear path under the river, but I want no casualties. Withdraw if you feel the situation warrants it. Use the Earth comms, they have longer range. Mira will advise."

"Understood. Commander?"

"Speak freely."

"Why do we risk the Omega in this fashion?"

A good question, and one with no good answer. But there was an easy one, and thought she didn't like it, it was good enough.

"Mira thinks it best to use a combination of artificial and natural senses. If someone else is using this system, we need to know about it. And as Mira says, these machines are very dangerous. If there is a potential threat in this region, we must eliminate it as soon as possible."

"Understood. Perimeter sweep ready in fifteen."

One click sounded in her ear, and Jantine disabled the scattercomm.

Jantine was in no particular hurry to rejoin the others, so she drew her hand weapon and sat down to watch her second sunset on Planet Earth. Even filtered through ruined buildings, Sol was a marvelous sight, and provided more than enough illumination to field strip her weapon.

She checked each piece for defects in the red-orange light, and snapped in a fresh energizer as she reassembled the pistol. There was more than half a charge remaining in the old one, but Mira's earlier warnings were still echoing in her head, and she saw no reason to face them at anything less than maximum combat readiness.

"Terrible weapons, capable of reprogramming themselves to overcome any threats. But in the end, there was no greater threat to the war machines than the people who'd invented them, especially those who'd expressed transgenic traits..."

MIRA

SOMETHING CRUNCHED UNDER MIRA'S BOOT, AND THE SOUND ECHOED OFF the tunnel's walls. So far, neither her own enhanced vision, the visor's optics, nor borrowing some of Jason's senses had detected anything more than a wide tunnel with ancient, rusting machinery.

Whatever made the scratches Katra found, it's definitely down here somewhere.

The darkness was almost a living thing, a deep, chilling black that clung to every available surface like tar. But they weren't using active sensors, which meant despite his Beta reflexes, Carlton tripped over every raised object in his path.

Mira put out a hand to catch him, but whatever it was he'd kicked went skittering off to the left and clanked off the side of the tunnel.

Mira froze, and felt both Katra and Jason's awareness spike at the sound. Seeing the tunnel though the Omega's eyes wasn't much different than the dim outlines drawn by her visor, but she at least had a more complete idea of where the major obstacles and walls were. Plus, since the Omega wasn't wearing a protective suit, she had access to his sense of smell. So far, he'd only registered dust, rust, and ancient hydrocarbons, but there was always a chance she might notice something Jason would otherwise ignore.

In contrast to the other mods' cool resolve, Carlton's emotions were like a hammer pounding inside of her head. Carlton knew only the basics of how to use his encounter suit, and as such had only Mira's hand to tell him where he was. He was completely out of his element, but Mira needed someone with no military training for this patrol, who would be afraid of everything they encountered. She was hoping the Beta's subconscious mind would give them some advance warning of an attack, and she hated herself because of it..

I'll get you back alive, Carlton. I promise. But I need you to be scared a little while longer, just in case.

Mira sent a thought to Katra, wincing at the pain that followed.

≈*We're going to wait here a minute until Carlton can proceed.*≈

≈*Understood. Fifty meters, then back.*≈

Once she lowered her defenses and allowed Mira in, the Gamma was surprisingly easy to talk to. Mira suspected that all Gammas had some kind of low-level psychic sensitivity, but given how little Mira know about them, there was no way to know for sure. Whatever it was made her a good soldier, and just like Carlton's inexperience, it was something Mira needed right now.

She slid her hand up from the Beta's chest to his shoulder, and then pressed him down to the floor. He resisted at first, fear spiking so high that she gasped with the pain. But then he relaxed just enough so she could think on her own again, and he crouched down next to her in a tight ball of nerves.

Sensing her discomfort, Jason sent her another recovered image from her past. This time it was one of herself and Tommy climbing down into the caves, about a month before she left Roswell forever. It was another inappropriate memory, but Mira was thankful for it all the same. Each one he was able to isolate and return to her was a gift that restored a bit of her emotional spectrum. A moment like this was something wonderful, and she was happy to have it back.

On the tour they'd taken during the day, the colors of the cave were fascinating. Greens and reds and oranges formed in a place where the sun never shone, and only when humans had come blundering in did simple sedimentary deposits transform into works of art.

At night, Tommy's ebony skin was part of the darkness, and the occasional flashes of his teeth and eyes in the chemsticks they carried made what they were doing more exciting.

Mira and Tommy had hidden a blanket and a bottle of his father's whiskey in a secluded grotto during the day, and tonight was going to be "special." She knew what Tommy wanted, and she'd more or less made up her mind to give it to him just so he wouldn't follow her around forever with his sad eyes.

But when they startled the bats, all thoughts of youthful indiscretion flew out with them into the night. Mira held on to Tommy as tight as she could when the leathery wings snapped by her head, and afterward the two teenagers laughed until they cried. Then Tommy made his move, but when his lips brushed hers she pulled away. The moment was gone, and as far as she knew the bottle and blanket were still stashed there, waiting for her to change her mind.

Maybe if I had, it would have been easier later. Maybe he wouldn't have...

The sound of the bats echoed in her mind again, but instead of tiny claws scratching at her ears and the musty smell she thought would never wash out of her hair, it was accompanied by the cold hiss of escaping air that even a first year middie feared.

≈Katra. Stop.≈

Jason was warning her of something, but there wasn't enough there to pass along. Katra didn't respond with words, but Mira felt the Gamma's awareness expanding. She knew what might be down here just like Mira did, but Mira had seen one of the death machines in action during her Academy days in Colorado, right on the edge of the Reclamation zone.

And that should make me even more frightened than Carlton. Chalk another advantage up for the transgenic virus, I guess. That, and having my brains scooped out.

Most of Katra's training involved sneaking up to the enemy and removing it as a threat before it knew she was there. Sealed up in her black encounter suit, Katra was nearly invisible when she wanted to be, but they'd agreed ahead of time that the mod shouldn't use her active camouflage save in emergencies. A stray electron here or there might make the difference between life and death when facing an adaptive killing machine with advanced sensor capabilities.

Down here, in the blackest night imaginable, there was nothing for her to aim at. No enemy to evade or capture, and with the Mississippi river a hundred meters over their heads, blowing their unseen foes up wasn't really an option either. But she was still in control of herself, and Mira borrowed as much of that feeling as she could.

Mira's own senses were stretched to the limit, but despite her plan Carlton's fear was making it hard to concentrate. Whatever made Jason think of the bats was also screaming a warning at Carlton's subconscious mind, and that more than anything made her want to abort the mission.

Come on, you metal freak. Show yourself.

Part of her wanted to be wrong. The consequences of being right were too horrific, especially on top of everything that had happened in the last two days. But all the signs were there, and if there was a pre-Reclamation killing machine in the tunnel ahead of them, Mira and Katra needed to buy JonB enough time to either defuse the charges on the bridge or find some way to succeed where she'd failed.

The whine of Katra's pulser coming to life told her that the time of "if" was over.

"Now, Carlton. Do it!"

The Beta's fear was nearly overpowering him, but with Mira drawing it away he was able to hit the switch on the device he'd been cradling for half a kilometer and roll it into the middle of the tunnel.

In terms of illumination, an infra-red heater was about the least effective device one could use on a battlefield. But when deployed against a monster that hunted by body heat, it leveled the odds faster than high explosive rounds.

Speaking of which...

The bloom of heat scrambled her visor's sensors, but Jason could still see just fine. As fifteen meters of robotic death powered up and uncoiled from a hiding place on the tunnel's ceiling, Mira relayed its movements mentally to Katra while she got a better grip on Carlton's shoulder and pulled him back toward the entrance.

Katra's pulser was firing nonstop, and the invisible packets of phased energy tore away large chunks of the hunter-killer's exoskeleton. She'd already crippled one of its legs, but according to the power usage Jason could see it had at least five more.

Thankful again that both of them had missed while shooting at one another during the firefight on *Valiant*, Mira dropped a second infrared heater and sent Carlton a strong desire to run to the surface. She felt his terror recede as he left, and turned her full attention to the monster twisting around as it attempted to destroy whatever was damaging it.

The robot's strategy was a sound one, given the technology it was programmed to fight. It was immune to most conventional weapons; Mira's slugthrower would be little more than an annoyance to the monster. But it wouldn't take long for its adaptive subroutines to come up with a defense against phased plasma pulses, and it was time for Mira to begin the next stage of the attack plan.

Now that Carlton was far enough away, Mira stretched out her mind, and made a full connection with Katra and Jason. Their thoughts melded with her own, until they were essentially one person with three different bodies and a single goal.

As Katra fell back to the second beacon, Jason picked up one of the decaying machines littering the tunnel and launched it at the robot's head. Katra rolled behind a rusted lump of metal and sent a pair of pulses at the monster's rear legs. Mira was momentarily dazzled by the way the pulses sparked as they encountered small bits of matter in the air, but Jason accepted it as a normal phenomenon, much like the X-ray bursts from Sagittarius-A he'd shown her last night.

The robot had a target and a direction now, and bounded forward fast enough to make Mira's heart skip a beat. Only the confidence she felt in Katra's mind gave her the will to stand her ground. The Gamma sent two more pulses into the robot's exposed inner workings. As they impacted with a shower of sparks, she relocated to a new firing position with a fluid grace that even Jason admired.

The Omega launched another improvised missile at the robot then sprinted to the side of the tunnel. His already low body heat was completely masked by the heaters, but even an Omega's thick skin had limits. A pair of cobalt lasers converged on the spot he'd just vacated, burning deep holes in the concrete and giving the creature a hot-spot to target.

But despite their impressive power, every cadet knew that the lasers weren't the real threat. The microwave emitter powering up in the robot's head was, and Mira charged toward the robot to spring the final part of their ambush.

Apart from a genetic super-assassin and a gentle telepathic architect who could see almost the entire EM spectrum, Mira had another advantage that hadn't existed during the Architect Wars.

A fully charged hardsuit, capable of amplifying her strength by a factor of five.

Maneuvers like this were best performed in zero-g, but the SDF spared no expense in training their officers and she'd learned her craft under the watchful eye of a grizzled and scarred sergeant deep inside Earth's gravity well. Most of the security forces assigned to *Valiant* came to the ship fresh out of training, with a host of groundside bad habits and poor suit discipline. But those under Mira's command either learned to use their suits at their intended level of performance or found another posting in the fleet.

For the last five years, *Valiant* had maintained the highest efficiency ratings of any ship in active service. Her damage control teams went through equipment almost as fast as they did recruits, but once Mira raised the Clarke Cup over her head for the first time, she knew she would never give it back.

And just because my ship is dead is no excuse to slack off now.

Mira's first stride was at normal power, but her second launched her three meters into the air and toward the tunnel's curved wall. When she hit, instead of surrendering to gravity's pull she bent her knees and flipped out over the still thrashing robot, firing all her attitude control jets and coming to rest on the ancient machine's back.

Its response was immediate, and predictable. It stopped thrashing its legs, tail, and manipulator arms in a futile attempt to find Katra's firing position, and it rotated every appendage it had into a configuration that would let it tear Mira apart. But Mira was already gone, having applied a thick paste of thermite gel to the back of the robot's head.

Rocketing backwards, she drew a borrowed hand pulser and held the firing studs down, remembering to shut her eyes just in time. The plasma discharge ignited the gel in a white-hot explosion, burning completely through the robot's head in seconds.

The robot was by no means disabled, but its energy weapons were now useless, and a hefty portion of its adaptive software was now tasked with reconfiguring itself to meet the threat of an airborne opponent.

Which gave Katra all the time in the world to completely discharge a fresh energizer into its exposed interior.

The machine fizzled and died in a cloud of smoke and electrical discharges. Mira twisted in midair and came down in a perfect three-point stance between the infrared lamps. She gave herself an imaginary pat on the back—not only had the three of them just defeated one of the most advanced weapons ever invented in less than thirty seconds with no casualties, but now they could forget all about the bridge and take their time guiding the train through the tunnel.

Not bad for an old lady. If you're watching, Captain, I did the side proud.

Mira dissolved the three-way link, and staggered as the pain in her head tripled. She closed her eyes against it, activating her suit's emergency lights with practiced hands.

Katra's spike of alarm added exponentially to Mira's headache, and the sight of Jason turning and running full out for the tunnel entrance was like a punch in the gut. But the Gamma's flare of emotion was gone in an instant, replaced by the cool emptiness she'd maintained during the battle.

The Gamma rose up from behind her cover, inserted a fresh energizer, and started firing over Mira's shoulder. Her thoughts weren't hard to decipher as she did, and it was Mira's turn to be alarmed.

≈I think we should be going now, Lieutenant Commander.≈

Even though she had an idea of what was there, Mira had to see it for herself. A second later she wished she hadn't, and was running with all the strength left in her legs after Jason's retreating back, with Katra just a few meters behind.

Oh, shit.

JANTINE

Jantine was standing outside the engine with Serene when the Earth comm unit sputtered to life. The child was wearing another one of Mira's modified garments, this time a heavy cloth jacket with the sleeves removed. It was near enough to the coveralls the mods used for the child to look almost dressed, and Mira had assured her that "M. Callaway" would not want the clothing back.

For once, O-6913 was not with her. The Omega was twenty meters away, staring down the tracks Mira and her team had followed to the tunnel mouth as if willing them to appear. It wasn't a defensible position, but having seen the Omega shrug off multiple barrages of micro-slugs, she wasn't worried about him. Besides, Artemus was standing at the edge of the bridge, with one pair of weapons pointed across the river and another in the direction the Omega was facing. If any threat came at them from either set of tracks, the Delta would know about it.

JonB and Serene were Jantine's real priority, and as ruthless as Mira's risk assessment had been, Jantine had to agree with it. Even with all the losses they'd sustained so far, the mission could still proceed if the Betas and the Alpha child made it to a place of safety.

But even before she heard Mira's voice on the comm, Jantine suspected that it was not going to be good news.

"JonB! Detach the trailing car and get the locomotive onto the bridge right now!"

"What was that?"

JonB stood in the door to the engine compartment, handheld in one hand and one of Mira's chess pieces in the other.

"Don't think," Jantine said. "Obey. I will move the train."

JonB slid down the ladder and ran toward the rear of the train, while Jantine picked Serene up with her free arm. She could have waited for O-6913 to finish his charge up the tracks and claim her, but she wanted to hold the girl, as if it might be her last chance to do so.

"Casualties?" Jantine handed Serene off as she spoke into the comm, then she vaulted into the engine's cab. Mira's response was close to panic, and the thought that Jantine had lost another friend distracted her from which of the controls on she was supposed to acti-vate to get the train rolling again.

"Not yet, but...damnit, Katra, keep up!"

Jantine wanted very badly to see what was happening, but the "backup plan," as Mira had explained it, was for her to get Serene across the bridge as fast as possible, and not look back.

Which control was it? Why can't I remember?

Jantine was afraid, and she didn't know why. It wasn't until she heard Carlton's voice yelling from outside the cab that she understood the feeling might not be her own.

"We have to go. We have to GO!"

"Jantine. Jantine! Is the train moving? We can't hold them back much longer."

Them?

Mira's voice over the comm was enough to at least get her mind working again. If she couldn't remember the control, Carlton or JonB would. Her first responsibility was to get Serene out of danger, and that she could do with just a word.

Jantine hurried to the ladder, and looked outside. O-6913 had Serene cradled to his chest, and she could see real fear in the child's eyes. She waved the comm unit at the bridge.

"Run."

The Omega was moving before she finished the word, and Carlton was not far behind him. There was enough starlight for them to make their way onto the bridge without difficulty, and as Jantine watched them pass Artemus and move onto the rusted metal structure she raised the comm to her mouth.

"It will be soon. Do you need support?"

Artemus started across the bridge, and by the way the Delta's footsteps were shaking the tracks, Jantine revisited her doubts as to how successful JonB's efforts to disable the detonation charges had been.

As if on cue, she heard hissing air from the rear of the train, accompanied by a soft clanking sound.

"Mira. Do you need support?"

Jason appeared out of the night, waving his arms over his head. The Omega did not turn and follow the rest of the mods onto the bridge, but instead moved to the rear of the engine and braced himself against it. There was a squealing sound as the train started moving forward, and Serene and her fear were far enough away now that Jantine realized he too was carrying out Mira's orders the only way he knew how.

Jantine thought she heard something from the rear of the train, but the sound did not repeat. She spent almost half a minute marveling at the sight of an Omega doing the work of a one-hundred ton machine, before turning her attention back to the control panel to find JonB already standing there.

The civvie had somehow entered through the entrance on the other side of the engine without her noticing, another indicator of just how paralyzing Serene's uncontrolled and contagious fear had been. The Beta's right hand reached out and threw several switches, and as the electric motors hummed to life, she noticed his face was flushed, his left arm was cradled against his chest, and there was a trail of blood leading from the entrance to where he was standing at the control panel.

Although she easily adjusted to the motion of the train moving down the tracks, Jantine was nearly pitched out of the cab when the engine rocked violently to the left. She caught herself before she slid completely out of the open portal, but lost her grip on the comm unit. It fell to the ground and bounced toward the tracks, and over the squeal of metal wheels on rails she heard a distinct crunching sound.

From her position on the floor, Jantine was facing the rear of the train and had an excellent view of not only Jason pulling himself up to the top of the engine, but lines of purple light illuminating two human-sized figures in the distance.

Before she could stand up again, the train's brakes engaged and Jantine nearly joined the com unit under the engine's wheels. Mira's chess pieces bounced past her head, and Jantine wondered why JonB had been carrying one of them in his hand when he ran toward the back of the train.

No time for that now. We have to get moving.

Jantine rolled back onto her feet, grabbed one of the supply packs that had slid to the back of the cab and threw it to JonB as he turned toward her. He looked like he was about to say something, but Jantine didn't wait to find out what it was. Instead, she shouldered several packs of her own and stepped off the engine and down onto the bridge.

There was another hissing sound, this time much closer. Jantine looked for the source, and saw Jason separating the remaining cars from the engine. Another pair of purple lights flashed in the distance, and out of the corner of her eye, Jantine thought she saw one of the figures rise into the air on a small column of flame.

Then Jason grabbed the bottom of the car in front of him, and lifted. The boxy container they'd been bouncing around in since dawn came up off the tracks, and veins stood out on his arms as he found a better grip on the heavy weight. Jason took two staggering steps forward, and then tilted the car to the left until it fell on its side with a loud crash. The car behind it jerked forward and jumped off the tracks as well, and came to rest with its length half on, half off the tracks.

Not content with simply tipping the container over, Jason braced himself against the nearest wheel assembly and pushed. Sparks flew off the steel bars as the container rotated until it was nearly perpendicular to its previous orientation. The trailing car separated with a shrieking, tearing sound, and rolled down the small hill toward the ruined city.

Then the bridge shook again, as O-6913 thundered past an awestruck Jantine to join Jason. The Omegas each took hold of a long metal bar on the underside of the container, and pulled the protesting container back toward her until its bottom surface came up against the metal support beams of the bridge's superstructure. On its side, the container nearly blocked access to the bridge, leaving only two meters of space and a slight inclined gap between them.

JonB landed beside Jantine with a small cry of pain, and she turned to look at him with incredulous eyes. He was lying on his side, helmet off, and facing away from her. When he rolled over, his face was even paler than usual. But what drew Jantine's attention was the blood-covered pack he was clutching to his chest with his right arm.

Jantine dropped the two she was carrying and rushed to his side. She lifted the pack away, expecting to see a horrible wound on his chest. Instead she saw a drying smear on the outside of his encounter suit, but no sign that the smart fabric had sealed over a puncture.

"I'm okay. I can't feel it. We should we should get moving."

Jantine put her left arm under JonB's shoulders and reached for his face with her right, turning it to the side and trying to spot any head wounds hidden in his dark hair. The starry sky gave off enough light for travel and most operations, but she couldn't tell if he was bleeding or not.

An explosion shook the ground, and yellow white light poured over the overturned car and dispelled the shadows for just a moment. Jantine blinked twice, fixing JonB's image in her mind, though in that brief glance she saw no blood in his hair or on his neck. She was about to ask him what had happened when a broad orange hand scooped her up and carried her away.

"No, wait. Put me down!"

Whichever one of the Omegas had tucked her under his arm ignored her shouted commands, and Jantine had a bouncing view of the river through the bridge's supports as he ran. She heard JonB grunt behind her, and then saw Katra skip by holding several grenades. The Gamma didn't slow down as she ran up one of the bridge's angled support beams, and then the Omega was past her, each step shaking the bridge until Jantine thought it might collapse just from the vibrations.

There was a second explosion as the Omega reached the other side, and Jantine was unceremoniously deposited next to the tracks facing away from the bridge. She spun around, drew her hand weapon, and tried to spot Katra or Mira coming across. Two columns of flame and smoke stretched up to the sky, but she couldn't see either woman.

Serene was crying just off to her left, but her fear seemed to be back under control for now. The Alpha was clinging to one of Artemus' legs, and as soon as she recognized Jantine, she disengaged and threw her arms around the Beta's waist.

Jantine was moving back onto the tracks at the time, helmet off and trying to get a better view as to what was happening on the bridge. The unexpected impact was enough to unbalance her, and she sat down hard between the metal bars with Serene still clinging to her midsection. The other Omega was charging hard straight in her direction, and not knowing what else to do she curled up around Serene and closed her eyes.

When there was no bone crushing impact, Jantine raised her head and saw the back of JonB's encounter suit just centimeters away. Serene stopped crying long enough to ask a question.

"What happened to your hand?"

Jantine didn't understand the question. Both her hands were on Serene's back, the left pressed against the child's spine and the right holding her hand weapon. She raised both, twisting her wrists in the starlight and trying to find some defect in her encounter suit.

"I fell down under the train, and it started moving." JonB said. "It's okay, I can't feel it. These suits have pain blocking medications."

His voice was flat, and full of the same artificial calm that Doria's had had at the end. Jantine tried to sit up, but with Serene in her arms she didn't have enough leverage to do more than raise her back up slightly.

When JonB twisted around to help her, the stump of his left arm hit her in the face and he started screaming.

KATRA

≈*Yes. JonB and Jantine are across now. She is fine, but he is…*≈
≈*Doesn't matter. Tell me when we're done.*≈

Katra nodded, not sure if the gesture would translate over the mental link with Mira. There was nothing either of them could do about the Beta's injury, and the machines now perched on top of the overturned container car would kill everyone if they were not stopped.

The pair of killer machines seemed impervious to the flames and smoke surrounding them. Whatever Mira had used to detonate the cars was still burning hot enough that Katra's visor optics couldn't make out many details. One thing she was certain of, though, was that the machines' heads were swiveling back and forth in an attempt to locate her, in motions eerily similar to those the Omegas had used aboard the *Valiant*. Beyond them, the remains of a third machine were indistinguishable from the wreckage of the first container.

The one that had our supplies.

Katra didn't think Mira made the wrong decision in destroying the container; it had bought enough time for the rest of the mods to cross the bridge. And although it had only eliminated one of the machines, it was an effective enough demonstration to make the other two pause before continuing their assault.

From where Katra was lying on the bridge's middle support frame, she had a good view of the entire span, including the packs Jantine had discarded when tending to JonB. If they were the ones from the engine compartment, among other things the contained the only replacement energizers in a thousand light years.

Katra wasted only a moment formulating a retrieval plan; it was clear to her that any such attempt would betray Mira's position in the engine to the enemy. Her pulser was of no use without a charge, but she definitely wouldn't be firing it if Mira wasn't around to perform another of her miraculous reversals.

Katra was not a strategist; in a society that produced Betas to formulate and execute battle plans, few Gammas were. But she recognized this failing in herself at an early age, and hoping to unlock the intricacies of war, she'd studied it obsessively for many years. Her knowledge of military tactics and history was extensive, but it wasn't until very recently that she'd had an opportunity to apply it practically.

Now she faced machines that did what she could not; adapt to changing situations and conquer. Moltke the Elder, a classic Earth strategist, maintained that no battle plan survived contact with the enemy. On the other side of the equation, the robots epitomized the "utmost use of force" Moltke's mentor Clausewitz warned against.

The humans invented them to kill us, but only succeeded in killing themselves.

≈Get ready to move. Sixty seconds.≈

Katra tightened her grip on the incendiary grenades in her hand. She wished there was more she could do to help Mira than offer a distraction, but Mira's bewildering plans had kept both of them alive so far, and there was no reason to question them now.

Without Mira's relentless optimism and the "fool's luck" common to so many military leaders from Earth's past, Katra would probably have been killed several times over by now. Her continued survival was proof enough that trusting Mira was the best strategy, and if there was a way to survive this latest encounter, Katra was sure the woman would find it.

One of the machines extended a metal leg to the edge of the support frame, and another into the gap leading down to the edge of the bridge. Unlike the solid ground the burning container sat on, the bridge's surface was a rusting nightmare of empty spaces and good intentions.

Mira's latest theory was that the demolition charges built into the bridge were meant to contain the machines, and the structure's current condition spoke to at least one previous attempt by the robots at a crossing. It would have been far easier to clear out any potential blockages in the tunnel than to disarm the charges, even assuming they'd found them all. JonB was supposed to have temporarily disabled the otherwise effective defense against them, at least over part of the span.

If the fifty meters separating the train engine from the robots was any indication, he must have been at least partially successful. But that distance was only a tenth of the bridge's total length, and the machines could run much faster than people. As the fires died down, time was running out for whatever contingency plan Mira was enacting inside the engine's cab.

≈*Almost done. Any change?*≈

≈*Fire's almost out. They're testing the bridge.*≈

≈*Good. That's what we want them to do.*≈

Katra trusted that Mira either knew what she was doing or was lying to keep her calm. It was a very different style of command than she was used to, and despite her impending violent death Katra had to admit that she liked it.

≈*I'm clear. Do it.*≈

Katra armed the first grenade, and let it drop to the bridge's surface. She set the second to detonate after a five-second delay, and set it down on the support beam she was using as a perch. She took two skipping, antigravity hops away from the grenade, and set up to observe the results on the next section of superstructure.

She didn't have long to wait. With the flames nearly extinguished, one of the machines was wedging itself between the overturned train car and the bridge's rusted frame. Metal shrieked as it extended two pairs of legs on either side of its body, shoving the container far enough back for the second machine to step cautiously down onto the tracks.

The grenades detonated on schedule, and just as Mira had planned the machines charged forward to attack the twin heat sources but found themselves blocked from advancing by the engine. Mira grabbed the packs and dove off the side of the bridge, body heat masked by both the fires and her hardsuit.

Not for long, though. The machines started pushing the engine forward, but found it much harder to move than the overturned container. The engine's wheels screamed in protest, and sparks flew as metal ground against metal. Meter by meter, the three technological relics advanced across the bridge.

Even filtered through her helmet, the sound was painful, and Mira's voice in her head was a welcome distraction.

≈*Five seconds. See you on the other side.*≈

Katra turned her back on the machines and selected a route down the superstructure to where the other mods were gathering around JonB. Jantine was holding his back to her chest, rocking back and forth while Carlton knelt in front of them.

Seeing the three Betas together was a painful reminder of the closeness she would never have now that Jarl was dead, and Katra tried to imagine herself in Jantine's place. She lingered a heartbeat too long on the fantasy of a raising children with a compatible mate and was caught unprepared when the bridge exploded.

As she tumbled headlong towards surface of the rushing river, Katra had just enough time to wonder how the encounter suit's impact systems would handle a fall from such a great height, and whether or not she'd remain conscious as she died.

AUTHOR'S NOTE

It's all "James S.A. Corey's" fault.

I've only ever met Daniel Abraham and Ty Franck in passing, but their work is the reason I wrote *Homefront* in the first place, instead of an overwrought, hard science masterpiece I couldn't sell anywhere else.

Let me explain.

In the summer of 2013, I offered a sprawling science fiction novel to Mark Teppo's incipient medium press, which in the fullness of time became Resurrection House. Several other imprints had already said no, and my hypothetical agent had broken down the likelihood it would see print with a major house in no uncertain terms. But Mark was looking for new voices and new stories, and I was optimistic enough to believe I was both.

Besides, Mark had already bought two books from me for the *Fore-world Saga*, and I was fairly certain he was looking to fill out the set.

He was, but at the same time, he wasn't. After a solid beginning, the book kind of fell apart in the middle, and as my friend and semi-patron, he also had to tell me the truth about its chances. So I put it aside (that's it over there in the trunk), and we tried to figure out what I *should* be writing instead.

To do that, we loaded up our kindles with recently released Space

Opera, and set ourselves a task to "crack the code." As luck would have it, we hit the motherload on the first try with *Leviathan Wakes*.

Here was a thrilling tale of nexteryear just like the ones I remembered. Here was classic science fiction recast for modern audiences hungry for escape. This was the far future I'd imagined I was writing, and the part where everybody else on the planet seemed to like it was just icing on the cake.

It was nothing like what I'd been writing. It was far more complex, and far more ambitious. I could see that future from where I was as a writer, but I needed a few more pairs of giants' shoulders to stand on before I could reach it.

So it was back to the drawing board for me. I read as much of their stuff as I could, drinking in the nuances and stylings of the EXPANSE the same way I'd devoured Heinlein, Burroughs, Clarke, Bova, and Bear in my formative years. I studied, I practiced, and I studied some more.

I pitched a new book at Mark, and in return received the best validation a writer can ever get.

I got paid.

A year later, I got published, and it was so close to what I thought I was writing that I honestly believed I was *at least* one giant closer.

That was five years ago. Things have changed, and the giants have only gotten taller. But I'm a few million words farther up the ladder than I used to be, and I hope you're enjoying the results.

Mahalo.

Scott James Magner
March, 2019

P.S. No preview this time, but *Beachhead*, the next (and final) book in the Homefront trilogy, is available for purchase right now, wherever it is you buy your books.

Give it a try, why don't you?

ABOUT THE AUTHOR

Scott James Magner has held down many jobs over the years, including circus promoter, warehouse manager, dog-sitter, professional role-playing gamer, and writer. He currently resides in Seattle with his partner of many years and several cats who don't understand why sitting down to write is not an invitation for lap-time.

You can catch up on all things him at his website:

scottjamesmagner.com